After the One

Cass Lester spent many years at CBBC having a fabulous time making award-winning programmes including *Jackanory*, *Big Kids*, *Kerching!* and *The Story of Tracy Beaker*. She has published a number of children's books and is now having a fabulous time writing adult fiction.

AFTER THE ONE

CASS LESTER

CANELO

First published in the United Kingdom in 2021 by

Canelo
31 Helen Road
Oxford OX2 0DF
United Kingdom

A CIP catalogue record for this book is available from the British Library.

Print ISBN 978 1 80032 309 4
Ebook ISBN 978 1 80032 308 7

Look for more great books at www.canelo.co

Printed and bound in Great Britain by Clays Ltd, Elcograf S.p.A.

1

for my mates

who've laughed with me and cried with me

and who laugh at me and despair of me

Chapter One

Some days the fates have really got it in for you. When Charley Taylor woke up on Thursday 16 April, with a leaden, flat weight squatting heavily in her stomach, she knew it was going to be one of those days. But then 16 April was always one of the worst days of the year for Charley, one of a handful of days when, instead of leaping out of bed with her usual verve, she wanted to stay put, pull a 10-tog security blanket over her head and hide from the world. All told there were eight duvet-hiding days in Charley's year, the others being, in date order: 8 August (her wedding anniversary), 22 September (her birthday), then Christmas Day, Boxing Day, New Year's Eve and Valentine's Day.

And then there was 25 February, aka the worst day of the year.

So, on this particular Thursday morning, all Charley wanted to do was hibernate with a pack of chocolate digestives until it was Friday. But it was gone seven o'clock and she had to get up and go to work, because, regardless of the date, and regardless of little things like births, marriages and deaths, life goes on.

If Charley had known how the day was going to pan out, and particularly the fact that she was actually only going to be in the office for about ten minutes, she would have hunkered back down and spared herself the monumental effort of slapping on a smile, holding it there and dragging herself into work. But not being in the privileged position of being able to predict the future, she bullied herself into getting out of bed.

'Come on, you… Get up, make up, go to work and do the day.'

Throwing off the duvet, Charley slung her legs out of bed, crossed the room and yanked open the curtains, only to be confronted by a soggy grey day as dull as ditch-water, with rivulets of rain running down the cold windowpane. It was in stark contrast to the photo on the bedside table where Josh, wearing Bermuda shorts and a suntan, with his shades pushed back onto his beach-scruffy hair, stood against the backdrop of an azure-blue Ibiza sea. He was grinning broadly at her, as was his way.

'You're not missing much,' she informed him, brightly. 'It's not exactly another day in paradise.' Then, almost as an afterthought, she added, 'Happy birthday.'

If he'd still been here to celebrate it, she'd be cooking him a birthday breakfast right now. The thought momentarily stopped her in her tracks and she stood, adrift in her memories for a while, until, with an effort, she brought herself back to the present.

You know how to do this, just make like it's an ordinary day, she told herself, padding barefoot into the bathroom. *It'll probably turn out a lot better than you think.*

She looked at her reflection in the mirror above the sink. It gazed back at her, gloomily, so she pulled a silly face at it. A thirty-one-year-old woman with long dark curly hair escaping a lopsided scrunchy, and with tell-tale smudges of yesterday's mascara round her eyes, made a face back. Charley wondered which one of them she was trying to convince.

Despite Charley's commendable optimism, the morning kicked off to a pretty lousy start. Her car, which had seen better days – and a good many of them before she'd even owned it – decided that today was the perfect day to break down. She'd barely pulled away from the kerb, when an alarming, and almost certainly expensive, rattling erupted from underneath.

'Bloody hell!' she swore and immediately manoeuvred back to the side of the road again. It sounded horribly like the exhaust was threatening to fall off, but she wasn't going to get out and clamber underneath to have a look, not in a work skirt and white shirt, that was for sure. She'd have to call the garage, *again*. Her heart sank; the last time the car broke down, less than six months ago, they'd been adamant it wasn't worth fixing.

'It's knackered, love. You want to trade it in before it dies completely.'

She knew they were right, but Josh had given the car to her, so she'd told the garage to go ahead and fix it anyway.

The mechanic had been admirably reluctant to rip her off. 'Honestly, it's going to cost a fortune, love, it's not worth it,' he'd protested.

Nevertheless, she had insisted. 'I'm just not ready to change cars yet,' she'd explained.

It wasn't that Charley was allergic to change, more that she avoided it like the plague. Losing Josh had torn into her life like a savage storm, leaving her shipwrecked, cast away on a sea of loss. Astonishingly, life had gone on, and somehow, she was expected to carry on without him. Her instinct, her coping mechanism, had been to grasp hold of the things that had remained, and nail them down in the

3

desperate hope of providing some sort of stability against the endless, buffeting waves of bereavement. Her car, their flat, her job, even the bloody broadband supplier, had all become her mooring posts.

Charley got out of the car, locked it and decided to worry about it later. Not least since her immediate problem was getting to work on time. A swift glance at her phone told her there'd be a bus in about five minutes, but she'd have to leg it. Kicking off her heels and clutching them, and her bag, tightly into her body, she hurtled down the road, her stockinged feet splashing through cold, gritty puddles. *Could this day get any better?* She turned the corner, panting heavily, her blood pounding in her ears. Taking advantage of a sudden break in the traffic, she went to dart across the road, but missed her footing. She stumbled off the kerb and pitched forwards. Her bag and shoes flew out of her arms and landed in the middle of the carriageway.

'Bloody, *bloody* hell!'

Charley scrabbled frantically to grab her things before they, or she, got run over, but as she retreated to the undignified safety of the gutter, there was a sudden squeal of brakes and a bloke on a bike screeched to a halt inches from her.

'Are you all right?' he asked, clambering off his bike and putting a hand out to help her up.

'Yes, I'm fine… thanks,' Charley assured him, but attempting to stand sent a sudden shooting pain into her ankle, taking her breath away.

The man put out his hand to steady her, his face clouded with concern. 'Are you sure?'

Bracing herself, Charley tentatively tried her ankle again. Although the pain made her wince, it was bearable and she could just about put her full weight on it.

'Honestly, I'm fine. Nothing's broken, but thanks for stopping.' She gave the man a slightly sheepish smile.

He smiled back, warm and easy. 'You're welcome. You're sure you're okay?'

She nodded, and he climbed back onto his bike and rode off, no doubt happy to have done his good deed for the day.

–

Charley was still naively hoping she might make it to the bus stop in time until, with impressive comic timing, the double decker smugly whooshed passed her, adding insult to injury by liberally spraying her with filthy water, and completely drenching her tights and skirt.

'Bloody, bloody, *bloody* hell!'

There wasn't another bus for half an hour, so now she *was* going to be late. She'd have to call in. She dug her phone out of her bag and stared at it numbly. The shattered screen looked like it had taken a gunshot – the image behind it reduced to a mass of meaningless multi-coloured pixels. Charley closed her eyes. *Oh, for crying out loud, could this day get any worse?*

As it turned out, yes it could.

Cold and soggy, and by now very late, Charley hobbled into work desperate for a pee, a chair and a hot coffee – not necessarily in that order – and ready to amuse her colleagues with her disastrous start to the day. But to her surprise, the office was deserted. Her boss shot out of his office so promptly it occurred to Charley that he'd actually been lying in wait for her.

He regarded her for a brief moment, as if taking in the sodden state of her, then, apparently choosing to ignore it, said, 'Ah, Charley. Can I have a word?'

It's probably fair to say that when the silver spoons and golden opportunities were handed out, Charley wasn't at the front of the queue – a position that was fine by her since she'd never believed that money made anyone happy. The pursuit of wealth had never been one of her life goals, which was fortunate because she hadn't exactly embarked on a gloriously high-flying career. She worked as an admin assistant, *the* admin assistant to be absolutely accurate, for a failing letting agency in an increasingly less-than-sought-after area of Bristol. Originally, the agency's next-door neighbours had been a Boots and a Ryman's, but now the office was marooned by a bus lane and double yellow lines, and found itself perched dismally between an anonymous vape store and the Dragon Inc. tattoo parlour.

So perhaps it shouldn't have come as a surprise to her when, after a stumbling start, her boss had said, 'I'm truly sorry, Charley, really… but I'm going to have to make you redundant.' But it had. Well, more of a shock than a surprise, really.

'Redundant?' Charley repeated flatly. The word hung in the air between them, perhaps because she simply refused to let it in and give it room in her brain.

It turned out that a property developer had offered him a buyout deal that was simply too good to refuse. *Frankly, any buyout would have been too good to refuse*, thought Charley, looking around at the grubby decor and outdated furnishings, but she said nothing and concentrated on not letting her emotions show.

'I'm going to retire,' he told her apologetically.

'Good for you!' said Charley, somehow managing to give him a cheery, sincere smile.

In all honesty she couldn't blame him for taking the money, she doubted the agency was even paying its way any more, and besides, he'd treated her more than fairly over the years, very generously giving her time off when she'd needed it after Josh died, and not hassling her to return until she was ready. He was a decent boss and a good man, and she genuinely wished him well, despite the small, sick waves of anxiety that were beginning to rise up inside her. She realised he was speaking to her.

'I'll pay you to the end of the month. And you'll get redundancy,' he was saying. 'But if you want to leave today, well, right now, even, I'll understand. I mean there's no point just sitting it out I suppose—' he trailed off, clearly dying with embarrassment.

'No. Probably not,' agreed Charley, giving him another smile.

Limping over to her desk, she belatedly realised her colleagues' desks were already bereft of personal belongings, a detail that had escaped her notice earlier. They'd obviously decided to ship out sooner rather than later, too. It was like the *Marie Celeste*.

Numbly, Charley started to pile her stuff into her bag: the 'Today Is Going to Be Awesome' mug her mate Tara had given her, a coaster that read, 'Be The Reason Someone Smiles Today', and a photo in a cheap pine frame from Ikea – the one of Josh and her standing on the Rialto Bridge with a gondola in the background, on their honeymoon. She had asked an American tourist to take it for them on her phone, and now there they stood, forever smiling and radiating happiness, raising glasses of fizz to the camera.

What the hell am I going to do? she asked Josh silently. He continued to beam broadly at her, which wasn't much help frankly, so she picked up the landline on her desk and called Tara.

—

The Reception of the Avalon Indulgence Spa and Conference Centre, where Tara worked, was, in Tara's humble opinion, grotesquely pretentious. Vast, overly ornate gilt mirrors posed against garish purple-and-black flocked walls, and enormous cream leather sofas, with cheap gold fittings, lounged on a mock-marble tiled floor.

On duty, sitting behind the massive cream faux-leather covered desk, Tara heard her mobile ringing in her handbag. *Technically*, she wasn't meant to take personal calls on Reception, but at this precise moment, her pimply young line manager was leaning over her shoulder scrutinising her screen minutely, or rather *insultingly*, to check Tara's ability to input the most basic customer details into a bog-standard spreadsheet. So she just couldn't resist. Not long out of university, with a smart new suit and a shiny new Business Studies degree, Tara's boss had the leadership skills of a minor dictator, the people skills of a sociopath and the mental capacity of a bread-maker. He took himself very seriously, which was interesting in itself, because nobody else did.

Taking pleasure in flouting the petty authority he so enjoyed wielding over her, Tara picked up her bag and took her phone out with a flourish.

'No private calls on duty,' he said, literally wagging his finger at her.

'Unless it's an emergency,' she reminded him, with a sickly-sweet smile. A glance at the screen revealed a number she didn't know. 'I'm sorry, but I'm going to have to take this. It's my daughter's school,' she lied.

Her manager hovered nearby, blatantly trying to listen to her call, undoubtedly to check if it really was an emergency, but all he heard was Tara saying, 'What!', followed by 'When?', and then, 'What do you mean *as of now*?', and finally, 'Don't panic, I'm coming round straight after work.'

Chapter Two

It was just after four when Tara pitched up at the bottom of the concrete steps leading down to Charley's garden flat.

'Sorry, I had to pick Monnie up and find someone to take her to Brownies,' she said, pausing in the doorway long enough to give Charley a hug. Following her friend through to the kitchen, she presented her with a Wild Fig and Vanilla scented candle, because she never arrived empty-handed, and then she fished a chilled bottle of Prosecco out of her tote bag.

'Thanks, but I'm not exactly celebrating!' laughed Charley.

'So?' Tara retorted, who had an unshakable belief in the restorative qualities of a bottle of fizz. Well, they both did. 'Never underestimate the power of Prosecco' was their maxim. 'And, anyhow, you should be,' said Tara, helping herself to the flutes from the cupboard before turning to Charley and adding, 'You didn't even like your job.'

'True,' admitted Charley, 'but that doesn't mean I didn't want it.'

It was no secret Charley had only taken the job in order to move to Bristol and live with Josh. At the time it was meant to be temporary, so that she could pay her share of the mortgage and the bills until she could find something better. And then afterwards, after Josh died, Charley had stayed put because it was safe, secure.

Tara opened the bottle with a satisfying *phup!* and poured the wine with an even more satisfying *fizzzzzz*. Handing Charley a foaming glass she headed into the living room, where they both sat on the sofa, kicked off their shoes and put their feet on the coffee table in one well-rehearsed, synchronised move.

'You were wasted there *and* you know it.' Tara raised a challenging eyebrow at Charley, defying her to contradict her. 'This is the fates telling you it's time to move on, find something better.'

'It's not the moving on that worries me, it's the moving out I'm trying to avoid,' replied Charley. 'There's the slight issue of the bills, and the even bigger issue of the mortgage!'

Tara waved a dismissive hand at Charley's problems. 'You'll easily find something else,' she said, taking a slurp of her Prosecco. 'Seriously, don't rush into the first job that comes up, Charley. Look around.'

'That's easy for you to say. You've got good old Baz supporting you; I haven't got a good old *anyone* supporting me.'

Tara looked at her over the top of her glass. It was unlike Charley to make a comment like that, she wasn't someone who begrudged another's good fortune, or harped on her own misfortune, for that matter. Chalking it up to Charley feeling a bit low, Tara deployed her usual rallying tactic. 'Come on, you! Look on the bright side! You're getting a redundancy payout, right?'

'Yes.'

'Then this is a brilliant opportunity to do something else. Something you really want to do.'

'What, like you do?' said Charley sarcastically, and Tara felt like walloping her with a cushion.

'No! Actually, yes! I hate my sodding job, you know I do. But it's mornings only, term-time, and it fits round Monnie, so I *am* doing what I really want to do.'

Charley raised her eyebrows.

Tara ignored the implied jibe and persisted. 'If you could do anything you wanted, *anything at all*, what would you do?'

Charley watched the bubbles fizzing upwards in her drink. *Anything at all?* she asked herself. *Well, apart from turn the clock back...*

Four years ago today, had been Josh's last birthday. It had fallen on a Saturday and she'd taken him breakfast in bed – eggs, bacon, toast, fried tomatoes, mushrooms, the full works. He'd sat up in bed all tousled-haired, and as excited as a big kid.

'I do not deserve you, Mrs Taylor!'

Charley had clambered onto the bed and sat cross-legged next to him, and they'd shared the plateful, taking it in turns to eat off Josh's fork. When they'd finished, he'd dumped the tray on the floor and pulled Charley towards him. They hadn't got up all day...

'Well?' prompted Tara, 'Any ideas?'

Charley forced herself back to the present. 'No, not really.' Then, catching the exasperated look on her mate's face, she went on, 'Sorry, I've just had a really rubbish day.' She took a breath before adding, 'It's Josh's birthday.'

Tara's face softened, her eyes flooding with empathy as she leant over to embrace Charley. 'Oh, my lovely, why didn't you say?'

Charley let herself sink into the comfort of Tara's hug, trying hard not to fall apart completely.

Birthdays. They both knew about birthdays, those agonising reminders that someone was missing, when opening a pile of cards which carelessly, thoughtlessly, wished you a 'Happy Birthday' was like rubbing salt into an open wound. As if you could have a happy day. As if everything was normal.

Bereavement had forged Tara and Charley's friendship. A few months after Josh's death, Tara's mum had also died, throwing the two friends into a closeness that was intensified by a barrier that somehow divided them from the rest of their friendship group. None of their other friends had suffered loss and they were unable to understand what Tara and Charley were going through. They were all too young to have lost a partner or a sibling or even a parent, but then so were Charley and Tara. Way too young.

Tara's mum, Kim, had died of breast cancer. 'After a bloody hard battle and an even harder life,' as Tara put it. Raising her daughter single-handed on a low income eked out by benefits had worn Kim down. She'd been easy pickings for cancer and was only fifty-six when she died. Everyone had given Tara hugs and sympathy cards and said how sorry they were... what a dreadful loss it must be... and to let them know if there was anything they could do to help. But only Charley had given practical help rather than platitudes: filling Tara's freezer with meals, picking little Monnie up from school, running the hoover round and doing the laundry. It was Charley who'd helped arrange the funeral, the flowers and the wake, and who'd helped Tara write the eulogy they were both too choked to read at the funeral, and it was Charley who, with her arm firmly around Tara's waist, had helped her friend stumble across the grass to the soft mud by the newly dug grave, their heels sinking into the ground, so that Tara could throw a sunflower down onto her mum's coffin. And afterwards, Charley, and only Charley, had known how to help Tara cope with the juggernaut of loss bearing down on her, and the harrowing, hollowing pain of the wound it left behind. Not just for the first few weeks, but in the months afterwards when people either assumed you'd be over it or seemed to have forgotten about it altogether.

There were two kinds of people, Charley had learned: the bereaved, who understood what you were going through, and the rest – the ones who were emotionally naive about grief, who couldn't understand, who weren't in the fellowship of the bereaved.

Lucky them.

–

What you really want, when you've got to grovel around in the gutter looking at the underbelly of your car to see if the exhaust is actually going to fall off before you can make it to the garage, is a nice dry day. So, naturally, it was drizzling when Charley headed out into the street the next morning in a tatty old tracksuit to check it out. *Oh, deep joy*, she thought, zipping up her top against the damp. She knelt on the pavement, her trackies instantly soaking through at the knees, and gave the exhaust pipe a tentative nudge. She was satisfied, if not exactly thrilled, when a clunking rattle confirmed her diagnosis was correct. Peering underneath, the exhaust didn't look like it was about to part company from the car, well, not immediately, and Charley decided she could risk driving to the garage. She wasn't going to waste money calling out a pick-up truck if she didn't have to.

The basic car mechanic course wasn't a total waste of time then, she told herself wryly, although she was probably the only woman who'd done the course to think so. But then the others, mostly single women or divorcees, had signed up hoping to 'meet someone'. Charley had only enrolled to fill one of her endless, empty evenings following Josh's death, along with a dozen other evening classes – *DIY, Fusion Cookery, Picture Framing, Drawing for All, Knitting, Beginners' Spanish…* They'd filled her diary and the hours, but the evenings were still empty, just like the flat, when she got home. Still, the course had paid off today.

Going inside to grab a quick shower and some dry clothes before heading to the garage, Charley was halfway down the outside steps to her flat when she heard the landline ringing indoors.

'Bugger!' She leapt down the last few stairs, burst through the front door, charged into the living room and breathlessly snatched up the phone.

'Hello?' she gasped.

'Sorry, darling. Have I called at a bad time?' It was her mother-in-law.

'Pam, hi! No, not at all.' Charley sank cheerfully onto the sofa, then realising her soaking clothes would make it damp, perched on the coffee table instead. A chat with Pam was always a welcome distraction.

'I'm popping into Bristol this morning and wondered if you might like to meet up for a coffee?'

Ordinarily, Charley would have happily gone, but not today. If she went she'd inevitably have to tell Pam about her redundancy, and for some reason she didn't feel ready to do that, not yet. So she lied. 'I can't do today, sorry! In fact, I'm busy all weekend.'

'Never mind. Another time, darling.'

'Yes! Absolutely!'

Putting the phone down Charley was instantly flooded with guilt and confusion. Why had she felt compelled to lie to Pam? To Pam of all people? She told herself it was because she hadn't wanted to worry her. *I'll tell her when I get a new job*, she decided.

She showered and changed, then drove into town to get the car repaired, very much against the advice of the garage of course, and then she bought a new phone. All told, she shelled out the best part of three hundred quid.

Bloody hell, she winced, *the redundancy money isn't going to last five minutes at this rate.*

Back home she made herself a strong, fortifying coffee, and then took a forensic look at her monthly bills and outgoings, to work out *precisely* how long she could live on what she'd got left in the bank. Apparently, not very long. Mentally rolling up her sleeves, she opened her laptop and started to look for a job, a task that would have been a lot simpler if she'd known what she actually wanted to do. There were, literally, hundreds of jobs advertised, some of which she'd never even heard of. But whilst the vast array of opportunities seemed initially exciting, it rapidly became overwhelming, and, after getting bogged down in a maze of recruitment websites, Charley soon realised she needed to be ruthlessly methodical in her approach.

She drew up a spreadsheet headed *Jobs I Want to Apply For*, with columns logging: the name of company; the location; job title; experience and qualifications and so on. Optimistically, she added columns for: date of interview; salary; and starting date.

Rather too optimistically, as it turned out.

It seemed she either needed qualifications she didn't have – like a degree, or a BTEC diploma – or experience in a bewildering list of things she hadn't even heard of.

What even is 'operations resource co-ordination' or 'people services administration' for crying out loud? And what the hell are 'procurement systems management' and 'supply chain operations'? She frowned. *I swear they're making these up.*

There was only one person she knew who could interpret this impenetrable gobbledegook – her friend Nisha. But she hesitated to pick up the phone. Nisha was the most successful of Charley's friendship group and she'd always found her slightly intimidating – actually, more than slightly. Cool, elegant and a little older than the rest of her mates, the woman worked twenty-four-seven, running her own marketing company. So, where Charley had decided not to tell Pam about being made redundant until she'd got another job, she didn't want to admit it to Nisha *at all* – she'd feel such a failure in comparison to her. She sighed, told herself to bite the bullet and picked up the phone.

'Hi Nishe, is it an okay time to call?' she asked, deploying her usual opening line with Nisha.

'Yes, of course. In fact, I was going to call you.'

'Oh?' said Charley warily, immediately assuming Tara had let the cat out of the bag about her redundancy, since she couldn't imagine why else Nisha would be calling her.

'I need cheering up,' announced Nisha, flooring Charley completely. Nisha was intensely private, an emotionally closed book who rarely confided in anyone.

'What's up?'

Charley could sense, rather than hear, Nisha taking a deep breath before announcing, '*La Bimbo* is pregnant.'

'Oh, Nishe,' said Charley, her heart going out to her mate.

'Can I come round?' asked Nisha hesitantly.

'Yes! Come now!'

Officially, Nisha's status was 'Happily Divorced', but Charley wondered if her friend's status was possibly better described as 'Stoically Divorced'.

Twenty minutes later Nisha arrived, the height of elegance in a pair of blue-and-white striped culottes, a navy shirt and heels, which made Charley feel like a grunge-queen in her old joggers and even older T-shirt.

Charley found herself apologising for the coffee. 'It's only instant, I'm afraid.'

'I much prefer instant,' Nisha assured her politely, and Charley didn't know if she was being truthful or diplomatic. Either way, Nisha sat opposite her at the kitchen table, nursing her coffee and venting spleen.

'He spent ten years telling me he didn't want bloody kids. Utterly refused to have any. So I kept taking the pill, and now... and now *La Fucking Bimbo* is up the duff, and I'm knocking forty and—' She didn't even bother to finish her sentence.

...and it's probably too late, finished Charley silently.

'I'm sorry, Nishe,' she said gently. With her other friends she'd have pulled them into a hug, but instinctively she felt Nisha wouldn't be comfortable with that.

'No, *I'm* sorry,' said Nisha. 'Sorry, to dump on you like this, but I can't talk to the others – they've got kids. They won't understand.'

'You're not dumping on me,' Charley assured her. 'I'm glad you shared it with me. It's huge. Devastating news.'

Nisha gave a faint nod and then said, 'Maybe I should have just stopped taking the pill and got pregnant, like *La*

Bimbo. Huh! Maybe she's not such a bimbo after all,' she finished bitterly.

Desperately wanting to find something, anything, that might make Nisha feel better, Charley said, 'If you'd had kids do you think you and Jay would still be married?'

'Probably,' replied Nisha. Then, after processing that notion, she visibly cheered up and added, 'Ghastly thought! Imagine being lumbered with him for rest of my life!' and Charley adjusted her friend's status back to 'Happily Divorced'.

Then, since she still needed Nisha's help with her job-hunting, Charley reluctantly fessed up about her redundancy. To her relief, her mate didn't seem to think it reflected badly on Charley at all, and after commiserating with her and assuring her she would be *bound* to get another job soon, Nisha turned her attention to the list of the job titles and duties Charley had found so confusing. She dealt with them easily, contemptuously even.

'Don't be put off by job titles. They're all just admin jobs, which you're eminently capable of doing. The job spec will tell you what the job really is. It's just title inflation. People bigging jobs up.'

'To attract more applicants?' asked Charley, thinking that if this was the case, it wasn't a tactic that was working for her.

'No, because the pay's crap. It's cheaper to give a job a fancy title than a decent wage. If I were you, I'd look at the salary first, then the job title.'

Chapter Three

Despite Nisha's advice, after two solid weeks of filling in applications and uploading her CV to countless websites, Charley had nothing to show for her efforts except several pages of a meticulously completed spreadsheet and an inbox full of rejections. Slowly but surely, Charley's self-esteem began to ebb away, and the fact that most of the rejections weren't even addressed to her personally, but to 'Dear Applicant', eroded her confidence even further. Worse still, dozens of the companies – *dozens* – didn't even think she was worth replying to at all. Despondency and a low-level persistent feeling of depression crept in as Charley altered the heading on her spreadsheet from *Jobs I Want to Apply For* to the more sobering title, *Jobs I Can Apply For*, and then, finally, to the more desperate-sounding *Jobs I Haven't Already Applied For*. The shortness of the last list alarmed her, raising the frightening prospect that she might perhaps not be able to get a job at all.

The screen on her laptop had gone to sleep and Charley realised she had been sitting staring at it blankly for a long time. A glance at the kitchen clock informed her it was, somehow, way past lunchtime and she hadn't eaten.

'I'm losing track of time,' she said. Then, realising she'd spoken out loud to a completely empty flat, told herself, *It's losing your* mind *you need to worry about.*

Charley was a people person who needed the camaraderie and conversation of others to bounce off and bring her to life. She hadn't spoken to anyone for days – no wonder she was talking to herself. Suddenly craving company, she picked up her phone. There was no point calling Tara or Nisha since they'd be working, but what about Angie? She had three kids, and only one of them was at school. She was almost bound to be home and up for a visit.

It was really, really tempting to go round to Angie's and muck about with the kids. Or she could go round to Pam's? The mere thought suddenly flooded her with a need for the reassuring presence, comfort calories and good old-fashioned mothering Pam always generously lavished on her. She would take herself off to Pam's, she decided, until she remembered that she hadn't been straight with Pam the last time her mother-in-law had called, and still hadn't told her about her redundancy. A visit now would entail an uncomfortable confession, plus the admission that she didn't actually have a job at the moment. She sighed heavily and put the phone back on the table. Bunking off to visit either Pam or Angie wasn't going to help her get a job, was it?

A grumble from her stomach reminded her she really ought to eat something. She scanned the contents of the fridge; its pathetically empty shelves depressed her even more. She should go shopping, but she just couldn't be arsed, and instead she forced herself to sit down in front of the computer again. There was a dull ping, and yet another job rejection joined the long list in her inbox, at which point she gave up and sat listening to the silence filling the empty flat. It was deafening.

In pure self-defence, she took herself round to Angie's.

'Come in, if you can get in!' laughed Angie, opening the door.

'I'll give it a go!' Charley grinned, trying to wade past Buster, the outsize chocolate Labrador who was bouncing around her dementedly, thumping his tail against her thigh, and the two small boys who had hurled themselves at her legs.

'Charleeeeey!'

'Hi, horrors!' She laughed and ruffled the boys' hair.

'It's chaos!' Angie informed her cheerfully. 'I'm painting the boys' room.'

'Again?' Angie had only painted it two years ago just before Finn was born. *Did the woman ever stop nesting?*

'Make some tea and come up.' Angie turned to head up the stairs.

'Tea?' queried Charley. 'Not coffee?'

'Tea,' Angie repeated casually. Too casually.

Charley hadn't seen Angie go through two of her three pregnancies without knowing exactly what *that* meant.

Trying very hard to conceal the pang of jealousy threatening to contort her face, Charley rushed over to hug her. 'Congratulations!'

Smiling blissfully, Angie turned and headed upstairs, the dog and the kids clambering after her.

It was hard not to envy Angie, who, quite simply, had the life Charley wanted. Where Charley had an empty flat and an emptying bank account, Angie had a house full of kids and animals. Piles of laundry, toys and games littered every surface, the smell of home baking permanently hung in the air and the whole place was a riot of colour, courtesy of Angie's artistic talents. Giant hand-painted sunflowers burst into bloom on the kitchen walls while an enormous beanstalk meandered along the hall and up the side of the stairs. Upstairs her eldest child, Beth, went to sleep under a seascape, her deep blue bedroom walls teeming with yellow starfish, mermaids and a giant purple octopus. In Finn and Eliot's room, adorably cute teddies drifted by on white fluffy clouds trailing rainbow bunting. Or rather, they had done – Charley wondered what was replacing them.

She made two mugs of tea, poured some milk into Eliot's Spiderman beaker and into a smiley face tippy cup for Finn, and raided the cake tin on the kitchen table. A waft of syrup from a pile of crumbly, homemade flapjacks promised to more than make up for missing lunch. Putting everything on a tray, Charley went up to the boys' room, where the furniture had been pushed into the middle and covered with a paint-splattered dust sheet.

'We're having pirates!' yelled four-year-old Eliot.

'Piwats!' His little brother leaped up and down ecstatically.

'Wow!' Charley breathed, gazing at the scene Angie was finishing painting on the wall.

A massive pirate galleon, in full sail and with a Jolly Roger flag fluttering above the crow's nest, sailed across the entire wall, cutting through an ocean of curly waves, while seagulls wheeled above it in a sunny sky. It looked like a backdrop for a panto at the Bristol Hippodrome.

'Blimey, Ange. You could do this professionally!'

'I wish,' replied Angie.

Charley shot her a look, but Angie merely shrugged it off. Charley put the tray on the floor, expertly pushed the optimistic Buster away with her foot, and then sat cross-legged on the floor. Finn immediately reversed his little bottom onto her lap, plonking himself down sure

23

of his welcome, and Charley slid her arms round him for a cuddle. A sudden wave of broodiness swept over her, catching her off-guard, and she couldn't stop herself from thinking that if Josh were still alive they'd have had kids by now and this would have been her life. She hugged Finn's busy little body to her.

'You're such a squidge-pot!' she told him, giving him a squeeze, and he giggled.

Angie sat herself down next to them, pulling Eliot onto her lap with one hand, and handing Charley a mug of tea with the other. 'How's the job-hunting?'

'Don't ask,' Charley groaned. 'I haven't got any qualifications. Apparently, you need a degree to do almost anything these days. I don't even know anyone with a degree, so why does everyone suddenly need one? It's ridiculous.' She rolled her eyes.

Angie flushed slightly pink and tucked her short bob behind her ears.

'Actually, I've got a degree,' she admitted sheepishly. 'Only Art,' she added, catching the deflated look on Charley's face. 'And Will's got a degree, but then he's a teacher, well, a Headteacher, so he needs one.'

'Well, that's different,' said Charley.

'And I think Nisha's got an English degree... or it might be Media? I can't remember, and of course, Tara's got an MBA.'

'Tara's got an MBA?' It was the first Charley had heard of it. 'Is this meant to be helping!?' she joked.

Angie pulled a face. 'Sorry.'

Once they'd finished their tea, they went down to the kitchen so Angie could wash her brushes, leaving the boys in their room burying fistfuls of brightly coloured plastic beads in a treasure chest Angie had knocked up out of a cardboard box.

Looking around Angie's house it was immediately obvious the woman was hugely talented, but Charley hadn't realised that her mate had actually been to art college and that, presumably, she'd had some sort of artistic career before she'd stopped work to have her children.

'You wouldn't really want to give up being a full-time mum, would you?' Charley asked as Angie plonked the brushes into the sink to soak, and then tried to cram the mugs into the already crowded dishwasher.

Angie sighed. 'Sometimes. I just feel like I'm missing out. Stuck here at home all day, every day. I envy you lot all working.'

I should be so lucky, thought Charley.

'It's just that… oh you know, four years at art college and then years working my way up as a designer, and now I spend my life painting bedrooms and my art box is full of wax crayons, felt-tip pens and finger paints.'

'But you love being a mum!'

'I know… it's just that sometimes it feels like I've completely disappeared in piles of dirty laundry, dirty dishes and dirty nappies.' Then, clearly seeing the concern on Charley's face, she shrugged carelessly. 'Ignore me. I'm just tired and hormonal. I love them all to bits, you know I do. And I really wouldn't want my life to be any other way, obviously, or I wouldn't be having another baby if I did!' She laughed. 'But sometimes, just sometimes, I wish I could be "Angie" for a bit and not just 'Mum' all the time.'

Somehow an afternoon at Angie's wasn't working its usual magic, and Charley left when Angie went to collect

Beth from school. She drove home and let herself into the empty flat feeling lower than ever, overcome with guilt for wasting an entire afternoon when she should have been job-hunting. The mortgage, she reminded herself, was not going to pay itself.

Financially, Charley had nobody to turn to, not even her parents, since she'd burned her bridges when she'd left home, in a sudden breathless rush of romance, to live with Josh less than a month after she'd met him. Her mother had told her she was a fool to move halfway across the country to live with someone she'd only just met on a Club Med holiday.

'It won't last. You'll end up alone and broken-hearted hundreds of miles away from home,' she had warned Charley.

As it turned out, her mum had been right, though not in the way she'd predicted. After Josh had died, Charley's mum simply couldn't understand why Charley had refused to give up the flat in Bristol and move back home to the family pub in Suffolk.

'There's nothing to stay for,' her mother had maintained and, when Charley had still refused to go home, her mother had taken it personally, baffled and hurt by her daughter's rejection of the comfort and care she wanted to give her.

'You can't mope around playing the grieving widow forever,' she'd snapped, and Charley had reeled, astonished by the cruelty of the remark.

Losing Josh had shaken the tectonic plates of her life so savagely that Charley had desperately clung to anything that still connected her to him. She couldn't bear to pack away her life with Josh into cardboard boxes and abandon their flat, the home he'd lived and laughed in, the sofa they'd sprawled on together, the rooms they'd made love in. It would have meant surrendering all her hopes and dreams, discarding them as if they, and Josh, had never existed, but she couldn't get her mum to understand. Pam had understood, of course, only too deeply, which had led Charley to turn to her instead, and her relationship with her own mother had suffered as a result – collateral damage in the fallout from grief. Charley had never been that close to her own mother in any event. The two had rarely seen eye-to-eye and had often clashed, especially once Charley had grown up. She did miss her dad, though, but he was easy-going and tolerant to the point of being conflict-averse and chose not to stand up to her mum. It hadn't been intentional, but inevitably she'd drifted away from her family.

Back at her flat, sitting hunched over her computer at the kitchen table, Charley told herself to be more realistic and to stop chasing jobs she wasn't qualified for, and to apply for something more modest and attainable, such as a bar job. She hadn't worked behind a bar for years, but her parents owned a pub and she'd grown up in one, which had to count for something, surely. It wasn't exactly a dazzlingly exciting prospect – in fact it was pretty grim, really – but it looked to be the best she could do.

Chapter Four

'You cannot possibly take a bar job. No. NO!' Tara yelled down the phone at Charley. 'You have *way* more to offer than that. I'm coming round. This evening.' She'd rung off before Charley could protest, but not before her heart had begun to sink. She knew her mate was only trying to help, but Tara in full flood was… forceful. And in all honesty, Charley wasn't feeling robust enough to stand up to her; there was every danger she'd end up being persuaded, or rather browbeaten, into doing something she'd regret.

Tara arrived at around half eight that evening, after she'd put Monnie to bed. She strode into the living room, and, pausing only to hand Charley a box of hazelnut chocolate pralines, ordered her to sit on the sofa whilst she propped up a pop-up flip chart on the coffee table and took out four different coloured marker pens from her bag.

'You,' she asserted, pointing an accusing finger at Charley, 'are *not* going to waste the rest of your life working in a sodding bar.'

Charley bit her lip and tactfully decided not to remind Tara that her parents had spent their entire working lives doing just that.

'You have a chunk of redundancy money and some savings. This is your chance to do whatever you want in life. Come *on*, Charley! This is your big chance!' Tara efficiently peeled back the cover page of the flip-chart pad to reveal a blank sheet of paper.

'Did you nick that from work?' Charley asked dryly.

'Yes. And don't change the subject.' Taking up the red pen, Tara wrote: WHAT I WANT TO DO in large letters. Then she turned to eyeball Charley. 'Right, Charley Taylor, what do you actually *want* to do for a living?'

'I don't know!' wailed Charley, half melodramatically, half in earnest.

'Well, do you want to carry on doing admin work?'

The unchecked grimace which crossed Charley's face said it all. Spending the rest of her life in admin felt more like a life sentence than a career choice. The problem was she couldn't envisage herself doing something else because she simply didn't have any idea what that 'something else' might be.

'We can put anything you like up here,' said Tara. 'You don't have to actually do it… We can just pretend it's a game if that makes it easier…'

It didn't. Charley's mind was as blank as the sheet of paper, and worse, under Tara's scrutiny, small flutterings of panic began to jitter away in her stomach, making it harder for her to think clearly.

Tara carried on, with evidently increasing desperation. 'Well, what did you always want to be… when you were little?' she prompted. 'Or before you met Josh?'

Before I met Josh? Charley couldn't even remember there being a 'before I met Josh'. Not very long after Josh had died, some people, thoughtless people who lacked empathy and imagination, had hurt Charley, really hurt her, by telling her she had *grieved for long enough* and that she should *go back to work and take her mind off things*, and then later, improbably, incredibly, they'd told her she should *move on and find someone else*. How dared they? Josh wasn't just the love of her life, he *was* her life. Losing him had cleaved her life in two: the wonderful part, full of fun and love and laughter, labelled 'After I met Josh', and the other part labelled 'After Josh died', which was where she lived now. The part labelled 'Before I met Josh' simply wasn't on Charley's life calendar. Maybe she had once had ambitions and dreams, but life had swept them aside. She shrugged helplessly at Tara and said, 'I don't know. Nothing, really. Sorry—' she finished, feeling even more of a failure.

But Tara wasn't giving up that easily. After a brief pause for thought, she changed tack. 'Okay. Let's look at this differently.'

She crossed out WHAT I WANT TO DO and wrote WHAT I LIKE DOING, then she folded her arms and looked at Charley. 'Well?'

'Knitting, reading, watching quiz programmes, being with mates...' reeled off Charley robotically, wondering what the point of all this was.

Tara rolled her eyes and tried again. 'What are you most looking forward to this year?'

Charley ran through the year ahead in her mind's eye... not her birthday, she still missed Josh too much, and she wasn't going on holiday because didn't have anyone to go with, and she wouldn't go on a singles holiday if you paid her. She frowned... and then suddenly, it was obvious. 'Oh, the Prosecco Night!'

'The Prosecco Night?'

'Yeah. Not just the fundraiser itself, but setting it all up, sending out the invitations, finding all the little Prosecco goodies to sell, getting in the fizz and the nibbles, not to mention totting up the cash at the end of the night!'

Tara nodded in agreement. 'Not a bad thing to look forward to at all!'

People grieve differently, as Charley had discovered. She couldn't bring herself to even light a candle on a cupcake to mark Josh's birthday, but Tara was different, she celebrated her mum's birthday every year with great gusto, affection… and Prosecco!

–

One bright autumn afternoon a few months after Kim had died, Charley and Tara had gone to Clifton Downs so that Monnie could ride her new bike, the first one she'd had without stabilisers.

'Mummy, Mummy, watch me!' she'd called, wobbling away in front of them along the path between the trees, putting her foot down every now and again to stop herself toppling off. The bike was bright pink, with glittery streamers fluttering on its handlebars and a tacky white plastic basket stuck on the front.

'Ghastly, isn't it?' Tara said.

'Yup,' agreed Charley. 'Did Monnie choose it?'

'Yup!' echoed Tara.

They'd both laughed, then Tara said, out of the blue, 'I'm going to hold a coffee morning on Mum's birthday. You know, a fundraiser, like a Macmillan's one.'

'What, for cancer research?'

'No, for the hospice.'

'That's a nice idea,' said Charley, with a hint of caution in her voice. 'But…'

'But? What do you mean, but?' cut in Tara good-humouredly. 'I think you mean: "What a brilliant idea, Tara, how can I help?!"'

Charley smiled at her mate. 'A fundraiser *is* a lovely idea, Tara, but people have jobs, so are they going to get to a coffee morning? Unless you do it on a Saturday?'

'Monnie goes to mini gym on Saturday mornings,' replied Tara shortly.

'Ah,' said Charley.

They drifted on in silence for a while, the rhythmic rattling of Monnie's bike trundling along the path ahead mingling with the soft rustle of the dry leaves swirling in the autumn breeze and the distant sound of dogs and children playing.

Then Tara sighed, 'Okay, so not a coffee morning then. But I don't want to let her birthday pass without… without, anyone knowing or caring.'

Hearing the catch in her friend's voice, Charley moved over to tuck her arm through Tara's, completely under-standing her sense of loss and hurt bewilderment. Josh's birthday, coming only weeks after he'd died, had loomed so monstrously and raw to Charley, yet it had slipped by unnoticed by anyone else, other than his family, as if it were just another day.

'You absolutely should do something to remember Kim on her birthday. Maybe something in the evening, when everyone's around. Actually, why not have a party? Kim was a real party girl!'

'Wasn't she just!' laughed Tara. 'Oh my God, Charley, you should have seen her at my wedding reception! She wasn't off the dance floor for a second. At one point she was drinking fizz and doing the twist with the vicar!'

'Oh my God, that's so Kim!' Charley could vividly imagine the scene.

'The only woman I know who could dance with a man of God in one hand and a glass of Prosecco in the other!' exclaimed Tara.

'Well, that's it then,' said Charley, as a flash of inspiration stopped her in her tracks. 'Don't have a coffee morning, have a Prosecco night!'

And so The Annual Kim Henderson Memorial Prosecco Night was born.

Charley had organised the fundraiser in her flat because Tara hadn't wanted to hold the event at her place, with her five-year-old daughter trying to sleep upstairs. And Charley had hosted it every year since. She could have stepped aside and let Tara do it as time went on, but Tara had never asked her to, and besides, it was her idea, her baby, and Charley looked forward to it every year.

However, much as Charley loved it, she couldn't exactly make a career out of running a Prosecco night, even Tara had to admit that. Dropping the pens on the coffee table, Tara sank down next to Charley, before helping herself to a chocolate, momentarily deflated.

'Look, the pub job is only until I can get something better,' Charly assured her.

Tara clearly wasn't convinced, but it was equally obvious she didn't have an alternative to offer, so, much to Charley's relief, she accepted defeat.

As it turned out, growing up in a pub did count for something and Charley got the first job she applied for, which was a shame because, whilst there are undoubtedly some exceptionally good pubs in Bristol, this job wasn't at one of them. Bang in the centre of the city, it was part of a new local chain, aggressively out to soak up the salaries of young office workers, binge-drinkers and party-goers. It was the sort of pub to attract lads who had an intimate knowledge of the meaning of the phrases 'legless', 'wasted' and 'rat-arsed', but who were baffled by the term 'drink responsibly', and young women who knew precisely how many calories there are in tonic water, but had no idea how many units of alcohol there are in a large gin and tonic, or more worryingly, how many units of alcohol were inside *them* at the end of a night.

Charley hated it. She hated the noise and the drunkenness, the sour smell of stale alcohol soaked into the carpet and steeped in the woodwork of the bar, and she hated going home with her clothes and hair reeking of garlic, lager and chips. Above all, she hated herself for being such a failure.

She had opted for evening shifts so she could spend the daytime looking for a proper job, which had seemed like a good idea at the time. Except she'd forgotten to factor in the all-too-critical *alcohol per punter ratio*, which at lunchtimes was reasonable, but in the evenings was off the scale, and tonight didn't look like it was going to be any different. A bunch of lairy lads, all smart suits and Amex cards, apparently hellbent on getting onto the office leader board for who could get pissed the quickest, managed to drop an entire tray of lagers on the outside patio. They cheered wildly as the bottles smashed onto the paving slabs, splinters of green glass exploding everywhere. Charley wouldn't have minded if they had at least apologised, or tried to help by moving their damn feet out of the way as she crouched on her hands and knees to clear it up, trying to avoid kneeling on the razor-sharp shards of glass surrounding her.

On top of that, the last half hour of the shift was particularly gross, featuring a mop and a bucket and an improbable amount of vomit that had erupted from a group of very young women who appeared to have drunk their own weight in Chardonnay. They'd certainly thrown up gallons of the stuff.

As soon as she got back home, Charley stripped off completely, flinging all her clothes into the washing machine, followed by her puke-splattered trainers. She showered in a vain attempt to shampoo the delightful scent of inner-city pub out of her hair.

'Definitely not another day in paradise,' she informed Josh as she clambered into bed and sank gratefully onto the pillows. 'Oh well, think of the money,' she told herself. Unfortunately, thinking of the money only served to remind her that the hourly rate was dire, barely above minimum wage, and well below what she'd earned at the letting agency. If she wanted to match that level of salary she'd have to put in more hours. She winced. *No way*. There were limits. But she didn't need a degree in Economics to realise that she either had to make more money, or spend less, so she lay awake wondering what the hell she could cut back on.

Obviously not the mortgage, or the council tax, but maybe she could cut down the gas and electricity? Barely, but it wouldn't be enough to make a real difference. Food then? Hardly, she was maxing out on pasta and budget brands as it was. Petrol? Yes! She could cut back on petrol by not driving to work. She didn't fancy walking back late at night, but she could get a bike, a cheap second-hand one... obviously there'd be the initial outlay, but surely it would pay for itself in a month or two? Buoyed by the thought that there was at least something she could do to improve her situation, Charley fell asleep.

The following morning, she caught the bus into a city centre that suddenly seemed full of cyclists: men in skin-tight Lycra, frankly revealing more than anyone would want to see, powering along furiously as if they were in the Tour de France; kids in brightly coloured helmets on their way to school, their little legs pounding away at the pedals, with a parent cycling protectively behind them. And students, hundreds of them, wheeling round the city as if they owned it and apparently without a care in the world. She told herself off for feeling jealous of them.

The second-hand bike shop she was heading for was down by the docks, in the Cargo area of the city, where the buildings were made out of open-sided lorry containers stacked two high with metal walkways linking them all together. Packed with trendy street-food places and quirky little shops, all run by equally trendy and quirky people, it positively ached with urban chic, pure Hipster Central, and Charley loved the buzz of the place. The bike shop was no exception, styling it out in 1960s retro chic. Complementing the look and making a style statement all of its own, a raffish grey lurcher with a blue bandana instead of a collar lay on its side, sunning itself in the doorway. Stepping over the dog, Charley walked into the shop, where the owner was busy with a young dad who was trying to persuade his son to choose a bike he didn't want.

The little boy's lower lip jutted out as he pointed at to a toddler-sized bike on the other side of the stop. 'I want that one!'

'Yes, but that one's too small for you,' explained his dad wearily, and having run out of both options and patience, he turned in mute, despairing appeal to the shop owner.

Charley watched as the bike man squatted down on his heels in front of the little boy to speak to him directly. It idly crossed her mind that, in his beige chinos, boat shoes and white linen shirt, he didn't dress like someone who worked in a second-hand bike shop. Then she told herself she was being ridiculous. What was a bike-shop man supposed to dress like anyhow, for crying out loud, oil-smeared jeans and a tatty T-shirt sporting a naff cycling slogan like 'Watch Out! Cyclopath About!'?

'Why do you like that one best?' the man was asking the little lad, and Charley was struck by the fact that he addressed the child in exactly the same way as he would an adult, without a hint of patronising the boy, but rather treating him as a valuable customer in his own right.

''Cos it's red,' said the boy. *Obviously*, his tone said.

'Ah, well here's the problem. I don't have a red bike that's big enough for you, but I have got some red stickers you could put on the other one.' The man got up and went to fetch a sheet of shiny red-and-yellow flame-shaped decals from behind the counter. He held them up against the frame of the larger bike. 'What do you think?'

The little boy's face lit up immediately and he nodded excitedly to his dad. 'Cool!'

'How much would they be?' the dad asked warily.

'Nothing.' The bike man smiled, sealing the deal.

While Charley waited for them to sort out the payment, the lurcher got up, stretched leisurely, then sauntered over to her and pushed his rough grey muzzle into her hand. She scratched his ears and he stood contentedly swiping his long tail and gazing up at her.

'Sorry to keep you,' said the bike man, finally coming over as the boy and his dad left with their new bike.

'No worries,' said Charley. Then she suddenly exclaimed, 'Oh, it's you!'

He frowned at her quizzically.

'You helped me up out of the gutter,' she said, then belatedly realising that she'd made it sound as if she'd passed out in the street after a late-night drunken binge, added hurriedly, 'I'd tripped over, on my way to work…?'

His face cleared in sudden recognition and he smiled at her warmly. 'Yes, yes, I remember.'

He showed her a handful of bikes he thought might be good for her, mostly old-fashioned sit-up-and-beg models with comfy padded seats which looked as if they'd been ridden straight off the set of a classic movie. Charley could instantly imagine herself on one, pedalling gaily through the city streets, with the wind in her hair…

'I rescue them from skips and tips and do them up,' the owner told her, bringing her down to earth.

Nevertheless, she fell hopelessly in love with an ice-blue bike with a cream leather seat and a wicker basket strapped to the front handlebars.

'D'you want to take it for a spin along the dockside and try it out?'

'Seriously? Aren't you scared I'll nick it?'

He looked her straight in the eye, as if he were appraising her. 'No, I trust you. And anyhow, I'm sending Security,' he joked, as he called the dog over. 'You won't outrun Carlo!'

So, a few minutes later, Charley was bowling along the dockside on the bike with the huge lurcher gambolling along easily by her side, with an expression of pure joy on its face. The feeling of fun and freedom was intoxicating.

'I'll take it,' she announced, slightly out of breath, when they arrived back at the shop.

'Great! Any problems, just bring it back.'

She paid, and then gave the lurcher a final ear scratch before cycling off. Pedalling homewards she reflected that it had been a good morning's work. It wasn't just that she'd done what she'd set out to do and had bought herself a bike, it was the added bonus of having bought it from someone who seemed to be a thoroughly decent, charming guy she instinctively felt was trustworthy. Optimism flooded through her. Maybe the morning would prove to be a turning point. That happy thought sustained her all the calf-tearing way up the hill home.

Chapter Five

It seemed that Charley might have spoken too soon, because the following day did not start well for her. Halfway through her shower the hot water suddenly cut out, deluging her with freezing cold water.

'Bloody hell!' she gasped. Towelling herself dry she figured that either the boiler or the shower were about to die, and hoped to God it was the shower, because the boiler would be far more expensive to replace. Wrapping the towel around her she tried the shower again, and this time it dutifully ran hot, so perhaps it was an intermittent fault. Frankly, she was none the wiser but she wished she'd adding Basic Plumbing to the list of evening courses she'd taken.

Then, less than an hour later, having shoved a load on to wash, an alarming squeaking sound suddenly erupted from the washing machine as it went into spin cycle. She groaned, then glanced round at the fridge and the cooker, both of which were equally elderly.

'Don't even think about it,' she warned them, then she grabbed her laptop, checked her bank balance online, did some rapid sums and promptly felt sick. As it was, she was going to have to live on Pot Noodles, not even pasta and sauce, if she was going to make the mortgage repayment this month. And that was without factoring in the additional expense of home repairs. She could take another chunk out of her redundancy, but she absolutely refused to do that, since that little pot of money was her safety net, her *only* safety net.

Pondering her dire financial position, it occurred to Charley that if she couldn't get a better job than working in the pub, or at least a better paid one, there was nothing to stop her taking an *additional* one. She was drawing up a list of things she could do alongside her bar job – cleaner, courier, part-time sales assistant – when the doorbell rang.

Tara stood on the step, clutching a bunch of bright orange tulips and a pack of Danish pastries. 'I've just dropped Monnie at mini-gym. Got time for coffee?'

'Are those cinnamon swirls?' asked Charley, narrowing her eyes in mock interrogation.

'Yup!'

'In that case, I am putting the kettle on…'

The women took their coffee through to the small back garden and sat on the wooden bench, balancing their mugs on the slats between them. The garden was unrecognisable from the mattress-and-junk strewn yard it had been when Charley and Josh had first bought the place. Together they'd cleared out the piles of rubbish, painted the fence sage green, sown a small patch of grass and planted up a dozen or so big earthenware pots. Glancing round, Charley noticed the lawn needed mowing and the pots could do with a bit of a weed, but she decided to worry about that later, because just right now chilling in the late spring sunshine with Tara was utter bliss. She kicked off her shoes and focused on the simple pleasures of feeling the warmth of the sun-baked patio slabs under her feet and the icing from the pastry melting on her tongue. She wasn't going to ruin the moment by thinking about money. Well, that wasn't until Tara popped her blissful bubble.

'Any news on the job front?'

Charley's mind raced to find a positive spin. 'Yes,' she lied, 'I've had a bit of a rethink, and I'm drawing up a list of things to apply for… so it's going pretty well.'

It was a good attempt at deflection, but futile – trying to deflect Tara was like trying to distract a charging rhino with a string of party bunting.

'Get your laptop, let's have a look,' she ordered, and Charley's shoulders slumped.

After briefly scanning Charley's list, Tara promptly rejected everything. 'These are all zero-hour contracts. There's no job security and they'll treat you like dirt.'

'There's nothing else!'

'Oh, there must be!'

Tara's scathing contradiction caused a sudden burst of temper to flare up inside Charley. Clearly Tara had no idea how intensely infuriating it was to be told that achieving something was a thousand times easier than it actually was in practice.

'I've applied for dozens, literally *dozens* of jobs and so far nobody's offered me so much as an interview, and half the time they don't even bother to get back to me at all!'

'How bloody rude!' exclaimed Tara, then, helping herself to a second Danish, she paused for a moment, before saying, 'You know what you *could* do? Get a lodger.' Charley frowned at her. 'Why not?' challenged Tara. 'Do you ever even use the spare room?'

There was a beat before Charley replied, 'Not really.'

As a point of fact nobody had *ever* stayed in the second bedroom, there wasn't even a bed in it, and Charley rarely ventured in there, only using it to store stuff. When she and Josh had first moved in, she'd envisaged it as a future nursery, picturing it furnished with a white-painted wooden cot, a musical mobile hanging above it, an old armchair for night feeds in the corner and a changing table under the window. If Josh hadn't died, there might even have been bunk beds in there by now…

They'd both wanted kids. On what had turned out to be his last Christmas, when they'd been at his mum's as usual, Josh had sprawled on the living-room floor building a Lego fort with Ben, his five-year-old nephew. Ben's little sister, Jessica, had been desperate to join in, but the bricks were far too fiddly for her tiny fingers, and, sensing a full-scale tantrum looming followed by an outburst of mass destruction, Charley had pulled the toddler onto her lap and read a pile of picture books to her. The warmth of the fire and the excitement of the day had soon overtaken the little girl, and she'd lolled backwards in Charley's arms, a soft, sleepy bundle. Josh had glanced up and smiled at her. 'Comfy?' Charley had smiled back in reply, loving the feel of the little body so trustingly slumped against her.

But whatever Charley's plans had been for her spare room, she wasn't going to need a nursery now. She realised that Tara had put down her pastry and was heading indoors to recce the room, so with a sigh, Charley got up to follow her.

'Actually, it needs a bit of a clear-out,' she warned, and she tensed as Tara pushed open the door to reveal a jumble of boxes, carriers and bin-liners spilled across the floor, all full, some to overflowing. It seemed to take less than a fraction of a second for Tara to realise what was in them, but then Tara's garage had housed a similar pile of baggage, for months.

After Kim died Tara hadn't been able to face the ordeal of sorting out her flat, so Charley had done it for her. She had diligently boxed and bagged everything up, and then discreetly handed it all over to Baz to store in the garage so that Tara wouldn't have to even look at anything until she was ready. Almost a year later, when Tara had finally felt she could cope with the task, Charley had helped her again, and they'd spent an emotionally exhausting morning, while Monnie was at school, sifting through Kim's possessions. There was nothing, nothing at all, of any monetary value, but a wealth of things with huge sentimental value. When Tara had clung onto Kim's chipped old Brown Betty teapot, and her tatty jam-stained cookery book and said, 'I can't get rid of these. I just can't,' and when she'd clutched Kim's favourite blue scarf to her face to inhale her perfume, and said she couldn't bring herself to give that away either, Charley had simply said, 'Then don't,' and had gently taken them out of her hands and put them into the box labelled 'Keep', along with photos and myriad other priceless treasures. Afterwards Charley had taken the rest of Kim's belongings to the charity shop to save her friend the heartache.

Nobody had offered to help Charley sort out Josh's belongings. She'd tried to do it, once or twice, but had been defeated by the seeming impossibility of psychologically separating Josh from his possessions. The thought of disposing of anything in the aftermath of his death had felt like an act of betrayal, as if throwing out his belongings somehow implied Josh no longer mattered, or was not wanted any more.

Tara put her arm round Charley, and breaking into her thoughts, said gently, 'Can I help you sort this lot out?'

Taking a deep breath Charley let it out slowly before shaking her head firmly. 'No. It's all right. I'll do it.'

Tara pulled back, looking mildly offended. 'Oh, okay.'

'I'll be fine,' Charley assured her, for all the world not wanting to hurt her friend's feelings. 'I'd rather do it myself. Honest.' She knew it was going to be a gruelling and unholy blub-fest, and she didn't want to inflict that on anyone or have anyone witness it.

But then suddenly Tara floored her by saying, 'I was rubbish to you when Josh died.'

Charley was completely taken aback. 'No. No, you weren't!'

'I was. I didn't do anything to help you. I didn't even come round. I just sent you a bunch of texts.'

A small, confused frown slid onto Charley's face. 'I thought you came to the funeral, with the others?'

'Yes, of course I did. But I didn't support you the way you supported me when Mum died.' Tara shrugged apologetically. 'I just didn't know what you were going through. I'm sorry.'

Those first terrible days after Josh died, Charley had felt numb and cut off from reality. It was the texts pinging to her phone, brief messages of care, which had cut through the thick fog of sorrow and kept her connected to the world, like a mooring line to the shore. 'You don't have to apologise, really,' said Charley, giving Tara a hug. 'Sending me texts helped. They let me know you were thinking about me.' Then she quickly changed the subject. Glancing around the spare room she said, 'I'll have to buy a bed and do the room up a bit.'

'Actually, the whole flat needs doing up,' Tara said bluntly.

Charley winced, but she knew the walls hadn't seen a paintbrush for years and the cheap magnolia paint that she and Josh had plastered everywhere, was now less Magnolia with a Hint of Peach and more Grey with a Hint of Grime.

'You'll have to get a double bed,' said Tara, wandering off on a tour of inspection round the rest of the flat.

'But it's a single room!' protested Charley, following her. 'I'm not having a couple.'

'No, but there might be a boyfriend, or girlfriend… or whatever. Unless you have a "no bonking" clause,' laughed Tara. 'Or let the room out to a nun.'

Charley suddenly got cold feet, icy-cold feet. *Two* people meant she'd be outnumbered in her own flat.

Tara carried on obliviously, 'And of course you'll have to let them use the kitchen and the bathroom, and probably the living room, too. You can't expect them to spend all their time in their room. Unless you gave them your room?' Tara hummed in apparent consideration. 'That might be big enough to put a sofa in as well as a bed.'

'No!' Charley said fiercely, so fiercely that Tara looked round at her in surprise. But there was absolutely no way she was giving up her and Josh's room to a couple of strangers.

'In that case you'll have to share the living room as well,' said Tara, not unreasonably.

'But that's the whole flat!' It was going to be more like a full-scale invasion than a room-let.

Charley spent the entire weekend in an agony of indecision. Never having shared a flat with anyone other than Josh, the logical practicalities of the term 'room-let' had simply not occurred to her – she'd interpreted the phrase literally. Having lived at home until she'd moved in with Josh, she hadn't understood the inevitably invasive nature of letting out a room. In theory, getting a lodger seemed to be the perfect solution to her money worries, but in practice… in practice, the thought of sharing her home, no, her and Josh's home, with a total stranger appalled her. There'd be someone else's toast crumbs in the butter, their dirty dishes in her sink and takeaway cartons in the pedal bin and her whole flat would reek of other people's cooking smells. They'd probably leave underwear on the bathroom floor, disposable razors by the bath and shampoo in the shower. And she'd have to put up with them sitting on her sofa, sitting at her kitchen table, not to mention them sitting on her bloody *toilet* for crying out loud. Charley shuddered at the thought. She didn't think she was being overdramatically squeamish, but these would be total strangers and she wasn't at all sure she could put up with that, even if it was the perfect – the *only* – solution to her money worries.

Chapter Six

On the Monday morning Charley woke to find a storm that had raged overnight, waking her with its ferocity, had blown the garden fence down. 'Bloody, *bloody* hell! More expense,' she groaned, cradling her hot coffee mug in both hands and gazing helplessly at the damage. Annoyingly, since it was the back fence, she couldn't even ask a neighbour to share the cost of replacing it. *But, looking on the bright side*, she told herself, *at least the back fence is shorter than the side fence, so it'll be cheaper to fix*. The thought didn't actually succeed in making her feel all that much better – but it was a good try.

After breakfast she called Tara to ask if Baz could get her some fencing panels, since he could get them cheaper through his building firm.

''Course he will. I'll get him to come over and put it up for you.'

'I don't expect him to do that!'

Tara laughed. 'No, but I do!'

The broken fence forced Charley to make a decision about the lodger. She ordered a bed – a double – then, after breakfast, she made herself go into the spare room and start clearing it out. She was dreading it, but perhaps it would be easier now, especially if she cut herself some slack and allowed herself to keep a few special things, like the Arctic Monkeys Tour T-shirt she'd bought Josh at Reading Festival, the Italian leather belt from Venice, his Hugo Boss body spray…

Sitting cross-legged on the floor she picked a bag at random and pulled out a pair of jeans and a couple of T-shirts. The jeans, she decided, were too tatty for a charity shop. 'Bin,' she decided, but the T-shirts were okay. 'Charity shop,' she said, starting a different pile. Pulling open another bag she took out a bubble-wrapped package. Without even opening it, she knew what was inside – a pair of engraved crystal wedding flutes. Carefully unwrapping them she held them up to the light to read the inscriptions: one said 'Love and Laughter' and the other 'Happy Ever After'. Josh had given them to her on their honeymoon and although the memory brought a brief, tender smile to her face she also felt a twinge of sadness deep inside.

In an uncharacteristically romantic gesture, Josh had hidden the flutes in his rucksack and had dug them out and presented them to her as they'd stood on the Rialto Bridge overlooking the canal in Venice. He'd then produced a bottle of Prosecco also stashed in his pack and solemnly poured them both a glass. She remembered laughing as the warm fizz had foamed up, spilled over and frothed onto her hand. It had been late in the afternoon and they'd stayed on the bridge, leaning on the cool stone balustrade, soaking up the warm sun, sipping the Prosecco and letting life go by all around them. She'd asked a passing tourist to take a photo of them. As the sky had darkened to the blue of Venetian glass, the city had lit up, lights reflecting on the dark water, and the lanterns hanging front and aft of the gondolas had hinted at a magical city full of romance, and so, when the bottle was empty, they'd kissed and headed through the narrow streets back to the hotel.

She never wanted to forget the feeling of Josh's skin against hers. She knew she would always, easily, be able to conjure up images of him, the way he'd looked at her, or something he'd said or done, but it was getting harder to remember his touch, his smell and the sound of his voice, and it alarmed her to think she might forget altogether one day.

'Oh, this is too bloody hard!' She put the flutes back into their wrappings, stood up and took herself off to the DIY store.

–

Grabbing a trolley, she ordered herself to think cheap and cheerful, with the emphasis on cheap. Naturally the shop had put the cheaper paints right at the back and she was forced to push her trolley through the shelves of gorgeous, eye-wateringly expensive paints. Studiously ignoring the to-die-for colours, she pushed on to the bargain corner.

Several large tubs of Rustic Red sat forlornly on a pallet labelled 'Half Price'. Immediately deciding 'Half Price' was her new favourite colour, she slung a couple of pots in the trolley for the living room and then splashed out on some cheap, industrial-sized tubs of Zesty Yellow for the rest of the flat. Then she found some chic curtains and bedding with an abstract, autumnal leaf pattern for the spare room. She was almost tempted to put them in her room, except her room absolutely wasn't part of the makeover, she reminded herself. Finally, she headed to the checkout and handed the cashier her credit card.

'Don't even tell me how much it is,' she begged. 'Just put it on the card.'

Within an hour she was cheerfully rollering the kitchen walls Zesty Yellow. It was an enormous improvement so, hugely encouraged, she decided to tackle the ceiling, using a chair to stand on. She'd barely begun when Baz arrived to fix the fence, and promptly gave her a bollocking.

'That's how people end up in A&E, and why God invented the stepladder!'

When she pointed out she didn't actually possess a stepladder, he got one out of his van.

'Hang on to it until you're done,' he told her.

She thanked him and offered him a coffee.

'I'll make it,' he said, 'You crack on.' He made them both coffee and took his outside to get on with the fence.

You are a damn good man, thought Charley, and not for the first time, wished Tara appreciated him a bit more.

By the time he came in to tell her he was all finished, she'd moved on to the hall, but she had a crick in her neck and cramp in her painting hand. She was flagging, definitely flagging.

'You're doing a grand job!' he told her.

She rolled her eyes. 'I wish! Anyhow, how much do I owe you?'

'I'll send you an invoice,' he said vaguely.

Charley looked him in the eye. 'Don't forget,' she said.

'Okay,' he replied, but they both knew Tara would ensure the bill was 'forgotten'.

–

It took Charley several, totally knackering days to paint the hall, the bathroom, the kitchen and the spare room. It didn't help that every night she had to stop around five, scrub up and go to the pub to work. The blisters on her hands, the aches in her muscles and the fact that she could barely move her neck reminded her *precisely* why she and Josh had only ever painted the flat once. She never wanted to pick up a roller again, which was a shame, because she still had to tackle the living room.

Covering her blisters with plasters, and the furniture with dustsheets, she scooped up all the ornaments on the shelving unit, including her wedding photo, which momentarily stopped her in her tracks. Josh was beaming at her like a Cheshire cat who couldn't believe he'd got the cream. He'd always been quick to smile, and perhaps it wasn't surprising that nearly all the pictures she had of him had captured him with his trademark grin. The only difference was that in this photo, for once, he had managed to tame his unruly hair.

'You are not going to recognise the living room by the time I'm done,' she told him, but even she wasn't prepared for the shock-and-awe effect of Rustic Red obliterating Magnolia. Charley rocked back on her heels and eyed the wall. *'Rustic?'* More like *'Drastic'*. And then suddenly and rather irrationally, she felt she was being disloyal, as if she was eradicating the memory of Josh with every sweep of the roller – painting him out of her life. She told herself she was being ridiculous. 'Anyhow, it's too late to go back now,' she told herself briskly. 'You need the rent.' So, flinging open the French doors to let the paint smell out and the fresh air in, she carried on, and by the end of the day the living room was completely transformed.

Going through to the kitchen, she dumped the roller into the sink, ran the cold tap, and started rinsing the paint out of it. An improbable quantity of dark red paint gushed out, as if it had been the weapon for a particularly bloody murder, while her red-splattered hands identified her as the killer. Naturally, just at that moment, her phone rang.

'Calm. Me. Down,' said Nisha's voice tightly down the line.

'What's happened now?' Charley sank anxiously onto a kitchen chair.

'He's demanding more money.'

Immediately grasping Nisha meant Jay, Charley replied, 'I thought you settled all the finances in court when you got divorced.'

'We did.'

'Is he allowed to ask for more money now? Legally I mean.'

'I don't know. Possibly. Probably. He says he wants the other ten per cent.'

It was a statement which meant nothing to Charley, so Nisha went onto explain that Jay had been so keen to leave her and buy a flat with *La Bimbo*, he'd agreed to take forty per cent of their joint assets, instead of the usual fifty-fifty split, because that was all she could raise. Actually, as Nisha pointed out, it was pretty much what he would have ended up with anyway since if they'd sold the flat, it would have cost them a fortune in estate agent and legal fees which would have taken a substantial chunk out of the pot. And considering she'd put down the deposit and paid the lion's share of the mortgage, it was more than he damn well deserved anyhow.

'But now *La Bimbo* is pregnant, he wants me to give him the other ten per cent.'

'Can you afford to?'

'No! It'd be twenty-eight grand! I'm mortgaged to the max and had to borrow off my parents to buy him out as it was. But apparently, and you're going to love this, he thinks he's got a case because they're expecting a baby and I have no dependants!'

'Bloody hell, Nishe.'

'Bloody hell indeed.'

Feeling utterly helpless, and angered by the injustice of Nisha's position, Charley sighed before saying, 'I wish I could do something to help.'

'You have helped,' Nisha assured her. 'I only called to vent. And I'm sorry to dump on you, *again*, but you're the only one who understands what it's like to be on your own, financially, I mean, as well as everything else.'

'I just wish I could do more—' Charley trailed off hopelessly.

'Don't say that, or I'll feel crap about calling you. It's not like I was expecting you to magic up twenty-eight grand!'

'Just as bloody well! I'd struggle to raise twenty-eight quid!'

Chapter Seven

At the weekend, the delivery of the new bed forced Charley to brace herself and deal with Josh's things in the spare room. She'd leant the flat-packed frame and the double mattress against the wall, but if she wanted space to actually build the damn thing, she'd have to clear the bags and boxes cluttering the middle of the room – it was as simple as that. She made herself a mug of tea, knelt on the floor, pulled the nearest bag to her and began to empty it onto the carpet. Out tumbled the tokens of their lives together... the blue knot cufflinks she'd bought him for their anniversary... a tangle of festival wristbands... his phone and GameBoy (for crying out loud), and then his wallet. The wallet had been her first birthday gift to him. She opened it and her face stared back at her, a few years younger but still very much the same – her slightly self-conscious smile, framed by a mass of unruly curls tumbling down over her shoulders.

She took a deep, shaky breath. She was only halfway through the first bag and she was already struggling. So when the doorbell rang about ten minutes later, although she wasn't proud to admit it, she was thankful for the interruption.

A woman in cropped slacks and a long T-shirt, with greying hair and a cabin-size wheelie-bag, stood on her doorstep, looking vaguely distressed.

'Pam?' Charley's mind raced frantically. Her mother-in-law never arrived unannounced or without an invitation. *What on earth was she doing here, completely out of the blue without so much as a phone call or a text and, crucially, with a suitcase?*

'I've left Geoff!'

'What!' gasped Charley.

'He's having an affair.'

'Bloody hell, Pam!' The expletives escaped before Charley could stop them, but beyond that, she was utterly speechless so, picking up the suitcase, she ushered her mother-in-law indoors.

'Tea?' she suggested, leading into the kitchen.

'I was hoping for something a bit stronger. Quite a lot of something a bit stronger, actually,' replied Pam, flabbergasting Charley for a second time in a minute.

Charley didn't have '*anything stronger*'. She never kept wine in the flat, worried that she'd be tempted to drink alone, and that was a slippery slope she wasn't going to risk even putting a toe on.

'Make yourself at home, and I'll nip out and get something,' she said.

'Oh, don't go out just for me,' Pam protested politely.

I'm not, thought Charley. *After a bombshell like that, I need a drink.*

-

Nipping to the mini supermarket around the corner, Charley grabbed a bottle of Prosecco then, thinking about it, changed it to a bottle of Pinot, in case it looked like she thought that Pam leaving her husband was something to celebrate. Then, thinking about it even more and remembering Pam's request for 'quite a lot of something a bit stronger' she picked up a second bottle. Then she added a couple of frozen pizzas to the basket, partly to mop up the booze, but also because, judging by the suitcase, Pam had apparently come to stay the night and, as usual, there was bugger all in the fridge.

Ten minutes later, sitting on the sofa with glass of wine in hand, Pam seemed surprisingly unruffled. Only the speed with which she knocked back her drink and held the glass out for a top-up gave anything away – that, and the fact that the total transformation of the living room had utterly escaped her notice.

'I feel so stupid… such a *fool*! He's been seeing this… woman, *sleeping* with this woman,' she corrected herself, 'for *years*! Years!'

Charley was lost for words, which wasn't, as it turned out, a problem, since her mother-in-law ploughed on, emitting a steady flow of words fuelled, no doubt, by a much-needed release of tension.

'Of course, all the time he was working I never knew – he'd get held up in the office or have to go to a work do or something and he'd get home late, and I'd be full of sympathy for him having worked such long hours, when all the while he'd been… *having it off* in some… some hotel room or whatever.'

Charley took a gulp of wine. Hearing the ins and outs of her father-in-law's sex life, as it were, and from her *mother-in-law*, was all a bit… hideously embarrassing, really.

'How did you find out?' she ventured, when Pam briefly stopped in her rant to take another glug of wine.

'Hah! After he retired, he got careless… no, *greedy*. He couldn't resist a bit of… *afternoon delight*' – she spat the words out viciously – 'and I caught him at it.'

Charley choked on her wine. 'You caught them having sex?' she spluttered.

'No! I caught him with *the other woman.*'

Charley could almost visualise quote marks round the phrase 'the other woman' in Pam's mind. Then the first crack appeared in Pam's demeanour. She closed her eyes, flinched at the memory, and said, 'Oh God, it was awful, Charley, absolutely awful.'

–

Once in a while, Pam and her friends treated themselves to a pub lunch, and this time they'd decided, rather last minute, to try somewhere new. They'd met up, in the pub car park, in a flurry of hugs and air kisses, and then headed inside. Laughing and joking, they made their usual noisy invasion, but within seconds, the laughter had died in their throats and they'd stood in shocked and absolute silence. There, in the middle of the dining area, holding hands with a younger, *much younger* woman, and laughing animatedly at some shared joke, was Pam's husband.

Pam had seen him before he saw her. 'Geoff?' she ventured.

Her entire entourage had stiffened while they waited for his response. It was instantly damning, the panicked, guilty look on his face had given him away completely – without that, they might perhaps have believed he was with an old work colleague, but instead he looked, for all the world, like a naughty boy caught with his hand in the biscuit tin. Deafened by the sound of her blood pounding in her ears, and burned by the heat of her face scorched by humiliation, Pam had turned on her heel and fled.

Behind her, Geoff had scraped back his chair and scrabbled to his feet. 'Pam!' he'd cried, and then pushed his way through her group of friends to follow her. They hadn't made way for him.

Sadly, Pam missed the moment, the glorious moment, when Zee, her oldest friend, had casually picked up a full jug of water from the table and thrown it in the younger woman's face. Screaming in shock and with indignation, the woman had reeled back and then risen to her feet, wiping her dripping face with her napkin.

'That's assault!' she'd yelled. Whipping round to the bar keeper who was standing at the bar, open-mouthed and frozen in the act of polishing a glass, she'd cried gleefully, 'You saw that! She assaulted me! You're a witness!'

'Oh, take me to court,' Zee had replied magnificently.

Outside in the car park, Geoff had caught up with Pam at Zee's car, where she was desperately, but futilely, rattling the door handle and cursing the fact that she couldn't bolt into the sanctuary of the vehicle and lock the door.

'Pam—' started Geoff, but she had turned on him savagely.

'How dare you! How *could* you?' Then suddenly, finding herself urgently needing to know the answer to another, more damning question, she had demanded, 'How long?' When he didn't answer, she'd repeated, 'How long? I have a right to know.'

'Five years,' Geoff muttered sheepishly, and Pam had wanted to hit him. He'd put his hand on her arm. 'I'm sorry...'

She'd twisted away from him violently. Suddenly the thought of him touching her physically repulsed her. Frantically she'd looked around for Zee, who was halfway across the car park. 'Zee!' she'd called urgently.

Instantly taking in the scene, Zee had grabbed the car keys from her bag, opened the doors remotely, and Pam had escaped to the safety of the passenger seat, slamming the door behind her. Ignoring Geoff completely, Zee had got into the car and driven Pam home.

When Zee had pulled into Pam's drive, she'd wanted to go inside too, but Pam had shaken her head. 'No... thank you, but no... I... I need to think,' she'd stammered, and had hurriedly clambered out of the car.

As soon as she was indoors, the sudden, empty silence had engulfed her, focusing her mind and clarifying her thoughts. Her single overriding, urgent need was to get away before Geoff got back, so running upstairs she'd frantically thrown together an overnight bag and had fled to Charley's.

—

'Is it okay if I stay?'

'Yes, of course,' said Charley but then, as Pam picked up her case and started to head for the spare room, Charley belatedly remembered what she had been doing just before her mother-in-law arrived. 'I was having a bit of a clear-out...' she started awkwardly, trying to catch up with Pam, to warn her. But she was too late, her mother-in-law had already stopped in the doorway of the spare room and was surveying the piles of Josh's belongings. Charley felt vaguely sick.

Pam merely swallowed hard, then turned to Charley, and with endearing, unemotional simplicity said, 'Do you want a hand, or would you rather do it alone?' At that moment, Charley suddenly realised that out of everyone, Pam was the only person she would, very much, like to help her.

Fetching the rest of the wine she then squatted down beside Pam, who proceeded calmly to help sift through the belongings of her dead son.

'I'm struggling to know what to keep and what to—' Charley couldn't bring herself to say, 'throw away'.

Pam rescued her. 'What to *give* away,' she supplied, before adding in a light, careless tone, 'Well, I've kept Josh's teddy, but then I've kept Luke's too, all the photos, and a lot of the books I read them when they were little, a few other things of sentimental value… and I've kept his bed linen, too, of course.' But Charley knew that was partly because Pam was aware of how much it meant to Charley to sleep under Josh's old duvet cover when she stayed in his bedroom at Christmas.

Christmas. That terrible first Christmas without Josh. Charley had never known how Pam had managed to create a normal Christmas that year for the sake of her other son, Luke, and his young family. Comforting smells had filled the house – mulled wine, roast turkey, the sharp pine scent of the tree – and a full three-course lunch had appeared on the table, crackers were pulled, jokes read out, paper hats perched on heads. After lunch, sitting round the tree it was as if it was just another Christmas: presents were opened, new toys played with, and Ben and Jessica ate candy canes and chocolate money. Pam had kept herself busy looking after everyone, endlessly doling out food, treats, hugs and cuddles, instinctively knowing that grief can't settle on a moving target. Charley had spent most of Christmas Day curled up on the sofa, numb, barely able to speak, letting the festivities wash over her like a relentless tide until she could retreat to the sanctuary of Josh's old room, where she could lie on his bed, wrap his duvet round her, close her eyes and wish it were him.

It took Charley and Pam the remainder of the afternoon to go through the bags, although they'd have done it much more quickly if they hadn't let themselves get diverted by memories or by laughing at the sheer hilariousness of some of Josh's possessions: a pair of socks printed to look like sandals, his barbeque apron that said 'Hot Man doing Hot Work. Pour me a Beer!' and a plastic inflatable Sumo suit. Charley remembered him putting it on first thing one morning.

'Help me blow it up!' he'd cried, his blue eyes dancing with fun.

'Don't be daft! You'll never get in the car!'

'Good point!' he had said, and then in all serious-ness, he'd stood in front of the mirror and solemnly put his tie on top of the Sumo suit, to go to work. She remembered laughing until she'd cried – he'd looked so utterly ridiculous.

Pam's voice brought her back. 'Oh my God, where did he wear that?' she was asking.

'At the showroom. For a dare!'

'Who dared him?'

'Luke.'

Pam laughed out loud. 'I might have guessed!'

Charley doubted anything that her sons had got up to would have surprised Pam. The stories Josh had told her about what he and his brother had got up to as kids had been hilarious.

In the end, the sort-out was nothing like the painful blub-fest Charley had dreaded it would be. 'Is there anything you'd like to keep?' she asked Pam.

Her mother-in-law smiled, but shook her head. 'That's very sweet of you… but I don't need anything.'

When Charley found the Arctic Monkeys T-shirt and the Italian leather belt, she steeled herself and put them both in the charity bag. The Hugo Boss aftershave had gone off, so she poured it down the loo and put the bottle in the recycling. She kept the Prosecco flutes, their wedding album and Josh's wedding ring, of course, all the photos, his blue cufflinks and wallet. She chucked the festival wrist bands out, but then had a swift panic and hoicked them out of the bin liner, much to Pam's amusement. She then promptly rescued the Arctic Monkeys T-shirt from the charity bag, as well. Pam rolled her eyes.

'What?' exclaimed Charley wide-eyed with innocence. 'It's a perfectly good T-shirt. I can wear it in bed!'

And that was it. Now all they had to do was make the bed – literally.

Chapter Eight

'Do you even know how to do this?' asked Pam, as Charley confidently ripped the packaging off the bed frame.

'It's a flat pack from IKEA!' exclaimed Charley. 'We're two intelligent women, armed with an Allen key. There ain't nothing we can't do!'

Pam looked unconvinced, so Charley went on, 'Trust me. I've done a DIY course, and it's nothing like the dark, mysterious art it's cracked up to be.'

Methodically she laid out all the bed pieces on the floor and then picked up the instructions, at which point, irritatingly, her phone rang. Glancing at the number, she saw it was the pub. *Bloody, bloody hell!* She was meant to be at work! She didn't want to take the call in front of Pam, not because she was ashamed of working in the pub, she tried to convince herself, it was more that she still hadn't told Pam about her redundancy. She wanted to explain her change of circumstances in her own way, and at the right moment, so Charley shot off to her room, calling over her shoulder, 'Won't be a sec!' It didn't even occur to her how Pam might interpret, or rather, misinterpret that action.

In the privacy of her room Charley garbled a profuse apology to her manager, and explained that a family crisis had come up unexpectedly. After assuring him she'd be in the next day, she pocketed her phone and went back to the spare room. Much to her relief, Pam didn't even mention the call. Less than an hour later, despite IKEA's best efforts to make the instructions as opaque and confusing as humanly possible, Charley had defied them, and her mother-in-law's expectations, and had built the bed.

Although Pam might have found building a flat-pack bed a challenge, an hour or so later she was completely in her element in Charley's kitchen.

'Where's the garlic crusher?' she asked, rootling through the cutlery drawer.

'Sorry, haven't seen it for ages,' fibbed Charley, reluctant to admit she didn't actually have one, and wondering how to break it to Pam that she didn't actually have any garlic either. Charley had bunged the pizzas in the oven and was now watching Pam conjure up a salad from the pitiful contents of the fridge.

'It's not the just the betrayal and the humiliation...' continued Pam, savagely sharpening a vegetable knife as if it were her chosen weapon of assassination. 'It's that he's made me feel so stupid. Look so... *ridiculous!*'

'Nobody will think you're ridiculous,' said Charley gently.

'I damn well do,' retorted Pam, viciously slicing up a slightly limp tomato. 'You'd think I would have guessed. Maybe not when he was working, but once he'd retired... when it took him hours to buy a light bulb for the down-stairs loo... or when he spent the entire afternoon at the garden centre because "it was raining too hard to get to the car"... or the whole day in Bristol "buying underpants", for crying out loud. What kind of idiot am I?' She turned to look at Charley, wounded bewilderment showing in her eyes.

'You're not an idiot, at all, Pam. Why on earth would you suspect him after, what, forty years together?' Charley nearly added, *and all you've been through*, but she swallowed the thought. 'Does he know where you are?'

'No.'

'You should probably just tell him you're here, otherwise he'll worry.'

'Let him,' said Pam, picking up the knife again and brutally chopping an innocent apple into chunks. 'I don't want anyone to know. I just want to…' she looked away, and drew in a shuddery breath. 'I just want to run away and disappear,' she finished, suddenly sounding exhausted.

'That's okay,' said Charley, going over to Pam and putting her arms round her. 'You're allowed to run away and hide.'

When Josh died, Charley had fled to Pam's. Overwhelmed by the aching emptiness, she had gone to ground in Josh's childhood home seeking solace amongst his things, and his family. It was the only place where she didn't feel stranded on an island of grief while the rest of the world drifted by, with what felt like heartless disregard for her agonising loss. And then there was Pam. Brave, loving, unbreakable Pam. The only one who really understood the ferocious, monstrous chasm of loss engulfing her, and the only one who could help her through it.

Pam had never been one to wear her bleeding heart on her sleeve or to pour out her sorrows in an unending stream like a broken record, so Charley was touched that the older woman had allowed herself to lean against Charley for a short while and take comfort from her. She rightly interpreted it as a gesture of trust and the affection they shared for each other.

'I'm sorry, Pam. You really don't deserve this.'

'Does anybody?'

No, thought Charley.

Pam gave her a quick hug, swallowed hard and pulled away. 'I lost a son. I can cope with losing a mere husband.'

–

Hardly surprisingly, the emotional roller coaster of the day took its toll on Pam and she woke late the following morning. Wandering into the kitchen in her dressing gown, she found Charley already sitting at the kitchen table at her computer.

'Tea? Toast?' Charley asked her.

'Please. What sort of time is it?'

'About half nine,' said Charley, getting up and slotting two slices of thin white into the toaster and flicking the kettle on.

'What?! Why aren't you at work? Please don't tell me you've taken the day off because of me?' Pam was mortified, until, somewhat sheepishly, Charley confessed she'd been made redundant.

Pam's initial sympathy rapidly switched to indignation that anyone would have the audacity to make Charley redundant. 'Why couldn't the new people keep you on?' she demanded.

Charley shrugged. 'Perhaps they have their own people.'

'Well, they don't deserve you,' declared Pam. 'Anyhow, somebody else will snap you up and it'll serve them right.'

Charley gave her a warm smile and then handed her a plate of toast, together with a mug of tea. A slightly alarming thought hit Pam, and she put down the knife she'd just picked up to butter her toast. 'Is that why you've done the flat up? Are you thinking of selling it?'

'No! Absolutely not!' exclaimed Charley.

'So...' Pam stopped, hesitating to pry into Charley's affairs since it really was none of her business; yet at the same time, she was anxious about her. Adopting a deliberately casual tone, Pam said, 'So, you're okay for money.' It was a statement, rather than a question.

'Yes, of course,' Charley said in rush. 'Actually, I've taken a pub job.' Concern sliced through Pam, and although she was quick to mask her feelings with a smile, Charley obviously saw something in her face as she added quickly, 'It's only until I can find something better.'

In the interests of banishing the mild air of discomfort now hanging between them, Pam briskly changed the subject. 'Well, don't feel you have to entertain me. I don't want to gatecrash your day.'

'You're not. I've no plans at all.' But as Charley's eyes slid from hers, concern slid right back into Pam. 'Do you have... any plans?' Charley asked her lightly and Pam wondered if she was being deflected.

'No. None at all. Apart from leaving my husband!' she replied, with a brave stab at humour which brought a small smile from Charley. 'But can I stay? For a while, just until I...' she paused, not sure how long she would want to stay. 'Well, until I get things sorted out,' she finished vaguely.

'You know you can. As long as you like.'

For a while it was quiet in the kitchen. Charley's head was buried in her laptop and Pam assumed she was job-hunting. However, it didn't take a genius to work out that since Charley didn't have a proper job, had given the entire flat a makeover, *and* bought a new double bed, she was planning on letting the spare room. So, after a while, and bracing herself for an argument, Pam said, 'If I'm going to stay, then I'm going to pay you rent.'

Charley's head shot up from her laptop. 'Absolutely not!'

'Absolutely yes!'

Charley shut the lid of her laptop sharply, as if to express her determination. 'Pam, I practically *lived* with you after Josh died, and I didn't give you anything!'

The older woman looked at the earnest young face before her. She knew Charley needed the money. Was it pride stopping her from taking it, she wondered, or generosity? She decided it was probably a mix of the two so, shooting Charley a wicked look added, 'I'll get Geoff to pay it.'

–

Shortly afterwards, while Pam was in the shower, Angie phoned. 'Fancy coming for coffee? Although I should warn you, the boys have just got water pistols. Some idiot put them in a party bag. They'd love to show them to you!'

'I'll bet they would!' Charley laughed. 'But can we make it another day? The thing is… I've sort of got a lodger. It's Pam, actually, she's just moved in and I don't want to abandon her on her first day.'

'Pam?' queried Angie.

'Yes.'

'As in your former mother-in-law, Pam?'

'Yes.'

'Blimey, Charley! How did *that* happen!'

Charley lowered her voice and shut the kitchen door to prevent Pam overhearing her. 'I know! Look, I don't

want to give too much away – it's her business. But she's…
well, she's definitely staying for a bit. And, bless her cotton
Marks and Spencer's trainer socks, she's insisting on paying
me rent.' For the first time in weeks, Charley felt the heavy
burden of money worries shift a little, if not actually lift
entirely.

'Fantastic!'

'Yes, isn't it—' she paused.

'Except?'

Except that… 'Well, I know I was thinking of a lodger,
but I wasn't thinking of my mother-in-law!'

Angie laughed. 'Look on the bright side, it could be a
whole lot worse – it could be your mother.'

Charley groaned out loud, then down the line she
heard Eliot urgently trying to get Angie's attention.

'Mum… MUM… MUUUM!' he bawled.

'Hang on, Charley… Sweetheart, I'm on the phone,
just wait half a second.'

'But Finn's done a poo in my shoe!' wailed Eliot.

Oh, how gross! thought Charley.

'Oh Finn! Not again!' Angie moaned.

Again? thought Charley. *Poor Eliot!*

Hurriedly, Angie came back on the line, 'Charley, I've
gotta go!'

'No shit!' quipped Charley.

'Oh, ha bloody ha.'

Chapter Nine

In her frantic haste to pack before Geoff could get home Pam had left her pyjamas behind, amongst other things and, since there was absolutely no way on earth she was going back for them, she'd have to nip into Bristol and buy some. There was every danger she might run into someone she knew, someone who, in all innocence, would inevitably ask how Geoff was, and then she'd have to open the Pandora's box of explaining she'd left him, and she just wasn't ready for that. Resisting the urge to ask Charley if she could borrow a pair of dark glasses and a big floppy sun hat (not that Charley possessed such a thing), she did the next best thing and asked her to go with her. 'I need back-up,' she begged.

By the time they'd found somewhere to park and Pam had bought some nightwear and a few other just-left-your-husband-in-a-flaming-hurry essentials, it was lunchtime. Not wanting to risk exposure by sitting anywhere she could be seen from the street, Pam headed for the sanctuary of the upstairs cafe in the Bristol Guild shop in Park Street, with Charley following in her wake. The cafe was already packed with shoppers surrounded by designer carrier bags, and young mums with buggies. They'd just sat down with their lunches still on their trays when Pam's phone rang. Glancing down at the caller number, she rejected the call.

'It was Geoff,' she explained to Charley, who nodded understandingly, but said nothing. Four seconds later Geoff rang again. Pam rejected the call again, then, when he rang a third time, she turned the sound off and left the phone on the table, face up, fielding calls. Pam was just congratulating herself for dealing with things rather well, when Charley's phone rang. Charley dug it out of her pocket and held it up to show the caller number to Pam.

'It's Geoff! Don't answer it!' panicked Pam.

Charley declined the call. 'He must be wondering where you are. Do you want me to text him, just to let him know you're safe?'

'No,' said Pam, decisively slicing a chunk off her quiche.

For the next ten minutes or thereabouts Pam's phone was dead and they concentrated on their lunches, but then the screen lit up.

'Him again?' asked Charley.

Pam glanced at the number. 'No, it's Zee. Geoff's probably calling everyone to see where I am.'

'Does she know you're staying with me?' Pam shook her head. 'She'll be worried about you. Maybe just give her a quick call now?'

Waving a hand to indicate the crowded cafe Pam said, 'What from here? No, I'll call her later.'

Pam lost count of the number of times her phone lit up during the rest of their lunch. She studiously ignored it, but then the texts started pinging in.

'Oh, for crying out loud,' she muttered and, snatching up her phone, shoved it into her handbag.

'Pam, you can't just disappear without telling anyone,' Charley pointed out reasonably. 'If nothing else, just text *someone* and let them know you're okay.'

Reluctantly conceding that Charley had a point, and sighing heavily, Pam quickly sent a text to Zee: *Staying with my daughter-in-law. Don't worry!*

She toyed with adding *Don't tell Geoff*, but somehow it seemed ridiculously childish. In the end, she just added *I'm fine. Catch up soon. Px* and clicked SEND.

The only other message she replied to was Luke's. He'd texted:

> Where are you? Are you okay?

In the interests of keeping things simple and not worrying him, she was economical with the truth and typed *Yes. I'm fine. Having lunch with Charley. Lots of love.* Then she made a mental note to call him later, in private, and explain… as best she could.

–

An enormous bouquet of flowers sat at the bottom of Charley's steps when they got back to the flat, with a card stuck onto the cellophane that read:

> *Please forgive me,*
> *Geoff*

Pam glanced at the note briefly then, to Charley's astonishment, she swept up the flowers, stormed straight back up the steps, dumped them in the dustbin and slammed the lid shut. Wordlessly, Charley watched her stomp back down the steps and into the flat, openly seething. Not two minutes later, when they'd barely had time to get inside and deposit Pam's shopping in her room, the doorbell rang. *They say fools rush in where angels fear to tread – well, apparently so do unfaithful husbands, but then perhaps they're the same thing*, Charley thought as she opened the door.

'Geoff!' cried Charley, in a voice she hoped would be loud enough to carry through to Pam in the kitchen. Then she stood at the doorway, not really knowing what to do. She'd always got on well with her father-in-law, and she was caught out by the anger now simmering inside her. Nevertheless, she couldn't just leave him standing at the threshold. 'You'd better come in,' she said coolly.

He hovered sheepishly in the hall, but Pam strode imperiously out of the kitchen to confront him. Taking in the Arctic drop in temperature, Charley turned on her heel and bolted out of the front door to Tara's.

–

Pam gave Geoff all of ten minutes before sending him packing, which was ten minutes more than he deserved, as far as she was concerned.

'Did Zee tell you where I was?' she demanded tersely.

'No. Nobody seemed to know where you were. I called Charley but she didn't answer. I drove round here on the off-chance and saw your car parked up the street, so I decided to sit and wait for you.'

He did try to apologise, desperately and repeatedly, promising to give up 'the other woman', who, it turned out, was a former work colleague called Barbara. Pam listened to his increasingly grovelling apologies and his pleading promises in utter silence, for nine-and-a-half excruciating minutes, and then, when Geoff finally ran out steam she said, with icy civility, 'Do you seriously think a bunch of flowers, an apology and then offering to end your grubby little affair can undo the…' she struggled momentarily to find the right word '…*betrayal?* The *years* of betrayal?'

When Geoff didn't answer, Pam simply showed him the door. How dare he assume an apology could even begin to undo the irreparable damage he'd done – not just to their marriage, but to her? As soon as she'd closed the door behind him, her paper-thin poise disintegrated and, taking herself to her room, she flung herself onto the bed like a broken-hearted teenager and gave in to a wave of rage and sorrow. After which she pulled herself together, blew her nose, splashed her face with cold water and made herself a mug of tea, before calling Luke and explaining the situation to him, as calmly as she could.

'I don't expect you to take sides, darling…' she tried to assure him.

But Luke cut her off, exploding with fury. 'He's having an affair, Mum! Of course I'm on your side. I'm bloody livid with him.'

For a moment Pam couldn't speak, and struggled to hold back tears of sheer relief. She genuinely hadn't wanted Luke to have to take sides, but she hadn't realised how deeply frightened she had been, that if he had done so, he might have sided with Geoff, and not with her. And then she would have lost both her sons.

–

Charley just managed to catch Tara before she took Monnie to her afterschool swimming lesson. She went with her and they sat in the viewing area on plastic chairs while Monnie and the other kids ploughed across the pool in dogged pursuit of their twenty-five-metre badges.

'The thing is I actually like Geoff, but I just feel so bloody angry towards him.'

'I feel bloody angry towards the man and I don't even know him!' retorted Tara.

'It's such a shock. I mean, who breaks up after forty years?' said Charley.

'Lots of people. They just drift apart, fall out of love. You don't even realise it's happening.'

Charley glanced at her sideways. 'You and Baz are okay, aren't you?'

'Yes. Of course.' But her friend had turned away to watch Monnie, and Charley didn't feel she should pry further.

'I can't imagine ever having fallen out of love with Josh,' she said.

'Yeah, well you really never got beyond the honeymoon stage. Wonderful as it is, it doesn't last forever,' said Tara, with an astonishing lack of tact. Charley let it go.

Monnie had just finished her last width of the pool and, spluttering and grinning fit to burst, she hauled herself out of the water and on to the side of the pool. Tara instantly leapt up out of her chair and started applauding wildly. 'Well done, Monnie-Moo!' she yelled.

Charley had no idea if the little girl could hear them through the glass, but she jumped up and clapped enthusiastically, too. 'Go, Monnie!' she shouted.

Catching sight of them, Monnie grinned even wider, endearingly revealing two missing front teeth, and gave them a double thumbs-up.

When Charley got home a few hours later, Pam's bedroom door was closed. Tapping lightly, she went in and found her mother-in-law lying on her bed surrounded by discarded soggy tissues. Hastily pulling herself together, Pam sat up and slapped on a bright smile, but her sore, swollen eyes gave her away.

'Budge over,' said Charley gently, sitting down next to her. 'What did he have to say for himself?'

'Oh, he said he was sorry... and he'll give her up, and come back to me.' Her world-weary tone implied she hadn't expected him to say anything else. Then, reaching for yet another tissue, she blew her nose loudly before saying, 'But d'you know what? I don't want him to. I don't want to be anyone's second choice; I'm not going to be a bloody consolation prize.'

Charley didn't blame her.

Chapter Ten

The upstairs room of the pub had been booked for a hen party; about twenty young women, all old enough to know better but too young to resist, were chugging their way through enough Prosecco to fill an Olympic-sized pool. They all sported garish pink sashes which read 'Team Bride', except for the bride-to-be, who wore a white 'Nearly Married' sash, novelty glasses with the word 'Bride' stuck across the top in plastic diamonds and a T-shirt that declared: 'Saskia's Hen Night. Last chance, lads!'

There's subtle, thought Charley. Then she told herself off for being judgemental. It was the bride's night and entirely up to her how she chose to celebrate it, she reminded herself, but then Charley's hen night had been a much more sober affair. Well, a bit more sober. *Yes*, there had been Prosecco – a lot of Prosecco – and *yes*, they'd all drunk more than they should have, but it had been just her and her best mates, and since they were all married, they'd all just come round to Charley's for a girl's night in, while Josh was out on his stag do. She smiled to herself remembering the ridiculous game of Prosecco Pong they'd played on the kitchen table with plastic cups and a ping-pong ball, and how ruthlessly determined Nisha had been to win and how equally determined Tara was to stop her. And then afterwards, how they'd had to abandon a game of Truth or Dare when Tara over-shared way too much about Baz's performance in the bedroom. Then they'd all watched *Love Actually* and cried themselves silly.

'Another bottle of fizz!' the bride-to-be demanded stridently, crudely breaking into Charley's reminiscing.

'More fizz! More fizz!' chanted Team Bride, waggling their half-empty flutes at her.

More fizz? thought Charley, swiftly totting up the number of empties on the table and deciding that applying any more alcohol to these already inebriated young women would be morally unethical and biologically unwise. Deftly avoiding actually saying 'no', she replied, 'Sorry, but it's nearly closing,' and then, she even more skilfully avoided an all-out riot by announcing it was 'Party bag time!' Team Bride squealed with excitement and Charley nipped off to get the party favours the pub had provided, on top of the hire of the room.

God, those are ghastly, she cringed, as the women up-ended their sparkly pink bags onto the table to reveal a plastic badge that said, 'I'm with the Bride'; a pink, heart-shaped balloon; a party popper and a mini bottle of Prosecco. And this time Charley didn't beat herself up for being judgemental, not least because she knew for a fact the pub charged a fiver for each bag, and there were twenty of them, which meant the bride had shelled out a hundred quid. *A hundred quid?* she thought. *Seriously! If you're going to spend that much on party bags, surely you'd want something better than that?* It was a scandalous rip-off.

It was well past eleven by the time the other bar staff and Charley had finally poured the last of the girls into a taxi and had started to clear up the room.

'Those party bags were atrocious,' Charley told her manager.

'I know,' Jacob replied with a shrug. 'But they didn't seem to mind.'

'They might when they sober up,' said Charley. 'Honestly, for a fiver a head, I could do a lot better.'

Jacob stopped piling glasses onto a tray and looked at her. 'Seriously?'

'Yes!'

'Okay then, bring us a couple of sample bags, and if they're good, I'll put in a word at Head Office.'

Cycling home through the dark, lamp-lit streets, Charley started thinking about the party bags, mostly to distract herself from the effort it took to pedal up the hill, but she was convinced she could definitely do something much better, much classier, and still make a profit.

Waking the following morning, Charley flung the duvet off and padded to the bathroom, but the door wouldn't open. Momentarily confused, she rattled the handle.

'Won't be a minute!' called Pam brightly from inside.

Dammit! 'Sorry!' Charley called, and went to put the kettle on.

A minute or two later, Pam came into kitchen, fully dressed and already wearing earrings and lippy – it wasn't even eight o'clock. *This is definitely not good for my self-esteem*, thought Charley, knowing only too well what she looked like in her baggy old PJs, dregs of yesterday's make-up, and with the remains of her top knot now closely resembling a bird's nest on a windswept clifftop. She sloped off to the bathroom, emerging less than ten minutes later to find that while she'd showered and dressed, Pam had set the table with a pot of tea, a plate of toast, butter and jam, and was now tucking into a boiled egg.

'Shall I do you an egg?' Pam asked.

'I don't expect you to make my breakfast!'

'I know.' Pam smiled, then added getting up, 'But do you want an egg?'

'Actually, I'd love one,' Charley said, sitting down and pouring herself a mug of tea.

When they'd finished eating, Pam reached for her dirty plate.

'No! You cooked! I'll clear.' Charley stood up and gathered up her crockery.

'Nonsense. I've got nothing else to do, and you've got to job-hunt.'

Taking everything from her, Pam ushered her out of the kitchen and Charley felt like a teenager sent off to do her homework, a feeling that intensified an hour or so later when Pam came in with a mug of coffee for her and asked, in a distinctly motherly kind of way, what she'd had for supper last night. Charley cringed and admitted to having had a burger and chips, like she did most nights in the pub – not that she was going to fess up to that particular habit. The pub did do healthier food, salads even, but halfway through a gruelling shift Charley craved junk – or *comfort food*, as she preferred to call it – telling herself she deserved it, or that at least she would burn it off on the ride home.

'Why don't we have our main meal at lunchtime?' Pam suggested. 'I'll make it, because I know how busy you are.'

Charley felt a pang of irritation at Pam's obvious attempts to organise her, and then, telling herself not to be ungrateful, replied echoing her previous statement at breakfast. 'But I don't expect you to do the cooking!'

'If you expected me to, I wouldn't!' Pam returned. 'I *want* to.'

'We'll take it in turns,' said Charley firmly, privately thinking, *we are really going to have to create some house rules, set some boundaries and draw up some rotas.* It was Charley's flat, not Pam's, and, much as she loved her mother-in-law, Pam was the lodger, not her.

'How about I make salmon *en croûte*?' Pam suggested.

'Oh my God, I love that!' groaned Charley, instantly giving in. She wasn't proud of herself.

A few moments later she could hear Pam rooting through the food cupboards and the fridge, and then shortly afterwards she appeared in the doorway and announced she was off to the shops.

'Have you got a spare key?' she asked.

'Yes, of course!' said Charley getting up to fetch one, before realising the only 'spare' key she had was Josh's. She went into her bedroom and dug it out of her bedside table. It'd lain there undisturbed for four years, but nevertheless Charley still felt a swift pang of loss as she handed it over.

Pam glanced at the keyring and smiled. It read, 'My Other Car's a Porsche.' 'I gave him that when he bought his first car!' Cheerfully pocketing the key, she headed off.

'We can sort out money later!' Charley called after her.

Once Pam had left, Charley gave up any pretence of job-hunting and threw herself into looking into what sort of party bag she could do for a fiver while still making a decent profit. And, as it turned out, she could do a pretty damn good one. But then Charley was on home ground here, since for the last three years, she'd sourced the various Prosecco-themed gifts they had sold at the Prosecco Night fundraiser. She knew her way round the suppliers, and she knew the sort of gifts and treats people liked to buy, and what they cost. So, after some swift research to double-check prices and availability, Charley settled on: a lip balm, bath bombs, white chocolate truffles, a small scented candle and the requisite mini bottle of fizz which she knew she could source at cost via the pub. All of which would be presented in a chic, white-and-gold striped mini paper carrier bag. She was just about to order up enough stuff to make up some sample bags to show Jacob, when it occurred to her that other venues might be interested in the party bags, and there might be other events she could cater for, such as birthday parties, pamper weekends, weddings…

Pam's key in the lock momentarily startled her, but then it had been four years since anyone else had opened the front door except her. Hearing Pam struggling up the hall, Charley went out to help, and it was just as well she did, since the poor woman was laden with bags.

'Blimey, Pam! Is there anything left in Sainsbury's?'

Her mother-in-law laughed and gratefully handed over a couple of full carriers to Charley to lug up the hallway. 'Just a few store-cupboard essentials!'

Between the two of them, it took nearly an hour to put away all the 'store-cupboard essentials', mostly because they had to have what Pam described as 'a bit of a sort-out' to make room for everything, which involved spring-cleaning the fridge and scrubbing out the insides of all the food cupboards. It was a mystery to Charley how so many unsightly smears and stains had been made over the years by cans and jars that to her certain knowledge had never even been opened, and by the time they'd finished Charley felt both invaded and vaguely rebuked. Apparently oblivious to that, Pam was keen to volunteer for more work.

'Is there anything else you'd like me to do?'

'Um… not really.'

'In the garden perhaps? The pots need a bit of weeding or I could paint that new bit of fence? Or if you haven't got the paint yet, I could clean the windows?'

The windows? Instinctively, Charley glanced at the windows and, noticing precisely how grubby they were, she cringed.

Pam followed her gaze. 'I'm sorry! I didn't mean to imply they were dirty...' She flushed pink, clearly mortified at having inadvertently caused offence. 'It's just that... I've got nothing to do!'

Charley sent a reassuring smile Pam's way. 'If you really want to clean the windows, then fine, go ahead, I mean... you live here, too.' Which was true, but it didn't stop Charley wincing at the thought.

Pam cheerfully cleaned all the windows, inside and out, including the frames. She refused to let Charley help her, and instead shooed her back to her job-hunting, and then afterwards, with the glass now sparkling and the paintwork gleaming, she started to prepare lunch for both of them. Charley hovered in the kitchen, once again feeling that she should at least offer to help, but Pam was adamant that she was fine and didn't need her. Then, as the first mouthwatering mouthful of Pam's salmon *en croûte* melted on her tongue Charley realised, with a sinking heart, that if they were going to share the cooking then she was going to have to up her culinary game quite a bit – well, a lot, actually. Ping meals and piles of pasta in packet sauces simply weren't going to cut it. It was either that or gracefully step aside and let Pam take over in the kitchen. Charley was beginning to feel like she'd been made redundant all over again, but this time, it was in her own home.

Chapter Eleven

'I've had an idea which is either bloody brilliant or barking mad!'

Charley had called Tara to pitch her the party-bag business idea, and Tara instantly pronounced the notion as 'bloody brilliant'.

'See, I *said* you were wasted in the pub! You're a born entrepreneur.'

'Ah, but if I hadn't been working in the pub then I wouldn't have had the idea in the first place!' countered Charley, which Tara reluctantly conceded was true. Charley then cut to the chase. 'Do you think I could supply the Avalon?'

'Maybe,' Tara said cautiously, 'but you'd have to approach the intellectually challenged youth who calls himself the manager...'

Charley laughed out loud. 'Okay, but could you do some research for me? You know... what kind of events are coming up, how many people are booked in... and crucially how much the Avalon charges for things, so I can pitch myself in the right level? I don't want to be too expensive. Or look too cheap, either.'

'Sure!'

Nisha was more cautious and businesslike in her response than Tara had been, warning Charley to cost the venture properly from the outset.

'Be sure you can make enough profit right from the beginning. If you have to go back later and charge more, you'll lose customers and you won't get them back.'

Dutifully, Charley made a mental note to double-check her sums, but she'd actually called Nisha to ask about things like paying tax and whether she should set herself up as a company... or whatever.

Well within her comfort zone, Nisha rattled off business advice with eloquent and easy expertise.

'As a sole trader you won't have to tell HMRC until your income is over a grand.'

'But I earn more than that from the pub!'

'That doesn't count,' replied Nisha, 'It's only the income from your business that matters, your self-employed income. Just keep meticulous records of any payments, and then, if you make over a thousand pounds, register the business then.'

'*If!*' thought Charley understandably deflated by Nisha's evident lack of confidence in her, but she tried not to show it in her voice when she said, 'Okay, thanks,' before going on to say tactfully, 'And... how are things with you?' She was deliberately oblique, leaving it up to Nisha as to whether she wanted to share more about her problems to do with her ex or not. Apparently, she did.

'Not great. I've told Jay I can't raise the money, so now he's threatening to take me to court.'

'Bloody hell!' exclaimed Charley, 'That's a bit heavy, isn't it?'

'Yes and no. If he wants to change the divorce Court Order he'll have to go to court. But I think he's bluffing. I'm sure it's *La Bimbo* pushing him. It'll be hugely expensive, plus I've pointed out he might not win, which means he'd have to pay all the costs – mine, as well as his.

'How did he take that?'

'He went rather quiet. I don't think he's got the guts to take me to court.'

Charley could only hope her friend was right. 'Well, you know where I am if you need me,' she said, 'Not that there's much I can do—' she trailed off.

'There's not much anyone can do.' Nisha sighed stoically. 'And anyway, worst-case scenario is I'll have to sell the flat and buy a smaller place. It won't be the end of the world.'

It would be for me, thought Charley, but then her flat was filled with happy memories of Josh, whereas Nisha's flat... well, that place had witnessed more acrimonious moments and bitter rows than wedded bliss.

'It's just that...' Nisha started again, but she broke off sounding anxious, and Charley wondered if she was worried how Charley might judge her. After a pause Nisha carried on tentatively, 'It's not about losing the flat, it's more the thought that he will have won. *La Bimbo* will have everything... everything I wanted... kids, a happy family. And I'll have lost. I don't even get to be part of the rest of his family any more, she gets them, too.'

Charley felt for her. That was a loss which hadn't even occurred to her, since she was still a big part of Josh's family.

'D'you want to come round?'

'I'm too busy,' said Nisha, pulling herself together, yet sounding regretful. 'But thanks for asking... and thanks for being there.'

'Of course I'm here for you!' exclaimed Charley.

Nisha didn't respond immediately, and then she said, 'Thanks. And fingers crossed he's bluffing!'

'Crossing everything,' replied Charley.

In contrast to Nisha's measured, professional approach, Angie was wildly enthusiastic, and immediately offered to design some customised gift bags for Charley.

'I was just going to order some snazzy ones off the internet to start with,' Charley told her. She was wary about the cost of getting some printed specially.

'You can't do that!' wailed Angie down the phone. 'It'll look really amateurish!'

Charley cringed. She hadn't even considered that.

'Come round, we'll do it together. It'll be fun!' pressed Angie, and Charley caved.

By the time she got there, Angie and the boys were already set up at the kitchen table, which was strewn with art materials. At one end were the kids' tubs of felt tips, wax crayons, finger paints, piles of garish stickers and bags of colourful fluffy pom-poms, while at the other end was a pile of decidedly more expensive-looking materials, including graphite pencils, charcoals, water colours, acrylic paints and oil pastels. They were placed well out of the reach of small fingers, Charley noticed.

'The boys want to help,' Angie explained, and Charley was horrified, until her mate went on to say, 'I thought you could help them at that end of the table, and I'll work at this end.'

'Okay,' said Charley ruffling the boys' hair and happily joining them at the nursery end. This is what she loved about Angie's house: there was always something going on, someone doing something, or making something, usually noisily, and always messily. If she and Josh had had kids, she'd have wanted her home to be just like it.

Angie was busy mocking up some mini carrier bags out of printer paper and sticky tape. It all looked a bit Blue Peter to Charley, until Angie said, 'It's important to design your logo with the end purpose in mind.' At which point Charley became immediately impressed by this new, professional version of her mate.

'Now, what are you calling yourself?' asked Angie.

'Sorry?'

'Your business name?'

'I haven't got one!'

Angie tucked her hair behind her ears and hummed pointedly.

'I suppose I could use my name? *Charley's Party Bags*…or *Charley's Pamper Bags*. Does that sound okay?'

'No! It sounds like you're the sex trade!' exclaimed Angie, and Charley snorted with laughter.

'What's that?' piped up Eliot.

Biting her lip, Charley slid Angie a panicked look, but nothing phased Angie.

'Just something grown-ups do,' she replied casually, which seemed to satisfy Eliot.

'Mummy, look!' Finn proudly held up a paper carrier he'd completely plastered with felt-tip pen scribbles and a mass of garish stickers and pom-poms. 'I done my bag for Charley!'

'That's lovely, sweetie,' said Angie, then turning to Charley and, apparently in complete seriousness, she asked, 'What do you think?'

'Awesome!' pronounced Charley, before adding tactfully, but just as seriously, 'But I was thinking maybe something a little less busy?' Angie suppressed a smile.

In the end, Angie designed her an all-purpose bag that said, 'A gift for you' in a simple, but bold, gold font. She'd added the word *'Charley's'*, apparently carelessly hand-written, across one corner, also in gold, with a few gold stars tastefully scattered around. The finished product positively oozed class.

'Oh my God, it's stunning!' exclaimed Charley.

Angie beamed. 'Thank you. And can I just say, you are a delight to work with!'

Charley laughed and shook her head in a self-effacing gesture.

'No, honestly! When I did this for a living there'd have been dozens of people all demanding changes, just for the sake of it, and we'd have gone back and forth arguing about different fonts and colours and whether or not to replace the dot over the 'I' with a star, and six weeks later it would have ended up exactly how it was in the first place!'

'Sounds like a nightmare!'

'You're not kidding! Fun though,' admitted Angie, a little ruefully it seemed to Charley.

'Er… how do I actually get the design on the real bags?' asked Charley, cringing at how naive that made her sound.

But Angie didn't seem to think it did. 'I'll email you a digital version you can upload when you order them,' she told her, and when Charley still looked a little startled, she added, 'If you get stuck, I'll help.'

–

A couple of days later, as she'd promised, Tara came round to Charley's with details of the events and bookings, including prices, at the Avalon, and a large box of sea-salted caramels. Pam tactfully took herself off to her room, even though they'd both assured her she was welcome to stay.

'I don't want to intrude,' she'd insisted.

'You won't be,' Charley had assured her. 'Honestly.'

'We have sea-salted caramels…' coaxed Tara, waggling the box enticingly towards her, but Pam was adamant. She limited herself to taking a couple of caramels and then left them to it.

Tara curled up on the sofa next to Charley and settled down to indulge in her favourite pastime: taking the piss out of her boss.

'Then he said, and I quote, "We have to cascade this information and capture our colleague on this," so I told him I'm not a sodding kidnapper.'

'What did he even mean?' laughed Charley.

'No idea,' said Tara with a straight face, but Charley guessed she'd known perfectly well what her manager had meant — she just couldn't resist the chance to wind him up.

Charley swiftly ran her eyes down Tara's list. 'Blimey. The Avalon's not cheap, is it?' Mentally she adjusted her ideas, and crucially her prices, towards the higher end. 'Okay, so, how about I offer a range of five or six different goody bags, and a range of prices from, say, a tenner each up to twenty pounds?'

Tara frowned and shook her head. 'Way too complicated. You'll have to keep it simple, otherwise you'll confuse the poor lad. Honestly, he's got the wattage of a toaster. And only a two-slice one, at that.'

Charley laughed and then had a rethink. In the end she decided to offer three products: pamper bags, party bags and gift bags, at two different prices.

'As long as you talk slowly and don't use words with more than one syllable, he might just get his little noddle round that,' said Tara. 'I'd offer to set the meeting up, but I think it'd put him off you. I'm not exactly his star employee. In fact, it might be better if you pretend you don't know me at all!' She sighed. 'I sodding hate my job.'

'Well, pack it in then!'

'You sound like Baz.'

'So why don't you?'

'Because he only wants me to give up working so that he can dictate what I spend money on.'

That, thought Charley, *simply isn't true.* Baz never begrudged Tara anything, and if he was the main bread-winner, well that was Tara's choice. She'd had a career before getting pregnant and deciding to stay at home for Monnie. She could hardly blame Baz.

'He thinks I spend too much on Monnie.'

Privately, Charley agreed. On one of the very rare occasions Tara had agreed to leave her daughter to go out with her husband, for some business do for Baz's firm, Charley had babysat Monnie. The poor kid had barely been able to get into her bed, it was so full of teddies and dolls and fluffy animals, and Monnie slept in a king-sized double larger than Charley's, for crying out loud. The funny thing was, the only soft toy Monnie had seemed to really want was a rather bedraggled and much-hugged gingham rabbit she called Bunny-May, which she had slept with tucked under her arm. Monnie's entire room was crammed with toys, and Charley reckoned she must have more than all of Angie's kids put together.

When Charley didn't say anything, Tara guessed her train of thought. 'I just don't want Monnie to go without things. I had bugger-all when I was a kid. It wasn't mum's fault,' she added hurriedly, 'she was skint, but I like treating Monnie. And if that means putting up with a pimply prat with the management style of an obsessive-compulsive sociopath and the intelligence of a coffee grinder, then that's my choice.'

Charley shrugged sympathetically. 'I'll ring the "pimply prat" tomorrow and let you know what he says.'

'Okay, but if you do get a meeting, remember, you don't know me. In fact, don't even look at me!'

Charley rolled her eyes. In a warped kind of way, she was actually looking forward to meeting Tara's manager, if only to put a face to the muppet.

After Tara had gone, Charley took a mug of tea through to Pam in her room.

'We need to set some house rules,' she said, sitting down on the bed where Pam was leaning back against the pillows, doing a crossword. Immediately, Pam sat upright and looked alarmed. 'You're not *intruding* if I invite you to join me and my friends,' Charley told her earnestly.

'It is if you feel obliged to invite me, just because I'm here.'

'I didn't feel *obliged*,' objected Charley. 'I wanted you to join us. We both did.'

Pam looked mortified. 'Well in that case, I'm sorry. I didn't mean to be rude. I'm just trying not to… overstep my welcome.'

'You weren't rude,' Charley reassured her, and was reassured to see the anxiety melt from Pam's face. 'I think we just need to work out how to share the flat together, how to work round each other's social lives.'

'It's harder than I thought,' admitted Pam with a charming frankness.

Me too, thought Charley, but she tactfully refrained from saying so, continuing instead, 'And you should absolutely feel free to invite your friends here, whenever you want to; it's your home, too.' Although, and she was ashamed to admit it, as she heard herself say it, the thought still made her feel thoroughly uncomfortable.

There was a brief silence until Charley said, 'D'you want to come and help me finish off the sea-salted caramels? I mean, don't feel obliged to!' she teased.

Pam smiled at her. 'I'd love to. Do you want to help me finish the crossword?'

'That depends,' deadpanned Charley. 'Do you feel *obliged* to ask me to help?'

'No.'

'Then, yes!'

The two of them went into the living room and sat side by side on the sofa, working their way through the clues and the remaining caramels with equal efficiently.

Chapter Twelve

Pam took Charley's 'house rules' talk to heart. The flat *was* her home, for the foreseeable future at least, and she must stop thinking of it as some sort of bolt-hole and try to carry on with her life and get back to some sort of… normality. So she invited Zee for coffee. Still reluctant to impose upon her daughter-in-law's hospitality, she had waited until she knew Charley was going to be out, and now here she was, pacing anxiously around waiting for Zee to arrive, feeling like a cat on a hot tin roof, which was ridiculous. Why was she restlessly plumping up cushions, checking there was loo roll in the bathroom and trying to find something to do, *anything*, to dispel the well of completely irrational anxiety mounting inside her? *What's the hell's the matter with you?* she asked herself. Zee was her oldest friend, and she of all people would be in Pam's corner, but that didn't stop the niggling fear wriggling its insidious way into her that people wouldn't approve of her leaving Geoff. It didn't help when Zee was uncharacteristically late, which plunged Pam into a deeper anxiety, wondering if her friend had had second thoughts, and wasn't going to come at all.

She was infinitely reassured when Zee finally arrived, bearing a packet of posh biscuits and a preposterously large bouquet extravagantly packaged in cellophane and ribbons. 'Sorry I'm late! I wasn't sure it was the right place,' gushed Zee as she handed her the flowers and embraced her.

'Oh my God! They're enormous!' laughed Pam, taking the bouquet. 'And lilies, my favourites! Thank you.' She led Zee through to the kitchen, wondering if Charley would even have a big enough vase.

'Oh, the flowers aren't from me,' Zee corrected her quickly, 'I bumped into the delivery chap at the stop of the steps, I just offered to carry them in. I did bring the biscuits though!'

'Oh,' said Pam tonelessly, then, after giving the card attached to the cellophane a cursory glance, she opened the pedal bin with her foot and crammed the flowers in, breaking the stalks and crushing the blooms. Turning to meet Zee's astonished look she said, 'They're from Geoff.'

'Ah,' said Zee and then she paused before adding, 'Seems a bit of a waste.'

'Yes. Like forty years of marriage,' replied Pam. The she leant with her back against the worksurface and said defensively, 'I'm not going back to him.'

Zee pulled out a kitchen chair, sat herself down and opened the biscuits. 'Good. I don't think you should.'

'Is that what everyone thinks?' asked Pam, busying herself with looking for a cafetière which Charley didn't actually possess.

Zee shrugged lightly. 'I don't know.'

Which Pam took as a 'no'. Her friends were all strong, independent-minded women, and Pam knew she was naive to think there would be a simple consensus amongst them, but nevertheless she found herself desperate wanting their approval, as well as their counsel.

Then Zee went on, 'No one's blaming you, Pam. You've done nothing wrong.'

Visibly relieved, Pam gave up on the cafetière and reached for the mugs and the instant coffee, while behind her Zee, her oldest friend, a woman she'd known for thirty years, calmly dropped a bombshell.

'Theo had an affair.'

Pam's head turned slowly, incredulously, towards her friend. It was the first she'd ever heard of it. She gave up on the coffee altogether and sank down in the chair opposite Zee.

'When?'

'When the kids were small. That's why I put up with it. For them.' She sighed.

There was a silence as Pam suddenly saw her closest friend in a new light. Not as a happily married woman living a comfortable life, but as someone living with an uncomfortable secret, who'd lived, and was probably still living, a decidedly uncomfortable life.

'Do you regret staying with Theo?' she asked, tentatively.

'Yes. And I've often wondered if he regrets staying with *me*. Which is probably worse, actually.'

Yes, thought Pam, *I imagine it is.* She leant over the table and took hold of her friend's hand. Zee wasn't one to cry for milk spilt long ago, neither of them were. 'God, Zee, I had no idea. I always thought you were happy together.'

'We muddle along. But it changed everything.'

'Yes, some things do,' said Pam, quietly.

They both sat in contemplative silence for a while until the practical Zee asked 'What are you going to do?'

Pam shrugged. 'I honestly don't know, apart from leave Geoff.'

'I didn't have the courage to leave Theo,' admitted Zee with painful honesty.

'You had small children, Zee. I'm in totally different circumstances. I don't have any kids to support or worry about. It's only me.'

'That won't necessarily make it any easier,' observed Zee.

–

Shortly after Zee had arrived to have coffee with Pam, Charley had walked, with what she hoped was an air of confidence, into the reception of the Avalon Indulgence Spa and Conference Centre. Dressed in her navy-blue work skirt, white shirt and kitten heels, she was determined to come across as cool, calm and, above all, businesslike. Which was a shame because her palms were sweating, her mouth was dry and her insides were churning like a dough paddle in a bread-maker.

Tara was sitting at the huge, leather covered desk. 'Can I help you, *modom*?' she asked in a jokey posh accent.

Charley laughed, a sudden welcome release of nervous energy, which instantly made her feel calmer. 'I have an appointment with the manager,' she said, trying to keep a straight face.

'If *modom* would care to take a seat on the pretentious leather sofa behind you, I shall telephone through,' said Tara. Then she grinned, and added in her normal voice, 'Good luck!'

Charley sat down to wait for the manager she'd heard so much about. The second she set eyes on him it was evident Tara hadn't exaggerated one little bit – he literally swaggered over to her, checking himself at least twice in the huge mirrors that flanked the reception area. Charley had to suppress her smile, and didn't dare look over at

Tara. Which was very wise, because throughout her entire pitch, while she was trying to display her samples and run through her prices and exude professionalism, Tara was pulling silly faces behind her boss's back. Charley studiously ignored her and tried to focus on the hotel manager's reaction. It was blatantly obvious that although he was impressed, he was trying hard not to show it, and Charley reckoned he'd probably seen too many episodes of *The Apprentice*.

'The thing is,' he drawled, 'there are a lot of companies out there offering this sort of thing, and cheaper.'

'Yes, and it shows in the quality,' replied Charley, remembering the pile of plastic tat that had tumbled out of the party bags at the pub. 'I'm focusing on the classier end of the market, with a quality product, because I think that's what the Avalon customers will want.'

He couldn't argue with that, and instead tried to beat her down on the price. 'We can provide the mini Prosecco bottles you've included, but that will cost us £2.00 a bottle, so I'd need to see that reflected in your price.'

Since Charley knew *precisely* how much the trade price was for mini Prosecco bottles she looked him coolly in the eye and said, 'Really? I can source them for half that,' and steadfastly refused to shift on the price.

The young manager blanched, knowing he was outmanoeuvred. Behind him, Tara was beside herself with glee. Finally, he said he'd take a pilot order of fifty pamper bags, and that the Avalon would add the mini Prosecco bottles themselves, which was fine by Charley. More than fine, in fact, since although it wasn't exactly a life-changing deal, it was a start. Out of the corner of her eye, Charley saw Tara giving her a discreet double thumbs-up and she finally felt it was safe to throw a smile in her direction.

Zee had left by the time Charley dashed back through the front door, bubbling over with enthusiasm. 'Pam!' she called, rushing up the hall, bringing a whirl of excitement with her. 'I've got my first order!'

'Go, Charley!' whooped Pam, dashing out of the living room to hug her warmly. 'Congratulations! Well done, darling!' Then she hurried off to her room to fetch her handbag, calling behind her excitedly, 'I'm getting some fizz! I'm so proud of you!'

All the way home in the car Charley been anticipating Pam's reaction and looking forward to sharing her good news. But then she suddenly remembered her shift at the pub and her excitement evaporated. Hating herself for ruining Pam's treat, she called out, 'Sorry, Pam. I can't celebrate now, I'm working tonight.'

'We'll have it when you get back,' declared Pam, returning with her purse, undefeated.

–

Charley arrived early at the pub in time to show Jacob her sample party bags. He was noticeably impressed, and even more so when he heard the Avalon had already put in an order.

'They're really classy, Charley.' Then he chuckled and went on, 'A bit of a step up from the crappy ones the pub doled out!' Which wasn't that much of a compliment, when she came to think of it, but he promised to really push them with Head Office, adding, 'They'd be mad to say no.'

She was in pretty good spirits when her shift started. She should have known the feeling wouldn't last long. A man in his forties sat alone at the bar, steadily working his way down more pints than he could handle until, fuelled with Dutch courage, he started chatting Charley up. Her colleagues thought it was hilarious, but it infuriated her. *Why do men hit on women working in pubs? They wouldn't do it in a shop, or a bank, for crying out loud*, she thought. Gritting her teeth and adopting her most courteous smile, she reminded herself to be professional, but when he ordered another pint, he leered at her and added clumsily, 'And have one for yourself, sweetheart.'

He was clearly drunk, but not so drunk that Charley could refuse to serve him. She put a pint glass under the lager pump and flipped the tap on, before politely replying, 'Thanks, but I don't drink at work.'

'Well, then I'll buy you a drink another night… when you're *not* at work,' he pestered.

She shook her head and said firmly, 'Thank you, but no,' then she added, fully expecting the statement would shut him up, 'I'm married.' Charley never lied about her marital status, and it angered her she felt she had to resort to doing so now.

'So?' he slurred, then, winking grotesquely at her he leant right over the bar towards her, his alcoholic breath foul in her face. 'You don't have to tell hubby, do you? What the eye don't see, the heart don't grieve over, as they say.'

Suddenly Charley wanted to hit him. She could barely resist the urge to pick up his drink and throw it straight in his smug, lecherous face. Stepping back to get away from him, she flicked the lager tap off while the glass was only half full.

Sensing trouble, Jacob came over. 'Everything all right, Charley?' he asked with studied calm.

'I think this customer has had enough to drink.'

'Bollocks! You were in the middle of pouring me a pint!'

Taking one look at the man who was still leaning over the counter, Jacob said politely, 'I think my colleague is probably right, sir. I suggest you'd better go home.'

'But I want another drink!' The drunk had raised his voice almost to a shout, and heads turned in the rest of the pub.

'Sorry, sir, not in here, not tonight.'

For a split-second, Charley thought the man was going to kick off, but, probably because Jacob was well over six foot and built like an international rugby player, the older man wisely thought better of it, and suddenly deflating, he practically slid off the barstool and zigzagged his way to the exit.

'Wanker,' muttered Jacob under his breath, but loud enough for Charley to hear. Then he turned and gave her a friendly nudge with his arm, 'Don't let him get to you. He's not worth it, love.'

Charley nodded. She couldn't have agreed with him more.

The next morning, she woke early. The sun was trying to get in through the curtains, so she yanked them open and then grinned at Josh's photo on the bedside and, as ever, he grinned back. 'It's not exactly another day in paradise,' she told him. It couldn't be, not without him, 'But it feels like it might be a pretty good day…'

She stripped her bed, bundled up the bedding and headed into the kitchen, only to find the washing machine was already on, churning away full of soapsuds. Pam had got there first.

'I'm sorry!' said Pam, abashed. 'I didn't realise you wanted to put some on.'

'It's not a problem,' said Charley brightly, dumping her laundry on the floor. Then, as she belatedly remembered the kitchen was now a 'shared living space', she scooped it up again. 'Sorry.'

'No, it's fine. I always leave laundry on the kitchen floor at home,' said Pam, and then she hurriedly corrected herself, 'I meant, back at the house,' she clarified unnecessarily, and then she blundered on as if she were embarrassed by her evident breach of flat-sharing etiquette. 'And anyhow, it's my fault. I didn't bring enough clothes. I have to keep washing everything. I suppose I should go back and get some more, but Geoff will be there and—' She stopped herself, and took a beat before saying, 'I'm being childish, aren't I?'

'No. No, you're not,' Charley assured her hurriedly, and then, much against her inner wishes, she felt compelled to add, 'Do you want me to go?' She didn't really want to. No, make that, really, *really*, didn't want to. The visit was bound to embroil her in an excruciatingly difficult conversation with her father-in-law, but she felt she had to offer. And seeing the expression of sheer relief that was now flooding Pam's face, she was glad she had.

–

In the event, they both went, but in Charley's car. Over breakfast they plotted the raid with the precision of a SWAT team: if Geoff was at home, Charley would go in, armed with the list of clothes that Pam wanted; if he wasn't, then Pam would go in and Charley would stay outside, parked up the street, on lookout. If Geoff arrived while Pam was in the house, Charley would phone Pam and she would nip out the back and sneak to the car once Geoff had had time to get inside the front door. Pam resisted the urge to suggest they synchronised watches – not least because she didn't actually own one. Anyhow, it all seemed like a fine well-planned operation… until Charley pulled into the driveway.

There were two cars in the drive. And Pam didn't recognise the second one. She panicked. 'Oh my God! *She's* there! Reverse, reverse!'

'Bloody hell!' cried Charley slamming the gears into reverse, and shooting backwards out of the driveway, gravel spraying from her wheels. Then she had to slam the brakes on, because a steady stream of traffic had suddenly appeared, blocking her in and leaving them stranded on the pavement.

'Go! GO!' yelled Pam, clutching the door handle furiously, her eyes trained on the front door, dreading that someone might emerge.

'I can't! There's a truck coming!' cried Charley, with the car half in and half out of the drive.

Pam slunk down as low as she could in the passenger seat. She felt vaguely sick. Suppose Geoff and *the other woman* had heard the car on the drive? If they so much as glanced out of the front window they'd see them. She prayed furiously to the traffic gods to give them a break and grant them a speedy getaway. As soon as there was a gap in the seemingly endless stream of cars, Charley reversed swiftly onto the street and they tore off.

'That was close!' Pam sat back up and then burst out laughing, tension erupting from her like the cork from a shaken-up bottle of fizz. They drove away, giggling like a couple of school kids.

Although Pam was enormously thankful not to have had an encounter with *the other woman*, she was infuriated that because of *the other woman* she still faced spending the summer with four tops, two pairs of crops, five pairs of knickers and a spare bra. Which was, when you come to think of it, completely irrational. There was *so* much more to blame *the other woman* for than that.

Chapter Thirteen

After her success at the Avalon, Charley felt buoyed and enormously encouraged. She made up dozens more sample bags and phoned every possible venue in Bristol that might be interested in taking them, trying to book pitch meetings. Of course, not all of them had bitten, but she had secured a few appointments. Four dozen snazzy gift bags stood stacked neatly on the kitchen table. Charley cast her eye over them critically. They looked good. She took a quick photo and sent it to Angie.

Taking advantage of the fact that Charley was going to be out for most of the day, Pam had invited her four closest friends for lunch.

'You're welcome to join us, if you're free at lunchtime,' she told Charley. 'They'd love to meet you.'

'That's very sweet of you, but I haven't given myself the luxury of a lunch break!' said Charley, instantly pitching Pam into full motherly mode, and sending her directly to the fridge.

'Shall I make something to take with you?' she asked, scanning the now laden shelves.

'No, honestly, I'll be fine. I'll grab a sarnie or something.'

'Well, mind you do,' said Pam earnestly, and Charley laughed.

To be honest, Charley didn't have a full day of meetings, but she didn't want Pam knowing that. It wasn't that she didn't want to meet Pam's friends, it was just that if she'd joined them for lunch she would have felt weird… like a guest in her own home.

'Wish me luck,' she said, slinging her bag over her shoulder, scooping up her box of samples and heading out of the kitchen.

'You know I do,' Pam called out to her retreating back.

—

In the kitchen, beginning to prepare lunch, Pam wanted someone to wish her luck, too. She knew Zee was on her side and wasn't going to try to pressure her into going back to Geoff, but she wasn't at all sure her other friends would think the same way. It was such a huge thing to do – to end a marriage after forty years – even if your husband was having an affair. Was she overreacting? She paused, the knife she was about to crush the garlic with idle in her hand, and stared out of the window. The persistent, niggling feeling simply would not go away. After all, Zee had put up with Theo's infidelity, and perhaps her friends might think she should do the same. Maybe she should? No, she told herself, she had too much pride for that. Levelling the knife flat over the garlic on the chopping board, in a swift, intensely satisfying movement she brought her clenched fist down on the blade and smashed the clove flat.

'Welcome to my new home!'

Pam flung open the front door and then stepped back, with an extravagant gesture, to let her friends into Charley's flat.

They came laden with flowers, chocolates and wine… and full of concern. As they bundled into the hall, their warm hugs, slightly tighter and longer than usual, spoke volumes. Pam had feared they might not want to come; after all they and their husbands were her and Geoff's *joint* friends. She'd left Geoff so suddenly, so unexpectedly, that she hadn't had time to think about the fallout, how it would impact on their friends and family, spreading like the circles from a stone kicked carelessly into a calm pond.

The four of them clustered round Charley's small kitchen table, plates and glasses and elbows all jostling for space while Pam tipped the mushroom risotto into a serving dish at the cooker. She couldn't shake off a curious sense of 'playing house' in Charley's flat. It was the same feeling she'd used to have in holiday cottages when the boys were small, when she'd been cooking a meal she'd cooked a hundred times, but in unfamiliar pots and pans, and dishing it up on crockery she'd never seen before in her life. She brought the dish to the table and started ladling out the risotto.

'Nice plates,' said Toni, eagerly taking hers.

'They're lovely, aren't they,' agreed Pam, then joked, 'But then I would say that. We gave them to Charley and Josh as their wedding present – and I have impeccable taste!'

They all laughed.

One of the benefits of being an older woman is having a licence to be candid. It comes with the bus-pass. Pam and her friends had given up tiptoeing around elephants in rooms years ago, and definitely weren't afraid of calling a spade a spade, a mistress a selfish cow, and an adulterous husband an absolute effing bastard.

'He's behaved appallingly,' announced Rachel, 'disgracefully.'

'Which is why I'm not going to go back to him,' said Pam firmly.

There was a pause while her friends each decided how to respond. Whilst they all agreed Geoff was in the wrong, it didn't mean there was consensus on what Pam should do now, perhaps because they were of a generation which didn't divorce readily. But just as likely it was because, pragmatically, they all knew the chance of Pam remarrying at their age was pretty slim, and her future prospects might include a lonely old age.

'Isn't it a bit early to decide anything?' ventured Toni.

Mona nodded. 'I know you're furious with him, Pam...'

'We all are,' Rachel assured her.

Mona continued, 'But you're acting in the heat of the moment. A forty-year marriage is not something to give up lightly.'

'Perhaps Geoff should have thought of that!' countered Pam.

'And a husband isn't something to give up lightly...' said Rachel.

'Well, I'm giving mine up!' retorted Pam, with defiant cheerfulness.

'But he's *your* husband. Are you just going to hand him over to this other woman without a fight?' asked Toni.

'Yes.'

'You're just going to give in and walk away? After everything you've been through together?' persisted Toni.

'Yes,' repeated Pam. 'Even after all that. He's made me feel... *stupid* and *foolish*, and *worthless*. He doesn't want me, and now I find I don't want him. Simple as that.'

'Why not just have a trial separation?' suggested Mona.

'What for?' asked Pam. 'I've decided to leave him. There's nothing to "trial".'

'No-one's saying you shouldn't leave him,' said Toni. 'All we're saying is don't decide in the heat of the moment without thinking things through.'

'Yes, there's a lot to consider. What about the house?' Rachel pointed out. Pam merely shrugged. 'That house is your home,' insisted Rachel. 'I think you might need to move back in and claim the house.'

'Make Geoff move out. He's the one in the wrong,' was Zee's opinion.

Pam shrugged the suggestion off. 'This is my home now,' she said, waving her hand airily, but the word jarred as she said it. The flat didn't feel like home, how could it, when it was empty of her things, her memories, her lifetime's collection of treasures? *Well, if a home is made up of memories*, she told herself, *then having lunch with my oldest, closest friends is a pretty damn good start.*

Zee shook her head. 'You can't live with Charley forever.'

'I know I can't. But it's a start. A *fresh* start.'

'What about all your things?' asked Toni. 'I mean, it's a lovely flat, but it's hardly palatial, and there's nowhere for you to store anything.'

'I don't know...' Pam looked around the kitchen vaguely. 'Maybe things don't actually matter very much, when it comes down to it.'

Her friends exchanged anxious glances.

'This is all going to take time to sort out, a long time,' Rachel started, 'And you might not feel ready to go back right now...'

'I'm not going back at all!' cut in Pam hotly.

'Nobody's saying you should,' said Zee soothingly. 'But it's all been very sudden, Pam, and you need to take time to consider your options.'

Mona nodded sagely. 'Yes. We none of us know the legal ins and outs of getting a divorce or whatever, but all we're saying is, be careful, and don't do anything that might make you… vulnerable, or weaken your position.'

'Don't make any hasty decisions, or do anything rash,' begged Rachel.

'And don't agree to anything without talking to us first,' said Toni.

'Or a lawyer,' advised Zee. 'And for God's sake don't *sign* anything!'

Pam shot the group a withering look. 'Geoff might have made a damn fool out of me, him and *his other woman*,' she said, 'but I'm not a complete bloody idiot.'

–

The Orangery was Charley's last call. The other meetings had gone pretty well and although nobody had made any firm orders, several hotels had been sufficiently impressed to keep some of the bags and had promised they'd get back to her. Technically this was a loss, since she'd have to write off the cost of the sample bags, but then again, some of the hotels were huge and part of national chains, which might mean some lucrative deals. But anyhow, here she was, now standing outside what was probably Bristol's favourite wedding venue, and probably its most expensive, too. She could see why. Set against the backdrop of the clear blue June sky, the beautiful stone-built orangery, with its full-length Georgian windows framed with perfectly clipped ivy, looked like a film set. Its immaculate, land-scaped lawns surrounded an ornamental pond, complete with fountain and statues. The grounds were bordered by dozens of cream rose bushes, in full bloom; it was the perfect setting for a costume drama – or an extremely expensive wedding.

Needless to say, her own wedding had been a considerably more modest affair, but still very beautiful. She and Josh had been married in August, in a sunlit village church filled with friends and family, hope and happiness. The church was near Josh's family's home and her parents had had to travel over from Suffolk, much to her mother's annoyance.

'It's traditional to be married from the bride's house,' she'd said pettily. Charley had been determined not to let her mother's jealousy take the edge off her day.

As her dad had walked her down the aisle, Charley had never been so nervous in her life. She had concentrated on not tripping over her dress and trying to stop her wedding bouquet trembling in her hands. But when she reached the altar Josh had turned, smiled at her proudly and mouthed *I love you*, and her nerves had dissolved. Just at that moment, she'd thought everything, everything in her entire life, was going to be all right, forever.

Coming back to the present with a bump, Charley realised she was a little early for her meeting. The doors to the Orangery were locked, so she peered in through one of the windows. The sunlight poured in, and the light interior decor made the most of it. The room was already laid out for a wedding reception, with crisp white tablecloths covering around twenty enormous circular tables. Tall cut-glass vases full of white lilies adorned the centre of each table, around which stood about a dozen chairs, draped with white cotton covers tied with thick gold sashes. She could just imagine her gold-and-white gift bags on the tables – they'd look perfect.

As it turned out, the Orangery Events Manager felt the same. But unfortunately, she told Charley that the venue already had a regular supplier for wedding favours, which was gutting. She promised she would bear Charley in mind if they ever wanted to change suppliers.

Giving the woman her best professional smile, Charley thanked her effusively, and tried not to let it feel like she'd just been handed the consolation prize of the decade, instead of the big lottery win.

Since it was only just after two o'clock, and knowing that Pam's guests would still be in her flat, she took herself round to Angie's.

'Wimp!' exclaimed her friend, leading the way into the kitchen where she was sorting through a mound of laundry.

'I'm not!' objected Charley. 'It's not that I'm scared of meeting them! It's just I want to give Pam some privacy in…' she paused, struggling to finish her sentence, 'in her own home,' she finally managed, yet recoiling at that thought. Perceptive as ever, Angie raised a questioning eyebrow at her. Not wanting to be drawn, Charley changed the subject. 'Everyone *loved* the look of the bags.'

Angie positively beamed at her. 'Four years at art college wasn't a complete waste of time, then!'

'If you miss it so much, couldn't you maybe just do a little bit, part-time?'

Indicating the mountain of laundry, the piles of washing-up still stacked by the sink, and the chaotic jumble of toys and games strewn over the floor where her two youngest were crawling around engaged in a high-speed police chase involving two plastic cars with flashing blue lights and a good deal of noisy sound effects, Angie exclaimed, 'When?!'

Then, patting her rounded belly, she rolled her eyes and added, 'And there'll be even less time when this one arrives.' She turned away, but not before Charley had seen a look of mild dismay flick across her face.

'Nee-naw, nee-naw!' yelled Finn.

'Stop! Police!' bellowed Eliot.

'Boys! Pipe down!' snapped Angie suddenly, much to her sons' surprise and Charley's too, since she'd rarely ever heard Angie raise her voice to her kids. Angie suddenly busied herself digging into the laundry basket in search of missing socks. Moments later, having recovered her usual cheerful tone, she turned back to Charley, and smiled. 'Anyway, this is absolutely the last one!' Then glancing at the clock, and noticing it was almost school pick-up time, she added, 'I have to get Beth, coming? Or do you think it's safe to venture back to your place yet?'

To Charley's intense relief, Pam's friends *had* gone by the time she got back. They were probably lovely women, she told herself, but she hadn't wanted to get home to find her flat invaded by a bunch of people she'd never even met. It wasn't a feeling she was proud of, but then, although she was ashamed to admit it, she wasn't finding living with Pam altogether easy. It wasn't Pam that was the problem, it was the intrusion of someone else's possessions in her space, strangers in her house coming for lunch, or coffee. But at least it was Pam's things, and Pam's friends, she reminded herself; it would be a hell of a lot worse if she was living with a lodger she didn't know at all.

–

'I'm not sure any of them really understand,' Pam said to Charley later that afternoon, as the two of them sat on the sofa in the living room, the French doors flung wide open, with mugs of tea and slabs of Pam's mango cheesecake.

'They're all married,' she went on. 'Not necessarily *happily*, but... well, for better or for worse, I suppose. We didn't divorce so quickly, so easily in my day. "You've made your bed, now lie in it," as we used to say.' Catching the mildly horrified look on Charley's face, she went on hurriedly, 'Oh, none of them are unhappy or anything.' Then she thought of Zee and corrected herself. 'Not *desperately* unhappy. It's more that they're just all... muddling along. You know, like slouching about in a baggy old bra because it's comfortable, rather than buying a new one.'

When Charley pulled a mock-grimace, Pam hurriedly back-pedalled and said, 'Not that I'm expecting you to understand about the comfort of baggy old bras! I'm sure your underwear more than passes muster!'

Charley laughed. 'Actually, I don't think it would, but fortunately there's no danger of it having to.'

Something about Charley's cheerful, frank assertion rang a small alarm bell in Pam's head, but before she could pause to consider it, Charley had continued.

'What did they say?' she asked.

Pam sighed heavily and marshalled her thoughts into a bite-sized upsum. 'Toni says I should fight to get Geoff back. Mona says I shouldn't give up on a forty-year marriage. Rachel thinks I should move back home and stake a claim on the house, and Zee says I should make Geoff move out!'

'Oh,' said Charley and sat thoughtfully for a while.

Pam misinterpreted Charley's silence. *Just because Charley needed a lodger, didn't mean she wanted that lodger to be her mother-in-law*, she told herself. *Let's face it, who would want their mother-in-law cluttering up their home, invading their life and… cramping their style?* She remembered how Charley had left the room to take a phone call on the day she'd arrived. A young woman like Charley would be… well, having a love life… a *sex* life, for goodness' sake. How could she do that with her mother-in-law in the next bedroom? Even just thinking about it sent a hot fluster of embarrassment through Pam, and it suddenly, belatedly, occurred to her how selfish she was being, imposing herself on Charley.

'Perhaps it would be best, for *everyone*, if I went back home,' she said slowly.

'No! What's *best* is that you do what *you* want to do,' said Charley earnestly. 'I'm sure your friends are trying to help, but like you said, none of them have been divorced, so they don't know what's the best thing for you to do, do they? Why don't you stay here, get some proper advice, and then make an informed decision about what you want to do.'

'But what about you? What about *your* life? I must be… in the way,' Pam suggested, with evident discomfort.

'I was going to get a lodger anyway,' said Charley. 'You know that.'

'Yes, but you'd have got someone more your age.'

'What's age got to do with anything?' Charley seemed genuinely baffled.

'Well, you know, living more your sort of lifestyle. A young person's lifestyle.'

'Blimey Pam, what sort of things do you think I get up to?'

'Well you must have... friends to stay... occasionally,' Pam finished weakly.

It took a while but then suddenly it clicked for Charley. 'You mean men!'

'No!' lied Pam. Then, feeling sharply skewered by the candid, challenging look in Charley's eye, she admitted, 'Well, yes.'

Charley's face softened, but still holding Pam's gaze, she said, 'I'm not seeing anyone, and I'm not *interested* in seeing anyone, either. And if I'm going to have to live with someone I'd much rather it was you than a stranger... or anyone. Believe me.'

Clearly, Charley meant Pam to find this statement reassuring, but in all honesty, she didn't.

Chapter Fourteen

Towards the end of the week, Tara called Charley from the Avalon to let her know the pamper bags had proved an enormous hit, so much so, they wanted to order another hundred. She then invited herself round on the Sunday, while Monnie was at a birthday party, to celebrate. She arrived with scones, a pot of strawberry jam and a carton of clotted cream. Pam tried to do her usual I-don't-want-to-be-in-the-way-so-I'll-disappear-to-my-room routine, but both Charley and Tara protested.

'I've bought two packs of scones! Don't make me eat them all, I'll inflate like a barrage balloon,' begged Tara, and eventually Pam relented.

Outside, it was a beautiful, sunny day, so while Pam made some tea, the other two carted the kitchen table and chairs out into the garden and set them up under the shade from the next-door neighbour's tree.

'Got any other orders?' Tara asked Charley, as Pam arrived with the teapot.

'Not yet. But a few of the hotels were interested, I just need to chase them up.'

Pam glanced over to Charley. Her eyes had lit up with excitement, but then Pam watched the light switch off just as suddenly when Tara asked her how the job-hunting was going.

'Well, I'm not actually looking just right now. I've got the pub job, and a lodger…' she paused to smile at Pam, who returned it warmly. 'And I'm busy with the party bags…'

Tara rolled her eyes. 'Oh, don't do this, Charley!'

'Don't do what?'

'Don't get stuck in another crap job you hate… just because it's easy.'

'I'm not!'

'But you're not even looking for anything better!' exclaimed Tara hotly.

Charley didn't reply and Pam shifted uncomfortably in her chair and wondered how, or perhaps whether to intervene.

Tara charged on, 'You *said* you were only doing the pub job until something better comes along. You can't spend the rest of your life pulling pints!'

That's Charley's choice, thought Pam, bristling at Tara's aggressive approach, despite privately agreeing with her.

'You need to look for a proper job, something challenging and fulfilling.'

'I'm not sure I want that right now,' said Charley, defensively.

'Well, you should.'

Who says? thought Pam. Surely Charley had enough on her plate with losing her job and coping with everything on her own? It irked her that Tara was being so unsupportive of Charley, and she wondered why. And then Charley nailed it for her when she said, 'Why should I? Because you do?'

'This isn't about me,' retorted Tara.

'Yes, it is. That's what you'd want from a job. You're bored at the Avalon and fed up with working for a pathetic little prat, and, can I just say that having met the little jerk, I can completely see why… but just right now, I'm happy as I am.' She picked up the teapot and strode off to the kitchen.

'Charley, come back!' called Tara.

'I'm putting the kettle on,' shouted Charley, before disappearing through the French doors.

Prudently, Pam didn't said anything.

But then Tara turned to her and said, 'Honestly Pam, she's just wasting her life.'

What Pam wanted to say was, 'Back off, butt out and leave Charley alone,' but she bit her tongue, and limited herself to saying carefully, 'You know, a big change, like a redundancy or whatever, rattles everything, and it takes time to recalibrate. Charley's doing okay, and she's not "wasting her life", she's trying to set up a business, and I think it would be good if we could all get behind that.'

The subtle rebuke in Pam's remark was not lost on Tara, and she sat back in her chair. Charley got back with teapot to find her looking chastened.

'Your party-bag business,' said Pam cheerfully, 'I was just wondering what else you could do to build it up? Maybe make it bigger than just gift bags?'

Charley shrugged, and topped up the mugs, not wanting to be drawn into a further discussion about her career choices.

There was quiet for a while, and then Tara said, very tentatively for her, 'You know what you could think about maybe doing…'

'What?' asked Charley warily, and Pam found herself tensing on her behalf.

'You could have a little shop.'

'What, selling party bags?'

'No, you'd have to do more than just that, maybe sell a whole range of Prosecco-themed goodies. You know, like at the Prosecco Nights.'

That, thought Pam, *is not a bad idea.* She could just imagine Charley running a shop – she had bags of enthusiasm and precisely the right bubbly temperament to make a go of it. She held back from saying anything, not wanting Charley to feel like she and Tara were ganging up on her, but she was hopeful the idea might have appealed to Charley since she seemed to be giving it serious consideration.

'Just Prosecco stuff? Isn't that a bit too niche?' said Charley.

'No, it could be your USP!' enthused Tara, sitting forwards and warming to her theme. 'And anyway, *never underestimate the power of Prosecco!*'

'As if I would!' Charley laughed, but then, after a pensive moment, she shook her head and said, 'No, it's too risky.'

Pam felt a brief pang of disappointment, but Tara wasn't giving up on her idea that easily, and for once Pam was glad of the woman's tenacity.

'No, it's not,' said Tara, obviously dismissing an objection she didn't want to hear. 'Look at Nisha, she runs her own business. Why not you? You've got your redundancy, I think there might even be grants or loans or something. Nisha will know. Come on, what have you got to lose?'

'You mean apart from my redundancy, my flat and my security?'

'Oh come *on*, Charley!' groaned Tara, and then she caught Pam's eye, and said more gently, 'YOLO, Charley. You know that.'

'YOLO?' queried Pam.

'You only live once,' interpreted Charley quietly.

'Well, that's very true,' said Pam. Looking round she perceived that all three of them were, sadly, better placed than most to fully grasp the full meaning of that statement. It seemed to her to be something Charley had rather lost sight of.

–

For some reason the fantasy of being in her own shop, surrounded by happy, smiling customers all clutching handfuls of Prosecco-themed goodies, kept coming back to Charley. On the one hand she knew she should dismiss it, on the perfectly sane grounds that it was too risky. But on the other hand, the thought of doing yet another shift in the pub, or more accurately, endless, never-ending shifts in the pub, kept the fantasy pinging back. Not to mention the thought of having to face Tara if she didn't at least explore the idea.

So, early on Monday morning, Charley googled 'How to run a business'. There were pages of sites, littering the internet, offering advice with headings such as 'Fifteen Steps to Start your Own Business' and 'Ten First Steps Towards a Successful Business'. One site had whittled it down to a mere 'Seven Steps'. So, maybe it wasn't as hard as she feared…

Twenty minutes later she was convinced it was even harder. *Way* harder. The titles of those allegedly simple steps were bad enough: 'Choose your Optimum Business Structure' and 'Develop your Brand'. Statements which left her baffled and daunted, while the heading 'Understanding Legal Issues' was genuinely alarming. Worse, the advice was totally conflicting, with one website telling her to start by writing a business plan, while another said it was the thing to do last, after you've 'made sure you're compliant and you've got your business image in order', whatever the hell that meant. But it was the official government website that scared her off most: 'As a sole trader you're personally responsible for your business's debts', it informed her gravely.

Clearly, setting up a business was way more financially perilous than Tara had realised. Mustering up every ounce of courage, Charley called her, determined to put a stop to the idea. Fat chance – this was Tara she was talking to.

'Okay, so I've looked into it and it's too difficult, and too—'

'No, it's not,' cut in Tara.

'How do you know? You don't run a business,' countered Charley.

'Baz does.'

'Again, you don't.'

'Nisha does.'

'Nisha's got a degree!'

'So?'

In the end Tara bullied Charley into promising to at least talk to Nisha before she came to a decision.

'Of *course* you could run a shop!' Nisha exclaimed, before knocking Charley sideways by adding, 'But that's not to say that you should.'

'Why not?' asked Charley, taken aback.

'Is this your idea or Tara's?' asked Nisha bluntly.

Charley fessed up that it was initially Tara's idea. 'Has she already mentioned it to you?' she asked. She wouldn't have put it past her.

'No, it was just a hunch.'

'The thing is, I kind of like the idea,' Charley went on, 'and I can sort of see myself doing it.'

'It'll be exhausting, working flat out, seven days a week, and even then, hard work alone won't guarantee success,' Nisha warned.

It wasn't the work, or even the risk of failing, that was frightening Charley. It was the financial jeopardy, so she asked, 'Is it too risky?'

'Depends.' Nisha's reply was pragmatic as ever. 'If you have to invest money you can't afford to lose, like say mortgaging your flat to finance it, then, yes, it's too risky. But if you're just putting some of your redundancy money into it, and you don't mind writing that off if you have to, well, that's a lot less risky.'

'So, do you think I should do it?'

'I think you should do what *you* want to do. You're undoubtedly more than capable of running a shop – but I don't think you should do it just to please Tara!'

'I'm not,' Charley assured her firmly, and honestly, as the seductive image of her serving a crowd of happy customers, with the credit card machine bleeping away, flipped into her mind again. Bringing herself back to reality she asked Nisha cautiously, 'Heard anything else from Jay?'

Nisha sighed. 'No. It's all gone very quiet. My solicitor is sending him a letter reminding him the court order is legally binding and that he'd have justify challenging it.'

'Does that mean he *can't* ask you for more money then?'

'Sadly no. But she said a legal letter might frighten him off.'

'Will it?'

'Maybe, he always was a bit of a wuss.'

124

'Sounds like it's worth a try.'

'Definitely.'

'Fingers crossed then!'

'Yup. Although it's difficult to cross your fingers and type,' Nisha joked.

Charley laughed. 'Actually, can I just ask you something, for Pam? Do you think she'd be in a stronger position if she moved back into her house? To make a claim on it, as it were?'

There was a brief pause. Then Nisha said, 'No. At least I don't think so. I didn't get to keep the flat because I was living in it. It was only because I could buy out Jay's share, well, very nearly.' Then she added with a laugh, 'Why, is it driving you crazy living with your mother-in-law?!'

'No!' replied Charley, not entirely truthfully.

Chapter Fifteen

After the abortive raid on her house with Charley, Pam was still short of clothes. But wild horses wouldn't have dragged her back there, not if there was even the slightest chance of *the other woman* being there, so she called Zee and asked her to go instead.

'Come with me,' coaxed Zee. 'You don't have to go in.'

'Absolutely not! She might be there – Barbara.'

'Don't be such a coward! We can park in the next street. And then we can have coffee in town somewhere afterwards.'

It was very tempting. Too tempting to resist. Pam was thoroughly bored of being cooped up at Charley's, although she felt like a spoilt brat admitting it. She was used to having an entire house with much larger rooms, and most of all, she missed her garden. Here she had no vegetable patch to tend, no shrubs to prune, no flower beds to weed, and it only took five minutes to push the little electric mower round.

She'd picked Zee up and then driven to her old home, parking up just around the corner. Handing Zee her keys, overnight bag and a list of clothes, she said, 'If the case isn't big enough, there's another one in the wardrobe.'

'Won't be long,' said Zee getting out. Then as an afterthought she popped her head back into the car, 'Any message for Geoff if he *is* there?'

'Nothing repeatable!'

'Ha!' retorted Zee and then she sobered. 'And what about if *her* car is there? What shall I do?'

'Let the tyres down.'

Zee laughed and slammed the car door.

Waiting for Zee in the car, as the minutes ticked by improbably slowly, Pam belatedly began to worry about what she'd potentially let her friend in for. She felt herself slide into catastrophising. *What if Geoff was there and he and Zee ended up having a horrible confrontation? What if he wouldn't let Zee into the house? Worse, what if the other woman was there – how on earth was Zee supposed to deal with that?* She regretted her earlier flippant reply to Zee, which, she now realised, had been carelessly glib. Increasingly anxious, Pam looked at the clock on the dashboard, a pointless gesture since she had no idea what the time had been when they'd parked up. The catastrophe fantasies continued. *What if Zee lets it slip that I'm here? What if Geoff follows her to the car –* and with Barbara?!

Oh, for crying out loud, pull yourself together, she told herself brusquely, but nevertheless, the wider implications of leaving Geoff, including the impact it would have on their friends, were slowly dawning on her. Their friendship group was made up of couples who'd known each other for years, actually, make that decades. Would they find their loyalties divided and torn? How could they socialise if she and Geoff divorced? Would Toni invite them both to her annual New Year's Eve party, or just one of them, and if so, which one? And what about getting everyone together for supper or a drink? Would she and

Geoff have to take it in turns going? She laughed out loud at the sheer, childish, ridiculousness of the suggestion, until another, more disturbing thought slid into her mind, causing her laughter to catch in her throat. Over time, would her friends find it easier to stop inviting both of them at all, or worse, carry on inviting Geoff, but with the other woman, because they were a couple?

Divorcing Geoff, she reflected, wasn't simply something she was putting herself through, she was dragging all her friends through the mess too, and Pam wondered how she'd been so naive as to not realise that before.

A movement through the window alerted her to Zee's return.

'Was anybody there?' she asked as Zee hurled the case onto the back seat of the car.

'No, thank God!' gushed Zee, breathlessly clambering into the passenger seat, as eager to get away as Pam was. 'I've no idea what I would have said to Geoff if he had been there. And if he'd had *that woman* there…' she broke off, clearly having appalled herself by picturing what she might have done.

Pam started the engine 'I shouldn't have asked you to do that.'

'It's not a problem!' said Zee, hauling her seatbelt on.

'No. It was selfish and thoughtless of me to ask.'

Zee shook her head lightly. 'It's fine, Pam,' she assured her. 'Why do you say that?'

'Because I've just realised that just because Geoff and I are divorcing, it's not fair to drag everyone else into the whole thing, too.'

'I think that's probably unavoidable,' replied Zee, as Pam pulled away from the kerb, heading into town.

They went to one of the countless coffee shops clustered around the top of Park Street, in need of cake and caffeine.

'How is it, living at Charley's?' asked Zee, as they settled into a huge comfy leather sofa with their coffee.

'It's fine…' said Pam in a voice that suggested it wasn't.

'But?'

'I think I'm in the way. Not in *her* way. More, in the way of her getting on with her life.'

'How do you mean?'

'Well, she's not going out with anyone, or dating or whatever it is they do these days. And she says she not interested in finding anyone else.'

'Perhaps she's just saying that not to hurt you. Maybe she thinks it would upset you to see her with someone else. Someone other than Josh.'

'Maybe…' *But if that's the case*, she thought, *then I can't stay there. I can't let her put her life on hold.*

Zee put down her coffee looked her friend in the eye. 'How *would* you feel if she found someone else? Honestly.'

Pam didn't answer for a while, as she tried to interrogate her inner thoughts truthfully. Something about the idea upset her, deeply, she knew that, she just wasn't sure what, exactly. It wasn't the thought of someone replacing Josh. He was gone. He wouldn't be hurt, so what was causing that sharp unease inside her? 'I think… if I'm being really honest, it's the thought of her getting married, because then she'd have a new mother-in-law.'

'Replacing you.'

'Yes. I don't want to lose my connection with her, or my role in her life.' Pam's throat tightened and she finished in a strained voice, 'I'd lose her, Zee. I'd lose her, as well.'

Zee leant over and gave her friend's arm a loving squeeze. 'Come on, let's drink up and then walk.'

Pam readily acquiesced, knowing there was more privacy in a crowded street than in a half-empty cafe. She let Zee tuck her arm into hers and they headed down the hill, towards College Green, through a steady stream of shoppers who were entirely wrapped up in their own worlds and completely disinterested in the conversation of two older women.

'When Josh died, I didn't realise how much else I would lose, as well,' confided Pam. 'I know it's... illogical to miss something you've never had, but losing Josh meant he'd never have a family. So, in a way it feels like I've lost out twice. I've lost him and everyone else that would have been in his life.' Zee listened without commenting, and Pam carried on. 'I know I don't have a right to have Charley in my life, or to expect her to want to stay part of our family. I'm not expecting her to carry on coming to us for Christmas, year after year forever. I know I have to accept she will want to... that she *needs* to build a life without Josh, without us. But, and I know it's selfish, it saddens me, because then I'll lose her, and I'll lose her connection with Josh. Her memories of him. Their past lives together.'

'It's not selfish,' broke in Zee gently. 'We can't stop ourselves loving people. But I suppose it's like loving any child, we have to love them enough to let them go.'

No, thought Pam. *Somehow it's not the same*, but she couldn't immediately articulate why.

They walked on in silence for a while. As they approached College Green, at the bottom of the hill, they both watched a little girl, dressed in a pair of sunshine-yellow cotton dungarees and white sandals, run around between the trees with her arms outstretched like a wind-mill. Her mother, who was probably about Charley's age, Pam reckoned, ran to catch up with her and, sweeping her off her feet, swung her up into the air. The child squealed with delight, and suddenly, it hit Pam harshly that if Charley did have a child, it wouldn't be Josh's, and it wouldn't be her grandchild. She'd have no right to expect to be part of its life.

Although she genuinely wanted Charley to be happy and fulfilled, and not to be lonely for the rest of her life, up until now she hadn't grasped that Charley's future would unavoidably confine Josh to the past.

Chapter Sixteen

The words HOW TO RUN A BUSINESS stared down at Charley from the top of the flip chart where Tara had written them in bright red pen. Tara had summoned Nisha and Angie round to Charley's on the Sunday afternoon, so they could all get behind her and help her draw up a business plan. Charley had baulked at the idea to start with, but Tara had threatened to frogmarch her to the pub and make her resign on the spot if she didn't agree. And since Charley wouldn't have put that drastic deed past her, she had capitulated. Now she was hovering with mugs of tea for everyone and watching Tara in her element – bossing everyone around.

'Angie, you sit on the sofa because you'll never get up off the floor…' said Tara. Angie sank her now very pregnant self onto the sofa. 'And Pam, you can sit next to her…'

'Because?' challenged Pam with mock offence. 'You think I'm too old and decrepit to sit on the floor?'

'Er…' Tara appeared momentarily lost for words.

'Because you're revered and respected,' said Angie, bailing Tara out, and patting the seat next to her.

Nisha perched herself elegantly on the arm of the sofa, openly amused by Tara bossing everyone around.

'Charley, grab a cushion and sit where you can see the flip chart,' ordered Tara, and Charley did as she was told. 'Right. Where shall we start?' asked Tara, turning questioningly towards her.

'Um...' Charley felt like a rabbit caught in the head-lights. There was an uncomfortable silence during which everyone turned to look at Charley, and she instantly clammed up, intimidated and acutely aware that all of her mates were cleverer than her. They all had degrees for a start, and Tara had an MBA for crying out loud. How was she supposed to know how to run a business, wasn't that what they'd all come round to help her do?

When Charley didn't offer anything, Nisha cleared her throat and said, 'Draw up a business plan.'

Tara wrote that on the chart. 'Next?'

Nisha looked pointedly at Charley. 'Come on,' she prompted cheerfully, 'It's your business. We're all happy to help, but we can't run it for you!' The lightness of her tone took the sting out of her words, but Charley could still feel everyone's eyes all fixed on her.

Her mind went a complete blank and she blurted out the first thing that came into her head. 'Er... find a shop?' Then she immediately cringed, thinking that since all she'd done was state the most blindingly obvious thing, everyone would think she was stupid.

But nobody seemed to and in fact Nisha was nodding at her encouragingly. 'Absolutely. That'll be one of the first priorities, and it'll be crucial to find the right one.'

Tara wrote: 'Find the right shop', underlining the word 'right' three times, and Charley began to relax a little, because if Nisha said she was right, then maybe she wasn't a complete idiot. Now that Charley had broken the ice, Tara was immediately bombarded with ideas, a good many of them from Charley herself whose confidence grew every time something she said was written on the chart with equal weight and importance as everyone else's words of wisdom. Tara scribbled furiously, underlining things, circling others, switching pens, adding a forest of asterisks and arrows. When they finally came to a halt, they'd filled about twenty scrappy, chaotic pages, which Tara ripped off the chart and laid out on the floor.

Casually, Nisha stood up, 'Right. Let's pull all this together.' Tactfully nudging Tara aside, she picked up one of the marker pens and held it out to Charley, subtly handing control of the meeting to her along with the pen. Even Tara couldn't miss that hint, so she sat down.

'Go on, Charley,' said Nisha, 'It's your business plan.' Reluctantly, Charley took the pen. 'Don't look so anxious!' Nisha laughed, sitting herself back down on the arm of the sofa. 'You've got this, Charley.'

Charley took a deep breath and uncapped the blue marker pen and wrote: 'BUSINESS PLAN' on the top of the next clean sheet, then she began to gather all the chaotic points together logically. By the end of the afternoon she was in possession of a six-page business plan, numbered, bulleted, and prioritised in three different colours, which she had literally written herself, and which, essentially, she completely understood. She wasn't sure whether to be reassured or downright bloody terrified.

'Well done, Charley,' beamed Pam.

'Absolutely. Yes, well done,' echoed Nisha, and it was Charley's turn to beam.

'See, I *said* you could do it,' gloated Tara. Angie merely rolled her eyes at Charley.

–

Item one on the business plan was 'Find the right shop'. Drawing on her knowledge of Bristol estate agents from her previous job, Charley contacted the biggest commercial letting agent in the city. They sent her a list of every available shop in her price range – a very long list. She couldn't possibly see all of the properties. Nisha came round to help filter it down, utterly ruthlessly, as it turned out.

They clustered round Charley's computer, scoffing slabs of Pam's freshly baked almond and apricot tart. Well, Pam and Charley scoffed theirs, while Nisha ate hers delicately, with a fork. Nisha vetoed some of the shops outright. 'That one's in the back end of nowhere, that one's under a flyover and that one looks like it's next door to a brothel!'

Pam snorted with laughter and nearly choked on her tart.

Nisha carried on savagely culling, until they were left with a shortlist of five shops to consider. 'Think about customer parking, footfall, the quality and type of other shops and businesses nearby, street lighting, bus routes, unloading bays for deliveries…' she advised Charley, who was making meticulous notes.

'It won't just come down to the rent,' Nisha told her, reminding her that getting the right shop was *vital*. 'It'd be a bad business decision to take the cheapest shop if it's the one where you'll do the least trade. Go and look at all of them. Get a feel for the area and check out the other shops nearby. You don't want to set up slap bang next to someone selling the same sort of stuff. And don't choose a shop just because it's cute and you fall in love with it.'

'So, it's just like getting married,' quipped Pam. 'Marry in haste, repent at leisure!'

'Precisely,' laughed Nisha.

When they'd finished, Charley went to the door with Nisha, and asked her discreetly if there was any news from Jay. She hadn't felt it appropriate to ask her in front of Pam, not least since, as far as she knew, Nisha had only confided in her.

Nisha shook her head. 'He's not replied.'

'Is that a good thing?' ventured Charley.

Nisha shrugged. 'Maybe. Maybe no news is good news. But it means I don't know what's actually happening, so I'm sort of left in limbo, waiting to see what he decides to do. Or, more likely, what *La Bimbo* tells him to do. And I'm not going to prod him. The solicitor said if he doesn't reply, I should let sleeping dogs lie.'

'Very wise,' agreed Charley. 'There's no need to poke the bear, or the dog, or whatever,' she said, muddling her animal metaphors, 'if you don't need to.'

Nisha smiled, and then surprised Charley by reaching out and giving Charley a swift hug. 'Thanks. You're a good mate.'

'So are you,' Charley reminded her.

After Nisha had gone Charley looked at the list of shops again. Only one of them really appealed to her – a cute, old-fashioned looking store with a bow window, in a classy part of town near the Downs. Naturally it was the most expensive, but Nisha had said a more expensive shop might be better for business, hadn't she? Charley could see why Nisha said not to go rushing in, but what if the one she wanted, the only one she really wanted, got snapped up? She called the agent and asked him to set up viewings for all the premises on her shortlist. 'But I want to see the shop just off the Downs first,' she insisted.

They were meeting the agent at nine, the following morning. Holding her scrunchy in her teeth, Charley deftly swept her hair up into a simple twisted topknot and smiled to herself in the mirror. Somehow, a confident-looking businesswoman smiled back. Then she grabbed her bag, the file of potential shops and a notepad. It was nearly half eight. 'Pam,' she called, 'let's go!'

They drove to the shop through the morning traffic. As they drew near they both looked out for somewhere to park.

Pam suddenly flung her arm out. 'There!' The space was on the other side of the road. 'Quick, before someone else nabs it!'

There was a brief gap in the oncoming traffic, and Charley skilfully did a speedy U-turn. No mean achievement in the rush hour.

'That was lucky!' she exclaimed, reversing into the space.

They walked up towards the shop checking out the area as they went. Upmarket delis jostled with designer furniture stores and bespoke kitchen fitters. And exclusive hand-crafted jewellery hung next to original paintings and sculptures in the sort of art galleries where, if you had to ask the price of something, you definitely couldn't afford it.

'This is a *perfect* position,' enthused Pam.

'Isn't it!' Excitement rose up inside Charley, and she reminded herself not to let it show too conspicuously in front of the agent.

They met him outside the shop which, it turned out, was sandwiched between an antiquarian bookshop on one side and a chic gift shop on the other. Charley sighed. It was *perfect*. She could just imagine the little bow window full of Prosecco goodies and herself standing at a counter, wrapping a pair of glass flutes in gold tissue paper, with the credit card reader busy in the background. She exchanged what she thought was a subtle look with Pam, but nothing escaped the estate agent. Suddenly, he couldn't sing the praises of the shop highly enough, insisting that although the rent was *a little* on the high side, it was a terrific business investment.

'The whole area is awash with affluent customers, and an extremely high footfall – you won't even need a marketing budget,' he claimed.

'Parking's a bit tricky,' Pam pointed out.

'We managed okay,' said Charley, dismissing Pam's anxiety.

–

Mildly concerned that Charley's judgement was being skewed by how much she wanted the shop, Pam wandered off to objectively check out the area, starting with the gift shop next door. A few seconds later she came back and beckoned Charley over to her. 'I think we might have hit a bit of a snag,' she said quietly, then turning to address the agent said more loudly, 'We'll be back in a moment.'

Charley followed Pam into the gift shop. It was awash with Prosecco products and Pam saw Charley's face fall at being confronted by candles and coasters, body washes and bubble baths, tealight holders and tea towels. There was hardly any item with a Prosecco theme that the shop didn't seem to stock. Charley groaned and Pam shot her a sympathetic look and mouthed, 'Sorry.'

'Nothing wrong with a little healthy competition!' said the estate agent, when they broke the news to him. 'It's all about the *location*,' he told her. 'Location, location, location!' he quipped.

'Sorry. This time it's all about the competition,' said Charley. 'Competition, competition, competition!' she quipped back.

His face hardened. He obviously didn't appreciate Charley's little joke. 'Look, I don't want to pressure you, but there's a lot of interest in this shop, and I mean a lot. I showed some people round yesterday. They were extremely interested.'

Pam wasn't at all sure she believed him, until Charley moved closer to her and, turning her back to the agent, whispered softly in Pam's ear.

'I hate to say it, but I think that's probably true. If I learnt one thing from working at the letting agency it's that when a property stands and shoulders above anything else on offer, like this does, it generally gets snapped up instantly.'

Clearly sensing Charley was weakening, the agent pushed his advantage. 'I can promise you there isn't anything else around nearly as good as this anywhere in the city. Not for what you have in mind.'

Pam watched Charley's face anxiously. She was wavering, and it was obvious, so, scenting blood, the agent went in for the kill.

'This really is a unique opportunity. You don't want to miss out.'

A small, slightly helpless frown settled over Charley's eyes as they flicked over to meet Pam's. Worried that Charley was about to make a rash decision, Pam said,

'Why don't you just take a look at the others before you decide?'

The agent turned his back on Pam and addressed Charley directly. 'Well, it's your decision, but…' He said, and deliberately left it hanging.

'Let's see the other shops first,' said Charley, much to Pam's relief.

The rest of the shops were pretty dire. Most of the time it was barely worth parking the car, and on one occasion, it was impossible to park the car, since the shop was stranded in the middle of a one-way system with double yellow lines stretching as far as the eye could see. The only vaguely possible property was a former book cafe – a traditional, double-fronted shop with a wood-and-glass door in a slightly run-down corner to the east of the city. It looked like a shop in a child's picture book, with its windows still bedecked with sun-bleached, polka-dot bunting. But it was right at the end of a dead-end street.

'No footfall,' assessed Charley despondently. 'If there was decent footfall it would be ideal.'

'If there was decent footfall, it would probably still be a book cafe,' said Pam sagely. The agent shot her a filthy look, which she took delight in ignoring.

Nevertheless, Pam was saddened by the sight of the shop, with its faded decor, its flaking and battered wood-work, and its general air of neglect. It had obviously housed someone's passion project, but was now aban-doned and in desperate need of some TLC. In its heyday she guessed it might have been a bakery or a grocery store, and in her mind's eye she could see it thronging with customers, the lively central hub of the local community.

But now it was unloved and not needed any more. *You have my sympathy*, she thought wryly.

'So, now how do you feel about the other shop?' the agent was asking Charley. It wasn't really a question. More a prompt, confirming that he'd been right all along.

'Well I did absolutely love it, and you're right, it would be the best one out of all those we've seen today...' Charley paused, and Pam held her breath and mentally crossed her fingers that Charley wouldn't make a foolish decision. 'But I'm still worried about the competition from the gift shop,' said Charley, and Pam breathed out and mentally uncrossed her fingers.

'You're worrying unnecessarily.' The agent replied smoothly. 'If you set up next to a rival, and you're the better shop, with better products and competitive prices—' again, he trailed off provocatively.

'Setting up a shop is going to be hard enough,' Charley told him, 'without launching an all-out trade war with the one next door.'

'Yes, but setting up a shop is going to be impossible if you haven't got a shop,' he pointed out. Which was undeniably true. He left the thought hanging for a while, then, when Charley still didn't bite, he said, 'Well, I think you're going to regret this, I honestly do.'

Pam mentally put two fingers up at him.

They were both in low spirits as they headed back to the car. Pam suddenly stopped in her tracks. 'Lunch!' she suggested. 'Somewhere nice. On me.' Then, seeing a look of protest begin to cloud Charley's face, she added, 'I insist.'

Charley led the way to an inexpensive Italian restaurant by the dockside. They cut through one of the city's oldest squares with a central, tree-lined lawn, bordered by tall

Georgian houses, and then walked along the cobbled quayside to the restaurant. It was a beautiful, warm sunny day and despite the fact that the water was its usual muddy brown, the colourful bustle of the waterfront lifted their spirits.

Holding open the door of the restaurant for Pam, Charley joked, 'After you, madam. Age before...'

'Don't even finish that sentence!'

Charley laughed. 'You're not old, you're...'

'Vintage,' Pam offered.

'Classic!' decided Charley.

'Precisely.'

The waitress let them to a table in the window.

'I thought we'd be celebrating,' sighed Charley. 'I mean, I wasn't expecting to actually sign on the dotted line today, but I honestly thought I'd have at least found the right shop.'

They both ordered the special, spaghetti carbonara, and very soon two steaming bowls of pasta arrived in a tantalising waft of warm garlic.

Twirling spaghetti round her fork, Pam said, 'I did *not* like that agent. Far too pushy.'

Charley shrugged lightly, 'He was just doing his job. Everyone's like that in the business.'

'No wonder they're the most hated profession in Britain,' retorted Pam.

'They're not the most hated!' replied Charley, indignantly defending her old profession. Pam raised an eyebrow. 'They're the *fourth* most hated,' Charley admitted weakly. 'I looked it up,' she finished, and Pam had to chuckle.

'I did like the book cafe though,' said Charley, 'That could be lovely, if you painted it up a bit.'

'But no footfall,' reminded Pam.

It didn't matter how many times they went over all the shops, they had to face facts, none of them were right – not even the cute-but-costly one on the Downs.

'I completely fell in love with it,' Charley admitted wistfully. 'But I know Nisha's right – it would be *crazy* to set up a shop in direct competition to the one next door.'

Pam pulled a sympathetic face, but thanked her lucky stars that Charley had the good fortune to have friends who could advise her, and was smart enough to listen to them.

Chapter Seventeen

Never having been one to hanker after the impossible, by the time they'd driven home Charley was stoically telling herself that *what would be, would be.* 'These things are meant,' she told Pam cheerfully, pulling up outside the flat.

'Absolutely!' agreed Pam. 'Something else, no, something *better* will turn up.'

Which was possibly true, but Charley couldn't actually imagine *anything* better than that lovely, bijou little shop in Clifton Downs. The doubt must have shown on her face, because Pam carried on, 'One day, maybe not today, but one day you'll be saying, "Thank God I didn't take that little shop near the Downs!" I promise you.'

Charley laughed and headed down the steps to the flat, but she stopped in her tracks halfway because, on the doorstep stood a huge bouquet of cream-and-yellow roses. Charley guessed there must have been about a dozen of each. Pam groaned and rolled her eyes.

Tactful of Geoff not to send red ones, thought Charley.

Josh had always sent Charley red roses every Valentine's Day. Sometimes a bunch, sometimes just one, but always red roses. One year he'd sent her a card that read:

Will You Be my Valentine, Mrs Taylor?
I won't tell Mr Taylor if you don't.

On their first Valentine's Day, before they were married, Charley had assumed Josh would send her a daft, jokey card, and probably a rude one. She'd chosen his carefully, nothing overly romantic, and absolutely avoiding the word 'love'. She hadn't wanted to make any assumptions, or to indicate any expectation of a level commitment or affection that might not be reciprocated, so she'd sent him a light-hearted, colourful card, plastered with smiley face emojis which simply read: 'Happy Valentine's Day'.

Josh had sent her a card too large to even go through the letter box. Deeply romantic, and extravagantly expensive, it had featured a vast, plush red velvet heart, set against a background of red roses, and in fancy copperplate writing it read: 'Will you be my Valentine?'

When she opened it, he'd written in his untidy scrawl:

> *Please say yes*
> *Because I love you*
> *Josh*

She'd kept it, along with all the other Valentines cards, birthday cards and Christmas cards, he'd ever sent her.

Attached to the cellophane wrapping of Pam's bouquet of roses was an envelope. Pam didn't even bother to open it, and scooping up the flowers, she thrust them at Charley. 'You know where to shove those,' she said, indicating the dustbin at the top of the steps.

Charley looked at the flowers sadly. They were beautiful, and it wasn't their fault they were unwanted, innocent victims caught up in a marital battle. 'It seems a waste to chuck them out.' She doubted anyone would ever send her a bunch like them. 'They'd look lovely in the living room…' She glanced over to Pam.

'Okay. But I'm not reading the note.'

'You don't have to.'

'And I'm not putting them in a vase.'

'Fine.'

'And I'm not being childish,' asserted Pam, and then asked with endearing uncertainty, 'Am I?'

'Maybe… just a little bit!' laughed Charley.

In the flat, still clutching the enormous bunch of roses in one hand, Charley had only just got out a vase when her phone rang. Dumping the flowers on the draining board she dug it out of her back pocket. It was the estate agent. There was, he told her good news and bad news.

'The bad news is I've let the shop near the Downs.' He left a beat before gloating. 'I did warn you.'

Bugger, thought Charley. Even though she knew in her heart of hearts it wasn't right for her business, she still felt a pang of regret that someone else would get to run a business from it, and it wouldn't be her.

'The good news is,' the agent was continuing, 'the people I've let it to had first option on one of the units at Cargo, down in the docks. I suggest, if you're interested, you should meet me down there immediately, before anyone else finds out it's up for grabs.'

Charley knew he wasn't stringing her a line. 'We'll be there in fifteen!' she promised.

She and Pam jumped back in the car. Giggling with adrenalin, Charley floored it.

'Go, Charley, go!' cheered Pam.

'If I can't find a parking space, you leap out and keep him talking until I get there!' said Charley as they neared the docks, both of them scanning the side streets for spaces. As it happened, they were in luck, and spotted an empty meter space only a couple of streets away.

'It's an omen!' cried Charley gleefully. 'I have a really good feeling about this! I'm sooo excited!' She slung the car into the spot.

'Yes, but calm down, play it cool, and don't look too keen,' advised Pam.

Charley breathed deeply, then did it again for good measure, before clambering out of the car. 'Don't worry. I'll be the ice maiden.' She looked at her watch, she was going to be late if she didn't leg it. 'Dammit! I'll run on ahead. Okay?'

'Yes, of course, but remember, be cool!' Pam shouted after her.

'Got it!'

Cursing her heels, Charley hurtled along the dockside and arrived breathless and panting to find the estate agent already at the entrance waiting for her.

'Blimey, you're keen,' he said dryly.

'NO!' wheezed Charley. 'Not at all, I just didn't want to be late!'

'Of course,' smirked the agent, and Charley could have happily knocked the smug smile straight off his face.

There couldn't have been a bigger contrast between the units at Cargo and the old-fashioned, bow-fronted shop near the Downs. The minimalist, open-fronted lorry containers that formed the shop units were stacked into two blocks, one painted a bright urban blue, the other a matt olive green. From the distance they looked like a stack of temporary Portakabin offices for a dockside building development, but close up their glass front-ages revealed a hive of small start-ups. *Thriving* start-ups, thought Charley, looking around her. The whole area screamed entrepreneurial vision and vibrant chic and, more importantly, it was *heaving* with people, even in the middle of a weekday afternoon.

In all honesty there was hardly anything to show Charley when the agent unlocked the door and ushered her inside. It was just an empty, white-walled container box, the front of which was filled with a glass display window. But once inside, Charley was already conjuring up an exciting vision of shelves and tables all laden with mounds of Prosecco products, surrounded by, of course, a throng of happy punters.

The agent took a different tack with Charley this time and didn't try to browbeat her with a hard sell. He didn't have to. It was clear to Charley that there would be dozens of enterprising start-ups who would have torn his arm off to get one.

'What you see is what you get. It's a three-year contract with four months' notice.'

Charley was desperately trying to be businesslike, desperately telling herself *not* to fall in love with it, *not* to make any rash decisions and above all, *not* to make it obvious to the agent that she'd had already fallen in love with it and would have signed on the dotted line, there and then, in her own blood if necessary. It was when he told her the rent that she completely buckled. It wasn't suspiciously cheap or improbably low, but it was reasonable, and crucially, *affordable*!

'When would I need to let you know?' she asked, trying to sound casual, as they went outside to join Pam, who had been peering in through the window.

He paused to shoot her a straight look. 'I've given you a head start on this one. But I can guarantee if you don't take it today it'll be snapped up tomorrow.'

Charley's mask slipped. A small anxious frown fleetingly clouded her face and she shot Pam an agonised look, then turned back to the agent. 'I'm just going to talk to my...' she paused, thinking that 'mother-in-law' didn't sound very professional.

'Mum?' he suggested, patronisingly.

'Colleague!' replied Pam, raising an eyebrow witheringly. Taking Charley by the arm she led her some distance away, out of earshot of the agent.

'Oh-my-God-I-so-want-this-place-but-I-don't-know-what-to-do!' garbled Charley.

Her 'colleague' instantly stepped up to justify her newly acquired role of business associate. 'Is it in a good location?'

'Yes.'

'Is there enough footfall?'

'Yes.'

'Can you afford it?'

'Yes!'

'Is it, without any doubt, the best we've seen all day. And is it the only unit likely to come up here in a month of Sundays?'

'YES!'

'Go for it!'

'You think I should go for it?'

'Yes!'

'Sure?'

'Yes! Go for it!'

'I'm calling Nisha,' said Charley, suddenly getting cold feet, but Nisha's number went straight to voicemail. 'She must be in a meeting,' said Charley. She looked at her watch. It was half past four. The estate agency shut at five.

'Charley.' Pam took her by the shoulders and locked eyes with her. 'Trust your judgement.'

Charley frowned anxiously. 'Let me just call Tara!' Tara's response was instant and typically blunt.

'She says, "Stop being wimp and go for it!"'

'So what are you waiting for?'

'I don't know!' wailed Charley, in an agony of indecision. It was such a huge, momentously huge, *terrifyingly huge*, decision.

'Need any help?' asked a man's voice. They both turned. 'What sort of bike are you looking for?'

Charley was momentarily dumbfounded, until she realised they were standing outside the second-hand bike shop. 'Oh! Sorry, no, no. We're not bike shopping. Sorry.'

Carlo, the huge grey lurcher, plodded up to her and nudged Charley's hand with his nose, as if she were an old friend, and at the same moment, the bike man recognised her.

He gave her a warm, easy smile. 'Hi there. How's the bike working out for you?'

'Fine. It's all good,' said Charley hurriedly, trying not to be irritated that he was distracting her when she really, really needed to think.

'No problems with it then?'

'No, no.'

'You know you can just bring it back if there are.'

'Yes, yes. Thank you.' Nice as the man was, Charley wished he'd go away and leave her to think.

'We're actually looking at renting the empty unit three doors up,' volunteered Pam.

The man's face broke into a broad smile. 'Oh, that's great,' he said to Charley, maybe just a little too keenly.

'I'm *thinking* about it,' she stressed.

'Well, if it's any help, I can tell you being here's been good for me. We're all in the same boat, all trying to get our businesses off the ground,' he said, and then added with charming openness, 'It's really tough setting up a business, much tougher than I thought, especially on your own, and you need support.'

'Right, well, thank you,' she said. Then, realising he genuinely *had* just helped her make her decision, she looked at him and, holding his gaze, added, 'No, seriously, thank you.'

She was rewarded with a slow, sincere smile that spread to his eyes, as he replied, 'You're most welcome.'

After the briefest of moments, Charley gathered herself together, turned and walked off.

'If there's anything I can do...' he called after them, as she and Pam headed back to the estate agent.

'Thank you!' called Pam, over her shoulder.

When he saw them coming, the agent tapped at his watch pointedly. 'Cutting it a bit fine, aren't you?'

'Sorry,' said Charley. 'But I needed to have a think... and I've decided it's a no. I'm sorry to have wasted your time.'

His mouth literally dropped open. If she'd slapped him round the face with a wet kipper, he couldn't have looked more shocked.

Pam was also visibly stunned, and Charley studiously avoided making any eye contact with her. Meanwhile the estate agent tried everything he could think of to get Charley to change her mind, but she was adamant.

All along she'd feared she was chasing a dream that was too difficult, too risky, too ambitious for her, and the frank admission from the bike man, about how hard he found it running the shop by himself, had brought her down to earth. Life was tough enough on her own, why was she even thinking about making it even harder? She wasn't someone who thrived on risks, she liked, no, she *needed*, the security of things staying the same. She realised now that she'd been foolish to even contemplate taking on such a challenging adventure. It was beyond her. Simple as that.

Compared to the buzz of the drive down to town, there was a flat, uncomfortable silence in the car on the way back. Charley didn't volunteer any explanation for turning the shop down, and Pam didn't pry.

'Nice-looking chap,' Pam eventually remarked lightly.

'The estate agent?' spluttered Charley incredulously, thinking of the sweaty, balding, middle-aged man and how he'd unwisely squeezed himself into a shirt at least two sizes too small, with his beer belly bulging through the buttons.

'No, the bike shop man!'

'I didn't notice.'

'Really?' Pam fixed her with a gimlet eye.

But Charley met Pam's gaze, wide-eyed and innocent. The bike man *was* a nice-enough-looking chap, she admitted to herself, not particularly good-looking, nice enough, but she wasn't remotely interested in him.

'I think he noticed you,' said Pam.

Charley didn't rise to the bait. She'd had years of managing people who were trying to matchmake her. She wasn't interested in finding anyone else so, skilfully, she deflected Pam with a joke. 'Pam! I am not discussing my love life with you! You're my *mother-in-law*!'

A mischievous sparkle glittered in Pam's eyes. 'Well, you could think of me as your lodger, rather than your mother-in-law!'

'I'm not discussing my love life with my lodger either! And anyhow, I told you before, I'm not interested in anyone.'

Pam didn't reply.

Chapter Eighteen

'Why? Why did you turn it down?' Tara demanded, storming her way into Charley's flat. Pam had taken one look at Tara's dark expression and had turned to Charley, saying 'I'll leave you two to it,' before taking her coat and handbag and fleeing.

Charley felt slightly sick. She hated rows at the best of times, and Tara was the last person in the world she'd want to fight, partly because she was her friend, but mostly because Tara seriously outclassed her as a fighter – outspoken and fearless, with no holds barred, and no territory off limits.

Charley tried to defend herself. 'I wasn't a hundred per cent sure about it. So I made the *wise* decision not to commit myself to something in the heat of the moment, that I couldn't get out of. Nisha warned me not to make a hasty decision,' she finished, hoping that wheeling in Nisha would divert Tara's anger from her.

Tara snorted and rolled her eyes. 'Huh! You bottled it, Charley. Wimped out.' Charley opened her mouth to protest, but Tara ploughed on. 'Call the agent back. Tell him you've changed your mind. Go on. Now. Before it's too late.'

'No.'

'YES!'

Charley folded her arms, pointedly leaving her phone in her jeans pocket, which seemed to provoke Tara into losing all patience with her.

'Oh, for God's sake, Charley. We've only got one life. You of all people should know that. Don't be so *pathetic*. For once in your sodding life embrace change, take a chance.'

'I can't afford to!' snapped Charley, infuriated by Tara's self-righteousness. 'I can't take the risk. Your husband pays your mortgage – and all the other bills. I have to pay my own.'

Inadvertently, Charley had lit Tara's blue touchpaper, and she turned on Charley, her voice dangerously quiet.

'I don't need a man to support me, Charley. My mum raised me on her own and I could do that for Monnie if I had to.'

'But you won't ever have to, will you? Because you've got Baz. I haven't got a husband to support me,' retorted Charley.

'Neither did Kim,' Tara shot back. 'She didn't have a Baz or a Josh. She didn't need a husband, and neither do you.'

Charley gasped and reeled backwards as if she'd been struck. She would never stop needing Josh, not for the rest of her life. Furious tears streamed down her face and her body trembled. 'How *dare* you! How dare you tell me I don't need Josh.'

Charley watched as horror dawned on Tara's face, her hands reaching out to her in a pleading gesture, and she instinctively veered away, out of reach.

'Charley... I'm sorry... I didn't mean...'

But Charley wasn't listening, couldn't hear what Tara was saying over the hot raw anger burning inside her and making her blood pound in her ears. She lashed out to wound. 'You have a husband. A good man. A bloody good man and you completely take him for granted. You never do anything with him, or for him. It's all Monnie, Monnie, Monnie. And poor old Baz just puts up with it, all the while he's working his bollocks off to support the both of you. Kim might have raised you single-handed – but don't kid yourself that you could do the same. Because being on your own is a lot damn harder than you realise, so don't get on your bloody high horse and lecture me about not needing anyone, while you're sitting there *living* off a man. A man you don't even bloody well deserve!'

Wordlessly, Tara swept up her bag and stormed out.

Charley sank onto the sofa, clutched a cushion for comfort and cried her heart out.

–

Tara drove home and was still fuming when she got in. Slamming the back door, she headed straight to the kitchen and poured herself a glass of wine – a large glass. Her hand was shaking so violently that the neck of the bottle knocked against the glass. Baz wandered into the room and gently took the bottle out of her hand.

'What's happened?'

She took a big gulp of wine before she replied. 'Sodding Charley, that's what!'

Baz looked completely taken aback. He guided her into the living room and onto the sofa, switched the television off, and sat down beside her. 'What's she done?'

'She turned the damn shop down.'

'Did she say why?'

'Said she wasn't ready to commit to it… or something. What actually happened was she chickened out.' Tara swallowed some more wine. 'I knew this was going to happen. The minute she took that pub job I just knew she'd just… settle for it and get stuck there. In a crap job.'

'Maybe she doesn't see it like that. Don't her parents run a pub?'

'That's not the point!'

Baz looked baffled.

'The point is,' Tara said, 'she's a really bright woman. And she's wasted enough of her life stuck in a dead-end job she didn't even like. She only took it for Josh's sake, for crying out loud! And now she has the chance to do what she wants, and run her own business, and she won't take it.'

'It's stressful running your own business,' said Baz carefully, 'Maybe she doesn't want that.'

Tara shot him a look. 'It was your decision to set up on your own. I didn't make you.'

'I didn't say you did,' said Baz, sidestepping neatly. 'But look at it from her point of view. She's got a lot to risk. It's tough for a woman on her own. Tough for *anyone* on their own,' he corrected himself.

'I know exactly how tough it is for a woman on her own!' snapped Tara. 'I was brought up by a single mum, and she supported me as well as herself. Charley doesn't even have anyone dependent on her. She's free to do what she wants.'

'She *is* doing what she wants,' Baz pointed out mildly. 'Keeping a steady job and protecting her home.'

Tara rolled her eyes. Baz was obviously not going to see it from *her* point of view, so she finished her wine and changed the subject. 'Is Monnie asleep?'

'I think so.'

'You *think*? You didn't even bother to check?' She stomped off upstairs, furious with her husband, not because he hadn't checked on their daughter, but because she wanted to be right and he'd made her realise that she wasn't. And because, at that moment, it was far easier, and preferable, to be angry with him, and angry with Charley, than admit to herself that she was wrong.

–

Driven by the need to bolt from what was threatening to be an excruciating scene in Charley's flat, Pam had blindly fled to her car. She had started the engine before realising she had no idea where to go. For a few indecisive moments she sat by the kerbside with the engine running, wondering what to do. It would be too awkward to drop in on any of her friends unannounced, especially since she hadn't seen any of their husbands since she'd left Geoff, and she really wasn't ready to have the uncomfortable and challenging conversations which would inevitably ensue.

So, since it was still light on a balmy July evening, on the spur of the moment, Pam drove to a garage and bought a bunch of flowers before going to Josh's grave. She visited the village churchyard regularly and had come to enjoy and be comforted by the changing of the seasons – life's cycle endlessly turning and regenerating itself. At this time of year, the lingering evening sun slanting through the trees and onto the old church brought out the warm gold of the stone walls, and even managed to lift the sombre hues of the headstones. The haunting solos of blackbirds and robins floated in the air, but other than that, it was silent and peaceful in the churchyard.

As she walked back along the winding gravel path, round the headstones towards where Josh was buried, Pam noticed a small stone teddy bear, on what was obviously a child's grave, which had fallen over on its side. The headstone informed her that the teddy was for Hannah, who had died aged seven.

Seven, thought Pam, and her throat tightened on behalf of the little girl's parents. She'd had over thirty years with Josh. *At least I had him long enough to watch him grow up*, she thought. She'd always known, as all mothers do, that she wouldn't be gifted the care and custody of her children forever, but only for a short time, until the boys grew up and left home or until they found someone they'd rather spend the rest of their lives with. But Pam had never even begun to consider that, devastatingly, her allotted time with Josh would be cruelly cut so short. She stood the little bear back up on its feet on the grave.

'There you go, Hannah,' she said tenderly. 'Sleep tight, sweetheart.'

The flowers on Josh's grave were still fairly fresh, so Pam didn't throw them out, but merely added the new ones she'd brought, interspersing the fresh, bright purple asters between the pink and white carnations already in the vase. Then she sat on the cool grass, hugging her knees. Over these last few years she'd found it easier to talk to her son, easier to cope with the one-sided conversation, by pretending they were both in the kitchen at home. In her mind's eye, she could see him sitting on the work surface, in a T-shirt and torn jeans, his knees poking through the rips.

'I'm worried about Charley,' she told him.

In what way? she heard him say.

'I hadn't realised how lonely she must be, on her own… with nobody else to put the bins out for her, or mow the lawn, or cook her a meal, or even just take her a cup of tea in bed.' She paused, and he waited patiently for her to continue. 'The thing is, she says she never wants to find anyone else.' She hesitated, then went on, 'But I think she should. You wouldn't mind, would you. You'd understand.'

They were statements, not questions, but then she knew her son, better than anyone, even his young wife.

He gave her his slow smile. *I just want her to be happy, Mum. You know I do.*

'Me too,' she told him.

Brooding on Charley as she drove home, on the choices she had recently made and the chances she was so readily turning her back on, it occurred to Pam that, regardless of whether she and Josh wanted her to be happy, what was more significant was for Charley to want that, too. After a few weeks of living with her daughter-in-law, she was finding it painful, physically painful, watching her ask for so little, settle for so little, and apparently value herself so little. *You have so much more to offer*, thought Pam, *and you have your whole life in front of you. Why don't you want more?*

–

Nursing the remains of a now cold mug of tea, Charley gave Pam the edited highlights, or rather the select low moments, of the horrendous row she'd had with Tara.

'She says I'm wasting my life, but not everyone is ambitious! We don't all have to... *strive*, and be driven to achieve things. Josh was only a car salesman, but he was happy. He didn't want to run his own dealership or anything, and I was just an admin assistant, but I was happy doing that.'

'Were you?' queried Pam.

'Yes!' said Charley. But she felt a flush heat her neck and spread to her cheeks.

Pam paused before saying evenly, 'Josh was happy being a car salesman because it was easy.'

'He was good at it!'

'Yes. But he did it because he was lazy.'

Charley opened her mouth to protest, but Pam continued. 'Forgive me, Charley, but it's true. He was always. Even as a boy he always managed to nip off to the loo if the dishwasher needed unloading or the table needed setting. I bet he didn't pull on a pair of Marigolds and insist on doing his share of the cooking or the house-work, did he!'

'No, not really.' Charley smiled in spite of herself at the image of Josh in a pair of pink Marigolds.

'And I never could get him to put the toilet seat back down!' added Pam, the humour of the image taking the sting out of her remarks. 'Or put the rubbish out without being asked at least twice or put his laundry in the bin. I was forever finding his socks and boxers littering the landing…' She rolled her eyes in an exaggerated fashion.

Charley laughed. That was *exactly* the Josh she knew, the Josh she loved. He wasn't perfect, but then nobody was, and what did it matter if she was guilty of ignoring, or even denying, his flaws because she loved him? We all do that – it's human nature.

'It always seemed to me that you made the sacrifices, Charley,' said Pam gently. 'And if I'm honest, I don't think you did really love your job. You never talked about it, and it didn't exactly challenge you.' She paused, but Charley said nothing. 'Maybe you *should* think about doing something you'd enjoy more. And if that's working in a pub, then fine, but honestly, I don't think it is. I think Tara is right. You should chase your dreams, Charley, and be happy.'

The uninvited image of herself wrapping up a pair of Prosecco flutes in gold tissue paper in her own shop came into Charley's mind's eye. She pushed it away and shook her head. 'I can't run a business. Honestly, Pam, it'd be too much for me.'

A couple of beats passed before Pam said, 'I think you could, Charley, otherwise I wouldn't be encouraging you.'

Chapter Nineteen

It might have been the airlessness of the hot summer night that stopped Charley sleeping or the way her legs kept tangling in the sheet as she tossed and turned, trying to find a cool part of the bed. Or it might have been the row with Tara going round and round in her head. Maybe Tara was right, perhaps she was too scared to take on a business. So what if she was? There was nothing wrong with knowing your own limitations. But Tara was plain wrong about Josh, she thought hotly, wrong, and way out of line. She would never stop needing Josh, ever; he was the other half that made her whole.

What she needed now, she eventually decided, in fact *all* she needed now, was a safe, steady job so she could keep their flat. And she was having fun with the party-bag business, and that was enough. Having come to a decision, she manged to clear her thoughts, and tried to relax and let sleep come. But clearing her mind left space for a small, niggling voice to creep in. *Is that all you need?* it said. *A crap job in a pub, a flat and some party bags?* She ignored it. *Is that it?* persisted the voice. *For the rest of your life? No one to share your life, no children, and nothing to fulfil you, or make you happy? Is that all you want?*

Exasperated, she sat up, clicked the bedside light on and quietly slipped out of bed to look for a book, or a magazine, just something to read, anything, even the back of the bloody cornflakes pack. Something to banish that insidious, insistent voice telling her she was deluding herself, lying to herself. Because, deep down, she knew that she *did* want more. But what was the point of wanting something when you knew you weren't going to get it? Even if you did get that something or someone you wanted –

wanted with all your heart and soul – they could so easily be taken away, breaking you and crushing your hopes and dreams. Wanting was dangerous, it exposed you. It was much safer to deny you wanted anything, then you couldn't be disappointed if you didn't get them. Or if you lost them.

Over the next couple of days Tara must have texted and called Charley a dozen times to apologise, and when Charley didn't respond, her friend resorted to sending a card. It showed a hand-drawn illustration of two young women sitting back to back, leaning against each other, supportively. Charley had thought it was very nearly something Angie might have painted, but not quite as good. The caption on the front of the card read: 'I'm so lucky to have a friend like you.'

Inside the card Tara had written:

> *Charley—*
> *Please don't let us fall out over this.*
> *I value our friendship too much.*
> *Love,*
> *Tara x*

Charley read it. Twice. She wilfully allowed the words to reignite her anger.

'Bloody typical, Tara. Couldn't even bloody admit to being in the wrong or bring yourself to say "sorry",' she muttered, stuffing the offending card into the kitchen bin and allowing herself to seethe for a good while afterwards.

When an enormous bouquet of flowers arrived for her the following day, with a card entreating her to please call Tara, Charley took a leaf out of Pam's book. She nipped up the steps to the street, shoved the flowers into the dustbin and slammed down the lid with enormous satisfaction, and then she'd gone back to helping Pam paint the garden fence, a task she didn't particularly want to do, but felt duty bound to.

Pam, on the other hand, was gleefully slapping sage green paint onto the bare timber. 'It was good of Baz to do this for you,' she said, either inadvertently rubbing salt into a wound or obliquely reminding Charley that life was too damn short to bear a grudge against your best mate. Probably the latter, assessed Charley.

'Yes,' she replied, picking up the paintbrush and trying to ignore the stabs of guilt prodding her, since it *was* good of him and he hadn't even sent her an invoice. Half of her wanted to text Tara telling her to remind him, but she knew she'd be doing that for the wrong reason, either out of pettiness or to stop her feeling beholden to her. Either way, it didn't make her feel particularly proud of herself and she took her irritation out on the fence, savagely dobbing blobs of paint into the joints and all but trashing the brush.

'Is Tara coming round soon?' Pam asked lightly.

Charley glanced over at her, suspecting her question was more loaded than it appeared. 'No,' she replied, deliberately matching Pam's light tone.

'You should get her round and show her. When we've finished painting it, I mean.'

'It's a fence,' replied Charley caustically, now totally convinced her mother-in-law was trying to get her to patch things up with Tara. Then, feeling remorseful, she tried to soften her sharp retort by adding jokily, 'I think she's seen one before!' She went on, 'And anyhow, it's nearly the school holidays. She's always out of bounds in the holidays, doing stuff with Monnie.'

Which, to be fair, was true, but in reality, Charley *was* avoiding Tara. And both she and Pam knew it. Cluttering up the work-surface in the kitchen were a hundred pamper bags Charley was due to deliver to the Avalon but, perhaps cowardly, she'd decided to wait until the holidays and avoid a potentially difficult conversation with Tara in Reception. Charley told herself she was only being professional and not letting a conflict in her personal life affect her business relationships.

Uncomfortable as it was to admit it, Charley's decision to turn the shop down had impacted on all her friendships. Perhaps this shouldn't have surprised her, given how much time and enthusiasm her friends had invested in helping her – especially Nisha. While Tara had been angry, Nisha had been disappointed, and Charley wasn't sure which was the harder to cope with.

To her deep shame, Charley hadn't had the courage to call Nisha herself. But of course, Tara had tipped Nisha off, and so Nisha had phoned her.

'What happened?' she asked, the disappointment all too evident in her voice.

Assuming that Tara had given Nisha very much her own interpretation of events, no doubt telling her that Charley had bottled it, Charley found herself already on the defensive.

'You said yourself I wasn't to rush into anything, and the agent was pressuring me to make a decision there and then, on the spot, and I just wasn't one hundred per cent sure, so I turned it down.'

'But you're still looking for somewhere, right?' demanded Nisha. 'You've not given up the idea?'

Charley made a very noncommittal response, but Nisha wasn't prepared to let it go that easily.

'Charley, listen. It's a good idea for a shop, and you have a solid business plan, and the assets to make it work – and I don't just mean financially. So, give it a go! Give yourself a chance. I think you'll regret it if you don't.'

Feeling beleaguered, not to mention a little bruised from the knowledge that Pam, Nisha and Tara all clearly felt she was making a mistake, Charley turned to someone she thought would agree with her, and pitched up at Angie's.

The boys were engaged in some serious construction work in the garden involving Eliot's ride-on dumper truck, some plastic buckets, a small blue wheelbarrow and an impressive amount of mud.

'They're building a fort,' Angie informed her, carrying out a tray of cold drinks and oat cookies, which immediately got the construction workers downing tools and rushing over.

'Hands,' said Angie, and the boys reluctantly trooped indoors to wash. Charley dreaded to think what the state of the sink and towels would be like when they'd finished.

Angie heaved her pregnant bulk down into a plastic garden chair. 'Shame about the shop.'

Oh God, don't you start, thought Charley shooting her a sideways look, before admitting, 'Tara thinks I should have taken it.'

'Do you wish you had?'

'No.'

'Then what does it matter what Tara thinks?'

Nothing, Charley lied to herself. 'Actually, we've had a bit of a falling out. I love Tara to death, but she can be very… opinionated.'

Angie said nothing, but waited patiently for her friend to continue. Charley assumed that Tara had already told Angie about their row, so she gave her friend her version of the story, editing out Tara's comment about Josh entirely, and completely failing to mention Tara's numerous attempts to apologise afterwards.

Angie's response caught Charley on the backfoot. She'd expected Angie to be on her side, but her friend said, 'Don't let this come between you two, Charley. Please. I know Tara can be a bit… outspoken.'

'Just a bit.'

'And sometimes she doesn't think before she speaks…'

'Only sometimes?'

Angie ignored the interruption. 'But she's very fond of you and she's trying to help you.' Charley looked away, unwilling to hear what she already knew was the truth. 'And if I'm honest, Charley, well… I think she might be right.' Charley sighed, wishing everyone would stop making her feel like she'd bottled out and let them all down. 'I mean, isn't it better to at least *try* to do something you want to do, rather than stick at a job you hate?' finished Angie.

The boys reappeared, their hands only slightly less muddy than before, but nevertheless Angie handed them their drinks and cookies. 'Take them to the tree house,' she suggested, skilfully giving her and Charley a child-free zone for a while longer.

'A job has a guaranteed salary,' Charley said to Angie.

'Not always! You got made redundant,' Angie reminded her. 'Nothing's guaranteed in life, Charley, you of all people know that.' When Charley didn't reply, Angie went on. 'I just think you might look back and regret not doing something that might really fulfil you.'

'Like you do,' remarked Charley pointedly.

'Yes. Like I do,' Angie freely admitted. 'I loved being a designer, and I loved people telling me how good I was at it, but then I met Will. I thought we'd just have a couple of kids and then at least I could have a part-time career working round the children, but Will wanted a big family, and… and it turns out you can't have everything.'

Charley reeled inside. She'd always assumed it was Angie who'd wanted a large family, with all its attendant chaos and never-ending stream of demands, but clearly she hadn't. Suddenly she saw Will in a different light, not as the loving husband and father she'd always assumed him to be, but as a rather selfish man, who'd put his own desires before Angie's. Her thoughts must have shown in her face, because Angie leant forward and put her hand on Charley's arm, and she was moved by the look of love softening her face.

'Don't judge him, Charley,' she said, lowering her voice, and clearly not wanting the boys to overhear her. 'He had a lousy childhood, in and out of more care homes and foster homes than you could shake a stick at.' As if that explained everything to Charley, which, in a way of course it did. 'I just want to give him the big, happy family he missed out on and always dreamed of.'

'But what about you?' asked Charley gently.

Angie looked her friend squarely in the eyes. 'I have full hands and a full heart. Not to mention a full dishwasher and an overflowing laundry basket! What more could a girl need!'

Cycling back from Angie's house, pangs of doubt began to niggle away at Charley. If even Angie reckoned she might come to regret turning down the shop, then perhaps she should have taken it. Well, it was too late now, she told herself, unless of course...

But she didn't even get to finish that thought, because it was violently interrupted when her front wheel crunched into a pothole in the road. Desperately she grabbed at the brakes, but she was way too late; and the bike juddered sideways, flinging her off. Fortunately she fell towards the pavement rather than under the wheels of a passing truck. With a sickeningly pounding heart and trembling knees, Charley scrambled to her feet and dragged her bike off the road. *Bloody hell! That was close.* For a moment she was too shaken to do anything but stand leaning on the bike and try to get her breathing back under control. Running her eye over the bike she couldn't see anything obviously wrong, but when she tried to ride it, the front wheel scraped against the front fork with a decidedly unhealthy grinding noise.

Bloody, bloody, bloody hell!

-

'I can fix it now if you want to wait?'

Relief flooded over Charley. She'd taken the bike back to the nice bike man she'd bought it from, and if said he could mend it while she waited, then hopefully it wasn't going to cost too much.

'How much will it be?'

He looked across at her. 'It's not going to need a new part, and it'll only take me a few minutes, so… will a fiver be okay?'

'Yes. Absolutely. Is it something I could have done myself?' she added, beginning to feel vaguely foolish since it was obviously only something minor although, funnily enough, they hadn't covered straightening bike forks in the car maintenance course.

'That depends,' he replied deadpan, before picking up a metal tool with a ratcheted hook attachment and continuing, 'Have you got one of these?'

'Oddly, no, I haven't!'

'Then, no!' His face broke into a broad smile and, rolling up the sleeves of his white shirt, he knelt down and started to mend the bike.

She watched him idly, impressed by how easy he made the task look, and struck by how content he seemed in his work. Pam was right, she found herself thinking, he was a good-looking bloke.

He must have felt her looking at him, because he turned round. She flushed and looked away, but luckily the lurcher strolled over and nudged her hand, providing a distraction for both of them.

'Carlo, don't be a pain. Push him away if he's a nuisance.'

'He's fine,' said Charley. 'Honestly, I like dogs.' She did the ear-scratching routine she knew the dog liked and he wagged his tail appreciatively.

She'd always wanted a dog, but thought it was unfair to leave one alone all day. Her mother had always said dogs were too much work and she'd not been allowed one when she was a child. She had planned to get a dog when she stopped work and had kids, like Angie. Fleetingly she let herself slip into a fantasy of her and Angie pushing their buggies across the Downs with a couple of Labradors gambolling around a gaggle of kids, a couple of which she knew were hers. She pushed the ridiculous, pointless fantasy away, just as the bike man spoke to her.

'What happened?' he said.

His question momentarily confused her. 'Sorry?'

'To the bike?'

'Oh! I hit a pothole.'

He pulled a face. 'You were lucky you didn't do more damage or get hurt. You know you can sue the council? Well, you can try to.'

She shook her head. 'It was my fault, I wasn't looking where I was going. Too busy thinking about something else.'

'Not a great thing to do when you're cycling,' he remarked.

'No,' she had to admit.

There was silence for a while and then he said, 'You didn't take the shop then.'

Oh, for crying out loud, she thought, *not you too…*

'I decided against it.'

'I hope I didn't say anything that put you off.' He turned to her and she thought she saw genuine concern in his eyes.

'Of course not,' she said, glibly fibbing to reassured him. 'I just… wasn't quite ready to commit to it.'

On her way down to the bike shop, Charley had passed by the unit and had seen it already been let to some crafters. The window was dotted with flyers announcing 'Crafty Crafters Coming Soon!' She'd felt a twinge of regret, which she'd instantly crushed.

A few moments later the man stood up and span the front wheel experimentally, announcing, 'All done.'

She thanked him and paid him, then she ruffled the lurcher's soft grey ears, 'Bye, Carlo,' and wheeled her bike towards the door.

'Take care,' said the bike man. 'Keep an eye out for potholes!'

'Will do!' she promised.

Cycling off she reflected that, stupidly, she hadn't even asked his name. *You can't keep calling him 'the bike man' for the rest of your bike-riding life!* she chided herself. She took the long route back to the main road, deliberately avoiding the soon-to-be crafters' shop, but all the way home she just couldn't shake off the dismal feeling that she'd disappointed everyone, including herself.

Chapter Twenty

'Letter for you,' said Charley, holding out an envelope to Pam, who took it somewhat guardedly. Glancing at the envelope she saw her home address had been crossed out and Charley's address had been written to the side – in Geoff's handwriting. Intrigued, she flipped it over and opened it.

Charley started making pot of tea, but noticing that Pam had gone quiet, she turned to her with a look of concern on her face. 'What is it? Is it bad news?' She hurried over to sit with her at the table.

'No,' said Pam evenly. 'It's an invitation.'

'Oh?'

Silently, Pam handed her the card.

'Blimey, that's a bit posh!' Quickly, Charley scanned the invitation. In embossed copperplate letters, on a white card decorated with ruby-red roses, it rather grandly informed her that:

Geoff and Pam
are cordially invited to a party to celebrate
the joyous occasion of
Laura and Martin's
40th Wedding Anniversary.

Charley handed the card back to Pam, who merely smiled tightly at her before getting up and taking herself off to her room where she could call Zee in privacy.

'How am I supposed to reply?' she asked her friend. 'It's been sent to both of us, to our house, and Geoff's forwarded it to me.'

Zee was practical as ever. 'Do you want to go?'

'NO!' exclaimed Pam heatedly. Too heatedly, she realised, and she forced herself to continue more calmly, 'No, not if Geoff's going. I honestly couldn't face that.' In fact, she didn't think she could face going at all. 'They obviously don't know we've—' she paused, struggling to find an appropriate euphemism, 'we've "split up", and they're expecting us to turn up like some... happily married couple and I'll have to spend the whole evening explaining to everyone what's happened. It'll be excruciating!'

'You don't have to go,' said Zee mildly. 'Just give Laura a call and explain. It's not like you're one of her close friends, she'll understand.'

The thought of phoning Laura, a woman she knew more as an acquaintance than a friend, to decline her wedding anniversary celebration because her own marriage had broken down, threw Pam into a white-out panic, and she had to fight back the childish desire to ask Zee to make the call for her. Fortunately, to her intense relief, she discovered she didn't even possess a phone number for Laura and had to resort to using the RSVP email instead, which made it a little easier, but she still struggled to find the right words to explain her current situation.

'I have left Geoff' made it sound like she'd thrown some adolescent hissy-fit and stormed off in a huff, so she deleted that sentence and typed, 'We have recently separated'. Reading it back however, the words seemed to imply their separation was an arrangement they'd mutually agreed to, amicably, which was far from the truth. She deleted that too, and retyped: 'We are getting a divorce', but again that sounded like a mutually agreed scenario. It was the 'We' that was doing it, she decided, and so, hoping that it didn't make her sound like a melodramatic, aggrieved wife from some 1950s black-and-white movie, she typed: 'I am divorcing Geoff.' It was a statement drenched in accusation, with the blame firmly laid at Geoff's door.

'Well, that's the truth of it,' she told herself decisively, before she rapidly finished the email, and clicked SEND.

–

Late that night, Charley got back from the pub to find Pam still up and printing off reams of paper. The coffee table was strewn with piles of it.

'What are you doing?'

'Just looking stuff up. How was work?'

'Fine,' lied Charley, kicking off her shoes and curling upon the sofa, sincerely hoping Pam wasn't going to ask any more about her evening. There'd been some sports event playing on a mega screen which the pub had hired in specially. Charley neither knew nor cared what the match was; all that mattered to her was that the bar was heaving. It was standing room only, and it hadn't been humanly possible to pour the pints quickly enough. Drunken tempers had flared, and the shift had been one long stress-out. She'd barely had the energy to cycle home.

Stifling a yawn, she asked, 'What *sort* of stuff are you looking up?'

'How to get a divorce.'

'Oh!' Charley didn't even try to keep the surprise out of her voice. 'Isn't it a bit late to be doing that?'

'Only by about five years,' quipped Pam.

'I didn't mean that! It's nearly midnight.'

'Is it? Oh, good grief, I've been doing this for hours! I thought it was meant to be easy to get a divorce these days,' complained Pam, printing off yet another wodge of paperwork. 'I swear I read somewhere that you could get a divorce in six weeks.'

'*Six weeks!*' Charley was astonished.

'Yes. It was on a website… I printed it off some-where…' Pam starting sifting through the mound of papers on the table. 'There are all these companies who can help you… for a great big fat fee, no doubt.'

I'll bet, thought Charley.

'But then I also read that you can do it online,' Pam continued.

'Online? No, that *can't* be right.' To her certain know-ledge, Nisha's divorce had taken eighteen months, two lawyers, a visit to court and an eye-watering amount of money.

Sighing heavily, Pam picked up the stack of papers and started trying to sort them out. 'Honestly, half of these say one thing and the rest of them something else,' she said irritably. And then suddenly she gave up, tossing the paperwork onto the table in despair and sinking down next to Charley on the sofa. 'I'm even more confused than when I started.'

'We'll ask Nisha. She'll help you.'

'I can't do that, I hardly know her!'

'Yes, you can,' said Charley, stifling another yawn. 'And anyhow, you don't have to ask her. I will.'

Pam was about to protest, but Charley stopped her with a look. 'I'll call her tomorrow. Trust me, she's the font of all knowledge and *everything* will seem much better when you've talked to Nisha.'

Then she stood up, stretched wearily and went to shower away the delicate aroma of inner-city pub before she dropped into bed.

–

Since it was bit of a cheek, well a hell of a cheek really, to expect one of Charley's friends to do her a favour for nothing, Pam reckoned the least she could do was feed the woman. She'd laid out a light lunch with a spinach-and-ricotta frittata, three salads, a fresh-baked ciabatta with a balsamic dressing dip, and a cheeseboard, followed by a summer pudding.

'If you get bored living here, move in with me!' said Nisha, helping herself eagerly.

'Hey, hands off my lodger!' laughed Charley.

Pam smiled and tore the ciabatta into chunks.

Charley had warned her that Nisha was usually very reserved about her private life, so she was surprised when the younger woman seemed happy to be open with her. But then, perhaps few things hurl two women towards an instant and binding friendship faster than discovering that they've both been dumped by *an effing bastard* of a husband for a *younger* woman. It catapults them into the elite corps of the *cheated on*.

'Five years. *Five years!* And I didn't rumble him,' sighed Pam. 'All those countless nights "working late" and the improbable number of "leaving parties" he had to go to. The company must have been haemorrhaging staff.

HR must have been in triage! Then there were endless excuses for getting home late: punctures, flat batteries, breakdowns…'

'Heavy traffic, road closures, flash floods…' added Nisha knowingly. 'And of course, he could never call to let me know… because his phone had died. Or he'd left it on his desk.'

'Geoff dropped his down the loo in the Gents.'

'Ha!' Nisha shrieked with laughter. 'Jay told me that one, too.'

'There's probably a website with lists of excuses cheating husbands can download,' said Charley. 'Excuses 4 U.'

'Or Bastards R Us,' suggested Pam with a laugh. Then she suddenly deflated. 'I just wish I didn't feel such a fool.'

Nisha threw her a sympathetic smile. 'Welcome to my world.'

Pam winced, recognising that this was very much now her world.

'Anyhow, enough of the whinge-fest,' announced Nisha, putting down her fork, as if to signal she was giving Pam her full attention. 'How can I help *you*?'

Plucking up her courage and still worried that the sky would fall on her head if she uttered the 'D' word, Pam confided that she needed some advice about divorce.

'I don't think my husband will be difficult about it. I just want to know the quickest and easiest way to do it.'

'There is no quick, easy way to get a divorce,' said Nisha bluntly. 'It takes months. Years, even. My divorce took much longer than I thought it would. It was way more complicated, and painful, than I'd imagined. And it hurt more. It really hurt having to accept that my marriage had failed. People say going through a divorce is a bit like a bereavement…'

She stopped abruptly, having caught, as Pam had done, the look of hurt incredulity on Charley's face.

Nisha looked as if she wanted the ground to swallow her. Pam realised the poor woman hadn't meant to be dismissive of Josh's death, or to claim that her divorce had been as traumatic and tragic as losing him, but it was nevertheless a careless thing to say in front of a woman who'd been widowed at twenty-seven and to a woman who'd lost a son.

'I hope it's not,' said Pam serenely, assiduously keeping her own face expressionless.

Over the last four years, Pam had often been astonished, offended even, by some people's clumsy attempts to empathise with her. A neighbour had sympathetically told Pam that since their much-loved dog had died she understood about grief and could imagine what Pam was going through. Pam remembered being rendered speechless by the comparison, but she had learned, on these occasions, to remind herself that life's tragedies do not sit on a sliding scale. And that even if they did, how would anyone measure it – a points system set by the magnitude of grief? Five points for the death of a parent, three points for a divorce, one for redundancy, perhaps? The full ten points for losing a child, of course. She now believed that whilst none of us are in a position to judge if our loss or pain are greater than another's, only those who hadn't suffered loss would liken bereavement to divorce, or redundancy, or with anything really.

'Anyhow, back to the divorce,' prompted Pam, feeling the need both to move the conversation on for Charley's sake, and also to ease Nisha's evident discomfort.

Nisha shot her a small, grateful smile, before saying, 'Well, for what it's worth, my advice would be: One, don't make any rushed decisions. Especially if it's just because you want to get through the damn thing quicker. Two, don't make any plans or agree to anything until you've taken legal advice. And three, don't even talk to your husband, if you can avoid it. Well, not without a witness, and make sure you screw him down to a financial arrangement he can't try to wriggle out of later.'

Pam caught Charley shooting Nisha a concerned look before Nisha carried on.

'My ex,' she explained bitterly, 'is currently threatening to take me back to court to get more money from me. I've had to get my solicitor to write to him to remind him that he agreed to the financial arrangements and that they're legally binding.'

'Has he replied?' asked Charley.

'No, but I'm hoping it's scared him off.'

It was evident to Pam from the anxiety on Nisha's face that she wasn't one hundred per cent sure it would. Not even close.

So much for 'Everything will seem a lot better when you've talked to Nisha', thought Pam wryly.

–

Nisha had highly recommended the solicitor she had used, so Pam made an appointment, and Charley offered to go with her to make notes, a strategy Nisha had also recommended.

'I was so stressed I could barely remember any of the things she'd said,' Nisha had admitted sheepishly. 'I'd made notes, but it was like I was on auto-pilot, writing everything down without actually taking any of it in.'

To both Charley and Pam's surprise, on the day of their appointment they drew up at the address they had been given on the phone, and the solicitor greeted them in shorts, T-shirt and flipflops. It turned out she worked out of an office in her back garden.

'I guess Nisha didn't warn you I work in a shed!' said Serena, leading the way across the garden.

Hardly a shed, thought Charley when they got inside. The light, airy log cabin smelt of pine resin and flower-scented candles, and was a mile away from the cold, impersonal office they'd imagined they'd be visiting. Adding to the warmth, colourful cushions were strewn onto a variety of cream-painted kitchen chairs, all clustered round a battered old wooden table. Serena brought them coffee in what seemed to be her own, homely kitchen mugs, and a pack of chocolate-chip cookies.

'Excuse the packet,' she said cheerfully, handing them round.

After asking Pam some key questions about her circumstances, Serena briefly outlined her position. 'Basically, in your situation a fifty-fifty split would be usual. You'd get half the value of the house, half of your husband's pension and half of any savings or any other assets you have.'

'Half the house?' queried Pam.

'Half the value,' Serena corrected.

'So… we'd have to sell the house.'

'Does he have somewhere else to live?'

'I've no idea.' Pam looked at Charley, appearing momentarily flummoxed. 'I suppose he could live with his other woman, but I don't know…' she shrugged help-lessly.

'In that case you might not be able to keep the house,' said Serena, and Charley glimpsed a tinge of panic flicker across Pam's face. 'The courts look at needs,' the lawyer continued, 'You both *need* somewhere to live. So, unless you have a lot of other assets, you might have to sell the house to provide homes for you both.'

Pam bridled visibly. 'How come the courts have the right to decide what happens to our home? It's our damn house!'

Serena gave Pam few seconds to calm down before she answered, with steadying calm. 'Divorce is emotionally charged. People agree things in the heat of the moment, perhaps because they feel guilty, or they're desperate to get out of a marriage at any cost. But later on, if they think the financial arrangements aren't fair, they'll come back and want to renegotiate and then things get messy, and expensive.'

Like bloody Jay, thought Charley.

'Which is why the courts endeavour to ensure the agreements are fair and workable from the outset. Your husband might not want his share of the house now, but what if this other woman goads him into demanding it, a little down the line? They usually do,' she finished dryly, and Charley wondered if Serena was talking from personal as well as professional experience.

'This is just totally *effing* unfair!' exploded Pam. '*He* has an affair and *I* have to lose my home?'

'I'm sorry, Pam. Believe me, I really do know that's not what you want to hear. But my job is to tell you the truth, in order to help you make the best decisions you can.'

Pam sat slumped back in her chair.

Neither she nor Charley spoke as they walked back through the garden and onto the street. Charley slipped her arm through Pam's.

'You okay?'

'Not really.'

It was only when they were in the privacy of the car that Pam let go. 'How dare he do this to me? How effing *dare* he? Did he even think about what was going to happen to me? Where was he expecting me to live? Did that even occur to him?'

Tears of rage scorched down her cheeks, dragging her eye-liner and mascara with them. Charley rootled about frantically, but fruitlessly, in her bag, and then in the door pocket for a tissue. She eventually tracked down a tatty, second-hand one in her jeans pocket, but rejected it as definitely not fit for purpose. By then Pam had fished out a new, mini pack of tissues from her handbag, and Charley had had a chance to gather her thoughts. Geoff simply hadn't thought through, probably hadn't known, what the consequence of his affair would be, she realised. It was carelessness, not selfishness, she was convinced of that. 'Look. I'm not defending Geoff. Not for one minute. He's behaved like... well like a...'

'Complete bastard.'

'Absolutely. But you're right, he probably *didn't* think. Didn't think for one minute that you might have to lose the house, and if he had thought that, well... maybe he wouldn't have done what he did,' she finished, less certain of her last line. Completely uncertain of it, to be truthful.

Pam sniffed and wiped her nose. 'That doesn't make it any better, Charley,' she said quietly. 'It doesn't help to know that he didn't even *think* about me. My whole life is in that house... our marriage, our children... my memories. And there won't be any more memories of Josh anywhere else,' she finished.

It was the last thought that broke her, that hauled up sobs of raw grief. Struggling to hold back her own tears, Charley leant over to put her arms round Pam and held her, while the flood of tears raged and flowed, until, finally, it subsided, leaving Pam exhausted. Pam sank back in her car seat wearily, completely spent, and thoroughly mortified at having sobbed all over her daughter-in-law.

'I'm sorry...' she started to say, but Charley interrupted.

'Don't you ever apologise to me for crying,' she said fiercely, 'I've cried buckets... *oceans* all over you. Now it's my turn to be the sponge,' she added, trying to lighten the mood, and lessen Pam's evident, but unnecessary, embarrassment.

Pam wiped her eyes, then she took a few deep breaths, calming herself. Eventually she turned to Charley. 'Does it look like I've been crying?'

There was so much mascara and eyeliner smudged round her eyes she looked like a panda, and one that had had a very heavy night, too.

'Little bit,' admitted Charley.

Chapter Twenty-one

Pulling endless pints, stacking dirty glasses, wiping down tables and mopping up vomit isn't everyone's idea of a great summer. It's not everyone's idea of a great job either, an assessment Charley would have wholeheartedly agreed with, but she'd taken on extra shifts to cover people's leave, and to earn herself some extra cash to repay the money she'd taken from her redundancy pot. Needless to say, she was regretting it already. A group of drunken lads, with delusions of hilarity, had taken over two of the outside tables one particularly hot lunchtime, and she'd spent the last couple of hours ferrying bottles of lager to them, clearing away the empties and adroitly repelling their loud, clumsy advances. She was glad when they finally drifted off to make a nuisance of themselves elsewhere. Clearing the tables down she suddenly heard a voice calling out to her, and then the slap of footsteps running along the pavement towards her.

'Charleeey!'

She turned, just in time to catch a small girl in a summer dress and flipflops who'd hurled herself at her, flinging her arms round her tightly. It was Monnie. Tara wasn't far behind her, absolutely the last person Charley wanted to witness her slogging away in the pub. However, that wasn't Monnie's fault, she reminded herself, so she greeted the little girl enthusiastically.

'Monnie!' she cried, hugging her back warmly, while inwardly chanting, *Shit, shit, shit*.

'We're going to the 'quarium!' garbled Monnie excitedly. Grabbing Charley's hand, she pleaded, 'Can *you* come?' Without waiting for an answer she rushed on breathlessly in an effort to persuade her, 'There's sharks and a giant octopus and sting rays and starfish *and* you can walk underwater! It's going to be *awesome*!'

Charley smiled down at her thinking how amazing it was that such a spoilt child could be so generous-hearted. 'Sorry, sweetie, I'm working.'

Monnie's face fell.

'We'll do something another day with Charley,' her mum promised her.

Charley shot a look at Tara, but she seemed to actually mean it.

Blissfully unaware of the palpable tension in the air, Monnie was chattering on. 'We've been sailing!' she cried. 'For two whole weeks and I got to steer the boat!'

'Greece,' supplied Tara, smiling down at her daughter.

'Oh, how cool are you?!' said Charley, and she put up her hand for Monnie to high five, which the small child did gleefully.

'Where else have we been?' prompted Tara, keeping her attention focused on her daughter, to avoid looking at Charley.

Monnie struggled to remember it all. 'Um, Alton Towers and Cadbury World and the seaside and the zoo...' she trailed off.

'Wow, you have been busy!' Charley was rewarded by one of Monnie's gap-toothed grins.

'We must catch up,' said Tara. 'We're doing day trips this week, but I'm around in the evening,' and she looked at Charley expectantly, clearly hoping she'd invite her round.

Charley pulled a face. 'Sorry, I'm working every night this week,' she lied.

'Oh, okay.' Tara visibly deflated. 'Well, next week we're off to Centre Parcs and then it's back to school after that.'

'Boo,' moaned Monnie, pulling a face.

'Bad luck!' said Charley, gently tugging the peak of the child's sunhat down over her eyes.

Monnie giggled and pushed it back up.

'Let's sort something out when we get back from Centre Parcs,' suggested Tara.

'Sure,' Charley said noncommittally.

Turning to her daughter, Tara put her hand out towards her, 'Come on then Monnie-Moo, let's go and see some ferocious sharks!'

Monnie slipped her hand into Tara's, and Charley watched them walk off, playfully swinging their arms together. She wanted to cry.

Apart from that one encounter with Tara, and seeing Pam every single day, which wasn't necessarily good for either of them, Charley didn't see anyone else all summer. Instead she took every extra pub shift available and went to ground. When Nisha called, inviting her out for a drink, she declined, blaming an urgently needed economy drive, and when Angie suggested she join her mob for a picnic at the beach in Weston-super-Mare, Charley excused herself, saying she'd committed to working pretty much every day.

It wasn't that she didn't want to see her friends – she did. She desperately missed their company, their support and their affection. But she couldn't cope with facing up to the contrast between their lives, which were all happy, successful and fulfilled, and her own. She knew she was a failure. And she didn't need anyone, or anything, rubbing it in.

–

Ordinarily, Pam would have been able to lift Charley out of the doldrums she'd sunk into, but Pam's spirits and confidence ware sinking even faster than Charley's following the unexpectedly cold shower of truth at the lawyer's. Pam spent a lot of time in her room thinking things through.

When Zee suggested they all meet up for one of their occasional pub lunches, Pam declined, but with a cheery-enough laugh, 'You must be joking! Not after last time!' Then, the following week, she feigned a summer cold to avoid going on a shopping trip with Zee.

A few days later, Mona phoned to invite her round to a supper party at her place.

'Sounds lovely. Who's going?' asked Pam warily.

'Don't panic! I haven't invited Geoff,' Mona assured her. 'It'll be just be the usual couples – but minus Geoff.'

Pam didn't feel she could refuse, but as the dreaded evening loomed closer she grew increasingly anxious, and then unbearably anxious, until eventually, after a sleepless night and full of apologies, she called Mona and cried off.

Full of tact and sympathy, Mona had assured Pam that she understood, and that she certainly didn't want to pressure her into doing something she didn't feel ready to do. Explaining her change of plans to Charley, Pam fully expected her to understand too, but to her surprise her daughter-in-law took a different stance.

'I know it's daunting going to things on your own, Pam, believe me, I really do. But you just need to take that first step. The longer you leave it, the harder it will be.'

Pam's heart went out to Charley. There had been so much more the young woman had had to contend with following Josh's death, which Pam hadn't even appreciated. 'How did you manage it? That first step?' she asked.

Charley sighed thoughtfully before she answered. 'Well, to start with I did accept invitations from couples, from Josh's friends, but it was always horribly awkward. Nobody knew what to say, and people treated me differently, like they were tiptoeing round me on eggshells all the time. I hated it, and I knew I was spoiling everyone else's fun. Eventually I stopped going and only went out with my girlfriends – Tara, Angie and Nisha. But looking back I wish I wish I'd stuck it out, been a bit braver – because now I've lost that part of Josh's life, too. Which is why I think you should go,' she finished.

'But I've got nothing to wear!' claimed Pam, resorting to a different, if time-honoured, excuse. 'I've left nearly everything at home.'

'You can borrow something of mine,' Charley said, in a voice that brooked no argument.

'Don't be ridiculous, darling! I'd look like mutton dressed as lamb!'

Charley regarded her mother-in-law's slim figure with her head on one side. 'No, you wouldn't.' Then she slipped off to her room and a few minutes later came back with a couple of mini dresses and a pair of black leggings. 'Either of these, over those, will look great on you,' she promised. She then cajoled Pam into calling Mona back to tell her she could go after all.

'Ah,' said Mona, down the line, and Pam could hear the distinctive sound of a metaphorical brick being dropped from a great height and landing heavily. Her friend continued, 'The thing is, when you said you couldn't make it... I called Geoff and invited him instead.'

Hearing the acute discomfort in Mona's voice, Pam said hastily, 'Oh, that's fine! Absolutely fine!'

'I'm sorry, Pam—'

'No, it's my fault,' Pam assured her. 'I'm the one messing you around.'

'You'll come next time, yes?'

'Absolutely,' said Pam, instantly hating herself for feeling so improbably, childishly, disappointed – no, *jealous* – that Geoff was getting to go and she wasn't. She wanted to cry. She just bloody well hoped he wasn't taking that effing Barbara.

–

Much as they wanted to, Pam and Charley couldn't simply go off-grid and disappear from everyone's radar forever. A couple of days after the new school term started, Angie called Charley.

'Will's gone back to school and sanity has returned to the house! It is officially safe to come round!'

Charley laughed, knowing that Angie was only half-joking. Despite being the Headteacher of the local primary school, or perhaps because of that, Will's parenting style was best described as 'playful pandemonium'. Charley knew Angie's summer would have been spent in endless garden campouts and dinosaur digs, treasure hunts and pirate battles, mini-Olympics and water fights. Not for the first time Charley found herself feeling jealous of her friend's full-on family life. Normally, she'd have happily gone round at the weekends and after work, and joined in. But this year Charley had exiled herself, and she'd missed out on the fun, and she was missing Angie too.

It was tempting. It would be really good to see Angie and clear the air so that they could pick up as things were, before she'd turned the shop down and disappointed everyone. Angie, she knew, was the least critical of her, the least judgemental. But right at that moment, Charley was busily sorting out three hundred gift bags for two hen parties at the pub, plus a fiftieth birthday celebration and a series of pamper weekends at the Avalon. Her kitchen table was strewn with little bottles of bubble bath, mini scented candles, chocolates, lip balms, bath bombs and drinks toppers, so she hesitated.

'If you're too busy to come here, I'll come to you,' offered Angie. 'Of course, I'd have to bring… The Boys,' she warned, making it sound like a dire threat. Charley laughed and gave in.

She popped her head round Pam's bedroom door. 'I'm off to Angie's. Want to come?'

Pam was sitting on the bed, doing a crossword. She shook her head. 'No, thanks.'

'You'd be more than welcome,' pressed Charley.

But Pam shook her head again.

'Why don't you invite some of your friends for coffee here? Or go out somewhere…'

'Could do. Another day, maybe.'

'Okay,' said Charley, knowing she wouldn't.

Finn and Eliot were in the garden playing football with Buster the dog, when Charley arrived at Angie's. She stood leaning on the kitchen work surface watching them through the kitchen window, while Angie made them both some tea. It was chaos. The boys careered round the garden, kicking out wildly, tumbling over the dog, each other and the ball.

'Are they even in teams?' Charley asked.

'I *think* it's boy versus dog.'

'My money's on the dog.'

'Oh, good kick, Eliot!' shouted Angie suddenly, then she followed it up shortly with 'Good try, Finn!'

Charley gave her a sideways look. 'Angie, Finn just got tackled by Buster and lost.'

'Don't mock me, I'm doing my job. Will's desperate for one of them to play for England.'

'It'll be Buster,' said Charley.

Angie laughed, then called out, 'Up you jump, Finn. You'll live! Get back in the game!'

Finn scrambled to his feet and hurtled happily after the ball.

'How's the pub?' asked Angie.

'Fine,' lied Charley.

When it became clear Charley wasn't going to volunteer any more information, Angie changed the subject. 'How's Pam?'

Charley pulled a face. 'Turns out getting divorced is a lot grimmer than she expected. It's a lot grimmer than *I* expected. She's a bit low, a bit… a bit lost, I think. She doesn't seem to want to do anything. She hasn't seen any of her friends for weeks.'

'That doesn't sound too good,' said Angie sympathetically. Then she completely floored Charley by saying, 'Why don't you take her for a makeover?'

'A makeover?!' spluttered Charley.

She looked across at her mate: no make-up, baggy old T-shirt smudged with finger paints and God only knew what else, stretched over a huge belly, and tatty torn-off

193

jeans worn under-the-bump. Angie didn't even possess a pair of heels or an LBD, and Charley would have put a tenner on her make-up being in the bottom of the kids' dressing up box, yet here she was, seriously suggesting a makeover would help Pam? It seemed oddly shallow, coming from her.

Catching the look on Charley's face, Angie defiantly tucked her hair behind her ears. 'Listen. I could paint Pam's portrait in six different ways. They'd all be Pam, but there'd be one which she liked the most – the one that shows her the Pam she *wants* to be. So, if you think she's a bit lost, get her to her reinvent her look, help her find herself again – or rather, find the person she now wants to be.'

For a moment Charley went quiet, surprised by the psychological depth of Angie's reply, but she could see the logic behind it, and found herself wondering how her friend had become so wise.

'If nothing else, it'll be a laugh,' continued Angie, before provocatively adding, 'You could have one, too!'

'How very dare you!' laughed Charley. She wouldn't have a makeover if you paid her.

–

I'll kill that Angie.

Charley sat gazing dismally at her reflection. Harsh, unforgiving lighting showed up every flaw in her features and every blemish on her skin. Pam had refused point blank to have a makeover unless Charley had one too. And so here they were, sitting side-by-side in the salon, with no make-up, and swathed in shapeless, polyester gowns, in front of enormous, candidly critical, mirrors. Charley looked over at Pam. The lights mercilessly picked out her wrinkles, the dark shadows and bags under her eyes. She looked ten years older. Catching Charley's eye, Pam gave her a grin. A brave grin. Or maybe it was a grimace.

This was a terrible idea, thought Charley, not for the first time that day.

Their personal stylists hovered behind them, and regarded their clients' reflections with what seemed to Charley to be thinly disguised despair, as if they faced a Herculean task to render either woman barely presentable. Both of the stylists were Instagram-beautiful, with flawless skin, impeccable make-up and perfect hair. They were excruciatingly elegant, and above all, overwhelmingly intimidating. Charley felt the little confidence she had left in herself evaporate.

Pam's stylist offered her a style magazine to flick through. 'Just to give you some ideas,' she said.

Pam smiled at her, but politely refused it. 'Do what you want. Whatever you think will look best,' she said.

Is she insane? thought Charley.

Even the beautician seemed taken aback. 'Are you sure?'

'Absolutely,' Pam told her, adding logically, and with a disarming laugh, 'You're the expert.'

Charley's stylist had lifted Charley's thick mop of curls up to hold them level with her chin and was looking at her critically in the mirror. 'Have you ever thought about going short. Really short? You've got the face for it.'

'No. Absolutely not,' said Charley, more forcefully than was necessary. Pam frowned lightly and glanced across at her, and the stylist looked more than a little offended. 'Sorry. But I want to keep it long,' she explained somewhat defensively.

Josh had loved her hair. He would wind her curls round his fingers as they sat snuggled up on the sofa watching TV.

'Don't ever cut it!' he'd once begged, and she'd promised she wouldn't. For her wedding she'd been more anxious about choosing her bridal hair than choosing her dress. Everyone had told her to wear it up, even the hairdresser, but she knew Josh loved it loose, so she'd asked the stylist to sweep the front pieces into a simple twist, and then dress the rest of her cascading dark curls with dozens of tiny white flowers.

Cutting her hair short would mean looking in the mirror every day and seeing a different version of herself, a Charley who Josh had never known.

Pam's stylist was, rather tactlessly, inspecting the grey hairs on her client's head. 'Have you thought about having it coloured?' she asked.

'Absolutely not!' exclaimed Pam, echoing Charley seconds before. 'It's taken me a lifetime to get those grey hairs! And besides, grey is the new blonde.'

The young beautician looked deeply offended at this thoroughly anarchic notion, and Charley had to bite her lip.

Since Charley had refused a new cut for her hair, her stylist was now concentrating on her make-up.

'We all do the same make-up for years, but every now and then we all need to refresh ourselves and keep ourselves up to date. We just need to use something a little different,' she said patronisingly.

'Like Polyfilla?' offered Pam, from the next chair. Charley laughed out loud, and the stylist nearly poked her in the eye with the mascara brush.

'So, what's brought on the desire for a "new you"?' Pam's stylist asked as she snipped away with the scissors.

'I'm getting divorced.'

'Oh, me, too!'

'Been there. Done that. Twice, in fact,' boasted Charley's stylist. Then turning to Charley she asked, 'How about you? You getting divorced, too?'

'No,' replied Charley steadily. Normally she would have gone on to explain that she was widowed, but then she would have had to explain that it was Pam's son who'd died and then their two poor stylists would be acutely embarrassed and lost for words, so she merely said, 'I'm not married.'

'Lucky you!' quipped the stylist.

Pam visibly winced and Charley felt sick. It was as if she'd denied Josh had ever existed, like she'd brushed him under a carpet, and in front of Pam. God, what would she think of her? She vowed to never lie about her status again, whether or not she was with Pam. She wasn't 'not married', she was a widow, Josh's widow, and she wasn't ever going to deny that, or him, ever again. Her face burned, and her throat felt tight. She couldn't even bring herself to look across to Pam.

Chapter Twenty-two

If the makeover wasn't a complete success, it wasn't a complete failure either. Charley's new look boiled down to her applying some concealer, a bit of blush and a slightly shinier lip-gloss, but Pam's bold gamine haircut really suited her. Although it didn't make her look any younger, she hadn't expected it to, or even wanted it to, but it did make her *feel* more youthful somehow, trendier. Catching sight of herself in a shop window as they left the salon, she stopped and beamed at her reflection. 'I love the "new me"!'

Charley looped her arm through Pam's. 'You should! You look fab.'

'How about a glass of fizz to celebrate?'

'Why not!'

The women headed off, still arm in arm, to one of the dockside bars to sit outside in the early autumn sun and drink Prosecco. They chose a table overlooking the water and Charley went to get their drinks, leaving Pam gazing out over the harbour. The dull brown watery expanse was alive with people on paddle-boards and kayaks. Yellow water ferries chugged along and small dinghies ducked their way between the larger ships. The seagulls, the city's constant soundtrack, noisily squabbled for scraps or keened mournfully as they arced their way across the open sky.

Charley returned with the drinks, and sat down opposite her mother-in-law. She raised her glass.

'To the new Pam!' They both laughed and clinked glasses.

Charley had only taken a couple of sips of her drink when her phone rang. She glanced down at the screen. As did Pam, although entirely involuntarily, but she could clearly see Tara identified as the caller. Not intending to pry, she immediately looked away. Charley rejected the call, turned the phone to silent, but left it on the table.

Feigning indifference, Pam looked at the boats sliding past them on the water. Frankly, she thought Charley was taking this spat with Tara too far. Life was too short to be petty or to bear a grudge against a close friend. But whatever she thought, it was nothing to do with her, and whilst she'd done her best to encourage Charley to make it up with Tara, she had failed. Then Tara called again, and again Charley ignored the call, letting it ring, silently, until Tara hung up.

Then Tara called again, and again…

Thoroughly exasperated, Pam was just about to snap, *For crying out loud, Charley, don't be so bloody stubborn and answer your damn phone!* But Charley had already buckled, and picked up the call.

'Hi Tara,' she said tonelessly. Then there was a silence before she said, in a completely different voice, 'Are you at home? I'm coming over.'

Pam immediately put down her glass. 'Is she okay?'

'I don't know. No. She's crying. I've got to go.' Clearly flustered, Charley grabbed her bag.

'You go on,' Pam told her. 'I'll catch the bus back.'

Charley hesitated. 'Are you sure?'

'Yes! Go!'

Pausing only to nod gratefully at her mother-in-law, Charley turned on her heel, and ran all the way to her car.

—

The sight of Tara's face, when she opened her front door, blotched and puffy, eyes red-raw from crying, sent a rush of cold fear slicing into Charley and twisted her stomach. 'What's happened?' she demanded.

'I found a lump,' said Tara.

For a moment, all Charley could hear in her head was a voice screaming, *No!*

NO.

She forced herself not to overreact, or at least not to show it on her face. But her hand reached out for Tara's.

—

Oblivious to the hot water needling her skin in the shower that morning, Tara had stood numbed and terrorised by the lump she'd just discovered in her armpit. She pressed it. It didn't hurt, and it wasn't a large lump. *Maybe it's just a swollen gland. Maybe I'm just a bit run down. It might not be…* she couldn't even bring herself to finish the thought with *cancer.*

Tara had turned off the shower and leant her head against the glass door, trying to stop the creeping panic from overwhelming her. Somehow, she had to pull herself together enough to get Monnie up, make her some breakfast and get her to school, without letting her know there was anything wrong. She'd dressed, with shaking hands, barely noticing what she'd put on, and then slipped softy into Monnie's room. The sun, filtering in through the yellow cotton curtains, had filled the room with a soft golden light. Tara had stood for a moment, gazing at her sleeping daughter, her little chest rising and falling with each soft breath, so small and vulnerable underneath a yellow quilt covered in rainbows and unicorns. *Please don't take me from her, please, she's too little.* Then she'd wrenched open the curtains, letting the brightness of the early autumn day flood in. She'd swallowed hard and said brightly, 'Good morning, Monnie-Moo!'

Straight after the school run Tara had come home, called in sick, and phoned the doctors' surgery to ask for an appointment that day.

'Is it an emergency?' the receptionist had quizzed.

'Yes.'

'If it's an emergency you should go to A&E.'

'It's not that sort of an emergency.'

'Can you tell me what the problem is?' queried the receptionist.

Just right now, you're the problem Tara had thought, but she'd bitten her tongue, having had run-ins with this particular Rottweiler before.

'If you tell me what the condition is, then I can decide whether or not it's an emergency,' the receptionist had insisted.

Tara had lost it. '*If* it's any business of yours, which I don't think it is, I have a lump in my armpit which may or may not be breast cancer, and since my mother died of breast cancer four years ago, and since these things can be genetic, I would like to see a doctor *today* because if it is cancer, then the sooner it is diagnosed the better chance I have of surviving it, and I have a little girl who *needs* me. She's only nine, and so I really, *really* don't want to die.' Stopping only to take breath, she'd added, 'If you don't give me an appointment *today*, I'll come down there and sit in the waiting room and scream and scream and scream until I see a doctor.'

There was a stunned silence before the receptionist had said, 'The doctor can see you at 11.45.'

'Thank you,' said Tara before she had rung off. Shaking violently she'd sunk to the floor and had given into the tears and the terror.

–

'What did the GP say?' asked Charley, spooning sugar into Tara's tea before putting the mug into her friend's hands.

'She says it might be fine. Might be nothing to worry about...' Tara's face contorted with fear, and Charley knew Tara couldn't believe that, and much as she desperately wanted to, neither could she. Because they both knew that finding a lump was how it had started with Kim. Exactly how it had started. The doctor had referred Kim for tests almost immediately, but even then it was too late, and the last few weeks of Kim's life had been reduced to waiting. Waiting for more tests, waiting for results, waiting for doctors, waiting for chemo, waiting for a bed. And then, towards the end, there was only waiting. Cruel, heartbreaking waiting. Waiting for it to be over.

The fear that something might happen to Tara, that someone else would be taken from her, clutched at Charley. Her heart felt tight, it was hard to breathe and she couldn't trust herself to speak.

'She's sending me for tests. Will you come with me?'

'What about Baz?'

'I haven't told him.'

Charley frowned. 'Why not?'

Tara shrugged. 'I don't want him to let it slip to Monnie. And don't tell the others, Charley. Please. I don't want a fuss.'

Charley promised. Momentarily she found herself hoping the pub would be understanding and would give her time off if necessary, then she told herself she'd go anyway, even if they bloody well fired her.

They spent the next couple of hours curled up on Tara's sofa, watching ridiculous rom-coms, too frightened about what lay ahead to want to talk about it. Charley left when it was time for Tara to pick up Monnie. She cried so hard on the way home she could barely see to drive.

Funnily enough, Charley hadn't really warmed to Tara when they'd first met. She was a bit too gobby for Charley's taste. They'd met at a Zumba class on a Wednesday evening, not long after Charley had moved to Bristol. It wasn't really Charley's thing, but Josh played five-a-side footy every Wednesday and she was left on her own.

'Join an exercise class,' Josh had said. 'Make some friends.'

So she'd signed up for Zumba. It was either that or Spin, and given the sweat-drenched agony the Spin trainer clearly put his class through, Zumba was definitely the lesser of two evils. Or it would have been, had it not been the apparent intention of the Zumba teacher to dance them all to death.

'Come on people. Put some fizz in it!' she'd exclaim, as thirty exhausted people, Charley included, tried to Swing their Salsa, Make with the Merengue, Pump their Reggaetón and Get Down with the Cumbia.

'Smile! You know you're loving it!'

'No, we're not!' Tara had cried. 'It's agony!'

'Come on folks, keep up! It's not that hard!'

'Yes, it sodding is!' Tara had contradicted. And, getting a laugh from the class, she'd continued in that vein all through the session.

After the class she'd surprised Charley by inviting her, and another woman who was on her own, Nisha, to go to the pub with her and her mate, Angie. A few weeks later they all wisely decided that the Zumba teacher was a certifiable sadist, and had given up the dance class. But, even more wisely, they had kept the pub sessions.

It was only when Tara's mum was dying that Charley saw a different, more vulnerable side to her friend. Or maybe the harrowing ordeal of watching her beloved mum dying slowly, in terrible pain, day after day, had changed Tara. Looking back, Charley could remember the moment their acquaintance had deepened into a close friendship. It was when Kim had been moved from the hospital to the hospice to die – for 'end-of-life care' as the nurses preferred to call it. Kim hadn't wanted Monnie to see her grandma that ill, so Tara had left her small daughter with Baz to look after.

It was Charley who had volunteered to take Tara to visit Kim, since Tara was in no fit state to drive, and Charley who had helped her get through her agonising vigil of watching her mum slowly wither away, and so it was Charley, and only Charley, who had known what Tara was going through.

–

Towards the end, Tara knew she only had a few days left with her mum and that she should cling to every last moment, but inside, too ashamed to admit it, she was longing for Kim to die. Charley was the only person Tara had felt safe to confide in.

'I just want this to be over. Not for her, for me.' Then she'd added in a small voice. 'I just want her to die. That's terrible, isn't it?'

'No. No, it's not.' Charley had put her arms round Tara and rocked her while tears of guilt and relief poured down her friend's face.

Sometimes, very often in fact, it's the bereaved who suffer the most, who feel the most pain. Charley could have told her that. Three days later, in the middle of long, quiet night, Tara got what she wanted. Heavily sedated, Kim died in her sleep with her daughter holding her hand. It had been just the two of them when Kim had brought Tara into the world, and it was just the two of them when Kim left it. Tara felt her go, felt her lift, and float away.

'Bye, Mum,' she had manged to whisper through her choked throat. 'I love you.'

She'd stayed for a while. The nurses had made her tea and let her leave in her own time. When she was ready, she had called Charley. 'She's gone. It's all over.'

Charley had driven through the dark, empty streets to pick her up.

Too distraught to go home and break the news to Monnie and Baz, Tara had spent the rest of the night on Charley's sofa, until the cold light of dawn broke and the reality of death had to be faced up to. And now Tara was potentially facing the same, agonising end.

–

When Charley got home from Tara's, Pam was there, waiting for her.

'Why? Why do the people we love have to die?' Charley wailed at her.

They went through to the kitchen where Pam poured Charley a glass of water and sat down opposite her at the table.

'One step at a time, Charley. You don't even know if it *is* cancer. And even if it is, lots of women survive breast cancer.'

'And a lot don't.' Charley's eyes welled with new tears. 'I can't bear the thought of losing her, too.'

Pam caught a glimpse of the bewildered and heart-broken young woman who had bolted for sanctuary when Josh had died. She hadn't seen that Charley for a long time and it troubled her to witness her daughter-in-law's distress again now.

To begin with, after Josh's car crash, Pam had been terrified something would happen to Luke, too. The thought of him driving anywhere had made her feel phys-ically sick. She'd had to fight the urge to beg him to constantly text her to let her know he was safe. She'd had to force herself to stop thinking like that. And to prohibit herself looking at life through the prism of the past and not to let that painful prism distort her view of the present or the future. She'd had to forbid herself to give in to her morbid, irrational fears. It wasn't fair to smother Luke in the net of her own grief, she reminded herself, he had to be free to live his life. With effort, she'd made herself let go. It hadn't been easy, and even now if he arrived later than he said he would, she had to consciously crush the fear rising in her. But she had refused to become a hostage of the past.

Leaning across the table Pam gently took hold of Charley's hand. 'We can't live our lives terrified that we're going to lose the people we love, sweetheart. We mustn't spend our lives fearing the worst, we have to hope for the best. We need to hope that everything will be fine.'

But Charley shook her head, 'Don't tell me to hope that Tara will be okay. Because she probably won't be. Hoping for the best isn't coping. It's pretending.'

Charley's statement left Pam at a loss for words.

Chapter Twenty-three

Less than a week later Charley got a text from Tara.

> Hosp. appt next Tues 11.15. Still OK to come? T x

> Of course. Are you okay? Want to talk?

> Can't. I'm on my way to work.

> Want to come round after?

> Got to take Monnie to ballet.

> Okay. You know where I am if you need me.

Tara replied with an emoji of a smiley face with a halo. Nothing, literally nothing short of an earthquake, would have stopped Charley from taking Tara to her appointment. Not even Pam, although she tried her utmost. She made it plain to Charley that she thought that Baz should take Tara, not Charley, and further, that she believed Charley was wrong to collude with Tara to keep Baz in the dark.

'It's her body, she has a right to deal with it how she wants to,' Charley argued.

'But it is Baz's role to support her. He's her husband.'

'Well, it's not my role to tell him. I'm her friend.'

Pam didn't reply, but her expression said it all. She obviously disagreed with her and Charley found herself on the back foot.

'It's to protect Monnie,' Charley said defensively. 'Tara doesn't think she can trust Baz not to say anything to Monnie.'

'Really?' queried Pam. 'That sounds a little overprotective to me, if it means keeping things like this from her own husband.'

Charley went rather quiet. It now occurred to her that Tara was perhaps not so much protecting Monnie, as protecting her *relationship* with Monnie. And at the expense of Baz, as Tara often did, and the thought of colluding with that, now made Charley feel uncomfortable. 'The thing is,' she explained, 'Tara never had a dad, it was always just her and her mum, Kim.'

'Ah,' said Pam perceptively.

'And so I think she doesn't always know how to involve Baz.'

'Or when,' said Pam pointedly, then she paused before saying more gently, 'You did have a dad though, didn't you? Perhaps, as her friend, you could help her with that.'

It was said mildly and, Charley was sure, with best intentions, but nevertheless she felt the hint of rebuke. She nodded. 'Yes. I'll try.'

As she drove Tara to her appointment, Charley chattered away, filling the car with the kind of empty conversation that fills space, kills time and then evaporates leaving nothing. But as they pulled into the carpark, the sight of the grey concrete hospital building brought them both harshly back to earth and, turning to Charley, Tara said, 'If it's bad news, I've decided I'll jack in my job and spend the rest of my time with Monnie. I might take her out of school and go on some once-in-a-lifetime trip.'

'With Baz?'

'He can come if he wants, if he can leave the business.'

'I'm sure he'd want to...' ventured Charley.

'Maybe. But it's Monnie that matters. I want every single precious, tiny little moment I can have with her before—' Tara couldn't finish her sentence, and turned away, blinking hard, clearly struggling to control her emotions. Charley didn't comfort her, knowing it would only make it worse. She just waited, giving Tara time to pull herself together. Yet the agony in Tara's eyes tore into Charley and a savage fury raged inside her at the unfairness of life, the injustice of death. Picking off its victims so casually. It was just so *bloody* unfair. Bereavement doesn't make you scared of death, she thought, it makes you scared of dying, frightened of the damage your death will do to the ones you leave behind, the pain it will inflict on the ones you love.

The waiting room was crowded, but Tara and Charley manged to find a couple of seats next to each other. A tense silence filled the room while the distant, echoing noises of the rest of the hospital filtered through the double doors. If they spoke at all, people talked in hushed voices. Tara picked up a magazine and started flicking through it, but Charley doubted she was even focusing on the print. Charley let her gaze drift round the room. It was mostly filled with couples and almost everyone was a good deal older than them. One elderly pair were holding hands, not speaking, just holding hands. Looking at their hands, wrinkled and liver-spotted, with their gnarled fingers entwined, made Charley think how wonderful it must be to still to be loving, caring life partners after all those years. But then she thought how terrified they must feel, realising that their long journey together might soon end, leaving one of them to carry on alone.

Turning to Tara she said softly, 'I know you want to protect Monnie, but maybe you *should* tell Baz. You're a couple. You're partners. He wouldn't want you to face this alone.'

'Maybe,' was all Tara said.

And then Tara was called in.

'Shall I come?'

Tara shook her head. 'No, I'll be fine.'

Waiting for Tara to return, the minutes ticked by and Charley flicked through a magazine, not really taking anything in. An advert for pro-biotic yoghurt showed a woman pushing a little girl on a swing in a garden. The sun shone, of course, as it always does in Ad Land, the mother smiled and the little girl was open-mouthed with laughter. Even the damn golden retriever in the background had a stupid grin on its face. *How the hell was Monnie going to cope with losing her mum?* thought Charley. *How was anyone that young supposed to cope with death?*

Then, suddenly, Tara was standing in front of her.

'All done?' asked Charley as lightly as she could, absently reaching for her handbag and getting up.

Tara nodded tightly. 'They'll send the results to the GP in a couple of weeks.'

'*Two weeks?*' It seemed a cruel, protracted delay to Charley, but she swallowed her outrage as they walked out, knowing Tara didn't need her negativity right now. Two weeks would be a gruellingly long wait. 'Did they give you any indication at all?'

'No.'

Charley tucked her arm into Tara's. 'Come on, let's have a coffee.'

They went to the Friends of the Hospital cafe and ordered huge slabs of fruit cake with old-fashioned milky coffee in comfortingly thick cups. Charley got out her purse, but Tara refused to her Charley pay, as usual, and they sat watching the steady stream of staff and patients flow by.

'The problem with hospitals,' said Tara, 'is that they're places where crap things happen.'

Yes, thought Charley. *Really crap things.* And suddenly it all came flooding back. Four years ago. Her desperate rush to get to Josh. Her lovely, kind, funny Josh, lying in Intensive Care, smashed up and broken after the crash. She remembered running, in a nightmare-kind-of-race where she couldn't feel her legs, and could only hear her blood pounding in her ears as she ran and ran and ran along the never-ending corridors which stretched away forever in front of her. And even then she had arrived too late. She had vomited over the floor in shock when they told her he was dead. She didn't even get to say goodbye. Now, she closed her eyes. She bloody hated bloody hospitals.

'We need to think of the *good* things that happened here,' Tara exclaimed suddenly, bring Charley back to the present. 'Monnie was born here.'

'Yes,' nodded Charley, and then manged a smile before adding, 'And *all* of Angie's babies. And her next one will be, too.'

'Well, I'll drink to that,' said Tara.

They clinked cups.

–

Charley's birthday crept up quietly. She wanted to ignore it. Tara usually came round with a bottle of fizz, but she hadn't even mentioned her birthday this year. Charley assumed she'd forgotten, which was hardly surprising given the circumstances. Pam hadn't said anything either, which did surprise Charley, since her mother-in-law always sent her a card with a little gift, but then Pam, too, had other things on her mind.

On the morning of her birthday, she lay in bed listening to Pam clattering round in the kitchen, telling herself she ought to get up but, then again, since she was on the evening shift at the pub, she didn't really need to, not just yet. She turned to the photo of Josh on the bedside table and joked, 'I bet you didn't even get me a bloody present either, did you!'

He grinned at her, as usual.

He'd always bought her perfume, Charlie by Revlon, and often a bunch of other little things as well. To be honest, it wasn't her favourite scent. To be absolutely honest, she didn't like it much at all. She'd have preferred something lighter, more citrusy, but she'd never had the heart to tell him. He'd been chuffed to bits when he'd found it the first year they were together, watching her unwrap it, as eager as a small boy, and then because naturally she'd told him she *absolutely loved it*, he bought it for her every year. She smiled to herself and reflected that she'd been hoist by her own petard on that one. The last bottle had run out a couple of years ago and she'd never bothered to buy herself any more, which was probably a good sign. However, she still kept the empty bottle at the back of her knicker drawer, which was probably a bad sign. She sighed.

She was just about to chivvy herself into getting up when there was a tap at her door. 'Happy Birthday!' called Pam, before coming into the room bearing a tray laden with fresh croissants, a mug of coffee, orange juice and a pot of jam.

'Oh my God, Pam!' squealed Charley, shooting up in bed in delight. She couldn't remember the last time she'd had breakfast in bed.

Laughing, Pam plonked the tray down on her lap. There was no gift on the tray, but she'd propped a card up against the jam pot.

'I didn't get you anything because I thought you might want to choose what you want,' she said, sitting down on the bed.

'In that case I choose breakfast in bed every day!' laughed Charley.

It wasn't the most painful birthday she'd had to get through, but it was hard. In reality, each birthday spent without Josh had become a little easier to bear, but this year her fear of losing Tara intensified her feelings of loss. The day felt taut and brittle, and the passing of another year seemed more poignant. Her parents sent her a card, but no gift. They didn't call her either, an omission which she knew hadn't escaped Pam's notice but, tactful as ever, her mother-in-law let it pass without comment.

After breakfast, the two of them went for a long walk across the Downs and then Pam made a chicken and asparagus flan with a green salad for lunch, followed by raspberry pavlova with homemade meringues. Then they whiled away a giggly afternoon doing silly online puzzles and quizzes, discovering which type of dog breed they identified as (poodle and chihuahua), which type of bread they were (ciabatta and wholegrain), and which Disney villain alter ego they were most like (Ursula and Maleficent). After which, childishly, Charley found herself hoping that Pam had made her a birthday cake. But when the afternoon passed by without the appearance of a surprise cake, she felt absurdly disappointed. She told herself off for being immature.

Shortly after five, while Charley was in her room getting changed for work, the doorbell rang. Since she was standing in just her bra and pants, she called out to Pam, 'Can you get that, please?' But there was no reply and the doorbell went again. 'Pam!' yelled Charley scrabbling into her jeans, but there was still no answer. *Maybe she's in the loo.* Charley grabbed her blouse and struggled into it as she dashed up the hall. Whoever was outside had given up on the doorbell and had started to bang on the door instead.

'Hang on! I'm coming!' she yelled irritably. She yanked open the door to reveal a small flock of helium balloons, behind which her mates were, preposterously, all pretending to hide.

'HAPPY BIRTHDAY!' they chorused before tumbling into the flat, laughing and giggling, clutching presents and bottles, sweeping Charley along before them. In the kitchen Pam was already getting out the glasses and plates.

Charley skewered her with a look. 'Did you know about this?'

Pam tried to feign innocence, while Tara popped the fizz and handed Charley a foaming glass of Prosecco.

'I've got to go to work!' protested Charley weakly, but taking it nevertheless.

'No. You've got food poisoning today,' Pam informed her evenly. 'Didn't you know? I called the pub, so now, unfortunately, you can't go in for forty-eight hours. Poor you.'

Charley gasped in disbelief and awe at her mother-in-law. 'In that case...' She raised her glass. 'Cheers!'

Nisha presented Charley with a huge cake box and opened the lid to reveal a spectacular three-tiered red velvet cake, oozing with cream cheese icing and decorated with cream sugared roses with just a few token candles on the top. Pam slid the cake onto a plate and lit the candles.

'Make a wish!' cried Angie who really did need to spend more time with grown-ups, thought Charley fondly.

Charley's eyes flicked to Tara, who gave her a small, tight smile in response. Charley blew out the candles and then closed her eyes and wished. She knew it was a pointless, naive gesture. As if cancer could be defeated by wishful thinking and half a dozen sparkly candles.

Angie passed her a colourfully wrapped package and an even more brightly coloured homemade card. When Charley opened it, an astonishingly lurid pink cardboard cake popped up, instantly showering her with a cascade of purple glitter. Charley was filled with affection for Angie's kids. 'Tell them it's the best card *ever*!' Then she opened

Angie's gift, which turned out to be a hideous giant plastic raspberry, filled with shower gel.

'The kids chose it,' Angie told her, a trifle unnecessarily. 'It was a toss-up between that and a Super Spaceman Laser Bubble Gun.'

'Oh, tough call,' said Charley with mock solemnity, 'but ultimately the right one!' Then she laughed and said, 'Give them all a hug from me.'

Tara handed her a small white box. Intrigued, Charley opened it and her hand flew to her mouth. 'Oh my God, Tara! These are *gorgeous*!' Taking out the pair of silver-and-turquoise pendant earrings she held them up to her ears. 'Did you break the "less-than-a-tenner" rule?' she demanded.

'Of course not!' Tara wafted her hand in lazy dismissal. 'Anyhow, life's too short to worry about money. Much too short.'

Their eyes met briefly and then Tara looked away.

'Indeed!' cried Pam cheerfully, skilfully defusing the briefly tense moment. Charley gave her a small, grateful look, and Pam went on, 'And today is all about celebrating!' She raised her glass. 'Happy birthday, Charley!'

The others joined in the toast, chorusing, 'Happy birthday!'

Later, Charley managed to grab a second or two with Tara on her own while the others had gone into the living room.

'How're you doing?' she asked.

Tara shrugged. 'Fine. I'm fine.'

Charley hugged her and held her close.

They both knew she was lying.

Chapter Twenty-four

Going to the clinic to get Tara's results was an ordeal, for both of them. Charley's heart squatted heavily in her chest like a lump of cold lead, and she couldn't imagine what Tara must be going through. As they walked along the corridor to the clinic Tara suddenly stopped, and putting her hand on Charley's arm, asked her if she would do her a favour. 'A big favour,' she added seriously.

'Of course,' Charley assured her earnestly, assuming that it would be something to do with Monnie. 'Anything.'

'Promise?' persisted Tara.

There was a beat while the two friends looked at each other.

'Yes. I promise.'

'Whatever happens today…' Tara started, and Charley bit into her lip, hard. 'Whatever the results, promise me you'll give up working in the pub and start your own business.'

'What?!' For a second, Charley thought Tara was joking. It was so glib.

'I'm serious, Charley. Do it for me. Please.'

Charley looked away, annoyed that Tara had lured her into making such a big commitment.

'Don't be mad at me, please, Charley, hear me out. When Mum died, someone suggested that I try find the good to come out of her death. It wasn't hard, she was in so much pain her dying was a blessed relief for both of us. I'm just asking you to do the same for me. If I'm going to die I want something good to come out of it.'

The idea that *anything* good could result from Tara's death, or indeed anybody's death, left Charley dumbfounded. What possible good could have come out of Josh's death, for crying out loud? None. None at all. Charley thought it was the most ridiculous, heartless piece of advice, but Tara was looking at her with such intensity, she agreed.

'Okay. I promise.'

'And you have to call it "Tara's Grand Memorial Emporium!"' Tara said it with such a straight face that for a second, Charley thought she meant it. Then she caught in the spark in Tara's eye.

'Over my dead body,' Charley joked back.

'Or mine,' said Tara, and suddenly Charley had to fight back her tears.

Later, sitting in the waiting room while Tara was in with the specialist, Charley had time to reflect on her rash promise, and immediately regretted it. She would do anything for Tara, anything, she told herself, but the thought of running her own business frightened her, terrified her. Although not as much as the thought of losing Tara.

Hearing footsteps coming along the corridor from the consulting rooms she looked up, as did a lot of other people., but it wasn't Tara, it was a middle-aged couple. The husband had his arm round his wife who was leaning into him, crying silently. The man was clearly struggling, with enormous dignity, to control his emotions for the sake of his wife. Charley swallowed hard and looked away, not wanting to intrude. Somehow, when her friend emerged with her results, they were going to have to get out of that waiting room without falling apart. More footsteps and this time it was Tara. Charley scanned her friend's face anxiously, but it didn't give anything away.

'Let's go,' was all Tara said, before striding off through the double doors and out to the corridor. Grabbing her bag, and fearing the worst, Charley rushed after her.

Outside in the corridor Tara suddenly stopped and spun round towards Charley.

'It's fine. It's benign. It's nothing,' she gabbled, and then promptly dissolved into a flood of relieved tears.

'Oh, thank God!' cried Charley, as Tara literally fell against her and Charley put her arms round her almost holding her up. 'When you rushed out I thought—' she stopped, not even wanting to voice her darkest fear.

Sniffing back her tears and wiping her eyes, Tara pulled away before saying, 'I know. I'm sorry, but I thought it would be cruel to stand there beaming from ear to ear and punching the air.' She sniffed again and blew her nose. 'Some of those people in there are going to go home devastated.'

Charley thought of the middle-aged couple, and their quiet, brave display of composure in the face of heart-breaking despair.

Tara cut into her thoughts, grabbing her arm. 'Come on. Let's celebrate!'

Charley found herself leading them to the dockside bar where she and Pam had been on the day Tara had phoned to tell her about finding the lump. Perhaps she wanted to exorcise the fear that had descended on her that morning and had haunted her for the past two weeks. She made her way to nab the very same table, outside overlooking the water, while Tara went to the bar. It was only a couple or so weeks after that fateful day, but despite the sun and the blue sky, the autumn breeze made Charley grateful for her jacket. One of the bright yellow water ferries chugged by – the one with the model of Gromit the dog on its prow. *Only in Bristol!* she thought affectionately. A small boy waved at her eagerly from on board; he reminded her of Eliot. She waved back enthusiastically and his little face lit up.

Emboldened, he bawled excitedly at her, 'I'M FOUR!'

'Today!' called out the woman standing next to him, whom Charley presumed was his mum.

'Happy birthday!' Charley shouted back.

Four years old, she thought. Four whole years. Where had those four years gone?

The morning after Josh had died she'd woken up and sat in bed hoping, desperately hoping, that he hadn't. Desperately hoping it had all been a horrible nightmare, that it wasn't true, and that at any moment he'd walk into the bedroom and everything would be all right. She'd urgently, almost physically, clung onto that hope for several long seconds… but she'd been powerless to stop the hope slipping through her fingers, leaving her with nothing except the terrible reality. Josh was gone. At that precise moment, she'd given up believing in hope. To hope was a pointless, futile exercise. But now, today, Tara's wonderful, miraculous outcome began to rekindle, or perhaps more accurately, justify, a belief in hope. Maybe Pam was right, perhaps it wasn't tempting fate to hope for the best. Ruefully, she conceded that if she'd allowed herself to hope for the best, instead of fearing the worse, then the last two weeks wouldn't have been as bloody frightening, that was for sure. Maybe, just maybe, it was okay to hope that someone wasn't going to die. As long as you don't pin your hopes and dreams on it…

She was still unpicking her thoughts when Tara arrived back at the table carrying two glasses in one hand, and a bottle of Prosecco in an ice bucket in the other.

'A bottle?! Bloody hell, Tara, it's the middle of the day!'

'I know, I know,' Tara fended off Charley's protest airily. 'But hey, don't judge me! I was only going to get us a glass each, honest, but it seemed a bit of a feeble gesture, considering the sheer bloody wonderful miraculous brilliance of the occasion!'

'I'll let you off!' joked Charley.

'And anyhow,' Tara argued, 'It's a double celebration! One: I'm not going to die, and two: you're starting your own business.'

There was a nano-beat before Charley said firmly, 'No. I'm not.'

Tara put her glass down on the table and eyeballed her mate sternly. 'Charley Taylor, you promised.'

Charley looked away and focused on the water.

'I'm not going to let you wriggle out of it. You *promised*,' Tara repeated.

'Yes, but that was when I thought you were dying!'

'I know! It was my dying wish!' said Tara melodramatically.

'Most people have the courtesy to die before they expect their dying wishes to be granted,' replied Charley.

'Not me,' said Tara. 'I like to have my Prosecco and drink it, too! So now you're just going to have to do it because you love me.'

Not wishing to rob the joy from the day, Charley let the subject drop and, for probably much the same reason,

Tara didn't push it. In the event, since Charley was driving, and Tara had to pick up Monnie from school, they only had one glass of fizz each.

'Take the bottle home and celebrate with Baz,' said Charley, which seemed like a good idea to both of them at the time, so Tara swept up the bottle and, propping it up in the drinks' holder of her car, carefully carted it home to share with her husband, along with her wonderful news. Unfortunately, they had both massively misjudged how Baz would react.

–

'You had a biopsy?' Baz queried. 'Why didn't you tell me?'

'I'm telling you now.'

'I would have come with you!'

'It was fine. Charley came with me.'

With measured care, Baz put the glass of Prosecco Tara had handed him down on the kitchen side, his face tight with tension. 'You told Charley, but you didn't tell me?'

'I didn't want to worry you,' said Tara defensively.

'You took *Charley* instead of me?'

'Yes, I just thought…' she floundered.

His next question took her breath away. 'You don't love me any more, do you?' His tone was matter-of-fact, but the hurt in his eyes spoke volumes and sliced into Tara like a knife.

He stood there, a dignified, hardworking, modest man who'd never done anything to hurt her. Never done anything but adore her, provide for her, love her and care for her, and their daughter. A man who'd never done anything to stop her loving him.

Panic fluttered inside her like a trapped moth. She did still love him, very much, but she knew she'd stopped showing him, or even telling him.

'That's not true,' she said urgently, 'I do love you, Baz. I do.' She moved towards him, but he shook his head and pulled back from her, out of her reach.

'It's always you and Monnie. It's never you and me any more.' He looked heartbroken.

It would have been easier for Tara if he'd lost his temper. If he'd shouted at her. She was good in a fight, but his quiet dejection defeated her, that and the uncomfortable truth he'd voiced. Since Monnie had been born she *had* put Monnie first, had deliberately sought to be closer to Monnie than anyone else in the world, including Baz. But that was only natural, wasn't it? Just a normal mum and daughter thing, like her and Kim.

Then she remembered Charley repeatedly trying to encourage her to take Baz instead of her, and how she'd pointed out that Baz was her partner, her life partner. She realised that she had deliberately excluded him, and in all truthfulness, she didn't understand why.

'I don't know why I told Charley and not you,' she said at last, with open-hearted honestly. 'But I promise it's not because I don't love you. I do. I do love you.' And going over to him she put both her arms round his neck. This time he did not resist. He slid his arms round her waist, leant his head on hers, and then frightened her, really frightened her, by starting to cry.

'Don't cry. Please don't cry,' she whispered. Then she kissed him and led him upstairs.

Chapter Twenty-five

A promise was a promise, and a dying wish was a dying wish, even if nobody actually died. Dutifully, Charley called the estate agent. She wasn't surprised to hear there weren't any more shops available in her price range, and she wasn't particularly surprised to hear him gloating either. *Odious man*, she thought.

'The one in Cargo was snapped up,' he crowed.

'Will you let me know when the next one comes up?'

'I can't promise. They often go before they're even advertised. People hear about them through the grapevine. Sorry I can't be more help,' he finished in a tone that suggested he was, in fact, delighted.

'Actually,' said Charley, an idea taking root in her mind, 'you've been a great help. Thank you.'

Ten minutes later she was pedalling down to Cargo, planning to ask that nice bloke in the bike shop if he'd keep his ear to the ground and let her know if any of the units were coming up. As she cycled passed the shop unit she'd turned down she braked, climbed off her bike and looked in the window. Now called Crafty Crafters, the shop was filled with a variety – no, make that a jumble – of arts and crafts products, all jostling for space: polka-dot painted pebble doorstops shared a table with garish clunky wooden necklaces; rainbow-striped candles clashed with pottery pencil pots in neon colours; a whole wall was dedicated to some truly ghastly, amateurish pictures of flowers. She reckoned Angie's kids could have done better. To be fair, there were some rather nice pieces, too, they were just swamped by the rest. She fell in love with some adorably cute knitted baby cardigans and seriously considered buying one for Angie's new baby – until she saw the price. *All* the prices seemed massively optimistic to Charley, and appeared to be based, she suspected, on what the crafters wanted to be paid, rather than what the customers would want to pay. *How are they making any money doing this?* she wondered. *Actually, how are they even covering the rent?*

As it turned out, they weren't.

The bike shop man leant on the counter while Charley stood on the other side of it, scratching the big grey lurcher between the ears.

'They're definitely struggling,' he told her. 'I was chatting to them the other day. They're working all hours trying to make a go of it, but there's too many of them taking a cut. They've only been in couple of months or so, but I think they might have already given notice. I'll introduce you to them, if you like, then you can ask them what the situation is. Well, I could, if I knew your name!' he finished with a smile.

Charley thought she detected a hint of affectionate teasing in his tone. She smiled sheepishly. 'Sorry! I should have introduced myself. I'm Charley.'

'I'm Ricky. He put his hand out for her to shake. She took it readily, but she was suddenly aware of the warmth of his skin, and somehow the ordinary gesture of friendship felt like a heightened moment between them. Withdrawing her hand, she tried not to let it show on her face.

Apparently oblivious, Ricky led her over to the crafter's unit, leaving a disgruntled Carlo guarding the shop. As they passed the other units Ricky either waved or called out to some of the other owners and the camaraderie of the place was evident. But nevertheless, Charley was struck by how well-liked Ricky seemed to be, which didn't surprise her – it was hard not to warm to him.

As it turned out, Ricky had been right, the crafters had given notice and were desperate to get out of the four months' notice period they were still tied into. They suggested Charley contact the management company to see if she could take on the unit earlier.

Excitement and nerves, in equal measure, fluttered in Charley's stomach as she and Ricky walked back to the bike shop. Carlo thumped his tail in greeting.

'Why not give them a ring now,' suggested Ricky. There was nobody in the shop, but Charley hesitated.

Perhaps sensing she was reluctant to make the call in front of him he continued, 'Why don't I go and get us both a coffee while you make that call?'

Why not? asked a voice in Charley's head, and she couldn't come up with a single reason not to.

When Ricky got back with the coffee and a bag of pastries, she was standing in the doorway waiting for him, grinning like a cat that had got the cream along with a side order of Lobster Thermidor.

'It's all sorted!' she enthused. 'They're sending the paperwork over to the agent right now!'

'Fantastic!' He seemed so genuinely pleased for her she wanted to hug him. She didn't, of course.

Casually, he hitched himself up onto the counter and, apologising for the lack of chairs, indicated she could sit up there too. So, using her heel for leverage against the front of the counter, she hoisted herself up and sat perched next to him companionably. While they drank their coffee and ate their pastries, Carlo snuffled around the floor, hoovering up the crumbs, and Ricky asked her more about her plans.

'I'm opening a Prosecco-themed gift shop,' said Charley barely able believe the words as she said them.

'That could do really well here. No wonder the management are keen for you to have it.'

'Actually, I think it's more that the crafters aren't planning to sit it out for four months and they don't want an empty unit,' she replied, more realistically.

He shrugged amiably, dismissing her modest rebuttal, and raising his takeaway coffee said, 'Anyhow, welcome to Cargo!'

As she thanked him, it dawned on her how lucky she was to have bumped into him, and how generous he'd been with his time and help. She barely knew him, but she already felt way more comfortable with him than she ever had with her colleagues at the letting agency, and she found herself looking forward to the prospect of him being there, three shops down from hers.

After she'd finished her coffee, she thanked him again, and then took herself straight to the estate agent to sign the paperwork before she could chicken out again. The estate agent looked decidedly peeved that she'd managed to prove him wrong, and so soon, too. But Charley had merely smiled sweetly and tried extremely hard not to gloat. As she signed, literally on the dotted line, she realised her hand was trembling. Leaving the office, excitedly clutching her copy of the signed tenancy agreement and an impressively glossy letting brochure, Charley was suddenly engulfed by a blinding, full-on, white-out panic, as the enormity of what she'd just done hit her like a truck.

'Bloody hell! Are you *insane*?' she asked herself.

–

The women clustered eagerly round the glossy brochure Charley had opened out on the coffee table. Most of it was taken up with arty shots of the other shops at Cargo and a floor plan of the site, but there were a couple of unassuming photos of the interior of an empty unit.

'I know it doesn't look much, just a plain oblong box, but you should see some of the other shops, they're stunning!'

'No, it's great,' Angie enthused. 'It's a blank canvas which means you can do whatever you want. You could do hand-painted logos and Prosecco slogans all over the walls and the window, and paint the shop name in the same style.'

'*You* could, I couldn't,' laughed Charley.

'I'll happily do it for you!'

'Ange! You're *huge*! How are you going to even reach over the bump?' Tara raised her brows at Angie's rather impressive stomach.

'Long-handled paintbrushes!'

Pam eyed her sternly. 'Well, don't overdo it.'

Angie rolled her eyes affectionately. 'It's my fourth!' she reminded Pam.

'Even so...' Pam left the implicit warning hanging.

'I was thinking maybe do everything gold and white?' suggested Charley tentatively, prepared to bow to Angie's superior wisdom in all things design.

'Definitely!' Angie nodded. 'Simple, but classy.' She offered to come up with a number of logos for Charley to choose from.

'Can't we just base them on the 'Charley' logo on the pamper bags?' Charley asked. 'Then that would tie the two sides of the business together.'

'Smart thinking,' said Nisha, 'and you can use it on your website, too.'

'My website?' said Charley, mildly alarmed. Nisha made it sound like she could just pop out and get one from the Co-op.

'Yes. You'll need to make online sales to maximise your profits, and you'll have to be all over social media like a rash for marketing and promotion, and you'll have to try and get some influencers interested.'

Charley groaned. 'Must I?' Her previous forays into social media had been distancing and demoralising. She seemed to have little connection with, and even less to say to, the inhabitants of the internet, all of whom seemed to be living such adventurous, successful and fulfilled lives.

'Oh, choose me!' Tara put her hand up eagerly, like a primary-school kid in class. 'Finally, an excuse to waste my life, I mean *devote* my life, to social media.'

Pam leapt up and nipped off to the kitchen. 'I'm opening the other bottle of fizz!'

Charley put the budget she'd pulled together in front of Nisha. 'This is just a rough draft, obviously.' She pointed at the neat lines of figures. 'That's the shop rent, that's the amount I'll need to draw to live on for the first few months, and that's what I'll have left for stock. I've done a quick summary of the things I'd like to get to start with.' She presented Nisha with another list. 'Obviously I can build up more stock as and when the business grows.'

'Blimey. You've been busy,' Angie said, and Charley shot her a smile.

Nisha was looking at the figures, meticulously. 'So, can I just check,' she said after a few moments. 'Is this figure here the total of *all* the start-up capital you've got?'

'Yes. It's my redundancy *and* my savings.'

Nisha went quiet. Uncomfortably quiet, and when Pam came back in with the fizz she paused in the doorway, as if sensing the sudden tension.

'What's wrong?' Charley asked Nisha in a strained voice. 'Is there a problem?'

'No, not necessarily,' Nisha said carefully. 'It's just that I think there might be a few costs you haven't factored in.'

'Like what?'

'Business rates, insurance, the electricity bill – unless that's all included in the rent.'

'No, I don't think it is.' Charley bit her lip.

'And there's no display shelving in the shop. Plus there's broadband, website, domain names etc. I mean none of these are huge costs in themselves, but they will mount up and eat into the money you have left to buy stock.'

Nisha got her phone out and did some quick calculations, while Charley felt the colour drain from her face, rapidly followed by her enthusiasm, her optimism and finally, her confidence.

'How much is left for stock?' she asked when Nisha had finished her sums.

Nisha grimaced. 'Not a lot.'

'What the hell am I going to do? I've signed the lease! I can't back out now! How can I run a shop if I can't afford to buy any stuff to go in it?'

The joyous excitement inside her soured to anxious nausea.

'This is my fault, Charley,' said Nisha, running her hand through her hair and looking uncharacteristically ruffled. 'I work from home. I don't pay business rates or property insurance, or separate utilities. I simply forgot to tell you to budget for them. I'm sorry. I'm really sorry.'

'It's not your fault.' Charley reached out to squeeze Nisha's hand. 'It's *my* business. I'm the one who's screwed up.'

'Don't panic!' Tara said, plonking herself down on the arm of the sofa near Charley. 'We'll sort this,' she promised.

'How? HOW? I can't magic up a pot of money I don't have.'

'Baz will make you some display shelves for a start,' said Tara.

'I'm still going to have to buy the wood.'

'No, you won't. There's *tons* of timber left over from big building projects. More than enough to do a revamp on Harrods! Honestly, anyone would think it grows on trees!'

Charley managed a small smile.

'You can build a website yourself,' said Nisha. 'It's not rocket science, and I'll help.'

'Thanks, but what about all that other stuff… domain names etc.?' said Charley.

'Easy peasy to sort out, and cheap as chips,' Nisha assured her.

'Really?' Charley looked incredulous.

'Well, cheap as posh chips. You know, triple fried ones doused with Balsamic vinegar and pink Himalayan rock salt.'

'Blimey, Nisha, you eat *posh*!' laughed Angie. 'In our house the chips are posh if they're crinkle cut.'

'Ooooh, there's fancy,' said Pam, joining in with everyone's attempts to lift the mood.

'Okay, next?' said Tara.

Nisha looked at her list. 'Insurance. You'll probably need ten million pounds of public liability insurance.'

'Ten million!' gasped Charley, panic written all over her face.

'Calm down!' Nisha cried. 'Ten million is standard and nowhere near as expensive as it sounds. But you'll have to have contents insurance as well, and I would suggest you think about getting some income protection for if you're sick and can't open the shop.'

'She won't need that.' Pam shook her head decisively. 'If she's sick, *I'll* man the shop.'

Charley smiled at Pam gratefully, before turning to Nisha and asking, 'But what about the other costs?'

Nisha shrugged. 'You could get a small business loan...'

'I'm not borrowing money, and that's final.' Apart from the mortgage, Charley never borrowed money, she didn't even max her credit card.

Nisha hesitated before saying prudently, 'I think you might have to. Even with all these things taken care of you haven't really got a huge amount of money left for stock.'

Borrowing money was a deal-breaker for Charley. She made a snap decision. 'In that case, how much will I lose if I give up the shop?'

She was met with a chorus of disappointed wails.

Only Nisha remained level-headed and clear thinking. 'How much notice do you have to give?'

'Four months.'

'There's your answer – four months' rent.'

'Right, well, that's that then.' Charley slumped back against the sofa back before adding ruefully, 'Oh well. It was fun while it lasted.'

'You are not giving up!' Tara said fiercely.

'No way!' Angie shook her head vehemently. 'You just need to give us all some time to think about what to do next.'

'And don't do anything drastic,' warned Nisha.

'Okay,' promised Charley. Although, thoroughly browbeaten and defeated, in all honesty she didn't see what any of them could do.

'And try not to worry,' said Pam. 'It'll give you wrinkles.'

—

The swish of passing cars and the kaleidoscope of head-lights sweeping across her bedroom ceiling had Charley wondering why so many people were up and around in the middle of the night. As a small child, the rhythm of traffic driving past the pub had lulled her to sleep. As an adult it reminded her of endless sleepless nights. Lonely nights in an empty bed. She lay in the dark and gave up on sleep, giving in to the carousel of worries chasing each other round and round her brain. The only collateral for a business loan would be her flat, so, whichever way she looked at it, she was trapped in a vicious circle. She was trying to run a business to keep her home, but in order to run the business she would have to risk losing her home. Charley thought she was going mad.

She looked at her bedside clock. It was that drearily dismal hour when it was far too early to give up on the night and get up, but way too late to get decent sleep –

even if she could drop off, which she couldn't. She swung her legs out of bed and slipped barefoot to the kitchen to make herself some hot chocolate, taking out a mug and opening the fridge as quietly as possible to avoid waking Pam. She winced at the clunk of the microwave door, which seemed magnified in the stillness of the night, but was still startled when the kitchen door opened.

'I thought I heard you pottering about,' said Pam.

'Sorry. I didn't mean to wake you.'

'You didn't, darling. I just don't sleep as well if I'm not in my own bed. I think it's my age. I'm determined not to give in to it.'

'The sleeping or the ageing?'

'Both. Getting old is mandatory. Acting your age, on the other hand, is optional.'

Charley got another mug down for Pam. It was her old office mug, the one that read 'Today Is Going to Be Awesome'.

Pam glanced at the writing. 'Sounds like an omen,' she remarked cheerfully.

Charley read the slogan on her own mug: 'I'd give up Prosecco, but I'm not a quitter.'

'Hmmm. I'm less sure about mine.'

'Well you shouldn't be,' said Pam. 'You're not a quitter.'

'I'm not quitting. I'm giving in gracefully.'

Wisely, Pam didn't reply.

Chapter Twenty-six

By the time Pam had breakfasted the next morning, Charley was still sleeping. Not wanting to wake her, Pam scrawled a note on the back of an envelope and left it on the kitchen table:

> *Had to go out. Back sometime later today. Don't do anything drastic!*
> *Love P*
>
> *PS Red pepper and feta quiche for dinner.*

The first thing Pam noticed when she pulled into her driveway was that Geoff's car was there in its usual place, and that, mercifully, there wasn't another car parked next to it. Rather belatedly it occurred to her that it would have been wise to have called him beforehand to check. She parked on auto-pilot next to his car, and headed indoors. As soon as she'd put the key in the lock and opened the front door she was struck by a momentary panic. What if that Barbara woman *was* there? In her home? Just because her car wasn't there, didn't mean *she* wasn't, Pam realised. Involuntarily, her hand flew to her mouth, in a gesture of either shock or of suppressing nausea, possibly both. The thought of *her* being in her home, amongst her things, physically repulsed her. *Oh God, why didn't I think to phone ahead?*

It was too late now, she was on the threshold. She wondered whether to call out, in case they were… well, she didn't even want to think about what they might be doing. She compromised by shutting the door loudly before boldly walking into the kitchen. *It's my house*, she reminded herself. Then, bracing herself for any potentially uncomfortable encounter, she added, *I've every right to walk straight in.*

She flung her keys in their usual place beside the fruit bowl and went over to flick the kettle on. It was empty, which irked her, since she always refilled it. Going over to the sink she saw Geoff outside in the garden – on his own, thank God – raking up the leaves from the lawn, just like he did every autumn. Yet somehow, the scene wasn't the same. It was as if her world had spun round three hundred and sixty degrees and settled back in place but, crucially, slightly adrift or tilted from its starting point.

Pam watched him gather the leaves into a neat pile and thought back to when the boys were small and had mischievously grabbed handfuls of them and tossed them the air, scattering the leaves as quickly as Geoff could gather them. And how Geoff had chased them round the garden, pretending to be cross, before hurling them, one after the other, onto the heap of leaves, both boys squealing with mock fear. Where did those years go? If only you could hit 'pause' and hold back time before it charged away from you, blundering along ruthlessly and leaving you behind.

She sighed, and brusquely reminded herself that even if Josh hadn't died, those days would still be over. She put the kettle on, and while it boiled, she went to pick up a few more things she needed at Charley's.

As she walked through the house, memories of the boys came flooding back to her. All their secret midnight feasts she'd pretended not to know about, despite the almighty mess they'd always left in the kitchen. Luke breaking the kitchen window with his football, and the merciless pounding all the windows had taken from the inevitable barrage of snowballs whenever it snowed. The duvet dens they'd built on the turn in the stairs, and how furiously they had demanded the secret password before letting her pass. Mostly she'd managed to guess them, but at least once she'd had to clamber over the balustrade to get back down to the kitchen. She paused on the stairs, suddenly remembering Josh sitting on the bottom step to lace up his football boots, shedding dried mud and grass across the hall carpet.

'Can't you put them on outside?' she'd queried.

'It's raining!' he'd complained, as if it were entirely unreasonable of her to expect him to get wet putting his boots on, before going off to play an entire football match in the pouring rain. In her mind's eye she could see him as clear as day, and when he looked up and gave her his trademark grin, her breath caught in her throat.

All those birthdays and Christmases, she thought, remembering their stockings pinned to the fire surround in the living room, the piles of presents under the tree, their advent calendars on the dresser in the hallway counting down the days, and the build-up of the tangible, almost physical, level of excitement that had filled the entire house. She laughed out loud, remembering the Christmas when thirteen-year-old Josh had been rendered helpless with giggles, and pretty much legless, too, after drinking cider for the first time, and how Luke had sworn blind Father Christmas had given them the cans in their stockings.

Then, when they were older, she remembered the chaos of their teenage parties, and falling over piles of grubby trainers dumped by the front door, signalling that the house would be full of gangly, long-legged teenagers, and then, of course, there was coming home after the funeral… *No!* Pam told herself sternly, not that memory. Expertly she nipped it in the bud. Carrying on up the stairs, she deliberately stopped herself glancing into Josh's old room and marched straight into hers.

The bed was made and the room looked strangely unlived-in. Geoff's dressing gown wasn't hanging on the back of the door, and there were no stray items of clothing or dirty linen draped over the bed, no shoes kicked off and abandoned underneath it. *He's moved out*, she thought, *and moved in with her. He's only come back to see to the damn garden*. The thought panicked her. Sitting down hard on the bed, she was surprised to find herself close to tears. Not for Geoff, she realised, for herself. He'd left her and she was going to be on her own. She was going to grow old alone.

Oh, for crying out loud, pull yourself together, she told herself harshly. *There are worse things than being alone. You of all people know that*. Seeking distraction in action, Pam flung open the doors to her wardrobe, dug out a small suitcase from the back, and put it on the bed, telling herself that she might as well fill it, while she was there. Walking into bathroom to collect her perfume she saw Geoff's dressing gown hanging over the side of the bath, and a laundry bin overflowing with his dirty linen. Ha! He hadn't moved out then! *Well, not yet*. Once she had collected together what she needed, she headed back downstairs. She left her suitcase by the front door then went into the kitchen, where she made two mugs of coffee, automatically putting two sugars in Geoff's and stirring it for him. Then she took a deep breath and took them out into the garden. Putting their mugs on the patio table she called over to him. He looked up in surprise.

Watching his expression move from surprise to pleasure and then to hope as he walked towards her, Pam said bluntly, 'I've not come back.'

'Oh,' said Geoff, his face falling.

'I'm only here because I need to talk to you.'

–

Charley spent the morning considering her options. Having handed her notice in at the pub pretty much as soon as she'd signed the shop lease, she wasn't sure if they'd take her back, though there were other pubs she could try, of course. Maybe if she worked double shifts she'd be able to cover the shop rent and save enough to buy the stock. It would mean working something like a seventy- or eighty-hour week, but she could do it, for a few months, at any rate. And then there was her income from the gift bags, not exactly life-changing amounts, but it would all help. Opening a new spreadsheet she drew up yet another potential budget, but no matter how optimistically she juggled the figures she couldn't convince herself she could make enough money.

Slumping back in her chair she gazed at the screen, letting the lines of figures drift in and out of focus until the sound of the front door opening and Pam's footsteps coming up the hall brought her out of her trance.

'Have you got a minute? I mean, is this a good time for a chat?' Pam hovered in the kitchen doorway, looking a little anxious.

'Yes, of course,' said Charley, closing her laptop.

Sitting herself down opposite Charley, Pam said 'I've been back home to see Geoff.'

Oh, please don't say you're moving out! begged Charley, silently. She knew she was being selfish and self-centred, but after her complete screw-up with the business plan, she couldn't face another financial body blow. She forced herself not to overreact, and set her face to 'pleasant-interested-smile' mode and held it.

Pam carried on. 'I've had a chat with Geoff, and well the thing is, I couldn't do this without checking with him… not with everything that's going on between us… and I had to make sure I could do it… without him for obvious reasons—'

Charley honestly thought her smile was going to have to be surgically removed if she had to hold it any longer, but finally Pam got to the point.

'I'm going to invest five thousand pounds in your shop.'

Charley felt the pleasant, interested smile slide off her face. She wasn't entirely sure she could believe what she was hearing. 'Five thousand pounds,' she repeated.

'Yes. But listen, and I want to make this very clear,' Pam looked at her solemnly, 'I'm not going to intervene. It's *your* project completely, and I'm absolutely *not* expecting to get a return on the money. If the shop's a success, that'll be my reward. Those are the terms. No arguing.'

There was little danger of that. Her unexpected generosity had stunned Charley into silence.

Pam broke it when she said, 'I know you can make a success of this business, Charley, and I want to support you. This is the best way I can think to do so.'

Charley swallowed the golf-ball lodged in her throat. 'You went to Geoff for this?'

Pam gave her a half-smile. 'He told me to make it clear that it's an investment, it's not charity. He knew you wouldn't accept the money if you thought it was.'

Charley flung her arms round Pam and burst into tears.

'Oh my God! I can't believe you're doing this for me!'

Laughing, Pam drew her into a warm embrace. 'I can't believe you think I wouldn't!'

It was at this moment the doorbell rang, and regarding Charley's blotchy, tear-stained face, Pam volunteered to answer it.

Seconds later Tara exploded into the kitchen bursting with excitement, Pam following her.

'Charley, I have a business proposition for you,' Tara blurted. 'Baz and I will put three grand into the shop.'

Charley's eyes flicked to Pam, and then back to Tara.

'Don't panic, I'm not going to get all involved,' Tara promised her. 'It's still absolutely your thing. And I'm not expecting any immediate return. Except later, we'll take a small profit-share once the shop gets going.'

There was a brief, uncomfortable moment while Charley struggled to respond. 'Actually, Pam's already offered to invest some money,' she said finally, prudently deciding not to reveal that Pam was offering more.

'Oh.' Tara sat down abruptly the kitchen chair opposite Charley, in the one Pam had vacated to answer the door, as it happened.

Pam immediately offered to back out, 'I don't have to invest, if you'd prefer me not to.'

Nooo! wailed Charley's inner thoughts. Instinctively she would much rather Pam invested than Tara, because she knew she could trust Pam not to interfere, whereas her mate, despite her fervent promise not to meddle, would be all over the business like a rash.

Then, since Charley didn't take up Pam's offer to step down, and even more revealingly, didn't rip Tara's arm off to accept hers, Tara said, 'No, if Pam's already made an offer then you probably don't need mine.'

She looked gutted, and Charley found herself trapped in an impossible situation, forced to choose between the two people in the world she cared about most, and inevitably having to end up rejecting, and hurting, one of them. So, out of compassion rather than greed, Charley wondered if she could convert her predicament into a win–win – and take both offers.

'That'd be fine by me,' Pam assured her.

'Me too,' agreed Tara.

A huge smile slowly worked its way across Charley's face, lighting it up completely. Suddenly the idea of running a business seemed much less frightening now that she had business partners. Although they weren't necessarily the most obvious pair to put together, since Pam was cautious and wise, and Tara was smart, and… Charley sought for an alternative to 'bossy', and charitably came up with 'decisive'. She just hoped to God the two of them were going to get on – it would be a bloody nightmare if they didn't.

Chapter Twenty-seven

After Tara had left to pick up Monnie from school, Charley got out her phone. 'I must thank Geoff,' she told Pam.

'Actually, the money's just from me,' said Pam, stopping her. 'To be fair to him, he did want the money to come from both of us, he's very fond of you, too,' she added with a smile, 'But I thought that might make things complicated in the future.'

Just a bit! thought Charley. Then another thought occurred to her. 'It must have been incredibly difficult for you to go and talk to Geoff.'

Pam sighed. 'Yes. Well. He was obviously rather keen on talking about other things.' Then she caught Charley off balance by adding, a little too casually, 'He's offered to move in with Barbara, so that I can move back into the house.'

Bloody hell, that's huge, thought Charley. *Poor Pam*. It was one thing to have an affair with someone, but to leave your wife for them, after forty years of marriage, that was in another league altogether. 'Is that what you want?' was all she felt it was safe to say.

Pam didn't reply immediately, but looked away and gazed out of the window, as if she thought that somehow the answer to Charley's question might be out there, somewhere. Clearly it wasn't, but it seemed to have given her time to gather her thoughts, and after a moment she turned back to Charley, and shrugging lightly said, 'I don't know. If I'm honest, I don't want him to move in with her.' A position Charley could completely understand, but then Pam sighed heavily and continued, 'But if I am going to move back home then I don't want Geoff to be there as well. But having said that, I don't want to rattle about an empty house all on my own, with nothing but memories to keep me company.'

Charley could remember drowning in the silence of the flat after Josh died, its emptiness echoing the bleak, pointlessness she had felt inside. The shock of losing him had been so sudden, so traumatic, that to begin with, remembering any moments of their life together had been unbearable. Gradually, over time, a few memories had slid under her guard, and eventually she'd learnt to welcome them back: Josh, doubled up and almost crying with laughter at something funny on TV; him teasing her as she blubbed her way through a rom-com; both of them sitting round the coffee table trying to eat a Thai takeaway with chopsticks for the first time.

'Wait! I've got this!' he'd said, and had promptly stabbed a large prawn with a single stick.

'That's cheating!' she'd told him, laughing.

'I'll work up to two sticks next time!' he'd promised, shoving the prawn in his mouth.

Then there was the time when he'd rescued her from an enormous spider in the bath and she'd discovered he was almost as scared of them as she was. He'd gently cupped the hairy beasty in his hands and was gingerly carrying it out of the bathroom when he'd suddenly squealed and started shaking his arms around, hysterically yelling, 'It's run up my arm!'

'Memories aren't necessarily bad company,' she told Pam quietly.

—

A few days later, Zee suggested she and Pam head off to the coast for a walk in the autumn sunshine. They strolled idly along the beach, under a deep blue but cloudy sky, with the fresh, salty air mildly dampening their hair. The long sandy beaches that were crammed in the summer holidays were almost deserted now. They'd slipped off their shoes to walk barefoot over the cool damp sand in the kind of companionable, contemplative silence that only a long and close friendship allows.

'Geoff says he'll move in with Barbara if I want to move back home,' said Pam eventually.

Zee snorted with a mixture of derision and anger. 'That's a bit bloody rich. He's making it *your* decision then, is he, whether or not he moves in with her?' When Pam didn't answer, she softened her tone and asked, as Charley had, 'Is that what you want?'

Sighing heavily, Pam shrugged. 'I don't know. Deep down I don't want Geoff to leave me to move in with her. It's so...'

'Humiliating?' offered Zee.

'Yes! Bloody humiliating. But if I'm going to move back home, then I don't want Geoff to be there.' She shuddered involuntarily. 'Then again, I don't think I want to live there all alone in an empty house, reminding me that I'm not wanted or needed any more.' She sighed heavily and thought for a moment. 'Maybe I shouldn't move back at all? Maybe I should just accept that life is all about phases. Sell the house and move on.'

It occurred to Pam that she had got into the habit of just thinking about her life as two periods. Before Josh died, and afterwards. But there had been other phases, she now reminded herself. There was the one before she'd even met Geoff, and the one when they were first married before they'd had the boys, and now there was, apparently, going to be the one after she left Geoff, the one where she'd be on her own.

'Do you actually *want* to sell the house and move out?' asked Zee, sensibly sticking to the question of practicalities rather than addressing the more subjective question of 'moving on', which was altogether a far bigger mountain to climb.

'No, I don't,' replied Pam instantly, and the immediacy and clarity of her own response surprised her. She carried on talking, as much to rationalise her thoughts to herself as to explain them to Zee, 'I don't know if I can cope with the idea of another family moving in. They'll want to change everything.' Which sounded ridiculous and irrational, even to her. But if the house became someone else's home, it would stop being Josh's home, and part of his existence would simply be erased, as easily as her footprints in the sand by an incoming tide. The new family would paint over the pencilled height marks and dates by kitchen door frame, which she had meticulously painted around for nearly two decades whenever she'd redecorated. They'd Polyfilla the dent in the wall where Josh had tried to skateboard down the stairs and crash-landed in the hall. She'd have to remove the posters and festival tickets that were still Blu-Tacked to the wall in Josh's room, and they'd replace his lampshade, and his curtains, and obliterate the navy-blue ceiling. Of course, they'd make changes to Luke's room too, but Luke lived somewhere else now, Josh did not.

After a while, Zee said, 'It's a big step, Pam. Do you have to decide anything right now? I know things feel confused and uncertain, but it would be a mistake to go rushing into doing something you'll regret. Give it time.'

Pam sighed. She *was* giving it time. It was nearly four months since she'd left Geoff. But time didn't seem to be making it any easier to decide what to do.

The friends walked along in silence for a while, their footprints behind them leaving a long trail in the sand. Wandering closer to the shoreline, across the hard ridges of wet sand, they splashed through the cool shallows, letting the sea wash over their feet.

'You know, you don't *have* to get divorced,' said Zee. 'You could both stay in the house – but live apart. People do.'

'Is that what you and Theo do now?'

'No. Although now I come to think of it, I think I'd prefer it if we did. We still share a bedroom, and a bed, but more out of habit than anything else.'

Pam pulled a sympathetic face, but said nothing, and Zee went on. 'And I still cook his meals and do his laundry, and do the cleaning, and the shopping and run the house… and he does the gardening and the D.I.Y. Occasionally we even talk to one another,' she finished.

'So it's just like a normal marriage then,' quipped Pam.

Zee laughed. 'Yes, just without the wedded bliss!'

Pam tried to imagine what 'living apart' in the same house would be like, living *with* Geoff but leading totally separate lives: they'd sleep apart, obviously, but would they eat apart, cook separately, do their own laundry? It seemed an uncomfortable compromise – somehow spiteful and petty. A life of ridiculous pretence. And the mere thought of including *Barbara* in the scenario, accommodating her in any way, was just impossible.

'I don't know...' she sighed helplessly. 'I just don't want him to think we can simply go back to how we were. That if he just gives me some time and few bunches of flowers it'll all blow over and I'll forgive him. And I'm not going to live with him if he's still seeing that Barbara. I'm not putting up with that!'

'Is there any danger *she* might move in, if you're not there, I mean?' ventured Zee.

Horrified, Pam whipped round and stared at her friend. That utterly appalling thought simply hadn't occurred to her.

'Over my dead body!' she exclaimed. 'I am not having *that bloody woman* living in my house, sleeping in my bed, and cooking in my kitchen! And she is absolutely NOT having a shower or sitting on the loo in my en suite! I'll electrify the damn seat if I have to!'.

Zee laughed and volunteered to buy the wire.

After a while, Zee asked pragmatically, 'So, what's the worst-case scenario?'

'Having that Barbara in my house,' replied Pam instantly.

'Even worse than selling up?'

'Yes. I don't want another family living there, but that's a lot better than having her living there!'

Zee hummed in thought. 'Okay. So selling is the "least-worst" scenario. What's the best-case scenario?'

'Living there on my own, I suppose...'

'You don't sound very sure,' remarked Zee gently.

'I'm not.' But one thing Pam did feel certain of following their walk, was that regardless of the practicalities, whatever they might turn out to be, she didn't ever want to share her house, or her life, with Geoff again. Whatever the scenario – she wanted a divorce.

–

'The bastard's taking me to court!'

Nisha stood in the kitchen of Charley's flat, digging round in her bag for the letter she'd had from Jay's solicitor. She was shaking with rage. Her hands trembled as she found the letter and handed it to Charley.

'Shit!' said Charley, forgetting momentarily that Pam was also in the room. She took the letter and sat down abruptly at the kitchen table to read it. Pam didn't flinch one iota at the expletive, she merely crossed the kitchen and put the kettle on.

'What does this actually mean?' Charley asked Nisha when she'd finished reading. 'Are you actually been summoned to court, or what…?' She felt hopelessly out of her depth as she looked at her friend.

'No. It's just a warning that if I don't agree to settle, and give him a lump sum, then he'll apply to the court to challenge the court order.'

'Is he bluffing?' asked Pam calmly.

'It doesn't sound like it,' said Charley. 'Not if he's gone to the expense of sending this. Solicitor's letters aren't cheap, are they?'

'No,' said Nisha. 'And I don't think he's bluffing, or rather *La Bimbo* isn't. I've either got to pay him a heap of money I don't actually have, or spend a fortune fighting him in court… with money I don't actually have. I'm stuffed either way, and he knows it!'

'Bastard,' said Charley.

'Tea or coffee?' queried Pam mildly, standing by the kettle, which was nearly boiled.

Nisha looked at her vaguely as if the idea of drinking either beverage, or indeed any beverage, just at this moment was extraordinary.

'Or perhaps something a bit stronger?' suggested Pam.

'Preferably something a lot stronger,' agreed Nisha.

'We've only got wine,' said Charley apologetically, but Pam had already gone to the fridge. She poured Nisha a generous glassful.

Nisha put her hand out for it gratefully, and took a couple of large gulps, before setting the glass down on the table with a hand that was still shaking.

'I'm sorry to come round like this...' she started to say, but Pam interrupted her by leaning over and putting her hand gently on her arm.

'Why?' she asked simply, and Nisha seemed momentarily lost for words.

'It's what friends are for,' Charley reminded her.

'I just don't know what to do,' said Nisha in a small voice.

Charley glanced across to Pam, who was looking thoughtful. She hoped to God her mother-in-law had something useful to suggest, because she had absolutely no idea how to help Nisha. After a few thoughtful moments, when Pam did speak, she surprised Nisha and baffled Charley completely.

'How well do you get on with your mother-in-law?'

'My ex-mother-in-law?' Nisha queried, reminding Pam of her actual status.

'Yes.'

'I haven't seen her since we divorced.'

'How did the two of you get on before that?' Pam persevered.

'Fine,' shrugged Nisha, but her forehead was furrowed with a slight frown, and she was clearly wondering where all this was going. 'Actually, better than fine. I really liked her, and I know she liked me.' A small smile crept across her face. 'She's smart, very funny, and she was always lovely to me, forever wanting to take me shopping and spoiling me with little gifts.'

'Well, it's just a suggestion,' said Pam carefully, 'but if I thought my son was behaving like...'

'Like Jay,' provided Charley.

'Like a little shit,' corrected Pam, making Charley's eyebrows shoot up in surprise at her language. 'I'd shred him. And then I'd step in and try and stop him. So, maybe you should build some bridges, get in touch with his mother, and let her know precisely what her son is up to. Just a thought,' she finished.

Charley and Nisha exchanged astonished glances. Charley doubted either of them would have come up with a suggestion like that in a million years, but then, perhaps it was a solution only a mother-in-law could have dreamt up.

'But what if she already knows?' asked Nisha.

'And what if she doesn't?' countered Pam.

'It's got to be worth a try,' ventured Charley.

Nisha was less easily convinced. 'I'm not sure. We've sort of lost touch. Won't she think it's a bit cheap, me contacting her out of the blue, just because I want something?'

'Why not let her decide that?' advised Pam. 'She might be delighted to hear from you. Just because you've divorced your husband doesn't mean you have to divorce his whole family, too.'

'Actually, that's a really important point, Nishe,' agreed Charley. 'Like you said, why should *La Bimbo* get to be part of his family, and not you?'

'Because she's with Jay and I'm not any more.'

'That doesn't have to change anything,' said Pam. 'We can choose to keep the people we like, and love, in our lives if we want to.'

'Give her a ring,' encouraged Charley gently.

'What if she doesn't even want to talk to me?' said Nisha, in her quiet voice again.

Charley paused, not wanting to reassure Nisha with what might be naive assumptions based on her own relationship with her mother-in-law.

Fortunately, Pam rescued her. 'Well, I don't know you very well, Nisha, but what little I do know I like a lot, and speaking as a mother-in-law, I'd suspect your ex-mother-in-law will be only too happy to meet you for coffee.'

Chapter Twenty-eight

Technically, Charley wasn't meant to get access to the shop until her contract started, but since the crafters were keen to move out ASAP, and an abandoned shop gave out a bad image, the management had said that once the unit was empty she could begin decorating and shopfitting, as long as she wasn't actually trading. As it turned out, the crafters – evidently keen to cut their losses – had cleared out by the end of the week. Charley spent the week productively, setting up her business, sorting out a business bank account, building a website and drawing up an Excel sheet of potential products to sell, complete with prices, discounts and delivery details.

As soon as she got the keys Charley cycled eagerly down to the dockside, but when she got to the unit her enthusiasm evaporated. She'd expected the crafters to empty the shop, but in their keenness to strip it out they'd trashed the paintwork, left dozens of ragged screw holes in the walls, and a trail of rubbish and debris all over the floor. Momentarily she was infuriated, but making a conscious effort to rise above it, she told herself not to let it ruin her day. She dumped the bike inside the unit and nipped along to Ricky's shop to borrow a broom, dustpan and brush and a bin bag. Even just cleaning the shop would make it feel hers. Getting to work restored her mood, but as she'd actually come down to measure up and sketch the design for the shelves she wanted Baz to build, once she'd cleared up, she took a pad and pencil out of her rucksack, sat cross-legged on the floor and started drawing.

Before long, the shop door opened behind her, surprising her. She turned to see Ricky holding a couple of takeaway coffees. 'Cappuccino?'

She scrambled to her feet. 'Life-saver!' Then, looking round for the lurcher, she added, 'Where's Carlo?'

'Guarding the shop, so I can't stop long.'

He sat down next to her on the floor, looking over her shoulder at her sketch pad.

'A friend of mine's building me a dresser,' she explained.

'Great,' said Ricky. 'Useful sort of friend,' he added, but a shade flatly.

Charley didn't pick up on his tone. 'I'm going for a sort of shabby chic look.'

He nodded approvingly. 'You need a signature style. It makes a shop stand out.'

'Like yours. I *love* the retro sixties look!'

He rewarded her with one of his usual, easy smiles. 'Thanks. I was trying to find a way of making second-hand bikes look cool.'

'It worked!'

He smiled again.

'So, why second-hand bikes?'

Ricky paused as if he were marshalling his thoughts. 'Well, partly because I like bikes, they're good for the environment, and partly because new bikes are very expensive, so there's always a market for used ones, but mostly, I suppose, because I don't like things going to waste. Why junk a perfectly good bike when all it needs is a bit of TLC to get it back on the road again. What about you?' he asked. 'Why Prosecco gifts?'

Good question, thought Charley, still anxious that the idea might be a bit too niche. 'Well, I help run a Prosecco-themed annual fundraiser for the Patience House Hospice and I buy little gifts to sell for that. Everything always goes, plus I'm setting up a small party-bag business, you know for weddings, hen parties etc… and the two ventures just seemed to fit together.'

'Sounds like a good plan.' Ricky then added, 'Let me know when it is. The fundraiser, I mean. I'll come along. If I've not missed it already, that is.'

Charley briefly pictured Ricky at the Prosecco Night, probably the only man there, and mercilessly teased by Tara and the rest of her gang. Much as she would have liked him to be there, she couldn't inflict *that* ordeal on him.

'I should probably warn you that it'll probably be only women there.'

'Is that meant to put me off?' he asked, a glint of amusement in his eyes.

'No, not at all! You'll be more than welcome! It'll be in November.' As soon as she said that, she realised the next Annual Kim Henderson Memorial Prosecco Night was looming up soon, alarmingly soon. She made a note to mention it to Tara when she took the sketches round later.

Carlo then started barking. Ricky grabbed his coffee and got up. 'Sounds like a customer,' he said, heading off.

'Thanks for the coffee!' she called after him.

–

When Charley took the measurements over to Tara's that evening, Baz hadn't got back from work. Tara cast her eye over the drawing. 'He can easily make that for you,' she promised.

'Sure? I was worried it was a bit too fiddly?'

'Nothing's too fiddly for Baz! He'll knock that up in a weekend!'

Charley frowned, clearly unconvinced. 'If it's too complicated, tell him to make something simpler. Whatever he does will be great.'

'It'll be fine,' Tara assured her, then she opened the kitchen door and yelled up the stairs to Monnie who was playing in her bedroom. 'Five minutes, then bed-time, Monnie-moo.'

There was a protesting groan, and Tara rolled her eyes.

'Bedtime comes at the same time every night, but it's always a complete surprise to Monnie!'

Charley laughed, and then she reminded Tara about the upcoming Prosecco Night. 'Sorry, I've been so distracted I didn't realise the date was coming round so quickly! We'll have to get cracking.'

'Yes… right,' said Tara uneasily. 'Actually, I was going to talk to you about that. I think *I* should organise it this year.'

In point of fact, it was Baz who'd suggested that. 'Charley's got enough on her plate setting up her business. She can't run a charity event as well,' he'd said, and Tara assumed that Charley would be pleased to be relieved of the duty.

She wasn't. 'No!' she exclaimed, so heatedly that Tara must have looked startled by the forcefulness of her reply, because Charley laughed and said, 'Sorry, that was a bit full on! But it's just that I really love running the Prosecco night and hosting it in my flat. It's the highlight of my year, you know it is! I'm already looking forward to it.'

'Fine,' shrugged Tara, 'if that's what you want.'

'It is, and I'm sure I'll be able to cope with it. As a matter of fact, I'm going for a personal best!' Charley assured her. Tara conceded. She genuinely hadn't wanted to take over organising the evening. It was Charley's baby and she'd run it brilliantly every year, and Tara was only too happy to let her carry on doing it.

The first Annual Kim Henderson Memorial Prosecco Night had been a modest affair, with just their mates and a few of the mums from Monnie's class pitching up at Charley's one Thursday evening. They'd charged everyone a fiver for a glass of fizz, and laid on a few posh party snacks. Purely on a whim, Charley had had the inspired idea to buy a few little Prosecco-themed goodies to sell on the night to make a little more money and to make it more of an event. They'd raised enough to buy the hospice a Remembrance Book for the bereaved and Tara had been chuffed to bits.

Afterwards, she and Charley had taken the donation round to Patience House and then they'd driven to the cemetery to put flowers on Kim's grave, in celebration of her birthday. It had been a dull, grey day with a thin November mist hanging in the air. Tara had also brought a sparkly purple helium balloon, which was ostensibly from Monnie. It had looked completely out of place, bobbing along between the graves but Tara didn't care, it was her mum's birthday and she'd celebrate it how she damn well liked. She'd tied the balloon around Kim's headstone, where it bobbed about garishly wishing Kim a Happy Birthday in large, lurid orange letters, in stark contrast to the simple lettering on the memorial itself. It was a plain white stone with the words picked out in slate grey: Kim's name, the dates of her birth and death, and the message:

Mum – I love you
and I miss you.

They were simple, unfussy words and typical of Tara – no-nonsense and full of heart. She kept her mum's grave immaculately, always ensuring there were fresh flowers in the vase, because she believed fresh flowers on a grave meant far more than flowery words on a headstone.

'You know what I hate the most about Mum dying?' Tara had said to Charley, as she'd knelt to put the flowers into the vase on Kim's grave. 'She won't see Monnie grow up, and Monnie...' she broke off, gathered herself, and then continued, 'Monnie won't really remember her – she's not old enough.'

Charley had crouched down next to Tara, the wet grass dampening their shoes. 'We won't let Monnie forget Kim,' she promised. 'You've got stacks of photos, and we can share *our* memories with her.'

'It won't be the same though, will it? They won't be her memories.'

'Does it matter?' Charley had asked gently.

Tara had thought about it for a moment, then shrugged and said, 'Probably not.'

She'd stared to gather up the cellophane packaging from the flowers, and momentarily seemed lost in her own thoughts. Then she'd suddenly stopped and turned to Charley and flashed her a broad smile. 'D'you remember when Mum came to that 1970s disco?'

'Oh my God, yes!' Charley's face had lit up at the memory.

'That Tina Turner dress! It barely covered her bum!'

'And that wig! I can't believe she came on the bus!'

'I sodding can!' laughed Tara.

Laughing with her, Charley had stood up and held out her hand to help Tara to her feet, then they'd picked up their bags and headed towards the cemetery exit. Passing the newer graves, where the ground was still muddy and raw, they had noticed an elderly man sitting on a bench, alone. Wrapped in an overcoat and huddled in a woolly hat and scarf, he sat motionless, staring into the distance.

Tara never believed the old adage that 'fools rush in where angels fear to tread'. Frankly she thought it was an excuse made by those too timid to tackle something diffi-cult to offer help. Grief, she had discovered, was a lonely enough place without being marooned there, avoided by people too scared of saying the wrong thing. Even angels rush in sometimes, but they tread lightly, because the ground near a newly dug grave is soft.

'Mind if we join you?' she had asked the elderly man. He hadn't, and they'd both sat with him on the bench, and then they'd stayed a while talking. He told them he'd just lost his wife, after fifty years of marriage. It didn't take an angel to understand that he was the one who was lost.

'Where did you meet her?' prompted Tara.

He smiled, his eyes, old and rheumy, moistened with memories as he drifted back across the years. 'At a dance. She was a wonderful dancer...'

'Are you?' asked Charley.

'No! I'm terrible!' he confessed, with a smile. 'She always said I had two left feet.'

They sat there, the three of them, on a wooden bench at the edge of a graveyard – an elderly man telling two complete strangers about the love of his life. As he talked his face softened and lost some of the pinched look of grief.

When they eventually got up to leave, Tara said to him, 'When my mum died, someone told me that whenever I felt overwhelmed by sadness, and missing her, I should remember something fun we did together. Something that made us laugh.' She smiled at the old man gently. 'It works for me.'

—

When Charley got back from Tara's, she was surprised to find that Pam had company. She was sitting on the sofa chatting to Nisha. Charley plonked herself down on the coffee table, facing the two of them.

'I had coffee with my ex-mother-in-law,' Nisha told her, barely controlling the beaming smile creeping across her face.

'And?' prompted Charley.

'You were right! She was lovely! But, God, was I nervous?'

'I'll bet,' said Charley, and of the corner of her eye she caught Pam smiling fondly at Nisha.

'I'd decided not to tell her about what Jay was up to over the phone. I thought it might seem combative or confrontational. So I just asked if she'd meet me for a coffee and a catch-up.'

'Very wise,' said Charley.

Nisha shook her head. 'Not necessarily! I worked myself up into a complete state while I sat and waited for her. I literally felt sick.'

Charley found it hard to imagine Nisha ever getting flustered or anxious. In all the years she'd known her,

Nisha had always been the cool, composed one in the room, the one she could always rely on to be the voice of reason.

Rolling her eyes at the memory, Nisha went on, 'I was thinking, what if she'd called Jay and mentioned that I was meeting her and he'd told her not to come? What if she already knew what was going on, and thought that Jay was in the right and was only coming to pressure me into giving him the money? Or, worse, what if she *didn't* know, and then, when I told her she got angry and caused a scene and accused me of luring her to meet up under false pretences?'

Charley's hand flew instinctively to her mouth. 'I hadn't thought of that!'

'I know! I was almost ready to give up and scarper when she turned up.'

In the event, it turned out that her ex-mother-in-law had absolutely no idea that Jay was demanding money from Nisha. When she found out, she was livid and ashamed of him. Perceptively, she blamed his new partner, as Nisha did.

'Apparently she doesn't like her at all. None of them do. And then she said something that made me choke up.' Nisha paused and took another sip of wine, clearly in danger of welling up again.

'What?' prompted Charley gently.

'She said she missed me.'

Her voice broke and Charley slid onto the arm of the sofa and put her arm round her.

'I can well imagine she does,' said Pam.

Charley gave her friend an affectionate squeeze. 'Sometimes I don't think you realise how much you mean to people,' she told her, and Nisha flashed her the kind of smile Charley had never seen on her face before. An endearingly sheepish one.

And then Nisha told them her former mother-in-law had gone on to press home her point by taking out her phone she took and showing Nisha all the recent photos she had of the entire family.

'And I mean all! Which took a very long time!' Nisha said with a laugh. 'Anyhow, she's going to talk to Jay, or rather, his father is going to talk to him, which, believe me, is a much bigger deal,' she finished ominously.

Charley looked over to Pam, who was smiling contentedly to herself. *You*, she thought, and not for the first time, *are a very wise woman*.

Chapter Twenty-nine

On her knees in the shop, in her old decorating clothes, Charley was painting the shelving unit which good old Baz – good as Tara's word – had "knocked up over the weekend". With her earphones in, she was accompanying Adele as she 'Set Fire to the Rain' at the top of her voice. When someone suddenly tapped her on the shoulder, she nearly leapt out of her skin. Whipping her earphones out, she turned to find a highly amused Ricky standing there.

She cringed, knowing that singing was absolutely *not* in her skillset, especially not acapella.

'I'm just on a coffee run. Want one?'

'It's my turn,' she insisted, getting up.

'You're busy.'

'I could do with a break. Honest. I'll bring it down to yours. Cappuccino?'

'Americano, please, if you're sure…'

Ricky was just finishing with a customer when she pitched up with the coffees. Carlo strolled over hoping for some attention, so she scratched his ears. *I could get quite fond of you*, she thought. Judging by the contented look on the dog's face, she thought the feeling might be mutual.

'Do you have a dog?' asked Ricky, coming over once he was free.

'No. I've always wanted one, but I used to work full-time. I didn't think it was fair.'

'What did you do?'

She hesitated. 'I worked in a letting agency.' For some reason she felt reluctant to admit it.

'What made you give that up and start a shop?' Ricky asked, peeling the lid off his coffee.

'Redundancy.'

He frowned sympathetically, 'Ah. Bad luck.'

Charley thought for a second and then said, 'No, not really. Well, not necessarily. It's giving me the chance to do something better, more fun. I might even get a dog!' She laughed and then, remembering the sense of pleasure she'd felt when the huge lurcher had lolloped alongside her when she'd first ridden her bike, added, 'Where did you get Carlo?'

'He was a rescue dog.'

Now why doesn't that surprise me? She thought it seemed typical of the man to take on an abandoned stray.

Ricky took a slurp of coffee, and then asked, 'Is there anyone else running the shop with you? It can be a bit lonely being on your own all day. That's why I got Carlo.'

Tell me about it, thought Charley. Josh's death had left her with an aching, permanent loneliness, even when she wasn't alone. She could be at a party, with all her mates, laughing and joking, but there was a specific loneliness – of someone being missing – that never went away.

'Well, it'll be just me in the shop, but I've got lots of people behind me. My mates are super-supportive, and you've already met Pam, my mother-in-law.'

He frowned at her quizzically.

'When we came down to look at the unit,' she explained.

'Oh, that's your mother-in-law,' he said evenly. 'I didn't realise that.'

'Sorry, no, of course you didn't.' Then, seemingly oblivious to having dropped a small bombshell, Charley gave Carlo one last ear scratch and said, 'Well, I'd better get on before the paint brush dries out,' and she put the lid back on her coffee and left.

It didn't take Charley long to finish painting the dresser, and then she tried to visualise a suitable store layout. 'I could have an old kitchen table here for the till, some wicker hampers for displays, some bookcases along that other wall...' she muttered to herself as she paced round the unit, setting out imaginary furniture. She had the nostalgic sensation that she was back in Reception class playing 'shop', setting out the little red-and-white painted wooden stall with tiny cardboard cereal boxes and plastic 'tins' of tuna and baked beans. She knew it was probably a very childish pleasure, but she absolutely loved it.

—

'What *exactly* are we looking for?' asked Pam.

'I'm not really sure... Some old bookcases, a couple of tables, maybe, and a chair. Anything with a bit of character,' finished Charley vaguely.

As they poked around the second-hand shops, they decided that most of the furniture fell into one of two categories: V*intage and too expensive*, or *Pre-loved*, almost to death, *but affordable*.

Pam's first find was an old, double-layer 1950s wooden tea trolley. 'Any good?' she asked, 'It's a bit battered, but if you paint it white, Angie could snazz it up with a logo or whatever... it could look quite sweet.'

Charley's eyes lit up. 'Actually, yes! With a bit of TLC that could be perfect.'

Over the next couple of days Charley's back garden filled up with an assortment of old tables and bookcases, wooden trays and crates, hampers and baskets, and a trio of wicker chairs.

'We're getting there,' remarked Pam enthusiastically, as she and Charley eyed the collection from the kitchen window, nursing their morning coffees.

Charley pulled a mock grimace. 'Are we? I was going for shabby chic, but it all looks more like a pile of crappy old tat.' She turned to Pam anxiously. 'I don't want to look like a junk shop. Be honest. Do you think it'll look okay?'

'It'll be lovely,' Pam assured her. 'Listen, when I first married Geoff we couldn't afford a bedroom suite. We just got some odds and ends from the second-hand shops and painted everything white. You'll be amazed at how it'll pull together. Trust me! But if you're worried, why not ask Angie?'

Charley did, but then Angie was determined to help with painting it all up, although, as Charley pointed out, they wouldn't get much done with Finn and Eliot running round like the gorgeous, little turbo-charged terrors they were. 'Unless you can take their batteries out?' Charley asked.

'Sadly, no,' admitted Angie.

'I'll look after them,' offered Pam.

'Are you out of your mind?' laughed Charley.

Pam merely smiled. 'I doubt they'll be any more of a handful than Luke and Josh were!'

The next day Angie arrived with both the boys, Finn's changing bag, and a bag full of toys and games. She looked slightly anxious as if she wondered whether Pam knew what she'd let herself in for.

'You can sit down and paint the trays,' Pam told her, steering her into one of the wicker chairs.

'Fine,' smiled Angie.

'Don't get too comfy,' Charley warned, 'I'll be painting that later!'

Pam had nipped into Bristol earlier to buy the boys some full-sleeve plastic painting aprons. 'You can help me paint a bookcase,' she informed them, helping them into their aprons, and giving them each a small paintbrush. Angie looked mildly horrified.

Naturally, Charley and Angie had put on old clothes, but Pam had covered her crops and top with a pristine, long white shirt.

'Isn't that a bit good to be painting in?' asked Angie.

'Absolutely. It's almost new,' agreed Pam, before adding with a mischievous gleam in her eye, 'It's Geoff's. I popped back to get some decorating clothes, but grabbed this instead!'

'You're a wicked woman,' said Angie.

'What's the point of being a woman if you can't be wicked?' returned Pam.

Pam let the boys loose on the back of the bookcase, which wouldn't be on show. They happily sloshed paint around for all of fifteen minutes, until it occurred to Eliot that it would be much more fun to slosh paint all over his brother, who eagerly returned the compliment.

'Boys! No!' cried Angie, aghast and clearly worried about what Pam would think of their behaviour, but the older woman just laughed, gently removed the boys' brushes, and lured them indoors with the promise of doing something else much more exciting.

'Come on lads, let's get cleaned up, and then we'll make some cookies!'

'Yaaaay!' chorused the boys, happily relinquishing their painting duties, peeling off their paint-splattered aprons and following her indoors.

-

'These are looking good,' enthused Angie, as Charley finished off the bookcase Pam and the boys had started.

'Yeah, it's amazing how everything seems to match now they're the same colour.'

'I was thinking I could paint some logos onto them, if you like? I could use the Charley's signature.'

Charley's face lit up eagerly. 'Yes! Thank you!' Then she went on, 'Actually I've been thinking. I wondered if you'd like to make some Prosecco-themed wall plaques or... something, for the shop.'

'What, to decorate it? Willingly!'

'No, I meant to *sell*.' Angie stopped painting and looked over to Charley, who carried on, keenly warming to her theme, 'And maybe you could design a range of greetings cards, or tote bags or anything else you fancy. You could do it in your own time, no deadlines or anything. But it'd be great to have something original to offer, as well as the stuff everyone else stocks.'

A slow smile swept across Angie's face. 'I'd love to.'

'You'd have to work out your costings carefully,' Charley warned her, taking a leaf out of Nisha's book, 'Otherwise you'll end up working for peanuts! I won't take a cut,' she said hurriedly, 'You can take all the profit.'

Frowning, Angie shook her head, 'No, you have to take a cut, the shop is your business.'

Charley put her paintbrush down and eyed her mate squarely. 'Two can play at that game. In that case I'd have to pay you for any artwork you do in the shop.' Angie gave a light, noncommittal shrug in reply, so Charley said, 'Here's the deal, you get the profits, but I want to be your *exclusive* outlet!'

—

The following day, Charley loaded as much of the furniture she could cram into her car and drove it all down to the shop. Technically, only delivery vehicles were allowed on the access road, but she'd seen other cars parked outside the units to drop stuff off, so, flicking her hazards on, she decided to take a risk. When nobody flagged her down, and the other shopkeepers just gave her a cheery wave as she passed, she relaxed and parked right outside her unit, hoping it would be okay. She was just hauling the first bookcase out of the back of the car when a shout stopped her in her tracks.

'Hey!'

She looked round, half expecting a jobsworth of a parking attendant to give her a ticket, but it was Ricky.

'Let me help,' he offered, hurrying across to her, Carlo at heel, as ever.

She waved him off airily. 'Thanks, but I can manage, honestly.'

'Did I say you couldn't?' he asked her, coming over anyway.

'Er... no,' she laughed.

She stood back while Ricky lifted the bookcase up one-handed as if it was a bag of sugar and carried it into the shop. It took them less than five minutes to empty the car, a fraction of the time it had taken Charley to load it.

'Give me a shout if you need me,' he said cheerfully, and headed back to his shop.

'Thanks,' she called after him, then she paused to watch his retreating back, with the faithful Carlo loping along beside him, and caught herself wondering what it was about seeing a man walking with a dog at heel that made him look so… cool and attractive. Sexy, even.

Charley dumped the car in the multi-storey for the day and then spent the morning arranging and then rearranging the furniture until she was happy with the layout. She thought it looked okay, but when Ricky dropped by at lunchtime she was glad of the opportunity to get his opinion.

'What do you think? Be honest. Shabby chic or pile of old junk?'

He looked around the furniture, giving it a candid appraisal. 'Actually, just chic,' he replied. 'Not even a hint of shabby.'

Relief flooded through her. 'I was really hoping you'd say it was okay! I wasn't sure.'

'It's better than okay, Charley, it's really stylish,' he assured her then, catching her eye and holding her gaze he added, 'You're better at this than you think you are. You should trust your own judgement more.'

She shrugged off the compliment lightly, hoping to God she wasn't going to blush like a teenager.

'Come and get some lunch and meet the neighbours,' he suggested.

Carlo was waiting patiently outside her shop. 'Not on duty then,' she said to the dog, ruffling his ears.

'It's his lunch break,' said Ricky. 'The security department is very keen on its meal breaks,' he added, much to Charley's amusement.

She loved the way Ricky treated Carlo. She bet he spoiled him rotten at home, easily imagining the huge dog lolling on the sofa with his head on Ricky's lap while he watched TV, or mournfully begging titbits from the table, and sleeping on Ricky's bed. She found herself wondering if anyone else shared that bed. She brought herself up short, telling herself it was none of her business, and totally irrelevant anyhow.

Carlo padded alongside them as Ricky introduced Charley to some of the other tenants. They were a welcoming, friendly crowd and it made her feel like she was already becoming part of the place.

'I usually get lunch here,' said Ricky, pushing open the door to the deli.

The woman behind the counter smiled at him warmly. 'The usual, Ricardo?'

'Please.' He nodded and then introduced Charley. She ordered a Sundried Tomato and Goat's Cheese Artisan Sandwich and some Sea Salt and Red Leicester Organic Potato Thins – or chunky cheese butties and crisps as Tara would have called them. She was really touched when the woman only charged her mates' rates – because she was one of the locals now. They took their sarnies back to Charley's shop, and sat in the wicker chairs to eat them, with Carlo leaning heavily against Charley's leg, his huge brown eyes following the progress of her sandwich optimistically.

'He thinks you're a pushover.'

'He's wrong,' said Charley.

'Bad luck, boy.' Ricky patted the dog's head in compensation.

Charley had noticed Ricky had a slight accent, Spanish or Italian, maybe. She was too embarrassed to ask him outright, so asked more obliquely, 'What brought you to Bristol?'

Ricky paused, his sandwich halfway to his mouth, and Charley wondered if he was considering whether to answer. Or perhaps how fully.

'Self-defence,' he finally said.

What the hell was that supposed to mean? she wondered, and it was such an opaque response she was immediately anxious she'd offended him by appearing to pry, but then he continued.

'I fell out with my family,' he explained.

'Ah,' said Charley, thinking, *join the club.*

Then, despite his initial evasiveness, Ricky went on with disarming frankness, 'There was a girl, Bernadetta. She was, *is*, lovely. Our families had known each other for years, and when we started dating they expected us to get married, they sort of assumed we would, but we didn't want to, either of us. I had a big row with my parents and… I decided to leave, to go travelling. And I ended up here.'

His openness touched Charley. She honestly hadn't been fishing to get his entire life story, knowing more than most how painful it can be to have people prying thoughtlessly, into your past life, and she felt privileged that he'd felt comfortable to share it with her.

'Where are you from originally?' she asked.

'Tuscany. What about you? Are you from Bristol?'

'No,' said Charley and then she paused for a moment, wondering how fully she wanted to answer him. In the event she decided to match his openness with hers.

'I came to Bristol to get married…'

'Oh, I see,' cut in Ricky lightly.

'But then my husband died, shortly afterwards.'

Ricky's face froze. 'I'm sorry—' he started, and then trailed off, clearly not knowing what to say.

Appreciating that the poor man was probably wishing he hadn't asked, Charley put him out of his misery. 'It's all right. It was a few years ago.'

After a brief pause, Ricky said, 'What happened? If you don't mind my asking?'

Charley didn't mind; nevertheless she took a moment before she replied. She'd never talked about Josh's death before to anyone who hadn't actually known him.

'No… no, I don't mind telling you,' she started, and then she was surprised at how easily the words seemed to tumble out. 'He had a car accident. He was a salesman and he was delivering a new car up in Leigh Woods. It was in February, and he hit a patch of ice, black ice, they said, so he couldn't have seen it, and the car…' She stopped and took a deep breath. Ricky waited patiently. He didn't prompt her, or interrupt to tell her she didn't have to say any more if she didn't want to, for which Charley was grateful. She wanted, maybe needed, to finish telling Josh's story through to the end. '…the car veered off the road and hit a tree. They took him to hospital, but he died in intensive care. Before I could even get there.' Her entire body had tensed up and she realised it was because she'd been wary he might try to put his arm around her, or take hold of her hand, but he did neither.

He just looked up, held her gaze and said, 'I'm sorry. I don't know what to say.'

She gave him a gentle smile. 'It's all right, you don't have to say anything.'

Chapter Thirty

The planning meeting for the fourth Annual Kim Henderson Memorial Prosecco Night was at Charley's flat, as usual. Also, as usual, Tara had brought several big bags of posh crisps, some pretzels and tortilla chips, half a dozen dips, and a couple of bottles of Prosecco 'to get the celebration started'. Unusually, an uncharacteristically exuberant Nisha also arrived clutching two bottles of fizz.

'Blimey, Nishe! Did you win the lottery or something?' joked Charley.

'One's for everybody,' announced Nisha, handing a bottle to Charley, 'and the other one is for Pam!' she finished, presenting the older woman with the second bottle, which was lavishly decorated with a snazzy pink ribbon and bow.

Clearly bemused, Pam took the offered bottle, 'Thank you. But, why?'

'Because you are a completely wonderful woman and I owe you an enormous thank you! Jay's mum has brought the full force of the family down on him and believe me, that's a big deal! He's just sent me a legal letter confirming that the court order stands, and that he will make no further claims against me!'

Tara and Angie exchanged baffled looks, but Pam and Charley erupted into cheers.

'Woohoo!' cried Charley, throwing her arms round Nisha and hugging her.

'What a relief!' exclaimed Pam.

'Well, I have absolutely no idea what that was all about,' said Tara baldly, 'but it sounds like we're celebrating, so I'm pouring that fizz!'

Taking their glasses through to the living room the women all settled themselves around the coffee table. Angie bagsied a seat on the sofa and eased her now very pregnant self down into it with a slight 'ooof'.

'How's the shop?' she asked Charley.

'Getting there. The furniture looks fabulous!'

'When are you planning to open?' asked Nisha, elegantly scooping guacamole onto a tortilla chip.

Charley shrugged. 'When I'm ready, I guess.'

Nisha looked up sharply. 'You'll have to have a big opening. It's a massive marketing opportunity, you can't just open the door. You'll need to make a splash of it.'

Charley could feel the panic showing on her face, but she recovered quickly. Shaking her head she said, 'I'm not going to put myself under any pressure. I haven't even ordered any stock yet.'

Nisha opened her mouth to respond but, fortunately for Charley, Tara interrupted her, reminding them of the purpose of the meeting.

'Okay, so this year the Hospice want to get a Tree of Life,' she informed them.

'What's one of those?' asked Angie, helping herself to the bag of sweet chilli crisps.

'I'm glad you asked that,' said Pam, who clearly didn't have a clue what a Tree of Life was either.

'It's a memorial tree,' said Tara. 'Like a Christmas tree. People hang a decoration on it in memory of their loved one.'

'Oh, that's a really lovely idea,' enthused Angie warmly. 'Like celebrating Christmas with them.'

Frankly, Charley thought it was a terrible idea. Christmas was hard enough, the *last* thing she'd want to do was hang a crappy ornament on a bloody tree in memory of Josh. She wouldn't need reminding that he couldn't be there to share Christmas with her, and never would be again, but it wasn't up to her. *People grieve in different ways*, she reminded herself.

'How much is it going to cost?' she asked Tara.

'They reckon a couple of thousand,' Tara replied nonchalantly.

'Two grand!' spluttered Charley.

Nisha nearly dropped taramasalata on her Ted Baker slacks. 'That's a bit of a step up!'

Adopting the most casual tone humanly possible, Tara said, 'Obviously I'm not expecting us to raise the whole two grand—'

'Very wise,' said Nisha dryly.

Tara ploughed on without breaking stride, 'But it would be nice if we could raise say...' she hesitated and the others exchanged wary looks. '...I don't know, say... half of it?'

'A thousand pounds?' asked Charley incredulously. '*A thousand pounds?!*'

Everyone stared at Tara in astonishment; ignoring them, she carried on blithely, 'So it would be great if we could really big it up a bit this year. Try and get a lot more people.'

'How many more?' asked Charley in alarm, looking round her small living room.

'There's a limit to how many people Charley can fit in,' pointed out Pam.

'Well, obviously,' replied Tara, then turning to Charley, she asked, 'How would you feel if we held it somewhere else? Be honest. Would you mind?'

Charley was desperately trying not to let her face give anything away, but she *did* mind. She'd hosted the Prosecco Night every year and it was more like a party than a fundraiser – and the only one she ever threw in her flat these days. Then, slightly harshly, she accused herself of being selfish, and immature. *It's not your party*, she reminded herself, *it's about raising money and remembering Kim and, above all, it's for Tara.* And if Tara wanted to think big, then that was fine by her. Setting aside her disappointment, she raised her glass of fizz and said, 'The bigger, the better!' She was rewarded by an affectionate hug from her mate, and a less obvious, sympathetic smile from Pam.

'Where were you thinking?' Nisha asked Tara, who shrugged.

'I hadn't actually got that far,' she admitted.

Determined to think *really* big, Charley suggested the Orangery, picturing everyone gathered round the gold-and-white tables she'd admired when she went there to pitch her party bags. 'It's fabulous,' she raved.

'Fabulously expensive, too,' said Nisha.

'Maybe they'd waive the fee for a good cause?' Angie sounded hopeful.

'Or good publicity?' said Charley, slightly less naively.

'No chance,' said Nisha. 'Honestly, it's shocking how much, or rather how little, any business will do for charity these days. Even though it's tax-deductible.'

'What about the Avalon?' suggested Pam, and everyone turned to Tara.

'I can ask…' she said dubiously, 'But don't hold your breath. It'll mean appealing to the better side of my pompous prat of a manager, and I doubt very much he's got one.'

'It might be a bit low-profile for them,' Nisha warned.

'There's always the school hall,' said Angie. 'Will would definitely be okay with us holding it there.'

Nisha looked suddenly optimistic. 'Now that's a good call, Angie.'

'Yes!' agreed Charley warmly.

They left it that Tara would approach the Avalon and Angie would ask Will. Charley knew which option she preferred, but she kept schtum, guessing it would probably be the default position anyhow.

'I hope Will says yes,' she confided to Pam later as they loaded the dishwasher with the glasses after everyone had gone.

'Really? It would be much more prestigious having it at the Avalon, plus you could invite all the hotel guests, too. You'd probably raise a lot more money.'

'True,' admitted Charley. What she didn't admit was her fear that if the event moved to the Avalon, Tara would completely take it over.

—

Will was head down at the kitchen table deep in work when Angie got home.

She went over to kiss him, 'Still hard at it?'

He wrapped his arms round her waist and held her to him. 'Governors' meeting.'

She grimaced on his behalf and then pulled away to head upstairs to check on the children. Not because she didn't trust Will to have put the kids to bed; she did it because she loved them and she wasn't going to beat herself up for that.

Baa–Baa, Finn's fluffy sheep, had fallen out of his bed. She picked it up and gently popped it under the duvet next to him. Then, adoring the way he crooked his forefinger over his nose as he sucked his thumb, she stroked his cheek softly before crossing the room to Eliot's bed. Eliot had taken his mega truck into bed with him. The truck had sharp edges so she carefully edged it out from under his arm and put it at the end of his bed. Then she ran her fingers lightly through his curls. Across the landing, Beth had fallen asleep reading, with her bedside light on. Angie eased the book out of her grasp and put it in her book bag for the next day. When she switched off the lamp Beth stirred. 'It's all right, lovely. Back to sleep.'

She went downstairs, made a pot of tea and sat down at the table next to Will.

'How was the meeting?' he asked, gratefully taking the mug of tea Angie handed him.

'Lovely. Lots of crisps!'

He chuckled before going back to his paperwork.

'Actually… can I quickly ask you something? Tara wants to make the Prosecco Night a much bigger event this year. Could we use the school hall?'

Will shrugged lightly. 'It'd be fine by me, but it can't be a school event, sorry. It'd have to be a PTA thing. You'll have to ask them.'

'Noooo!' groaned Angie. 'Don't make me talk to the PTA. That Felicity Whatshername's an absolute nightmare. Can't *you* ask her?'

'No, I can't. Anyhow she's not that bad. She's just a bit...' Will struggled to find the right word.

'Patronising... bossy... condescending?'

Will raised his eyebrows at her.

'Only trying to help,' she protested.

'Motivated,' finished Will, tactfully.

Angie sighed. 'Okay. *I'll* talk to her then. If I must.' *Felicity Whatsername's going to eat me alive*, she thought gloomily.

–

The following afternoon Tara sat at the Reception Desk of the Avalon, stressed to the nines and struggling to keep her temper, when Charley arrived to drop off fifty top-of-the-range pamper bags for a hen party.

'You okay?' she asked.

'No. I'm having a complete pig of a day wrangling the Hen Party from Hell, plus, Rent-a-Git said "No" to holding the Prosecco Night here.'

'You weren't really expecting otherwise, were you?' pointed out Charley, trying to conceal her inner relief.

'No,' sighed Tara, 'But he was just so sodding pompous about it.'

She'd spent a frenetic morning dealing with the never-ending stream of must-haves, don't-wants, and can't-eats of the Hen Party from Hell. When she'd finally managed to grab five minutes with her manager, and pitch the fundraiser to him, his little eyes had initially lit up greedily. He'd rapidly bought into the idea of a room full of women buying bucketfuls of Prosecco and demolishing a small mountain of bar snacks to mop it up, even offering to pitch the event to Head Office himself, until Tara poured cold water over his fantasy.

'No, you don't quite get it. *They* don't buy the Prosecco from the hotel, *we* bring the Prosecco.' He looked at her blankly. *God, it doesn't take much to confuse his tiny little brain, does it?* she thought, before explaining slowly, as if to a five-year-old child, how a charity fundraiser worked. 'We will bring the Prosecco, some nibbles, and a range of Prosecco-themed products, all of which the women will buy from us. The money we raise goes to the Hospice. All the hotel has to do is provide the room and the parking.'

'So, what's in it for the hotel?' he asked.

'Kudos, and a lot of good publicity.'

He thought about it for less than nanosecond before spluttering, 'No way! You can't bring your own food and drink to the hotel! I'm not asking Head Office if we can do that. It's a completely unacceptable request,' he finished highhandedly.

'It's for charity!' Tara had countered. 'For a hospice for the dying.'

'Absolutely not. And that's my final decision,' he said, all too evidently enjoying asserting his authority over her.

Tara seethed. For a brief moment she thought about going over his head and contacting Head Office herself, but realistically she knew that if they refused, the obnoxious little berk would never let her live it down.

'Seriously, Charley, you have no idea what a nightmare it is working for such a complete and absolute...'

'Jerk?' suggested Charley.

'Arsehole,' finished Tara, bitterly.

Charley hesitated, as if she were deciding what to say, or maybe whether to say anything at all. Then leaning across the desk, she bent her head closer to Tara's, and lowered her voice. 'Tara. Will you listen to yourself? The man *is* an arsehole, an utter arsehole, and he's making your working life miserable.' Tara rolled her eyes, but Charley didn't give up. 'Look, I know you keep joking about him, but honestly, now I've actually met him, and I've seen how unhappy you are here, I'm not sure it's actually very funny.'

Tara shook her head lightly, dismissing Charley's concerns. 'Don't worry, I can deal with a little prick like him. You've just caught me on a bad day.' Which was partly true, but what was also true was that the bad days were becoming increasingly frequent, although she didn't want to admit that.

Baz, on the other hand, was not as easily dismissed.

'Tara, just leave,' he'd said when he'd got home from work and heard Tara's Rant of the Day.

'I'm not quitting! He's the one with the problem, not me. And anyhow, I like earning my own money, then I can spend it how I want.'

Baz took a moment before he spoke. 'I know you want to buy things for Monnie, the things you never had…'

Tara interrupted him. 'That wasn't Mum's fault. She did her best.'

'I know,' said Baz steadily. 'And I'm not criticising Kim.'

'Well it sodding well sounds like it.'

Baz took a slow breath in and then let it out again. 'Kim did an amazing job, but you had a tough childhood, Tara. You went without a lot, and now you're…' he paused.

'Spoiling Monnie,' chanted Tara angrily. *Off he goes,* she thought, *same old argument, same old loop.*

'No. You're *overcompensating*,' he said.

The break from the usual script, his usual mantra, got Tara's attention.

'And since Kim died it's got worse,' he went on carefully. 'It's like you're trying to fill an empty space.'

Suddenly Tara's eyes prickled and her throat tightened. She swallowed hard. *Of course she was trying to fill a bloody empty space. There was a gaping hole in her life where her mum had been.*

'You can't replace someone with things, Tara,' her husband said gently.

'You can't replace them *at all*,' she said angrily, hot tears burning her eyes.

'I know,' said Baz, going over to her and pulling her towards him. She didn't resist, so he held her for a while, and then he said softly, 'Would you have loved your mum any more if she'd given you more things?'

'No, of course not.'

'Then will Monnie love you less if you give her less? You're what matters to Monnie, and what matters to me. They don't bloody deserve you at that hotel, Tara, and you don't deserve to be this unhappy.'

–

Earlier in the afternoon, when she'd got back from delivering the gift bags, Charley had called Angie.

'It's a "No" from the Avalon,' Charley told her and, crossing her fingers, asked, 'What did Will say?'

There was an audible sigh at the end of the phone before Angie replied. 'He said I'd have to ask the self-important, patronising harridan who chairs the PTA. So, I nabbed her at the school gates, and *tried* to give her the gist of what we wanted, but she's insisting on having a written plan, detailing exactly what we want to do: how many people, what we're trying to raise money for etc., etc. And then she wants a meeting! She's calling it a "pitch" meeting, for goodness' sake! Honestly, you'd think she owns the school! Anyhow, she can meet us on Friday at nine forty-five.'

'Us?' queried Charley.

'Yes. Sorry. I know you're busy, but you have to come with me, otherwise I'm going to batter her to death with Beth's recorder.'

'Fine!' laughed Charley.

'Do want to come round here and do the plan together?'

'No. It's okay. I've got this!' said Charley, wondering if Angie was actually barking mad thinking they could pull *anything* together with Finn and Eliot within a three-mile radius.

If the PTA wanted a detailed written request then they could damn well have one, thought Charley, opening her laptop. She hadn't spent seven years drawing up lavish letting brochures without knowing how to churn out a knock-your-socks-off presentation. She happily engrossed herself in creating a comprehensive, five-page document outlining their fundraising target, the success of the previous Prosecco Nights (with full figures), the projected numbers of attendees, a complete process flow schedule and a list of everyone's contacts, together with their potential requirements on the night, both technical and otherwise.

Chapter Thirty-one

'Do Not Be Late!' Angie had begged Charley. 'Felicity Whatshername takes no prisoners.'

So, a good five minutes early for their appointment on the Friday, Charley met up with Angie outside the school, with Finn in his buggy. Felicity Whatshername was already in the hall waiting for them. Immaculately turned out in a tailored grey dress, with perfect make-up and not a hair out of place, she looked pointedly at the clock as they walked in, a gesture which peeved Charley since they weren't even late. Angie hung back, ostensibly because she had to wrangle Finn's buggy up the steps into the hall, but in reality in order to let Charley take the lead.

Thanks, Ange, thought Charley, wondering exactly what it was about these flawlessly presented, yummy-mummy, professional women that was so intimidating. She told herself to calm down. *You've got this. You have a plan. You have a presentation. And you have paperwork – pages of it*. She took a deep breath, flashed Felicity Whatsername a bright smile and introduced herself. And then, with all the confidence she could muster, launched into her pitch.

'We run an annual fundraiser for the Patience House Hospice which provides end of life care for...'

'I know what it does,' cut in Felicity Whatshername brusquely.

'Oh.' Charley shot a look at Angie, who raised her eyebrows at the woman's rudeness.

Until Felicity Whatshername carried on, 'My brother died there. Last year.' Then she abruptly turned away, clearly struggling to stop her face collapsing with grief.

Angie just stood there, clearly at a loss as to what to say or do.

'Why is she crying?' asked Finn loudly, with embarrassing innocence. Angie crouched next to him to subtly hush the toddler up, but Charley had already moved closer to Felicity and put her hand on her shoulder.

'Oh, I'm so sorry... so sorry,' she said quietly. She waited, still with her hand lightly resting on Felicity's shoulder, respecting her moment of grief and giving her time to recover her composure, before she went on gently, 'He must have been very young to die.'

Felicity busied herself with digging a tissue out of her handbag. Then she sniffed hard and took a moment to breath out through her mouth to steady herself, before she spoke. 'Yes. He had cancer. He was thirty-eight.' She dabbed at her eyes with the tissue, trying to rescue her mascara.

'That must have been dreadful. For everyone,' said Charley.

Felicity blew her nose. 'Yes. Yes, it was.'

'My husband died,' Charley told her. 'He was thirty-two.'

Slowly, Felicity turned to look directly at Charley, as if she was having trouble processing what this young woman, this young widow, had just said. 'At the Hospice?'

'No. In Intensive Care. He had a car accident.'

'Oh, God. How awful. How absolutely awful.' Spontaneously Felicity's arms reached out to embrace Charley,

'I'm so sorry for you,' she said, her voice cracking, silent tears coursing down her cheeks.

Charley hugged her back. 'Thank you.'

Angie was now standing awkwardly off to the side. Unsettled by the sight of a grown-up crying, Finn twisted round to hold his arms out to her, his little face crumpled with concern. She stooped to take him out of the buggy and then stood up again, with him on her hip, where he sat eyeing the scene warily.

Shortly, Felicity pulled herself together, sniffed a few times, and then gave Charley a brisk pat. From then on, perhaps unsurprisingly, the meeting was unexpectedly easy.

Rapidly scanning Charley's pitch paperwork Felicity said, 'That's all fine. It's just a question of the date.'

'Anytime mid November onwards...' said Charley hopefully.

Felicity checked the calendar on her phone and after a lot of efficient scrolling through screens, while Angie and Charley exchanged glances, she finally pronounced they could hold the Prosecco Night in the School Hall on the last Saturday of October... in three weeks' time.

'Three weeks tomorrow?' Charley's eyebrows shot up in alarm.

'Yes. That's the only slot available this term.'

She and Angie exchanged anxious looks.

'I don't think we can scramble it that quickly,' said Charley, with a slight shake of her head.

'Of course you can!' replied Felicity briskly, before proceeding to effortlessly reel off a to-do list off the top of her head. 'You just need to bring the Prosecco, the glasses, maybe some yummy nibbles and cupcakes, the little things you want to sell and a cash float. Fifty pounds should do it. We'll supply tables and chairs, tablecloths if you want them, the kitchen, the PA system and a mic. You probably won't need a PowerPoint, will you?' She rattled on, without waiting for an answer, while Charley frantically made notes on the back of her pitch document. 'Parking's on the playground. We'll do the social media, Facebook and the school website. Give us some flyers next week and we'll put one in all the kids' book bags.' She barely paused for breath while Charley scribbled away. 'And you might want to do a bottle tombola and a raffle,' she raced on. 'We've got books of raffle tickets, you just bring the prizes. Oh, and you'll need to bring some flowers or bunting or whatever to brighten the place up. You see? Hardly anything to do. There's plenty of time.'

Charley and Angie could only nod weakly.

'How many flyers will we need?' asked Angie.

'One for each family. So, four hundred.'

'Four hundred?!' gasped Charley.

–

Pam hadn't volunteered to look after Finn that morning, much as she would have enjoyed it, because she'd arranged to go house-hunting with Zee.

'Don't you think you might be rushing things a bit?' suggested Zee, as they stood outside one of the estate agents in Park Street, browsing the houses for sale in the window.

'I'm not rushing, it's more…' Pam paused, looking for the right phrase, 'reality-checking. I'm not going to *do* anything yet,' she reassured her. 'I just want to know what my options might be.'

Zee looked at her, an expression of despair on her face.

'I'm just being sensible,' Pam assured her. 'There's no point me sticking my head in the sand like some petrified ostrich, is there!'

'No, but that doesn't mean you have to stare unflinchingly into the face of a blinding dust storm,' replied Zee. 'You are allowed to lie low for a while, let the dust settle, before forcing yourself to plough on.'

'I'm not forcing myself to do anything. I just think I'll feel less stressed, less impotent, if I know how things might stand in the future. Wouldn't you?'

Zee nodded. 'Yes. I can see the sense of that.'

Pam turned back to peruse the properties in the window and Zee joined her.

'That one's nice.' Zee pointed to a stone-built, two-bedroomed cottage in a village out on the northern side of the city.

'Yes! It's very pretty!' Pam peered more closely, scanning the details. 'But the garden's a bit small. It's even smaller than Charley's. More of a "yarden" than a garden!'

'Well, how about something like that?' suggested Zee, indicating a narrow, red brick Edwardian terraced town house. 'That's got a lovely long garden.'

Pam leant in to get a closer look at the picture of the garden. 'Ooooh, yes, and that's an apple tree!' She turned excitedly to Zee. 'A little town house like that would be perfect!'

'Can you afford it?'

'I have absolutely no idea. There's only one way to find out!' Flashing Zee a brave smile, she pushed opened the door to the estate agent's and went inside. Zee dutifully followed.

As it turned out, she couldn't afford either of the properties in the window. Not by a long chalk. Taking into account her postcode and the image of Pam's house on Google maps, the estate agent said he could give her a *very rough* valuation of what her house was worth. Or, more accurately, what her and Geoff's house was worth.

'But it'll be just a ballpark figure,' he warned her. 'I'd need to come round to do a proper valuation to give you anything in writing. When would suit you?' he said, opening his calendar and pushing for an appointment.

The mere suggestion alarmed Pam. 'I'm not looking to sell just yet,' she said hastily. 'I'm just looking around, seeing what might be available in my price range.'

'That's as may be, but even if you're just looking at your potential options, you won't be able to get a reliable mortgage quote without a proper valuation of your assets.'

A mortgage? thought Pam. The notion hadn't even crossed her mind, and how would she even pay for one, since she didn't have a job? Unless maybe Geoff could have one, on his pension? She had no idea. They'd paid off their mortgage about five years ago, that much she did know. Suddenly the prospect of having to navigate this potential minefield as well as everything else seemed overwhelming, and frightening.

Since Pam had gone rather quiet, Zee spoke up. 'Just a very rough ballpark is all we need now,' she told the agent firmly.

So, perhaps realising he wasn't going to be able to coerce Pam into booking an appointment there and then, and with a lot of unnecessary reminders that it was 'very much just a rough estimate' and 'not an expert valuation', and 'not even an estimate he could stick to until he'd done a proper assessment of the actual property', he gave them a figure.

It seemed a lot of money, until Pam divided it by two. 'What sort of property could I get for *half* of that?' she asked, wondering if there'd actually be anything at all.

'Half of that?' he queried, raising an arch eyebrow and clearly fishing for more information.

'Yes,' replied Pam, deliberately not giving him any. It was none of his business. Although she guessed he'd probably already put two and two together, or rather that he'd started with two and divided it, to come to the conclusion that she was divorcing.

'Just in the Bristol area?' he clarified.

'Yes.'

'There will be quite a few properties,' he said, perking Pam up considerably. 'Mostly flats and apartments,' he finished, instantly deflating her again.

'No houses?'

'Some…' he paused and his eyes flicked from Pam to Zee and back again, and Pam got the distinct impression he was appraising them and making mental assumptions about them as he did so. 'But they'll be a long way out of the city.'

'Well, that's not necessarily a problem,' replied Pam.

'Of course, if you can get a mortgage, that will increase your options greatly,' he told her.

Pam glanced over to Zee, who merely shrugged back noncommittally. 'I don't think I'm in a position to do that,' she said, partly to stall another attempt by the agent to badger her into letting him make a valuation appointment, but mostly because she didn't really want to have to confront that alarming territory just yet.

He pulled together a small bundle of brochures illustrating a range of the properties in Pam's price range and handed them to her. She'd adamantly refused to let the agent make any viewing appointments or to accompany them. 'We're just going to look around and get a feel for the areas,' she told him firmly, as they got up to leave.

'Don't worry, we won't knock on any doors,' Zee assured him, somewhat witheringly, and the agent had to settle for that. His disappointment was evident.

Popping into the nearest supermarket, they bought a meal-deal each and headed to the Downs to eat them. Sitting on a bench overlooking the Clifton Suspension Bridge they ate crisps and sandwiches, and swigged their drinks out of the bottle like a couple of day trippers.

'I used to bring the boys up here in the summer holidays,' said Pam. 'They loved it, even when they were teenagers. We'd bring a frisbee, or a football or their kites... and just... muck about.'

The days had seemed endless back then. As they'd grown older she'd often wondered, watching them larking around, how their lives would turn out, and what their futures would hold. She was thankful she hadn't known how very short Josh's future would turn out to be. It might very well have broken her if she had.

'Have you told Charley you're house-hunting?' asked Zee, bringing Pam back to the present.

'No. I'm not being evasive, it's just that I'm not planning to move out of the flat anytime soon, and I don't want to give her anything else to worry about. She's got enough on her plate without thinking she's going to have to look for another lodger in the not-too-distant future.'

Whatever Pam's ultimate life plan was going to be, she was very aware that her rent was a financial lifeline for Charley just right now, and she wasn't going to pull that particular rug out from under her.

Over their picnic they planned the most sensible route to take in order to see all the flats and houses which they thought were worth looking at. Or at least the ones Pam said she thought worth were looking at. Zee didn't voice an opinion on any of properties, which Pam had taken to mean she didn't hold out much hope that any would be even remotely suitable.

In the end Zee was proved right. Pam tried to be optimistic, they both did, pointing out the positives in each of the properties, and trying to make them outnumber the negatives, but as the afternoon wore on they both became increasingly downhearted. Pam found herself battling to keep her mounting anger towards Geoff under control. Why should she have to give up her house, her home for *decades*, because of him?

Neither of them could see her living in any of the properties, or even the areas, they looked at. Most were tiny high-rise flats, which might have been triumphs of stylish inner-city living, but they had no gardens, and when they read the details closely, they found the rooms were claustrophobically small. Whilst some of the houses had seemed a little more promising, they were way outside the city, and miles away from all of Pam's friends. She feared she'd become isolated and lonely, at a time of life when it would be difficult to make new friends and put down new roots.

At the end of what felt like a fruitless afternoon, Zee slung the brochures onto the back seat of the car contemptuously. 'You can't possibly live in any of those.'

'I might have to,' replied Pam bleakly.

Zee shot her an alarmed look. 'Why?'

'Because since Geoff doesn't have anywhere else to live, we'll have to sell up to buy us both somewhere.'

'But he does have somewhere else, doesn't he? He can move in with his other woman.' She saw Pam's look of dismay. 'I know that isn't your best-case scenario, but having looked at what you could afford to buy, I don't think selling up and moving is much of an option either.' An assessment Pam couldn't fail to agree with.

'Maybe you could buy Geoff out?' continued Zee.

'What with?!'

'Maybe you could get a mortgage?'

'Again, what with?!'

'You could take a leaf out of Charley's book.'

'Meaning?'

'Get a lodger! In fact you could have more than one – it's a big house.'

Pam pulled a face. 'Taking in lodgers? It makes me sound like a seaside landlady or a distressed Edwardian gentlewoman down on my luck!'

'Careful!' Zee warned her provocatively. 'One of my best friends is a lodger!'

Pam laughed out loud and the cloud of dismay, verging on despair, which had gathered over her throughout the afternoon, began to thin. Perhaps Zee was right. As worst-case scenarios went, having a lodger or two wouldn't be nearly as excruciating as living with Geoff, or, heaven forbid, having that Barbara living in her home, or having to sell up altogether.

'You don't have to decide immediately, Pam, in fact don't decide anything at all today,' counselled Zee sagely. 'Just think about it as another option.'

Pam could see the wisdom of that. But there was one thing she was now blindingly certain of. Whilst she might not be quite ready to move back to her house quite yet, moving back was going to be her 'best-case scenario', and she wasn't going to give up her home without a fight.

Chapter Thirty-two

Faced with the alarming prospect – no, make that the terrifying prospect – of *four hundred people* pitching up at the Prosecco Night, Charley called an Immediate Emergency Meeting.

As they gathered round her coffee table Charley could only hope someone would know what the hell to do. 'I can't possibly run an event for four hundred people!' she panicked. 'That's huge!'

'Four hundred flyers doesn't mean four hundred people will turn up,' reasoned Angie, but in a tone that very much suggested that she thought they might.

Nisha, on the other hand, clearly thought they wouldn't. 'There'll probably only be about two hundred,' she said calmly. Normally Charley would have found Nisha's characteristic unruffled composure reassuring. This evening she was trying hard not to find it infuriating.

'*Only two hundred* is still hell of a lot of people!' Charley reminded her, and to illustrate the fact she did the sums out loud. 'Two hundred glasses of fizz, with five glasses to a bottle… that's forty bottles. Oh!' She stopped. Actually, now that she had a much smaller number in her mind, and one in double digits rather than three, it suddenly didn't seem as daunting.

'Forty-five bottles to be on the safe side,' suggested Nisha.

'Make it fifty,' said Tara.

'Okay,' nodded Nisha. 'It'll be sale or return anyhow.' She always bought the fizz at a significant discount on her cash-and-carry card, which was a double-whammy for Charley, since not only did it take it off her own to-do list, it added to the profits of the night, too.

'I'll take care of the float,' said Tara, confident that she'd be able to sort it out at work like she usually did.

Charley scanned her list. 'Felicity suggested we sell cupcakes.' She pulled a face, not knowing what sort of reaction the notion would get, fearing that cupcakes were a bit more 'school fete' than 'Prosecco Night'.

'Not a *bad* idea in itself,' said Nisha, warily, 'as long as they're classy and have a Prosecco theme. We don't want piles of multicoloured fairy cakes plastered with brightly coloured sweeties leaking food dye all over the icing, looking like mould.' She visibly shuddered at the thought.

'Well, that counts mine out!' laughed Angie.

'I'm up for making them,' volunteered Pam casually, then turning to Nisha to get her seal of approval she said, 'I'm thinking vanilla-flavoured cupcakes with Prosecco butter icing, topped off with a sprinkling of gold sugar stars.'

'That sounds perfect!' cried Nisha, looking mildly astounded.

'Gold or white cases?' asked Pam.

'Gold!' answered Angie and Nisha in once voice.

'Are you sure you want to make them, Pam?' asked Charley. 'We're going to need two hundred.'

'Of course,' replied Pam, 'I'll do two hundred and fifty, just to be on the safe side.' Then, catching the look of alarm on Charley's face she added, 'Darling, I've made

298

literally thousands of cupcakes for fetes and fairs... football tournaments... charities, not to mention the W.I.'

'Well, okay... but we'll pay for the ingredients out of the profits.'

'Absolutely not!' retorted Pam, visibly offended, 'It'll be my contribution!'

Angie had printed off a draft flyer and she passed it round. 'It's only a first stab, I'm not wedded to it,' she assured them. But, after running her professional eye over it, Nisha pronounced it to be excellent, and Angie beamed at her.

'It'll do... I suppose,' deadpanned Tara, and Angie clobbered her with a cushion.

'Bunting,' said Charley, checking her list. Again she was a little worried about the tone it would set, but the school hall was markedly drab and would need something to set the party mood.

'The Avalon's got miles of the stuff,' said Tara. 'I'll *borrow* some. I might even ask first,' she added, getting a laugh.

'Do we really want a tombola or a raffle?' asked Charley.

'No,' said Nisha firmly. 'They're too—'

'Complicated?'

'Time consuming?'

'Hokey?'

'Dull?' suggested the others.

'Naff,' corrected Nisha.

The only thing left on Charley's list was sourcing the Prosecco gifts, which she didn't mind getting, like she usually did. Except this time she needed to get enough for *two hundred people* – most of whom she didn't even know.

It was a vast step-up from buying a couple of dozen or so little items for a group of mates and mates of mates.

'Charley, you *know* how to do this,' Nisha told her serenely. 'It's exactly the same as usual. Just ten times bigger.'

Which, funnily enough, wasn't anywhere near as reassuring a statement as Nisha meant it to be.

A few days later, Charley sat at the kitchen table, drawing up the list of Prosecco goodies to buy for the night. She supposed she could just base it on last year's list, which she could pretty much remember, and simply multiply everything by ten, like Nisha had said. Except that she always bought one or two more expensive items, like a reed diffuser or a cushion with a Prosecco slogan on it, to raise the standard on the stall, as it were, and the thought of lashing out on ten of the higher-priced items seemed way riskier than just buying a couple.

She was pondering this with Pam, when Tara arrived unannounced, in the middle of the afternoon, bearing a bottle of fizz.

'To what do we owe this unexpected pleasure?' asked Charley, taking the bottle through to the kitchen.

'I've handed in my notice!' Tara dropped her bombshell, utterly flabbergasting Pam and Charley, before calmly helping herself to the glasses from the kitchen cupboards.

'Woohoo, that's fantastic news!' exclaimed Charley, once she'd recovered.

Tara had already popped the cork from the fizz and was pouring it.

'What happened?' Pam put her hand out for the foaming flute Tara held out to her.

'Yes, what made you finally quit?' demanded Charley.

'It was the bunting,' replied Tara evenly.

'The bunting?' repeated Charley, before exchanging an incredulous look with Pam.

'Yup. After thirteen months and two weeks of putting up with working for that moron of a manager, no, make that a *major*-moron of a *micro*-manager, it was when he refused to lend us some bunting for the Prosecco Night that I finally flipped.' She took a slug of her drink, and then continued. 'He was just so sodding pompous and petty about it!'

And she proceeded to relate the conversation to them, adopting a ridiculously haughty, nasal tone to voice the words of her manager. A tone which Charley judged, having met him, as surprisingly accurate. 'He said to me, "I can't possibly authorise the lending of Avalon equipment to a private function off the premises. Any resulting health-and-safety issue would compromise our corporate responsibility and invalidate our liability insurance." Honestly, he was so full of himself I thought he was going to spontaneously combust.

'"It's a string of bunting, for crying out loud," I told him. "It's not like I'm asking to borrow a tanning machine or a massage couch." So then he got on his high horse and said, "It's the principle that matters, and it's completely against company policy." So I said, "In that case, I quit!" Which wiped the smug look off his face, I can tell you. But then he sneered at me, literally sneered, and drawled in that nauseating voice of his, "You're leaving because I won't let you borrow some bunting?"

'And I thought, no, I'm leaving because you are a complete and utter prat with the empathetic capacity of an egg cup, and the mental ability of a dung beetle, and if I have to spend any more time working with you I will strangle you, slowly, with your own ridiculous 'university' tie. And, because you don't bloody well deserve me!'

Charley laughed out loud. 'So, did you tell him that?' she asked. She wouldn't have put it past Tara for a second.

'No. I decided to leave that until my very last day. It'll be my parting shot. Something to look forward to!'

'Have you told Baz?' Pam wanted to know.

'Yes, I called him immediately.'

'What did he say?'

'About bloody time,' replied Tara, and Charley burst out laughing.

'Congratulations!' Pam raised her glass.

'Yes, congratulations!' echoed Charley, as all three of them clinked glasses.

'So, what are you going to do now?' asked Pam, once they'd drifted into the living room to settle on the sofa in a line, all three of them kicking off their shoes and putting their feet on the coffee table in one, well-rehearsed, synchronised move, with Charley in the middle.

'Well...' Tara paused for effect, before announcing grandly, 'I've decided to work with Charley, in the shop!'

Charley's glass paused in mid-sip. She loved Tara to death, but she wasn't at all sure about actually working with her. How would that pan out? Tara could be pretty *forceful*. You could probably measure her on the Beaufort scale and, like a full-on gale, it was hard to stand up to her.

Fortunately, the bigger issue wasn't whether she wanted Tara working with her, but whether she could afford it. Sharing the profits hadn't been factored into her business plan, which justified her saying, 'I'd love it, you know I would, but I'm just not sure the shop is going to make that much money.'

'Oh, I don't need any wages,' Tara said, waving a careless hand and dismissing any objections, in her usual way. 'I'm not doing it for the money… I'm doing it for fun.'

Ah, thought Charley, momentarily at a loss as to how to turn Tara's offer down without offending her. She took another slurp of her drink to buy her some thinking time and, as the fizz frothed in her mouth, the brief image of them larking around in the shop together flicked into her mind. It was undoubtedly more appealing than the thought of being stuck in the shop on her own all the time. And then she remembered that it was Ricky telling her how hard it was to run a shop on your own that had put her off renting the shop initially. So she decided to ignore her reservations and said, 'Well, it'd definitely be a laugh!'

Tara took it as a yes, and the two of them clinked glasses to seal the deal.

'I've got to work my notice. A month. Oh, deep joy,' Tara said flatly. 'But is there anything I can be doing to help now? I've farmed Monnie out to a mate's on a playdate this afternoon. I'm all yours until supper time.'

'In that case, actually, yes,' said Charley, putting down her glass on the coffee table. 'You can help us decide what to order for the Night.'

'Not for the shop?' queried Tara.

'Not yet.'

'Why not?' she challenged, and Charley was aware of a slight, almost imperceptible, intake of breath from Pam, sitting on the other side of her. She tried not to react, or rather to overreact, to Tara's bossiness, telling herself that it was simply her friend's nature.

Charley had already drawn up a spreadsheet of products she might want to sell in the shop, but had held off actually ordering anything, reluctant to spend the money until she absolutely had to. 'I'm not even sure when I'm going to open the shop yet. I'm still getting it ready.'

'But we may as well order stuff for the shop at the same time as the fundraiser,' Tara pointed out logically. 'We'll save on delivery and probably get more discount.' Then, since Charley appeared to remain unconvinced, Tara leant forward to peer round Charley to appeal to Pam and demanded, 'Won't we?'

'Er, possibly,' said Pam guardedly. Turning to her, Charley caught a glimmer of irritation in Pam's eyes. It was evident she was as peeved by Tara's high-handedness as she was.

'I just don't think we should rush into ordering stock, without carefully considering it beforehand,' Charley told Tara, trying to stick to her guns.

'We're not rushing in,' objected Tara. 'We already have to order a lot of stuff for the Prosecco Night and if it's things you also want to stock in the shop, then it makes sense to combine the two orders. It'll be more efficient and cost-effective.'

Tara's point made good business sense, and Charley knew it. The real reason she hadn't ordered any stock was that she was simply too frightened to make that huge step on her own. So she gave in, but, knowing that Tara could outnumber her even in a one-to-one, she roped Pam in too for back-up. When Pam hesitated, Charley reminded her that she was a business partner as well. She went to get her laptop and all three of them clustered round the screen.

There were, as Charley had already discovered, literally hundreds of Prosecco-themed products around… scented candles and tea-light holders, bubble baths and soaps, mugs and glasses, chocolates, sweets, truffles, tote bags, fridge magnets… Despite her earlier research, the choice was still bewildering and contentious, as it was soon all too evident that they didn't all have the same taste. Or the same assertiveness.

Tara passionately championed a pair of sparkly purple Prosecco flutes. 'Oh-my-God those are *perfect*!' she enthused.

Oh-my-God those are ghastly*!* thought Charley.

'I wonder if they might be a bit too sparkly,' Pam said diplomatically.

'No. They're perfect. Let's get a dozen pairs,' ordered Tara.

'Um…' Charley pursed her lips.

'What?' demanded Tara.

'I'm not keen,' rushed Charley, her gaze darting towards Pam for safety.

'Neither am I,' said Pam.

'Well I am.'

After a few such messy spats, in the interests of preserving their sanity, their friendship and the business, and because Tara *never* backed down even when she was out-voted, Charley introduced the 'rule of three'. They all three of them had to agree to put something on the final purchase list. Then the only issue was how many of each to buy, since with more than eight grand sitting in the business account, it would have been dangerously easy to get carried away. Everything seemed reasonably priced when they looked at the individual prices, but ordering them in packs of twenty and forty… or boxes of a hundred, the figures multiplied alarmingly.

By the time they'd got to the end of their shopping list on just the *first* supplier's website, Charley was already having kittens at the cost of everything they'd put in their basket.

She held the cursor over the pay-now button, but couldn't bring herself to commit to clicking on it.

'Shall I do it?'

'Yes,' Pam said.

'Yes!' cried Tara.

'Sure?'

'YES!' repeated Tara and Pam together.

'Should I just check the returns policy first?'

'No!' said Tara. 'We won't be sending anything back! *Sell, Sell, Sell* – that's our motto! For God's sake, Charley, just hit PAY NOW.'

So Charley did and the website politely thanked them for their order.

There was a nanosecond of silence while it sank in.

'Well, there's no going back now,' said Pam.

'Yup, we've got to open the shop now,' said Charley. 'Either that, or we've got to get through one hell of a lot of bubble bath and chocolates.'

'Bagsy the chocolates,' said Tara.

Chapter Thirty-three

Deliveries soon started to pour into the shop, and Charley went down regularly to unpack everything and check the contents off against the order forms, and to sort through which products were for the shop and which were for the fundraiser. Pam went along to help her – allegedly.

'It's like Christmas!' Pam cried, gleefully ripping open boxes like a five-year-old on a sugar high.

'Slow down! I've got to check everything off,' laughed Charley.

'Sorry!' Pam sang, but immediately she picked up the nearest box, and announced, 'Fifty boxes of White Chocolate Prosecco truffles!'

Charley checked her lists. 'Half for the shop, half for the fundraiser.'

'Oooh, they look delicious.' Pam efficiently divided the packs into two piles, then paused and, feigning seriousness said, 'But I wonder if we should just check? I mean, purely in the interests of quality control…'

She meant it as a joke, but Charley realised it was actually valid point, since she didn't want to sell anything that wasn't excellent quality. Pam didn't need any further encouragement to tear open a pack. Minutes later, still cheerfully 'quality checking' the chocolates, they ploughed on.

'Thirty sparkly gold tealight holders.'

'All for the fundraiser.'

'Twenty bottles of Prosecco and Rose Bubble Bliss.'

'Shop.'

Pam unscrewed the lid from one of the bubble bath bottles and sniffed. 'Oh, that's lovely!'

She shoved the bottle under Charley's nose, who dutifully sniffed it. 'Ooh, yes, lovely, but can we try and stay focused? Otherwise we'll be here all day!'

'Sorry!' Pam pulled out the contents of the next box. 'Six cushions which read "Smile, there's always Prosecco". Oh, I like these,' she said plumping one up. Charley rolled her eyes. 'Don't give me that look! I might want to buy one! How much staff discount do I get?'

'None at this rate!'

They sorted through everything, and then Charley checked her emails and frowned. 'The tote bags and the tea towels should have been delivered too, and the bath bombs.'

'Are they from the same company?' asked Pam, 'Perhaps the order went astray?'

'No.'

'That's worrying. When were they delivered?' asked Pam.

'According to the email, yesterday.'

'But nobody was here yesterday.'

'*Bloody hell!*' swore Charley. 'I hope they didn't leave them outside and someone's nicked them.' And with that unpleasant thought hanging in the air, they started clearing up the mountain of packaging covering the floor.

Shortly afterwards, when Ricky appeared with the three missing packages, Charley could have hugged him. 'Thank you *so* much! You've made my day!' she gushed.

Ricky gave her his easy smile and said, 'I only took some packages in! It's not that much of a big deal. You'd do the same for me.'

'Yes of course. But I thought they'd been nicked!' explained Charley, smiling back warmly. Then, suddenly acutely aware that Pam was watching her, she felt a hot flush creep up her neck and into her face. She turned away and busied herself opening the missing packages, creating a decidedly awkward moment.

Covering the uneasy silence, Ricky turned politely to Pam, 'I'm Ricky, I own the bike shop.'

'Oh, sorry!' said Charley. 'This is Pam, my—'

'Business partner,' said Pam.

'Mother-in-law,' Charley finished at the same time.

Ricky seemed amused, but then no doubt noticing the new sudden tension between Pam and Charley, he said, 'Well, I'd better get back, I've left Carlo guarding the shop,' and he slipped off.

Charley pointedly engrossed herself in finding all the delivery notes she'd left in the packaging, which she had now belatedly realised she needed to keep, while Pam started breaking up the cardboard boxes before taking them to the recycling bins. Both of them studiously avoided mentioning Ricky.

When they got back to the flat, Pam went to the kitchen to start cooking supper while Charley ran herself a hot bath and poured in a generous slug of the Prosecco and Rose Bubble Bliss she'd nabbed from the shop. Stepping into the warm, frothy water, she gratefully sank under the mountain of foam. Idly brushing the bubbles off her legs, Ricky slid, uninvited, into her mind. He wasn't her type, she reminded herself, but he was a nice guy, and he had nice eyes. Brown. Josh's were blue, blue and always smiling, always looking for the fun in life, whereas Ricky's eyes were more thoughtful, she mused. Then, picturing Ricky in an imaginary flat, she wondered what he was doing. Cooking supper? Watching something? Or listening to music? Or maybe he was a reader? Josh hadn't been into books. It was the one thing she wished she could have shared with him. They had never sat and read. Her mind wandered to an image of her and Ricky relaxing on his sofa, reading companionably together, Carlo sprawled on a rug in front of them. She brought herself up short and sat up abruptly, the bathwater splashing violently around her legs. She was furious with herself for even allowing herself to think about Ricky, to fantasise about him like that. Comparing him with Josh, and finding Josh wanting! She must not do that again.

And then, to her absolute mortification, she remembered that she'd blushed, actually blushed, when Pam had caught her smiling at Ricky. Cringing at the memory, she just hoped to God she hadn't given her the wrong idea – or Ricky, which would be even worse.

Getting out of the bath, she wrapped a towel round her and padded barefoot into her bedroom. Sitting down on the bed put her face level with the photo of Josh on her bedside table. He grinned at her, as usual, and she felt immediately guilty. Even thinking about Ricky in the bath seemed a disloyal act, a betrayal. Josh was The One. He always had been, and he always would be; no one could ever follow him and she didn't want anyone to even try. Pulling on some baggy joggers and Josh's old Arctic Monkeys T-shirt, she went through to the kitchen to help Pam.

A tantalising smell of mushrooms frying in garlic butter filled the kitchen as Pam stood at the cooker stirring them round, letting them crisp without burning. Charley wandered in, her hair still damp from the bath.

'Mmm! Smells amazing. Anything I can do?'

'You could make a salad, if you like.'

'Sure.'

Then, glancing over to Charley, Pam said casually, 'Nice of Ricky to take in those packages.'

'Yes,' replied Charley evenly, then she buried her face in the fridge.

'He seems like a decent bloke,' persisted Pam, and when Charley didn't answer she continued with a light prod, 'Don't you think?'

'Probably,' shrugged Charley. Then dumping the salad stuff on the table she added, 'I'm just not interested.'

There was a sudden hiss as Pam poured cream into the hot butter. She let it bubble furiously for a moment. She'd seen the way the two of them were together, and the way Charley's face had lit up when she smiled at him.

'It just seems such a shame, letting a good man like that go to waste!' laughed Pam.

'Well the field's clear if you want him!' teased Charley.

Pam was scandalised. 'I'm old enough to be his mother!' she spluttered, nearly dropping her spatula.

A mischievous gleam glinted in Charley's eye. 'Oh, I'm sorry, I thought you might be keen on him. It was the way you told him you were my business partner rather than my mother-in-law... I mean, obviously, being a "mother-in-law" does imply a certain *age*...' she trailed off provocatively.

Pam was almost hyperventilating at the cooker. She threw the oven gloves at Charley. 'I'm always happy to say

I'm your mother-in-law! You know I am, even though, technically I'm not any more, of course.'

'Well, I will *always* think of you as my mother-in-law' said Charley affectionately.

Always? thought Pam. *Always?* And that's when it hit her, and about half a dozen cogs clicked into place in her mind. She looked over at Charley. Her dark head bent low over the chopping board at the table, her damp curls captured in a loose top knot with an old blue hair scrunchy. A huge pang of affection welled up and caught in Pam's throat. Some women find it hard to love the people their children fall in love with – the people their children love more than them, but it had been easy to fall for Charley.

Sensing Pam was looking at her, Charley glanced up and smiled back at her lovingly. *God*, thought Pam, not for the first time, *you're far too young to be a widow. And you're far too young to be alone for the rest of your life.* She stirred the pan in thoughtful silence for a while, marshalling her thoughts and choosing her words carefully, hesitating to rush in where, in this case, even angels would tiptoe in cautiously. Finally, taking the pan off the heat she went over to Charley and sat down next to her at the table.

'Sweetheart, I don't want you to think of me as your mother-in-law forever.'

Charley's eyes widened in protest, but Pam silenced her by putting her hand on her arm. 'I will be whatever you want me to be in your life... a friend, a stand-in-Mum, a business partner... a lodger even!' Anxiety had clouded across Charley's face, so Pam went on hastily, 'I will always, *always* want to be part of your life, and I will never want you to stop being part of mine, but I think it's time you started to think... time we *both* started to think,' she corrected herself, 'that one day someone else might fill the wonderfully privileged role of being your mother-in-law.'

Charley swallowed hard and shook her head.

Seeing tears brimming in Charley's eyes Pam fetched her the kitchen roll. She unravelled a piece and handed it to her, before carrying on tenderly, 'It's okay to find someone else, Charley. It's more than okay, and in fact you should. You're a *wonderful* young woman and you deserve to find someone who will make you happy for the rest of your life. Josh would want you to be happy. And so do I.'

'There'll never be another Josh,' said Charley fiercely, hot tears scalding her cheeks.

'No. Of course there won't be. But there might be someone else you could love.'

'I'll never love anyone the way I loved Josh,' insisted Charley.

'Yes, that might be true,' said Pam sagely.

Then she went on to confide in Charley something she'd never admitted to a living soul before. 'When Luke was born, I didn't want another child. I loved him so much I was scared I would *never* be able to love another child as much as him. I just didn't believe I could.

'But Geoff was adamant we should have two,' continued Pam, 'He was adamant Luke should have someone to play with. So I did a terrible thing. I had another baby purely to give Luke a playmate.' Charley didn't say anything, but lightly touched Pam's hand in a gesture of support. 'And then Josh was born,' Pam went on tenderly. 'Out he popped, all scrunched up and wrinkled, and they bundled him into my arms, and then suddenly, there was this... this rush of love. It completely engulfed me – Josh brought it with him.' Her throat tightened threateningly. She took a deep breath, while her eyes sought Charley's and held her gaze. 'We can *all* love more than one person, Charley. Loving Luke didn't stop me loving Josh. Loving Josh mustn't stop you loving someone else. He'll always be a part of your life. As I will.'

Wordlessly, Charley put her arms round her mother-in-law, and Pam leant into the hug, resting her head against Charley's.

Chapter Thirty-four

'I'm not sure how to break this to you...' Angie's voice down the phone was hesitant.

Charley was in the shop trying to work out if she had enough power sockets. As it happened, she didn't. The crafters, she remembered, had crisscrossed the floor with multi-plug extension cables, which she doubted was even legal – it certainly wasn't safe. 'What's happened?' she demanded urgently.

At the other end of the line she could her Angie take a deep breath, and her mouth went dry. She hoped to God nothing had happened to one of Angie's kids.

'A pipe's burst in the school kitchen. A mains pipe. And the kitchen and the entire hall is flooded, so we can't use it for the fundraiser.'

'What?!'

Charley sat down hard on the nearest chair, her mind racing, and not quite understanding why they couldn't use the hall – how long did it take to mop up a floor, for crying out loud?

'Hang on, the Prosecco Night is nearly two weeks away. Surely they can get it cleared up by then?'

'No. The water's lifted the floor tiles. They've got to replace the whole floor.'

Bloody, bloody, bloody hell, thought Charley, sinking back into the seat. 'What the hell are we going to do?'

'We'll have to cancel.'

'Noooo!'

'I'm sorry…'

'It's not *your* fault, Ange,' Charley assured her, then added less tactfully, 'But Tara's going to be gutted.' Charley was already gutted, partly because she'd ordered more than nine hundred quid's worth of extra stock for the event, but mostly because she really, really didn't want to let Tara down.

'I can't see any other option,' said Angie, 'unless we go back to holding it in your flat.'

The idea was so ludicrous that Charley laughed out loud. 'We've sent out *four hundred* flyers! *Twenty* people in my flat is a squeeze!'

And then a notion slid sideways into her mind. She dismissed it, but it slid right back again. 'Ange. I'll call you back.'

Was it an *insane* idea to shift the fundraiser to the shop? She looked around the available space. It was just about big enough, but would people come down here? Would they want to trek all the way into town for what had always been a very local event? She wasn't sure, so she called Tara, who didn't pick up. She left the gist of the problem, and her solution, on Tara's voicemail, then she called Nisha.

'Good time, bad time to call?' she checked, as usual.

'Perfect time. Slogging through some accounts, and any distraction's welcome!'

'I've had what is either a very good idea, or a very bad idea. Or possibly a completely mad idea.'

Nisha pronounced the idea 'inspired'. 'It's the perfect venue, and you can use the event to launch the shop.' A suggestion which set off flutters of panic inside Charley.

'I don't think I'm ready to open yet,' she protested.

'You'll have to be,' responded Nisha brusquely.

'No, seriously, I'm not,' said Charley firmly.

'Again, you'll have to be. You can't hold an event in the shop and tell everyone you'll be opening soon, but you don't know when. How unprofessional will that look?'

Loath as she was to admit it, she could see Nisha was right. Charley was beginning to wish she'd never come up with this solution. Maybe it wasn't too late to back-pedal.

She heard a text ping in. 'Hang on a minute, Nishe.' It was from Tara. It read:

BRILLIANT IDEA! GO, CHARLEY, GO!

Shit, thought Charley. There was clearly no going back now. She took a deep breath and said to Nisha, 'Right then, let's do this.'

'Excellent. I'll get on to the local press. You get new flyers out promoting both the fundraiser and the shop opening ASAP. Get the other units at Cargo to give them out too, it'll drum up support with the locals and regular shoppers, and will help promote the area for them, too. Do six hundred flyers.'

'Six *hundred*!' gasped Charley.

'Don't panic! They won't all come on the night. But they will find all out about the shop, which will be great marketing.'

Six hundred flyers was, quite literally, six hundred invitations to an event in her shop. Charley looked round the small unit in dismay. 'Nishe, this is my little shop remember! It's not a Marks and Spencer's!' she cried.

'Trust me, it'll be fine,' said Nisha calmly and rang off. Taking a deep breath and trusting Nisha as instructed,

Charley grabbed an empty envelope and a pen and hurriedly wrote: 'Call Angie – 600 new flyers needed TODAY.' Then another thought occurred to her, and she added, 'Check she can paint shop logos in time.'

She then jotted: 'Call Felicity – post change of venue on PTA Facebook group and school website TODAY. New flyers to go out in book bags TOMORROW.'

Then Charley looked around the shop intending to list everything she still had to do to get ready for business, and realised the back of an envelope wasn't going to be anywhere near big enough.

She had less than a fortnight to get the logos painted, the shop name put on the window; order the rest of the stock; get shop-branded paper bags and carriers made; stock the shelves, set out all the displays; get an electrician to put the sockets in; get a card reader and a till working…

Not surprisingly, the panic already simmering inside her threatened to boil over. She crushed it down. *You can do this*, she told herself. *There's a lot to do, but if you're organised and drive it along and keep everything on schedule, it'll be fine.* Then she added, *But you do know you're insane, don't you?*

–

Since she was still working her notice, Tara pulled a sickie a few days later to help Charley and Pam in the shop. Charley was infinitely grateful to have all hands on deck. Most of the orders had arrived, and so now they were standing in the middle of the shop, drowning in a sea of products.

'Where's it all going to go?' Pam looked round the shelves in despair.

'I don't even know where to start!' cried Charley.

Tara doubted they'd fit everything in.

They spent the entire morning stacking things onto shelves, then promptly emptying them again, trying to work out where best to put everything. It was chaos. Jumbles of stock lay piled all over the floor.

'This isn't working,' said Tara.

'We need a plan!' said Charley. 'Let's make a list of all the display areas, and shelves, and then do a list of the products and *then*…'

She didn't even get to finish her sentence, because Angie arrived at that moment, ready to paint the logos on the walls and window. Eliot was at nursery, but she'd had to bring Finn. Naturally Pam was delighted, but Tara and Charley took one look at the energetic little toddler who was already wriggling impatiently, desperate to be released from his buggy, and promptly started sweeping everything up either off the floor or out of his reach before Angie could even unstrap him. She'd stuffed the changing bag full of toys and games to keep him amused and soon Pam and Finn were crawling around on their hands and knees setting up a farm. Watching them, it was debatable who was having the most fun, Pam or Finn, but it was probably Pam. No, definitely Pam.

'More flyers,' said Angie, handing over a wodge of them to Charley. 'For the other shops to hand out.'

'Thanks,' she said, making a note to run them down to Ricky later. He'd offered to take them round since he knew the other traders better than she did, but just right now they needed to focus on which slogan should go where.

'How about "Prosecco with Everything" on the window, because it sums up the shop,' Angie suggested.

'Then "Happy Prosecco Day" on the wall above the till, then, on the back wall above the clock, how about something like "Tick Tock, it's Prosecco O'clock?"'

'Perfect!' said Charley.

'Blimey!' said Tara, 'You've really thought this through. Charley was just going to go, "ip dip sky blue"!'

Charley poked her tongue out at her, and, of course, Ricky chose that precise moment to walk in, which made her feel like a complete idiot. Only to feel even worse when Tara and Angie both stopped what they were doing and turned to stare at Ricky. Pointedly.

Ricky styled it out with his customary easy charm. 'Morning,' he said, his eyes taking in everyone in the room and embracing them with an engaging smile. Then he turned his focus to Charley. 'Have you got those flyers?'

'Yes!' she said, handing them over. 'Thanks very much for doing it. I really appreciate it.'

'It's my pleasure.' He nodded at the others. 'See you later,' he said breezily, and left to go back to his shop, pausing only to look down at Finn who was pushing a tractor with a trailer full of plastic sheep around the floor. 'Cool tractor,' he said sincerely, and the little boy beamed up at him.

The second the door shut behind him, Tara and Angie did a slow turn to Charley.

'And who was that?' demanded Tara.

'He runs the bike shop,' Charley replied with studied carelessness.

'Nice-looking chap,' Angie said, her eyes glittering mischievously beneath raised brows.

'I hadn't noticed,' lied Charley, not daring to look Pam in the eye.

'Nice-looking *body*,' added Tara suggestively, her eyes not leaving Charley's face for a second.

Willing herself not to blush, Charley shrugged carelessly. 'Yes, well, he probably cycles.'

'So, you *have* noticed him!' teased Tara.

'He's a friend. Just a friend! A local shop owner!'

'He seems very keen to help you.' Tara was merciless.

'Very keen,' nodded Angie, straight-faced.

'Oh, pack it in! He's just being neighbourly.' Charley exclaimed. 'Just trying to help a fellow entrepreneur!' she finished, sounding way more pompous than she'd meant to.

'Oooh!' responded Angie and Tara before collapsing into childish laughter, which Pam was also clearly struggling to suppress. Charley studiously ignored them.

Clambering over Pam and Finn, and trying not to tread on them or inadvertently slaughter any farm animals, Charley and Tara went back to their monumental task of stocking the shelves, while Angie sketched the first slogan onto the wall. Then she filled the wording in with gold paint and outlined it with a fine line of black to make it stand out. Then she stuck her paintbrush over one ear and, apparently blissfully unaware of the streak of black paint now daubing her temple, she stood back and regarded her work critically.

'What do you think? Is it okay?' she asked tentatively. 'And be honest!' she begged.

'Stunning!' announced Charley.

'Absolutely,' nodded Pam.

'It'll do,' said Tara with a perfectly straight face.

Charley rolled her eyes, and a smiling Angie cracked on.

As the slogan on the back wall was going above the clock, this meant Angie couldn't quite reach to paint it standing on the floor. She picked up one of the wicker chairs, letting out a slight 'oof' with the effort of reaching around her huge bump.

'You shouldn't be lifting that,' Tara told her sternly, and immediately, both she and Charley moved to take the chair from her.

'Don't fuss. It's lighter than Finn,' said Angie, putting the chair in place under the clock.

'Be careful,' said Charley.

'It's not being up here that's the problem,' said Angie, 'It's the getting up and down.' Now over eight months gone, her enormous bump got in the way as she tried to step up on the chair, so Charley helped her climb up. Once she was up there she seemed steady enough, and Charley relaxed, leaving her to get on with her artwork.

The minutes flew by, with everyone involved in their own worlds of busyness, focused on their own tasks. There was nothing to alert Charley to what was about to happen, until it was too late.

Vaguely, she heard Angie cursing under her breath, and turning round Charley saw her stretching out, way too far, to reach to paint the very edge of the slogan above the clock.

And then it seemed to happen in slow motion.

The chair overbalanced and, yelping in fear, Angie toppled off sideways, crashing to the floor, her round belly hitting the corner of the table on the way down.

'Angie!' screamed Charley.

Charley leapt over Finn in her rush to get to her mate. Tara joined her only a fraction of a second later. Clambering to her feet, Pam instinctively swept Finn up into her arms to comfort him, where he struggled, wailing in distress with his arms out, urgently trying to get to Angie lying on the floor.

'Mummyyyyyyyy!'

'I'm fine! I'm fine!' Angie reassured him, before ungainly rolling over onto her hands and knees in order to push herself to her feet. Tara and Charley slipped one arm each under hers and gently helped her up. Angie was clearly shaken, and Finn's eyes were still wide with fear and his little lip was trembling. No doubt anxious to calm her frightened little son, Angie deliberately made light of her accident.

'It's all right, sweetie. Mummy just had a bit of a bumps-a-daisy!'

The fear in the little boy's face began to melt away and he settled more calmly on Pam's hip, but his fingers continued to grip her shirt tightly. Tara and Charley were about to help Angie to sit down into the chair when she suddenly froze, frowned deeply and let out a small moan.

'I think you'd better sit down,' said Tara, exchanging an anxious look with Charley, but before Angie could lower her huge bulk into the chair, she winced and groaned again, even louder. Then, taking a deep breath and abandoning the chair altogether, she stood up, moved across to the table, where she leant on it, clearly trying to steady herself.

'I'm calling an ambulance!' cried Charley, whipping her phone out of her back pocket.

'Mummy!' cried Finn, thrusting his arms out to her, immediately scared again.

'I'm fine, sweetie,' said his mum. Then turning to Charley, she added, 'Honestly. I'm only having Braxton Hicks.'

'Branston what!?' said Charley alarmed.

'They're sort of practice pains,' Pam informed her calmly. 'They'll probably die down in a few minutes.'

'Don't panic,' Tara said to Charley, then turning to Angie she asked if she'd like a cup of tea.

Tea? TEA? thought Charley, thinking everyone around her, apart from Finn, had clearly gone mad.

Angie nodded, and then uttered a long, loud groan. Charley made a decision. 'I don't care if they're bloody Branston Pickles! I'm calling an ambulance.'

'Charley, you're overreacting,' Tara told her. Pam and Angie both vociferously agreed with her, and all three of them started talking at once, telling Charley to calm down, stop panicking and not to bother the ambulance service... until Angie's waters broke and splattered onto the floor.

Everyone froze.

'Shit!' said Tara under her breath.

'Ah,' said Angie, visibly forcing herself to keep calm, for Finn's sake.

'Mummy done a wee-wee!' said Finn, scandalised.

'Don't worry, everything's going to be fine,' said Pam, to nobody in particular, but in an attempt to reassure everybody.

Thirty seconds later, Charley told them the ambulance was on its way. She just bloody well hoped it would arrive before the baby did.

Chapter Thirty-five

Charley paced up and down the shop like a panicking first-time father, anxiously nipping outside every now and again to see if she could see the ambulance. Eventually, after what seemed like hours, she spied a couple of paramedics in their dark green overalls, calmly walking towards her.

Walking? What's the matter with these people? she thought. 'Where's the ambulance?' she cried, rushing up to them to guide them to the shop.

'We had to leave it on the double yellows round the corner,' one of them told her nonchalantly. 'There was a van in the way.'

For crying out loud! Please, tell me this isn't happening to me.

Technically of course, it wasn't happening to Charley, it was happening to Angie.

'How often are the contractions?' one of the paramedics asked Angie, once they'd got to their patient. When she replied they were still several minutes apart he simply said, 'Can you walk to the ambulance?'

'For goodness' sake!' cried Charley. 'Haven't you got a wheelchair or something?'

'I'll be fine to walk,' Angie assured her, then she gave Finn a big hug and a kiss, and told him to stay with Tara.

'Want Baa-Baa!' wailed Finn. Angie stopped to fish the bedraggled and beloved fluffy sheep out of the changing bag and handed it to her son with a smile. Then, after plonking a kiss on the top of his head, she turned and calmly waddled off with the paramedics, Charley hovering anxiously at her elbow.

Charley had no sense of how long it took to get to the hospital. Every second seemed like ages, and although the calm, relaxed attitude of the medic looking after Angie was probably meant to be reassuring, for some reason it irritated the pants off Charley. She wanted to scream at him, convinced he wasn't taking the emergency seriously enough. She clung onto Angie's hand.

By now Angie's contractions were coming at more regular intervals, and she was frowning in concentration, focusing on controlling her breathing.

'Have you got a watch?' the paramedic asked Charley, with infuriating calm.

'No, but I've got a phone.'

'You might find it useful to time between the contractions,' he told her.

Charley's hands trembled as she took her phone out of her back pocket.

'They usually get Will to do that,' Angie told her. 'Although, in all honesty, normally at this stage, I wouldn't trust him to count to ten!'

I'm not surprised, thought Charley, as her fumbling fingers struggled to set the phone's clock controls to stopwatch.

Angie gave her arm a comforting squeeze. 'It's okay, Charley. You're doing fine,' she said with a perfectly straight face.

'Thanks,' said Charley in all seriousness.

Angie bit her lip, clearly trying not to laugh.

The ambulance swung into the bay outside the hospital and the paramedics wheeled Angie's trolley bed to Maternity. Charley hurried alongside her, still clutching her hand. Charley was hoping to God that Will would be there before them, and when they arrived at the maternity unit she frantically scanned the faces of everyone milling around. She couldn't see him. As soon as they were in a delivery room, and while the midwife was helping with Angie's cumbersome transfer from the trolley to the hospital bed, Charley texted Will.

> Where are you?

> Stuck in traffic. Don't leave her.

> I won't. Promise.

'Will's stuck in traffic, so you've got to hang on a bit,' joked Charley.

'No chance!' Angie gritted her teeth, bracing herself to cope with the pain of the contraction sweeping over her.

'It's the babies who decide when they're coming. Not us!' the midwife told Charley cheerfully, then checking Angie's notes, she added lightly, 'Even when they're a little bit early like this one.'

Soon Angie's contractions were coming thick and fast and it seemed to Charley that she barely had time to recover from one wave of pain before the next one engulfed her. Watching countless episodes of *Call the Midwife* hadn't prepared Charley for the reality of being in the same room as a woman actually giving birth. It definitely hadn't prepared her for the harrowing groans of agony coming from Angie in her final stages of labour, as if her whole body were being torn apart.

Nor did it prepare Charley for the overwhelming, joyous and utterly miraculous moment when the baby finally slithered out, and suddenly, astonishingly, there was a brand-new baby person in the room.

'Well done, Angie,' exclaimed the midwife, 'You've got a baby girl!' as Angie sank back onto the pillow, exhausted and drenched in sweat. Relief and joy surged through Charley and she burst into tears.

'You silly sod!' cried Angie, putting her arms out to give Charley a hug.

For a moment the sound of Charley's crying and Angie laughing at her covered the silence that had followed the birth and distracted both of them from the swift, urgent actions the midwife was now focused on performing with the baby. It was only when the midwife leant over and pressed an intercom button behind Angie's bed, and said calmly, but insistently, 'Baby doctor to room eight. Baby doctor to room eight,' that Angie and Charley realised something was wrong.

'What's happened?' cried Angie instantly struggling to sit forward, her face contracting in fear, but the midwife didn't answer. 'What's going on?' she demanded more urgently.

Suddenly the doors to the delivery room crashed open and half a dozen medics burst in, pushing piles of alarming-looking equipment and an incubator on a trolley. They surrounded the baby and neither Angie nor Charley could see what they were doing.

'What's wrong? What's wrong with my baby?' cried Angie, struggling to clamber out of bed and get to her baby. Instinctively Charley held her back. Icy panic swept over Charley, cold as death. *No, no, no, no, no, no...* was all she could hear, and she wasn't sure if it was Angie begging or a voice inside her own head. She and Angie clung to each other, frightened and impotent, as the agonising seconds, as long as a lifetime, dragged by.

Then, all of a sudden, fracturing the tension with the shocking intensity of breaking glass, came the furious, thin scream of a newborn, venting indignation at being born. Angie sank against Charley in relief, tears streaming down her face. They watched the medics carefully place the baby in the incubator, handling her as if she was as fragile as blown glass. Her scrawny little body seemed so frail and vulnerable.

'Can't I just hold her?' begged Angie, 'Just for a second?'

Going over to her, the midwife pulled a sympathetic face, and patted her arm comfortingly. 'Sorry, my lovely, not just now. We just need to settle her into the incubator and then she needs to go to into special care for a while.' Seeing the panic on Angie's face she put her hand on her shoulder and added reassuringly, 'Don't worry, you're coming, too.'

It was at this moment that Will arrived. He glanced at the baby, swamped by the incubator and surrounded by medics fiddling with tubes and wires, then went across to the bed and gathered Angie up into his arms and held her while she sobbed. Charley could see Will was struggling to hold it together, so, feeling utterly redundant and uncomfortable at imposing herself on their very private emotions, Charley left them to it, and slipped out of the room.

In the waiting area outside the delivery suites, a large sign read, 'No Mobile Phones'. Guessing that this was because the phones' signals might interfere with the medical equipment, Charley made her way to the hospital entrance before ringing Tara. Tara picked up almost immediately, as if she'd been hovering over the phone.

'Is everything okay? How's Angie? Has she had the baby? Is the baby all right?' she garbled, pelting Charley with questions.

Drained and weary, Charley leant back against the wall of the hospital. 'Angie's fine. Will's with her now, but they're taking the baby into special care.'

There was a beat before Tara said, 'But it's going to be okay, yes?'

The desperation in Tara's tone was evident to Charley. Her mate so obviously wanted to hear her say, *Yes, the baby's going to be fine*. She wished to God she could give that reassurance, but she couldn't.

'I don't know,' she replied dully. 'They didn't really say. It's a little girl. I think she came out okay, but then they called a baby doctor in and suddenly the room was full of medics and bits of equipment and oxygen and… and now she's in an incubator and—' She stopped, too choked to speak.

'Charley? You okay?'

Overwhelmed by the vulnerability of Angie's precious new baby, and by her own fear of what might happen to her, Charley replied in small, tight voice. 'Oh Tara, she's so little and helpless…'

For once Tara seemed at a loss for words. They both were. Neither of them wanted to exchange pointless platitudes and cliched inanities, such as telling each other to hope for the best, or that modern medicine can work wonders these days, because they both knew, only too well, that modern medicine can't always work miracles. Ultimately, the thread of life is spider-web thin, and once it's broken, it cannot, for all the world, be repaired.

Charley kept the conversation short as she needed to phone Pam before her battery ran out.

'Give Angie our love,' said Tara.

'Of course,' replied Charley, before ending the call.

In contrast to the fear that had been all too apparent in Tara's voice, Charley was thankful that Pam's tone was reassuringly calm and measured. Whilst her mother-in-law was obviously concerned and anxious for news, her sensible, practical advice was to tell Charley to try not to worry.

'Worrying doesn't change anything,' she told her, 'it just wears you out and leaves you less able to cope with things. How much longer are you going to stay at the hospital?'

Charley hadn't even thought about it. She was just taking it one minute at a time. 'I'll stay until I can find out from Will what's happening,' she told Pam, 'but don't wait up. I'll try and text you if there's any news, but my battery's low.'

'Don't forget to eat,' was Pam's final piece of motherly advice.

Charley's phone was now down to 2 per cent, so, anxious that Will might not be able to contact her, she went back into the hospital and followed the signs to the Neonatal ICU.

Outside the unit, Charley arrived at the nurses' station where one of them immediately intercepted her, stopping her from going in. 'Are you a relative?' she asked.

'No, just a friend.'

'Then I'm sorry but you can't go in. It's family only.'

'The thing is, I was there for the birth,' Charley started to explain. 'I came in with her, in the ambulance. And I just want to make sure my friend's baby is okay.'

'I'm afraid we can't give out any information if you're not a relative.'

The nurse was polite, and only doing her job, but a wave of frustration swept through Charley and she wanted to scream at her. She wanted to rant and demand to be told what was happening. Didn't she understand how much Charley needed to know, *needed to know* that the baby was okay? She forced herself to calm down and be rational, and to remember it wasn't the nurse's fault that Charley's phone had died and she couldn't text Will, nor that Angie had gone into labour early and ended up in intensive care. It was Charley's fault. Everything was Charley's fault. She should *never* have let Angie climb onto a rickety wicker chair just to paint a bloody stupid slogan on the wall, for crying out loud. And she should never have let go of her arm, or have taken her eye of Angie for a single second, then she would have been able to stop her from reaching out too far. Or at the very least she could have grabbed hold of her and stopped her from falling, and then Angie and the baby would both still be all right.

Chapter Thirty-six

In the end there was nothing Charley could do except ask the nurse to let Will know that she would be waiting outside in the corridor. There were no chairs, but then it wasn't meant to be a waiting area, probably because the last thing they needed lining the corridor leading to an intensive care unit was a row of chairs getting in the way of the trolleys and equipment, thought Charley. It felt inappropriate, somehow disrespectful, to sit on the floor, so instead she just stood and waited, leaning against the wall, hoping that Will would come out to tell her what was going on. There was no clock, and since her phone was dead, she had no sense of how much time had passed. It could have been minutes, it could have been hours, but finally Will, anxious and drawn, came out to find her. There was no change, he told her. The baby was still in the incubator.

'She's hanging on in there,' he said.

'But they think she's going to be all right?' Charley wasn't sure she even had the right to ask.

Will shrugged. 'I don't know. I hope so, but I don't think they make promises or guarantees in here. She's not in any immediate danger... she's just a bit early, thirty-five weeks, and she didn't start breathing right away. Angie's trying to express some milk for her.'

'Oh, Will, I'm sorry… This is all my fault…' Charley tried to say, but Will pulled her into one of his huge bear hugs, wrapping both arms around her tightly.

'Angie said you'd blame yourself,' he said, 'But it's not your fault, Charley… whatever happens. It's *not* your fault.'

Charley, feeling like a frightened lost child suddenly finding itself in a warm safe place, struggled to choke back her tears.

Will was going to spend the rest of the night in the unit with Angie and the baby, but, as he said, there was no point Charley being there. He promised he'd call her the moment there was any news, so Charley went home.

Going straight into her bedroom, she plugged her phone into the charger by the side of her bed. All she wanted to do was crawl under the duvet, curl up and never come out again, but Pam had waited up for her, and was hovering anxiously in her doorway. She followed her through to the kitchen, where Pam made a pot of tea for them both, and then, ignoring Charley's protestations that she felt too sick to eat anything, she made her a sandwich.

Charley shook her head at the food but took the tea numbly. Cradling the hot mug, Charley's hands started shaking uncontrollably, the tension that had built up in her over the past few hours needing to find its way out of her body somehow. Scalding hot tea slopped over her fingers, but she didn't seem to notice. Pam leant over and gently took the mug, then she held Charley's hands in hers, as if she were trying to absorb some of the shock herself.

'What if the baby dies?' Charley whispered, terrified to voice the thought out loud, her fingers gripping Pam's painfully hard. She closed her eyes and hot tears spilled down her cheeks. 'Why do things like this happen? Why?'

Pam had long ceased asking that question. There was no rational answer, no fair reason. The purpose of a death, especially that of a child, like the pain of loss, was unfathomable. In the first weeks and months after her son had died, the question had raged round and round Pam's head and heart, like a thunderstorm trapped in a valley. The question had echoed around the aching void of her loss, harrowing and hollowing, unanswered and incomprehensible. She'd long given up looking for an answer.

Still holding Charley's hands all she could find to say was, 'People die, Charley. It happens. Sometimes way too early, when they're far too young. Sons die, husbands die, babies die. It happens, but life goes on, and we survive – because we have to – and the act of surviving makes us strong.' A stray strand of hair had fallen down over Charley's forehead. Tenderly, Pam swept it back and tucked it behind Charley's ear. 'Losing Josh made me invincible, Charley. Nothing can ever hurt me more than that. But I survived, and *you* survived losing him. If Angie's baby dies, *if*,' she repeated, seeing the alarm that had flickered immediately into Charley's eyes, 'it will be terrible, dreadful. But Angie will survive, and you will help her, like you helped Tara when Kim died.' She then got up and fetched a box of tissues from her room.

It was well into the early hours when they finally went to bed. Charley was too exhausted to undress, and she crawled under the duvet, wrung dry and completely cried out.

–

The mid-morning sun was streaming in through the bedroom window when Charley woke the next morning.

She would probably have slept until well beyond lunchtime, but her phone was ringing. It was Will. She sat up, instantly wide awake and alert, desperate for good news. Sadly, there wasn't any real change, he told her. The baby had been tube-fed some of Angie's milk and Angie herself had managed to get a little sleep.

'How about you? Did you get any rest?' Charley asked him.

'No. I sat up all night with them. Now I'm going home to pick up Angie's overnight things and put on a clean shirt, then I'm going straight back.' Charley was only too capable of reading between the lines – Will was scared to leave Angie alone in case anything dreadful happened while he was gone.

'Can I do anything?' she offered.

'No. It's all covered. Tara's looking after the kids.'

'Can I come and see Angie?'

'I don't even know if you're allowed visitors in special care. Sorry. I'll find out and let you know.'

'Give her my love, won't you?' said Charley. And then Will rang off and she was left bereft, holding her phone numbly.

'Did I hear your phone?' Pam asked as Charley went into the kitchen.

'Yes. There's no news.'

'Okay,' said Pam carefully, 'Well, maybe no news is good news. Babies can be tenacious little buggers. They may be tiny but they can have a very strong grip.'

Charley sat slumped at the table while Pam made her some coffee and a mound of hot buttered toast, but Charley pushed the toast away. 'I'm not hungry.'

'You haven't eaten since lunchtime yesterday,' Pam reminded her. 'You need to eat,' and she pushed the toast back towards Charley, who ignored it.

Then Charley's phone rang, again, and she leapt out of her chair and ran to her bedroom to answer it. It was a very pissed-off electrician telling her that he'd been standing outside her shop for twenty minutes and was anyone actually going to turn up and let him in? She grovelled profusely and promised him someone would be there within fifteen minutes. Then she went back into the kitchen and asked Pam to go and deal with him.

'But I don't even know where you want the sockets,' Pam protested.

'I don't care.' Just right now Charley didn't give a flying banana about where the plugs went, she couldn't have cared less if the electrician had literally screwed one onto her forehead. 'Anyhow, I haven't even showered.'

'Okay,' agreed Pam reluctantly, 'but come down as soon as you can, yes?'

Charley shook her head. 'I can't face doing anything today, Pam, and anyhow, I need to stay here in case Will calls.'

'But you'll have your phone with you and the shop is nearer the hospital,' Pam pointed out logically.

But Charley wouldn't budge. 'I'm too tired,' she said wearily.

'Well try and eat something,' was Pam's parting shot.

–

Irritated, Pam sped down to the shop, cursing every red light. She didn't doubt Charley was tired, but Pam had been up most of the night too, and she was *twice* Charley's age. Then she groaned out loud. That was a sum she wouldn't do again. She slung the car on a meter – which would cost a fortune but would also save her a precious few minutes – raced to the shop and let the electrician in. Not wanting to make decisions without checking with Charley, Pam tried calling her a couple of times to ask where she wanted the socket for the till and the card reader, but Charley didn't pick up.

–

Back in the flat Charley had pulled the curtains closed in the living room, then she'd curled up on the sofa. What she really wanted to do was run away, run away and hide. Not to anywhere or to anyone in particular, she just didn't want to be *right here, right now*, because *right here, right now* was a crap place to be. Only a call or a text from Will, telling her that the baby was going to be fine would make it bearable. Picking up the remote from the coffee table she flicked the TV on, then she lay back down and closed her eyes. She didn't care what was on, she only wanted the sound of other people without having to actually talk to anyone. Switching her phone to vibrate, she put it on the table, only intending to answer it if it was Will. Then she turned the ring on the landline phone off, too. She couldn't cope with fielding calls from everyone, and it was pointless talking to them anyhow, since she couldn't tell them anything more. If there was any news, she'd text them. Meanwhile, she was just going to hide.

–

A couple of hours later, arriving back at the flat to find Charley lying on the sofa with the curtains closed, a box of tissues and the phone by her side, and some rubbish or other blaring out from the TV, Pam's irritation boiled over. Striding to the French windows she flung the curtains open. The daylight poured in, temporarily dazzling Charley, who scrambled to sit up and then fumbled to switch the TV off with the remote.

Pam stood in front of her, uncharacteristically confrontational, with arms folded. 'Falling apart is not an option,' she informed Charley brusquely. 'You can't just mope around like this.'

'I'm not *moping around* as you put it. I'm tired and I'm worried. *Extremely* worried. Any minute now, Will might call and say... and say—' But she couldn't bring herself to say the words she was dreading that she might hear Will say.

In anyone else Pam would have scented melodrama, and would have accused them of hijacking Angie's trauma, like some inappropriate outpouring of a 'nation's grief' after some tragedy on the news, a greedy, egocentric appropriation of other people's personal and private pain. But this was Charley... and Charley, she just now realised, had reverted to her *own* tragedy, ensnaring herself in the endless loop of her own loss.

Pam spoke to her gently enough, but with a slightly sharp edge to her tone.

'Charley, I know how worried you are, but if Will does call... with bad news,' even Pam struggled to openly voice their darkest fear, 'then Angie is going to need you to be there for her, to support her, not sitting here wrapped up in your own grief.'

Charley reeled backwards as if she'd been slapped.

'I'm not wrapped up in my own grief!'

'You are, Charley. This is how you were when Josh died. This isn't about Angie losing her baby, this is about you losing Josh.'

'It's not!' Charley's eyes blazed.

Pam pressed on, albeit more gently. 'It *is*, Charley. You're still mourning Josh, still bogged down in grieving for him. You cling to being his widow. You *define* yourself as a widow. You can't go on doing that for the rest of your life.'

The unfairness, the sheer, unkind, heartlessness of Pam's words shook Charley. This was Pam talking. Pam – who she'd always been able to turn to for support, and from whom empathy and sympathy flowed in a never-ending stream.

'Yes, I *define myself as a widow*, Pam,' snapped Charley, 'because I *am* a widow. I can't suddenly, conveniently, stop being a widow!'

'You have to, Charley. You have to stop seeing yourself as a widow.'

Incredulous that Pam would speak to her like this, Charley tried to protest, but Pam went on, ignoring the interruption.

'I'll never stop missing my son, every single day for the rest of my life. But I don't define myself as a "grieving mother". You have to move *on*, Charley. You can't keep thinking of yourself as Josh's widow.'

There was a long, painful silence before Charley spoke. She struggled to find the words, or even the energy to reply. To explain why she could never, ever stop thinking of herself as Josh's widow. Eventually, when she did speak, it was in quiet, tight voice that tore at her throat.

'You're still Josh's mother, Pam. Nobody tells you that you can't call yourself his mother any more now that he's dead. You'll always be his mother. But I'm not Josh's wife any more. All I *can* be is his widow. If I'm not even that, then... that's the end, the end of us. The end of us being anything together.'

Her shoulders hunched and she turned away. She could feel her face contorting itself with grief, and gave in to huge sobs that wracked her whole body.

Pam slipped onto the sofa beside her. 'It's not the end, my lovely,' she said, wrapping her arms round Charley, pulling her close and stroking her hair. 'There is no "end" of Josh. He was part of our lives, and he always will be.'

Pam let Charley cry for a while, before she continued. 'After he died, Charley, one good piece of advice I was given – in fact the best piece of advice I was given – was that I had to make a choice. I could either mourn what I'd lost, or I could decide instead to celebrate what I'd had. I decided to celebrate, and I still do. I still celebrate him daily – my lovely, funny, boy.' She broke off, her voice shuddering. Then, gently pushing Charley away so that she could look her straight in the eyes, she said, 'Let me ask you this. Given the choice, now that you know how much it hurt to lose him, would you have preferred not to have met him at all? Not to have fallen in love with him? Not to have had the wonderful time you did have with him?'

Charley replied without hesitation. 'No. Of course not.'

'Then focus on that. Remember the joy of being with him, not the pain of losing him. Choose to remember being married to him, not the sadness of being his widow.'

Chapter Thirty-seven

It wasn't until after supper, when Charley was loading the dishwasher, that Will called. Momentarily she froze, gazing at the phone screen for a second or so, too frightened to answer it. *Please, please, please, make it good news*, she begged. Then, crushing the panic tightening her chest and throat, she tried to make her voice as normal as possible.

'Hi, Will.'

There was no news, he told Charley. The baby was still in the incubator, but the nurses thought it would be good for Angie to have a visitor.

'Could you drop in for half an hour or so?' he asked her.

'When?'

'This evening? I've given them your name at the nurses' station. If you come now, I can go and check on the kids at Tara's.'

Garbling a quick update at Pam, Charley belted off to the hospital. She fumed at every traffic hold-up, and begged that there'd be a parking space. Fortunately there was and, thanking God she was wearing trainers, she ran hell for leather all the way from the car park.

The tense, unnatural quiet intimidated her when she walked into the Neonatal ICU. The last time she'd visited Angie on a maternity ward was when Finn was born.

They'd all turned up en masse – Tara had brought a bottle of fizz to celebrate, and the whole ward had echoed with their laughter and chatter, and a friendly fracas had broken out over whose turn it was to hold the baby.

Scanning the room looking for Angie, all Charley could take in was the alarming quantity of machinery and how terrifyingly frail and vulnerable all the babies seemed, dwarfed as they were by the medical equipment surrounding them. The unsettling quiet was underscored by a low-level mechanical hum, punctuated by urgent, insistent bleeps, and the soft rustle of the nurses' uniforms and their soft-soled shoes as they moved around, efficiently caring for everyone.

Suddenly an image of Josh slid into Charley's mind. The last moments of his life had been in intensive care, and he would have been wired up to machines like these, machines that would have counted out the last seconds of his life. Surrounded by people, doctors and nurses, all fighting to save him, caring for him, staying with him, until his very last moment. Up until now, because she hadn't been able to be there for him – had arrived too late – she'd imagined him dying alone. Now she understood, with immense relief, that he hadn't.

Looking round she noticed a couple of mums tending to their babies, inside their incubators, while another was leaning over and tenderly stroking her baby's bare tummy. Then she saw Angie, lying on her bed. Her baby was sleeping, encased in a domed incubator beside her. Charley went over, leant over the bed and hugged Angie.

'Thanks for coming,' said Angie tonelessly. She looked awful. Her eyes were red rimmed from crying, and her whole face was pinched and pale.

'Are you kidding me? I've been desperate to see you!' said Charley deliberately keeping her voice light. 'And to meet the little one properly. Congratulations!'

'Thank you.'

Then, willing herself to ignore the thick plastic sides of the incubator, Charley turned to look at Angie's newborn. *Act normally*, she told herself, *don't overreact and upset Angie even more.* But as soon as she set eyes on the scrawny, wrinkled little scrap all need for pretence tumbled away.

'Oh Angie, she's beautiful.'

The baby girl lay flat on her back, arms flung out either side of her. A tube, going up her cute button nose, was taped to her cheek. Her skinny legs stuck out of a nappy that seemed too large for her, and an outsize sticking plaster with a wire trailing from it was stuck onto the heel of one perfect, miniature foot. Charley gazed at her, awed by the miracle of new life.

To Charley she already looked a lot like Angie's other kids, especially Eliot, and even more like her dad. 'Oh my God, Ange, she looks like Will, poor thing!'

Angie managed a small smile.

'How's she doing?'

Angie shrugged. 'Okay, I think.'

'Have the others met her yet?'

'No. They're too young to come in here – it's a bit scary.'

And how, thought Charley, but she confined herself to saying, 'Have you sent them photos?'

'No. Not yet. Just in case.'

Just in case. Charley turned to look at Angie, but she looked away, avoiding her gaze.

'Angie…' started Charley, but then a nurse came up and interrupted her.

'I think the baby could do with another feed,' she told Angie, and she'd brought a large hypodermic full of milk on a small tray.

'Mum's own brew!' the nurse informed Charley cheerfully, then turning to Angie, she added, 'Well done. You're getting your baby off to the best start.'

Angie managed a tense smile.

Then the nurse handed the milk to Charley to hold and started taking the baby out of the incubator. Charley watched as she unplugged the monitor wire and wrapped the baby in a soft white blanket.

'Come on, poppet,' said the nurse, then turning to Angie she asked, 'Are you going to hold her this time?'

Angie shook her head. 'Maybe next time. When she's a bit stronger.'

'You know, I think she's stronger already,' said the nurse gently.

She might very well have been, but considering how vulnerable the baby still seemed, Charley could understand Angie's reluctance. Charley had never forgotten the first time she'd ever held a newborn baby. How fragile and limp it had been and how all the experienced mums in the room had constantly stressed how absolutely vital it was *to support the head*! She'd been petrified she might somehow break it, and she'd been mightily relieved when she could hand it back to its nervous mother. But not, she had suspected, as relieved as the mother. Angie, on the other hand, had always maintained babies were far more robust than Charley feared. This one was clearly different.

'Are you sure?' The nurse held the baby out towards Angie. 'I think she'd like a cuddle.'

Angie's hands stayed in her lap and there was a difficult silence. Charley wasn't sure whether the nurse particularly wanted Angie to take her, or whether she just wanted someone to hold the baby while she fed it.

'Can I help?' she volunteered.

The nurse looked towards Angie, obviously asking permission to hand the baby to Charley, and when Angie nodded, she carefully placed the bundle into Charley's arms.

'I won't drop her! Promise!' teased Charley.

'You'll be fine!' said the nurse. 'I wouldn't let you hold her otherwise. You should see some of the dads we get in here.' She shook her head affectionately. 'Quivering wrecks they are to start with, great big, ham-fisted fellas, all fingers and thumbs!'

Expertly, and with confidence-inspiring ease, the nurse began to tube-fed the baby.

'Have you decided on a name yet?' she asked Angie.

'No.'

Charley glanced over at Angie. 'I thought you'd decided on Lily for a girl?'

Angie shook her head. 'I'm not sure now.'

Alarm bells ringing deep inside her, Charley's eyes slid to the nurse, but she didn't meet Charley's gaze, deliberately, it seemed to her.

'Lily's a lovely name,' was all she said.

When she'd finished the feed, Charley expected her to take the baby back, but she didn't.

'Hang on to her for a while,' the nurse told Charley. 'She's enjoying having a little bit of a love, aren't you, sweetie?'

Out of the corner of her eye Charley saw Angie tense. Then, giving the baby a fond, parting pat, the nurse left, and Charley was literally left holding the baby.

Willing herself to relax, Charley could have sworn she felt the baby relax in turn. Her little body seemed to mould itself into Charley's, her head, covered in its white cotton hat, nestled into the crook of her arm. She lay there contentedly, regarding the world with the wise eyes of a newborn. Somehow the baby managed to look achingly vulnerable, heartbreakingly courageous and endearingly trusting at the same time, and Charley's heart did a double flip and a rush of love spilled over inside her.

And suddenly it became clear to her, in a way she'd never understood before, that anyone, even babies barely one day old, can bring the enormous gift of love with them, as if it's a fundamental, immutable part of who they are. Pam was right. *Of course* we can all love more than one person, love is not a finite resource. We're not limited to only loving one child, or only one friend, or only one man or woman.

She remembered Angie once telling her that she'd fallen in love with all her babies long before they were even born. With her firstborn, Beth, it was seeing her outline at the thirteen-week scan; while Eliot's first faint fluttery kicks had made Angie fall for 'The Butterfly', as she'd nicknamed him; and with Finn, it had been the moment she'd she seen the blue line on the pregnancy-test stick. But, as Charley knew, more than most, sometimes the people we love die, and so love always comes with the risk, the petrifying risk of the agony of loss. Having loved and lost, Charley recognised with painful clarity that the terror of losing her baby was stopping Angie from taking the risk of loving the little girl lying in Charley's arms.

She shifted up the bed so as to be within arm's reach of Angie. 'I think you should hold her for a bit,' she said, holding the baby out towards Angie.

'Actually, I'm a bit tired,' said Angie. 'I'll call the nurse and get her to put her back.'

'No. Don't do that,' said Charley quietly. 'Ange, you need to hold your baby. She needs it and so do you.'

Her friend still made no move towards taking her baby, so Charley pressed on.

'Your baby, Lily, needs your love, Angie. And you need hers. If—' she paused to find the right way to voice the unspeakable, '—if the unthinkable happens and you haven't shown her you love her, you will *never* forgive yourself. You'll never have the chance, it'll be too late. You have a chance to love this precious girl now, please take it. Love her while you can, and for as long as you can. Please, Angie. For me.'

Slowly, warily, Angie leant over and touched her baby's perfect, delicate fingers. Then she tentatively stroked her silky-soft cheek. The baby gave the tiniest of sighs, and Charley held her breath.

'Come on then, my Lily,' murmured Angie softly, holding out her arms for Charley to gently tumble Angie's newborn into her embrace. Closing her eyes in bliss, Angie cradled her baby daughter, and oblivious to the world, sank back and wilfully let love engulf them both.

Charley got up and left them to their moment. When she got to the door of the intensive care unit, she stopped and looked back for a moment. Then she slipped out, and closed the door behind her.

Driving home Charley remembered what Tara had said about finding something good to come from a bereavement. Well, maybe something good *had* come from Josh's death, if losing him meant Charley had been able to understand and help Angie. Whatever happened, Angie's love for Lily would be Josh's legacy, his memorial, she decided. Sometimes the thread of life is cut far too soon: sometimes after years, sometimes just months, days, or mere moments, but however long, or short, the thread turns out to be, Charley realised it could never be untangled from the lives it was interwoven with.

Chapter Thirty-eight

After a few worrying days, to everyone's joy and relief, Lily was strong enough and had put on enough weight to leave neonatal intensive care, and she and Angie were moved to a maternity ward.

The friends gave the family twenty-four hours so that Angie's other children could spend time some with their new sister. Then, at the next evening visiting hour they arrived together in a joyous gaggle to meet Lily. Angie slid the bundle into the first pair of welcoming hands. They were Pam's.

'Hello, lovely,' said Pam softly, while the others flocked around, arguing over whose turn it was next.

'Angie, she's adorable!' cried Nisha, 'My go next!'

'I think you'll find there's a queue!' joshed Tara.

'Yes, and you're after me!' Nisha good-naturedly elbowed Tara away.

Laughing, Tara happily turned her attention to opening the bottle of fizz she'd brought.

Sitting cross-legged on the bed, with Charley perched next to her, Angie slid her arm round her mate and gave her an affectionate squeeze. 'Looks like you're last in the queue. Bad luck!' she joked.

Charley smiled gently. 'I've already had my first cuddle with Lily,' she reminded her.

'True.' said Angie, then, holding Charley's gaze she mouthed silently, 'Thank you.'

Charley didn't reply. There was no need.

Meanwhile, of course, The Annual Kim Henderson Memorial Prosecco Night and combined Grand Shop Opening had loomed ever closer and was just days away now, because, regardless of little things like births, deaths and marriages, life has a habit of going on.

Nisha had sent details to the local press and radio, social media was awash with postings, alerts and tweets, and so, even though Charley's attention had been elsewhere, the event had gathered its own momentum, and Saturday was rolling towards them unstoppably...

On the Friday afternoon, Nisha had scheduled a last-minute rundown in the shop with everyone to double-check the arrangements. Tara arrived as soon as she could after work, but Nisha had given up her entire afternoon to help prepare for the launch.

'I've got the Prosecco from the Cash and Carry. I'll bring it down tomorrow,' she told them. 'I bought sixty bottles.'

'Sixty! We'll never get through that lot,' said Charley.

'Oh, I dunno,' replied Tara. 'I'll help!'

'How are we going to keep it chilled?' asked Pam.

'Ice-packs and cool boxes,' replied Nisha, who seemed to have thought of everything. Then she plonked a package on the table, and Charley discovered that Nisha's idea of a launch was a little more ambitious than she'd expected, and a great deal more *outrageous*.

'Tomorrow, in the afternoon, Pam and I will set up in the shop,' Nisha announced, briefing them as if it were a military campaign. 'Charley and Tara, you'll go round town handing out flyers wearing...' she paused for effect while she delved into the package for two fancy-dress costumes she'd bought online – 'these!' she cried, holding the outfits up dramatically.

Charley gasped. 'I— AM— NOT— WEARING— THAT!'

Nisha looked crestfallen. 'Why not?'

The outfits were ridiculously skimpy French Maid costumes with the shortest skirts and lowest cut tops Charley had ever seen. Their tasteless tackiness was topped off with frilly white aprons embroidered, or rather emblazoned, with the legend, 'Let Me Pop Your Prosecco!'

There was a horrified silence. Charley and Pam exchanged mortified looks.

'Oh, come on! They're perfect! You'll look great in them!' said Nisha. And going over to Charley, she held up the costume against her. It was barely going to cover Charley's arse.

'No!' said Charley, resolutely. 'I'm *not* offering to pop anyone's Prosecco.'

It was inevitable that Ricky would choose that precise moment to pitch up, ostensibly to see if they needed any help with the launch. When he saw Charley apparently trying out the costume, he said tactfully, 'Wow. Err, bold outfit. Are you all wearing them?'

'No, I'm not!' spluttered Pam. 'I'm sixty-three, for crying out loud!'

'It's for the launch,' explained Tara to Ricky. 'Tell Charley she'll look great in it,' she ordered.

'You'll look great in it,' he said obediently, but with a transparently appreciative gleam in his eye.

Pulling a face, Charley pushed the costume away, while a burning flush crept up her throat and across her cheeks.

Witnessing Charley's obvious discomfort, Pam said to her protectively, 'You don't have to wear it if you don't want to,' which caused Nisha's face to fall.

Guilt flooded through Charley at the thought of letting Nisha down after all the work she'd put into the launch. A guilt that only deepened when Tara cried, 'Well, I'm up for it! Come on, Charley, where's your entrepreneurial spirit?'

If she bottled it, Charley knew Tara would never let her live it down, but it was Nisha who ultimately won her over.

'Look Charley, I do know the outfits are trashy and vulgar, and you probably don't want to be seen dead in them, but – and it's a very big but – they are also an unforgettable gimmick which will get your business noticed, and remembered, for a long time.'

'Fine,' sighed Charley, outnumbered and defeated, knowing she would live to regret it. 'But I'm not wearing that apron.'

Hearing a choked-off laugh from Ricky, she whipped round to glare at him. He rubbed a hand across his mouth to try and hide the smile that Charley could still see twitching the corners of his lips.

'Go, Charley!' whooped Nisha. 'You won't regret it, I promise you! It'll have a *huge* impact. You'll be all over social media!'

'All over social media – wearing that. Oh, great!' Charley couldn't think of anything worse.

Regretting her decision already, she looked at Ricky and rolled her eyes. He merely shook his head in silent sympathy.

–

By late morning on Saturday, Charley and Pam had finally finished pricing up and displaying all the stock.

Stepping back and stopping for a moment, it suddenly struck Charley what they'd achieved in such a short time. It was astonishing. Looking around her, even to her self-critical eye she thought the shop looked amazing. The displays were methodical and professional-looking, full but not crammed. The dresser shelves were neatly stocked with soaps and toiletries, flutes and wine glasses, mugs and cups and saucers, and tote-bags and tea towels. Chocolates and confectionery were displayed in white wicker baskets scattered around on the tables, while a pile of the cushions Pam had had her eye on were neatly stacked on one of the chairs. The only thing unfinished was Angie's slogan on the back wall above the clock, but Charley had cannily Blu-Tacked a display of her gift bags over that, partly to conceal it, but also to advertise that side of the business.

She turned to Pam, who was busily tidying away the packaging.

'We did it!' she exclaimed.

Pam stopped trampling down some cardboard boxes and looked over. 'Yes! Well done you!'

'Well done *us*,' corrected Charley. 'I couldn't have done this without you, Pam,' she added earnestly, and when Pam opened her mouth to protest Charley put her hand up to silence her and continued. 'And I don't just mean the money, Pam. You've been incredibly supportive of me over the last few months. I wouldn't have had the guts to do any of this if you hadn't encouraged me and believed in me.'

'You've been supportive of me too,' Pam reminded her. 'Extraordinarily so. It's not every young woman who'd let her mother-in-law move in with her!'

'Ah, but then not every young woman has a mother-in-law like you!' Charley sobered before going on. 'If I'm honest Pam, I wasn't exactly…' Charley paused. She'd been going to say 'keen on the idea' but tactfully changed it to, 'sure it was a good idea. Us sharing the flat. Well not to begin with. But it's worked out well, hasn't it? For both of us.'

Pam nodded but she didn't reply, and Charley saw her face suddenly cloud over as if she were struggling with her thoughts. Eventually she said, 'Actually, I've been wanting to talk to you… but what with getting the shop ready, and Angie's baby and everything, I couldn't find the right moment.'

Intuitively, Charley guessed what the older woman was going to say. 'You're going to move back to your place, aren't you?' she said.

Pam sighed apologetically. 'Yes, I'm sorry, but I'm afraid I am.'

'Don't be silly! I think it's a really good decision. Really I do,' Charley assured her, and she meant it. Although the two of them had by now settled down into an easy living-together arrangement, she instinctively knew that, whatever her mother-in-law's future might be, Pam would be happier and better able to deal with it in her own home.

'I'm going to tell Geoff to move out.'

'Good for you!' said Charley.

'But I'll give you a couple of months' rent notice,' Pam went on hurriedly. 'I'm not going to leave you in the lurch!'

Charley shook her head. 'You don't need to, I can get another lodger. And anyway, with a bit of luck, if the shop takes off, I won't have to!'

'Fingers crossed for a roaring success tonight then!' replied Pam.

Charley crossed the fingers on both her hands and held them up. 'Absolutely!'

After lunch there was nothing for the two of them to do but wait and try not to get too anxious. It was the kind of tension that reminded Charley of throwing a party when, just for those last few moments before anyone's actually arrived, you begin to panic that you've either told everyone the wrong date or everyone's forgotten and gone to the pub instead.

'I just hope to God people turn up,' she said.

'It's the calm before the storm,' promised Pam. Prophetically, as it turned out.

Charley had already changed into her skimpy Prosecco costume when Nisha arrived at the shop shortly after two o'clock, but had concealed it under her coat.

'Let me see!' demanded Nisha.

Reluctantly, Charley undid her coat.

Nisha nodded approvingly. 'It's perfect!' Charley groaned. 'No, seriously, you look stunning!'

A few minutes later Tara arrived, also wearing a coat to cover up her Prosecco outfit. By contrast to Charley, however, she burst through the door, dramatically flung off her coat, struck a flamboyant pose and cried, 'Ta da!'

She was wearing the highest pair of heels Charley had ever seen her in, and possibly the brightest red lipstick available either online or on the High Street. Her voluptuous figure simply screamed sex appeal.

'Good grief,' gasped Pam.

'*Bloody hell, Tara!*' said Charley.

'I know, darling! Somebody call *Vogue*!'

Nisha laughed, then instantly switched to back her professional persona. 'Okay. Final checks. Baz is bringing the tablecloths and the glasses, check?'

'Check!' said Tara.

'And you've got the float?'

'Check!' repeated Tara, indicating her handbag.

'Cupcakes?' queried Nisha, looking at Pam.

'Under the table,' replied Pam.

Peering underneath the serving table, Nisha saw a stash of large transparent plastic tubs full of stunning cupcakes. She nodded approvingly at Pam, and then handed Charley and Tara a wodge of flyers each. 'Right, off you go. Back here half five, latest.'

Charley didn't move.

'Go!' urged Nisha.

Clutching the flyers and grasping the nettle, Charley followed Tara out of the door, still wearing her coat.

'Charley, coat!' demanded Nisha, holding out her hand.

'It's cold out there!' Charley clutched the garment tighter to her body.

'Coat!' repeated Nisha.

So, reluctantly, Charley slipped it off. She'd never felt so… exposed. Thank God she wouldn't have to pass Ricky's shop on the way into town. 'I think I need the loo…' she muttered, but what she actually needed was a longer skirt, a higher cut top and Teflon-coated self-confidence.

The woman who ran the florist called over to her as they passed. 'Big event tonight then!'

Charley nodded. 'Yup!'

'Good luck! I'll pop in later.'

'Great!' grinned Charley.

Nisha was right about the costumes – they certainly made an impact. The flyers flew out of their hands and there were barely any left when Charley and Tara headed back to shop at five thirty. They were both footsore and weary, half frozen and struggling to summon up the energy to face the launch itself.

But by six o'clock a sizeable crowd had gathered outside the shop. Tara was clearly elated, Pam beamed delightedly and Charley was a sweaty-palmed bag of nerves. Nisha, the personification of cool, calmly stepped outside to officially open the event.

'Ladies and gentlemen, welcome to The Annual Kim Henderson Memorial Prosecco Night and the official grand opening of Charley's Prosecco Pop-Up!'

There was a small cheer and people poured into the shop. Charley was frankly stunned by the turnout. She had feared that only family and friends and a few of the Prosecco Night regulars would turn up, and that the whole thing would be a bit of a let-down. As it turned out, the fourth Annual Kim Henderson Memorial Prosecco Night was *insane*. Nisha and Tara could barely pour the fizz quickly enough and Pam's Prosecco cupcakes sold out within the first half hour. The card-reader pinged virtually non-stop, and Charley thought a fight was going to break out over the last box of chocolate Prosecco truffles. It was pandemonium. The shop was heaving, like an inner-city pub on a match night. Charley had no idea how many people had crammed themselves into the shop. Ideally, she'd have liked to re-stock some of the rapidly emptying displays, but realistically she knew there was no way she could even get to the boxes of spare stock she'd stashed on top of Baz's dresser. Looking over, Tara caught her eye and grinned at her.

Despite being frantically busy, every now and again Charley caught herself glancing around and over the heads of the crowd, looking for Ricky. He had said he would come, but perhaps in all the chaos she'd missed him? Or maybe he'd been held up. Either way she didn't have much time to think about it – the endless queue of customers saw to that.

Halfway through the event, Angie and Will arrived with their whole gang. Wrapped in a soft white fleece with pale blue bunnies on, and wearing a white cotton hat and mittens, Lily lay snuggled in her dad's huge arms. Well, briefly. Pam instantly abandoned serving Prosecco to cuddle the baby. Charley took over from her, but made sure Angie's other kids didn't feel left out. Unscrewing the lid from a large jar of Prosecco gummy bears she offered them round, turning a blind eye at the size of the fistfuls they grabbed.

'Umm… have they actually got alcohol in them?' asked Angie, warily watching her kids stuffing their faces.

'Ooops!' Charley's hand flew to her mouth. 'Oh my God, Ange. I've absolutely no idea!'

Beth's eyes lit up wickedly. 'If we get drunk, it's all your fault!' she said, shoving another gummy bear in her mouth.

'Nooo!' cried Charley groaning in mock horror.

'Let's share them with Daddy!' said Angie, flicking an amused look at Charley, before shepherding her kids off to find Will. Charley watched them go and then she glanced around, still hoping to see Ricky. And suddenly there he was. In the doorway. He was scanning the room, and Charley knew he was looking for her. She gave him a slight wave and the moment he saw her, his face broke into a beaming smile, and he pushed his way towards her through the crowd.

'Congratulations! What a success!'

Suddenly acutely aware that she was still in her ridiculous costume, Charley slid round to take cover behind the till before handing him a glass of Prosecco. He took his wallet out to pay for it, but Charley held up her palm. 'Absolutely not! You've done so much to help me, you're not paying for it.'

'It's a fundraiser!' he reminded her, holding out a tenner.

She smiled. 'Well, okay then, but you'll have to let me buy you a drink another time.'

He glanced at her quizzically, and she realised her careless invitation was open to interpretation, to say the least.

As a matter of fact, Charley wasn't entirely sure what she'd meant by it herself. She'd been wrestling with her feelings over the last few days. Josh was The One, she had reminded herself, and he always would be… but maybe he wasn't The Only One. Maybe Ricky could turn out to be The One After The One, as it were or, then again, maybe he wouldn't, but she wouldn't know unless she gave him, no, gave *herself*, the chance to find out.

So, taking a deep breath, she said, 'Are you free next Saturday?'

He nodded. 'Yes.'

'Okay. So, that's a date.'

'A date?' he queried. 'Like a *date* date?'

'Yes, like a *date* date,' she said, feeling a coy smile work its way across her mouth, before realising, with excruciating embarrassment, that he might not want a *date* date. 'Unless, you just want it to be a drink,' she added hurriedly. 'I mean a *drink* drink, not a *date* drink. Oh God—'

She trailed off, realising how excruciatingly badly she was handling it. She was on tenterhooks until Ricky's face broke into his characteristic easy smile and he said, 'No. I'd much prefer a *date* date.' Which, Charley was a little surprised to discover, was fine by her. More than fine, in fact.

A heightened moment seemed to hang in the air between them until, with appalling timing, the woman from the florist suddenly pitched up, and the moment evaporated.

'Good turnout! Well done!' she said to Charley.

Swiftly recovering her poise, and her professionalism, Charley replied, 'Thank you, but it was very much a team effort, not just me!'

'Actually, I was going to ask you about that,' said the florist. 'Who did the artwork for you?'

Barely stopping herself in time from replying, 'My mate, Angie,' Charley corrected her thoughts, and said, 'The art designer is here, let me introduce you.' And, throwing a discreetly apologetic look over her shoulder towards Ricky, Charley led her over to Angie who, she discovered, was already deep in conversation with someone else who apparently needed a talented designer to give their shop a makeover. Charley introduced the florist and left them to it.

She'd intended to slip back to Ricky, but Pam, who by now was standing in the midst of a group of laughing older women, called her over to meet her friends.

Zee took one look at Charley's skimpy Prosecco outfit, turned to Pam and said, 'And where's yours?'

'Did she chicken out of wearing one?' Toni asked Charley.

'No!' said Pam.

'Yes,' lied Charley.

'I can't imagine why,' said Rachel dryly.

'I know, classy, isn't it?' She gave an ironic little shimmy to underscore just how classy it was.

Charley then watched as Pam's friends laughed good-naturedly while her mother-in-law dragged them around the shop, and piled them up with cushions, bath bombs, chocolates and even tea towels. Charley instantly liked them, struck by their big-hearted zest for life.

She looked around again for Ricky and soon located him in the middle of Angie's gang, holding baby Lily, chatting away to Will and looking thoroughly content. Smiling to herself, she left him to it, and went back to the till.

–

The shop was still packed at half seven, the time when Tara had decided to make her speech to thank everyone for coming and to explain the fundraising aims of the evening. Clambering onto a chair by the till, unaware of just how much her scanty costume revealed as she did so, she took a deep breath and bellowed: 'LADIES AND GENTLEMEN!'

Immediately, a sea of faces turned to look up at her expectantly and a polite hush fell on the room. Licking her lips, Tara took a deep breath and nervously started to read out her speech from a piece of paper which she held in a hand that was shaking considerably more than it usually had at the previous Prosecco events. 'Good evening, everyone. Firstly, welcome to Charley's Prosecco Pop-Up, and secondly, thank you all for coming to The Annual Kim Henderson Memorial Prosecco Night. This event is to celebrate my mum's birthday, and her life, and to raise money for the Patience House Hospice, which is where she died, four years ago.'

The expectant hush dissolved into a compassionate silence. 'The Hospice want to plant a memorial Tree of Life to remember those we have loved and lost, and who cannot be here to share the passing years with us,' carried on Tara, but to her horror, her throat suddenly tightened threateningly. *Do Not Lose It In Front Of All These People*, she told herself frantically. She took another deep breath and blew out through her mouth to steady herself. It was a tactic all too easily read by many of the people in the room, and prompted some of them to do the same. Out of the corner of her eye she saw a woman blink hard, while several others were digging into pockets and bags for tissues. Tara swallowed hard, sniffed, thought of Kim, and ploughed on. 'We're trying to raise a thousand pounds tonight, half the cost of the tree. So please do buy lots of things because the lovely Charley Taylor, proprietor of Charley's Prosecco Pop-Up, is donating a share of tonight's profits to the hospice.'

There was a spontaneous burst of applause, and everyone turned to look at Charley, who promptly went scarlet. When the clapping died down, Tara wrapped up her speech with simple but heartfelt sincerity. 'I can't tell you how much my Mum would have loved this evening – she was a real party girl! Or how much it means to me. Thank you all very much for coming.'

And that was it. The Annual Kim Henderson Memorial Prosecco Night was over for another year, and Charley's Prosecco Pop-Up shop was well and truly launched.

—

By the end of the evening, when only friends and family were left in the shop, Tara came over to Charley and draped an arm round her shoulders.

'What a triumph!'

'Never underestimate the power of Prosecco!' grinned Charley. Then she and Nisha emptied the till. They added up the takings, deducted the costs, double-checked, and then double-checked again, because they couldn't quite believe their own figures.

Finally, Charley said, 'We've made £1,234 and 37p!'

'Taken or made?' Angie peered over their shoulders at the figures they'd jotted down.

'Made,' confirmed Charley.

'Profit,' clarified Nisha.

For once, Tara was speechless.

'Where on earth did the odd thirty-seven pence come from?' asked Pam.

'Who knows?' joked Angie.

'Who cares!' laughed Charley.

Nisha was the first to head home. 'Sorry to leave you with the clearing up. I've got a mega-early start tomorrow.'

Angie and her gang left soon after because Lily needed a feed and it was past bedtime for the others. Charley gave Angie's eldest the rest of the gummy bears to take home.

'I *was* hoping to get them sobered up before bed,' said Angie.

'I read the label. They're alcohol-free,' Charley told her.

'Doh!' groaned Beth.

Then Baz told Monnie it was time for them to go, too, and Charley gave her a box of Prosecco Jelly Beans.

'I want to stay with Mummy!' cried Monnie, rushing over to Tara and wrapping her arms round her.

Much to Charley's surprise, instead of giving in to her daughter, Tara peeled Monnie's arms off her gently but firmly, and said, 'I've got to stay and clear up, Monnie-Moo. Go home with Daddy.' Baz put his hand out towards Monnie, who still hung back with Tara. 'Go on,' said Tara, gently pushing Monnie towards her dad.

'Come on, Monnie,' said Baz, and when his daughter moved over to him and slid her hand into his he gave it a squeeze and added conspiratorially, 'Let's get some chips on the way home!' Monnie beamed up at him, and they went off together happily.

Ricky departed shortly afterwards. He offered to stay to help clear up, but Charley wouldn't hear of it. He was initially reluctant to take no for an answer, but she gently ushered him to the door. 'There's three of us,' she reminded him. 'It's not like I'll be doing it all on my own.'

Moments later, Charley, Tara and Pam stood gazing round the shop, assessing the chaos. Prosecco flutes cluttered every surface, and cupcake cases littered the floor, and there didn't seem to be a single item of stock left in its allocated space on the shelves.

'Do we have a cleaner?' asked Tara.

'Yup,' said Charley, as she handed her the broom.

Tara took it, sighed melodramatically and said, 'I sodding hate my new job.'

An hour or so later, when they had *finally* cleared up, Tara said, 'Well, I think it's time for a well-earned glass of fizz.'

'Is there any left?' asked Pam looking round doubtfully.

Tara winked at her and pulled out a bottle she had stashed under the till table. She poured them each a glass. 'Make a toast, Charley!'

Charley dutifully lifted her glass. 'To—' she started, but was suddenly lost for words.

'To us?' ventured Tara.

'To the shop?' suggested Pam.

'No. To the future,' said Charley.

Acknowledgements

I owe an enormous debt of gratitude to my agent, the wonderful Gaia Banks, without whose persistence and wisdom this book would never have made it to first draft. Gaia – my eternal thanks for not giving up on the book, or on me!

I am also hugely indebted to the terrific Emily Bedford, Commissioning Editor at Canelo, for picking up on the MS and so skilfully guiding it to publication. Emily – working with you has been both a delight and a masterclass.

My sincere thanks also go to Sarah Whittaker for the fabulous, pitch-perfect cover illustration, and to everyone at Canelo who contributed to the final version. The book is far better for your input.

Finally, as ever, my heartfelt thanks to my four offspring. I honestly don't know how you put up with having a writer for a mother, but without you, your love and support, I wouldn't be able to write at all.